The Secret of Rose-Anne Riley

Shaw J. Dallal

Hamilton Books

A member of
Rowman & Littlefield
Lanham • Boulder • New York • Toronto • Plymouth, UK

Copyright © 2013 by Hamilton Books
4501 Forbes Boulevard, Suite 200, Lanham, Maryland 20706
Hamilton Books Aquisitions Department (301) 459-3366

10 Thornbury Road, Plymouth PL6 7PP, United Kingdom

Library of Congress Control Number: 2013942761
ISBN: 978-0-7618-6174-4 (paperback : alk. paper)—ISBN: 978-0-7618-6175-1 (electronic)

∞™ The paper used in this publication meets the minimum requirements of American National Standard for Information Sciences Permanence of Paper for Printed Library Materials, ANSI/NISO Z39.48-1992.

This novel is dedicated to all victims of rape
and to their families, who inspired it.

Acknowledgments

I would like to express deep gratitude to three women:

1. The late Mrs. Emma Newman, my beloved elderly and kindly land lady, who hosted me in her home in Ithaca, New York, when I first arrived at Cornell University as a teen ager in the early fifties. She introduced me to rural America through her quaint kitchen, which included a woodstove. Through the unforgettable and evocative descriptions of her own life on a farm in Upstate New York, Mrs. Newman left an indelible mark on me that is reflected in this novel.
2. The late Mrs. Betty Irene Osborn Young, my beloved first boss and mentor at Cornell University, who shared personal memoirs of her life on a farm in Kansas with me. She edited several chapters which describe life in rural America, and she helped me integrate that life, including the woodstove in a rural kitchen and other valuable rural items in the context of this novel.
3. Finally, my beloved wife Diana, who repeatedly and patiently edited *The Secret of Rose-Anne Riley*. Her editing, patience and diligence were crucial to its completion. Through her elderly and gracious maternal grandparents, Owen and Mable Griffith, who lived in Remsen City, a tiny village of less than one thousand in Central New York, she introduced me to the very essence of rural America. The Griffith home included the quaint and fascinating rural kitchen with a white rusted woodstove, which I marveled at, admired during our many visits and utilized within the context of this novel.

I thank my friend Walter Oczkowski, who accompanied me during many visits to several farms in Oneida and Herkimer counties in upstate New York.

He introduced me to gracious farmers who welcomed me to their rural homes and farms. These visits helped me describe rural America at its grandest. Walter was one of the early readers of the first version of this novel.

I thank my friend and former colleague at the Maxwell School of Syracuse University, Professor Stuart Thorson, who read and made helpful comments on a very early version of this novel.

I acknowledge the assistance of my beloved granddaughter, Justine Lindemann, who when she was barely fourteen, read and commented on the first, much shorter version of this novel. Justine's comments spurred me to continue revising the early version of this novel.

I thank my friend and law school classmate, Frank Giruzzi, who read and commented on an earlier version of this novel.

I thank my life-long friends, Kevin and Nancy Kelly, who read, edited and commented on several versions of this novel.

I thank my friend, Professor Clare Brandabure, Professor of Comparative Literature at the University of Indiana, who read an earlier version of this novel, reviewed it for prospective publishers and wrote a very kind and helpful blurb for the book cover.

I thank my friend and former colleague at Colgate University, Professor Kira Stevens, who read and appreciated the latest version of this novel.

I thank my former student at Colgate University, Teresa Kevorkian, who read and commented on an earlier version of this novel.

I acknowledge the special assistance of my very good friend and former colleague at Utica College of Syracuse University, Professor Eugene Nassar, Professor of English Literature Emeritus, who read and critiqued in writing the present version of this novel, and who kindly provided a blurb for the book cover.

I acknowledge the valuable assistance of my friend and former colleague at Colgate University, Professor Jennifer Lutman, Professor and Director of English Writing, who read and critiqued the current version of this novel, and who provided a very kind blurb for the book cover.

I thank my friend Professor Austen Givens of Utica College, who read, critiqued and discussed with me in depth the latest version of this novel.

I thank my former student at the Maxwell School of Syracuse University, Captain Brandi Shaddick, who edited, critiqued and commented repeatedly and most helpfully on the final version of this novel.

I thank my friends Timothy and Sharon Smith of Colgate University, who read and discussed this novel with me and with my wife at length. I especially thank Tim for professionally setting and formatting the final manuscript.

The greatest gratitude, however, must be reserved for my beloved granddaughter, Ruth Lindemann, who dedicated last summer, reading and editing the last version of this novel, with emphasis on the dialogue.

Chapter 1

Alexia, my dear, Alexia dreams her Grandma Rose-Anne saying to her, *I have something private I want to share with you.*

What is it, Grandma?

I'll tell you about it later, my dear, but I want you to stay away from those guns in the corner, the grandmother says in the dream.

But why, Grandma?

These guns are always loaded, sweetheart, and you mustn't ever, ever touch them.

Alexia is frightened. Her dream becomes a nightmare. *Why are they loaded, Grandma?* Alexia screams, as she begins to see Grandma Rose-Anne trip and fall down then get up while the grandmother, young, strong and beautiful, frantically chases rabbits and squirrels on a farm in upstate New York. Horrified and worried about her grandmother, Alexia screams again: *What're you doing, Grandma?*

The beasts are ruining Daddy's crops, my dear.

You've got to be careful, Grandma, I'm afraid you will fall down again!

Don't worry about me, my dear, I'm strong, I'll be all right.

Her heart racing, Alexia wakes up. Bewildered and confused, she sits on the edge of her bed and rubs her eyes and face in an effort to regain her composure. She stretches and stares out the window, recalling her grandmother's earlier conversations about rabbits and squirrels on a farm in upstate New York, where the grandmother grew up, and about loaded guns for hunting on the farm. She relaxes and stretches again. Oh, my Gosh, she then muses in amusement, Grandma Rose-Anne did look strong in the dream. She looked young and beautiful, as she once told me she used to be. Alexia rubs her face again, trying to fully awaken. I can imagine Grandma being strong, young

1

and beautiful all right, she continues to muse, but chasing rabbits and squir-rels! That was scary and hilarious, she smiles. And what's that private thing Grandma wants to share with me? Grandma mentioned that a few times, and she mentioned it again just a few days ago. Mystified, Alexia scowls, stretches one last time and jumps out of her bed to get ready for school.

Alexia wakes up at 6:20 every morning before school. Tall, thin and blond, she is a high school senior, and will graduate in June. She showers and dresses, but has no time for breakfast. Her school bus is due at 7:05. It will take her to the Valley Town Senior High School, in Valley Town, a town of about a hundred and fifty thousand in the state of Virginia, where she and her family live. She rides the bus with her twin brother Johnny, who sits in one section of the bus with some of his male friends. Alexia sits by herself in another section, waiting for her best friend, Joan Atkinson, who as usual will join her at the next bus stop.

When the bus reaches the next stop, Joan is not there. Alexia begins to wonder about her friend. Maybe she's sick, maybe she just overslept, maybe her mother will drive her to school this morning, maybe I'll share the dream about Grandma with her, she reflects. No, I shouldn't, I should just mention dreaming about Grandma, I'll keep what I dreamed private, she decides. She thinks about the day ahead, the fourth Monday of the fall semester of her senior year. She and Joan are taking physics, government for half the year, and economics for the other half, honors calculus and English (American and English Literature.) In English, which is a college level literature course, they do extensive reading and writing. They are assigned to read several novels and write a thoughtful essay about each. The two also have classes in Spanish and music, but they like the English class the most. They usually have four 80 minute classes each day. The first period is English, which begins at 7:45 am.

Alexia is relieved when she sees Joan waiting for her outside the classroom. "I wondered about you when you didn't get in the bus this morning," she says, hugging her best friend.

"I slept late, so Mom drove me. How was your weekend?"

"Great!"

"How's your Grandma?"

"Just about the same, I love Grandma's stories and she's always eager to talk about when she was young, and about her life on the farm in New York State where she grew up."

"Cool!"

"I'm enjoying it, but I feel sad."

"But why?"

"I just know she won't be with us very long, and I'm beginning to have crazy dreams about her."

"You shouldn't feel sad, Alexia. I know she's your Grandma and you love her very much, but she's an older person and has been quite sick, she's had a long and great life."

"I know," Alexia, blushes.

"Did you finish Jane Austin's novel?" Joan asks changing the subject.

"I have two more chapters to go, how about you?"

"I'm almost finished."

"What a great title, 'Sense and Sensibility.'"

"It *is* a great title," Joan smiles. Thin and blond like Alexia, but a little shorter, Joan has hazel eyes.

Alexia's eyes are sky blue. "'Sense and Sensibility,' it really fits the story."

"Yeah, it does!"

"Thank God we didn't have to submit our essays or discuss the novel today," adds Alexia.

"We do that Wednesday."

"I had a very busy weekend catching up on my homework and taking care of Grandma. As usual, that history assignment was too long."

"Mr. Nelson always gives us long assignments for the weekend."

"Does he think history is the only course we take?"

"He's a real jerk."

"Let's go in."

"Let's, did you notice Mat's new haircut?"

"It makes him look cuter."

"I wish he didn't smoke. Maybe if I bug him enough, he'll quit."

"The crew cut really makes him look like a fourteen-year-old."

"When I first saw it, I teased him about coming to school with his mommy."

Alexia giggles. "He's nice."

"Yeah, and he's very good-looking."

"He is."

The two girls walk into a crowded, noisy and unruly classroom, joining about thirty students. They sit next to each other and wait for the noise to subside.

Finally, the honors English teacher, Ms. Margaret Bates, enters and there is a sudden calm.

A petit, elegant and pleasant woman, in her middle forties, Ms. Bates is very dignified and attractive. She exudes confidence. She begins to speak distinctly and clearly. "The two sisters in 'Sense and Sensibility,'" Ms. Bates begins, "are symbols of two types of women, one is measured and reserved, who weighs every move she makes, every word she utters. The other is passionate and emotional, living by her emotions and instincts. I want you to read this novel carefully and thoughtfully. When you write your essays, I want you to apply what you have learned, not only here at Valley Town Senior High School, but also elsewhere. I want you to apply your common sense. What do you think of these two sisters? Are they real? Have you encountered women like them? Where? Which of the two do you like more? Why?"

Alexia is fascinated. She sneaks a look at Joan.

After class, the two girls walk to their homeroom for attendance and morning announcements.

"I like the sister who lives by her wits," Joan says.

"I guess most of us are like that," Alexia smiles.

"What type do you think Ms. Bates is?"

"Just see how she dresses and how she lectures."

"That may not be the whole story. I wonder why she assigned us this particular novel."

"She has a lot of sense!"

"That she does," Joan smiles.

After homeroom, they go to second period and then head to lunch.

"We should get to lunch, the line's going to be long today."

"Yeah, we should, they have chicken tenders."

"What are you going to get?"

"I'll just have salad, you?"

"I didn't have breakfast, and I'm very hungry, I'll probably have tenders and French fries."

"Good choices."

"Where do you want to sit?"

"Let's sit with Mat and Phil."

"Do you think we'll find them?"

"They'll find us."

At lunch, Alexia and Joan sit by themselves. They are soon joined by Mat Dodson and Phil Baker, both of whom are taking Ms. Bates' Literature class.

"I knew you would wait for us," Phil cracks.

"And we knew you would find us," Joan retorts.

"I love Ms. Bates," says Mat.

"She's cool," says Joan.

"Very," Alexia agrees.

"She's a great teacher," Phil says. "I really admire her."

"Are you guys going to the National Honor Society meeting after school?" Joan asks.

"Mat and I are," Phil says.

"Are you going, Alexia?"

"I can't, Phil, I need to go home to help my grandma."

"And you, Joan?"

"Yes, Mat, I'm coming."

"But I might go see Ms. Bates briefly for extra help," says Alexia. "Why don't you all come?"

"Yes, let's all go see Ms. Bates," says Joan.

"What do you think, Phil?" Mat asks.

"I can go."

"I can too," Mat agrees. "Let's all go see Ms. Jane Austin."

After school the four go to Ms. Bates' office briefly then Alexia takes the bus home.

Chapter 2

"Is that you, Alexia?" Grandma Rose-Anne asks in a feeble voice.

"Yes, it is, Grandma," Alexia says. "Need a pill?"

"I guess I do," Grandma Rose-Anne says. "The pain is coming back."

Widowed and struggling with terminal cancer at the age of seventy-one, the fragile Rose-Anne Riley Perry looks much older than her years. Her face is pale and wrinkled. She tries to sit up, but is unable to on her own. She had finally relented and moved in with her daughter and son-in-law, Carla and Michael Hartley and their seventeen-year-old twins, Alexia and Johnny. They live in a modest two-story home. Grandma's second floor bedroom is next to Alexia's.

After coming back from school, Alexia, who has been caring for her frail and ailing grandmother, peeks into her room, and finds her sleeping. Not wanting to disturb her, she leaves, but hearing the quavering voice, she comes back and reopens her grandmother's door. "Do you want it right now?"

"Yes, please."

Cherishing memories of the ailing woman's past favors, Alexia wants to return them. This attentiveness brings Alexia ever closer to her grandmother. Quietly closing the grandmother's door, Alexia hurries to the kitchen, fills a glass with water and places it on a tray with one large pill. She picks up a letter from a table in the hall and adds it to the tray. "Here you go, Grandma," she says, putting the tray down on a table next to her grandmother's bed and she helps her sit up.

"Thank you, dear."

"It's next to the water, Grandma."

The elderly woman reaches for the pill, puts it in her mouth, takes a sip of water and swallows it. "Thank you, Alexia. I'll feel better soon," says Grandma with a sigh.

"You will," says the smiling granddaughter.

Out of the corner of her eye, Grandma peeks at the letter on the tray. "What have we got here?"

"Do you want me to open it, Grandma?" Holding the letter, Alexia sits down on the edge of the bed next to her grandmother.

"Yes, please, where's it from?"

"New York."

"From the farm, from one of my brothers, either from Cliff or from Don, I'm sure."

"It's from Donald Riley."

"Please, hand me my glasses."

Alexia does as her grandmother requests. Then she notices the ancient eyes misting then tearing. "What's the matter, Grandma?" She rubs her grandmother's hand.

"I'm just being sentimental, sweetheart, remembering the hills and meadows where I was a little girl. I haven't been to New York in years, but someday I'd love for you to see the family farm. Maybe you'll go to college in the Northeast and visit the Riley homestead."

"Which college are you thinking of now, Grandma?"

"I'm thinking again about Ivy University, in Byron, New York, my dear. It's a really internationally outstanding university, Alexia. As I mentioned before, with your excellent academic record and high tests scores, you should keep it in mind."

"I will, Grandma." Alexia continues to hold her grandmother's trembling hand. "Do you honestly think I could get in?"

"I am sure you could. It doesn't hurt to apply, and apply for a scholarship my dear."

"I will, Grandma." She rubs her grandmother's hand gently. "Are you warm enough now?"

"Yes, dear, when I think about the Riley Farm and when I was young, I always think of you. You remind me of myself at your age."

"How is that?" Alexia smiles.

"Well, you're now seventeen, tall, blond and very pretty. You bring back a flood of memories and I sometimes worry about you."

"You mentioned that before, Grandma, and why do I bring back memories? How's that, Grandma?"

"Because you're lovely, and I want you to be careful, always very careful, Alexia."

"I always am, Grandma."

"I'm an old woman and old folks always worry about the young."

"You're still young at heart, Grandma. Please don't worry about me. I'll be O.K."

"Of course you will be." Grandma sighs again, and looks lovingly at Alexia.

"Grandma, what's your earliest memory?"

Taken aback by the question, she pauses, clears her throat and begins. "Well, my earliest memory is being stung by a wasp in my crib. So vivid is that recollection, Alexia, that I still close my eyes when I remember myself, a very young, curly-headed blond child screaming in my crib, which stood in a corner of my parents' room. I must've been a three-year-old at the time, because I had not been moved from my crib to share the bedroom with my older sister. Marilyn, your great aunt, was nineteen years older than me. She married when I was ten. Well, when I was seventeen, I was more outspoken than you."

Alexia smiles again, enjoying the newest recollection.

"Yes, I was outspoken, and I would express myself in earthy, even coarse vernacular, which arose from the farm environment I was born to. I lived with my parents, Carl and Juliana Riley, your great grandparents, on a dairy farm eight miles from Hamlet, New York, about two hundred miles south of Canada. As you know, I had four brothers and one sister. Hamlet was a small village of about four hundred. Around the countryside you would see hills, woods and lakes. And there were scattered white houses and red barns beside pastures and cultivated land. It was fifteen miles or so south of Stratford, home of a famous horseracing track, which attracted thousands of racing fans and tourists from many parts of the state. Stratford had a population of about thirty thousand in those days, some of whom worked in factories. Stratford was an industrial town twenty miles north of Ashton, New York. Ashton was a bigger city, about a hundred thousand. Most of Hamlet's population farmed but many worked in Stratford's industrial and agricultural factories, manufacturing equipment and tools that were marketed in New York City and in Canada. Our farm outside Hamlet was small and isolated, and life was very primitive, my dear. And it was especially challenging during World War II. Earnings fell sharply during the war. Many foods and other goods were in short supply and were rationed. My father, your great grandfather, Carl Riley, was in his seventies during the war. He was a big, rugged-looking, tall man, but a very sensitive soul. His furrowed, heavily wrinkled face hid his sensitivity. My mother, Juliana, was much younger and better educated. She was short and slender, less emotional, less vulnerable than Daddy. Mother only went to high school. She never went to college, and neither did Daddy. I don't think Daddy even finished high school. He was a farmer all his life."

Grandma pauses. "The farm was about seventy-five acres. It was situated near a bumpy country dirt road. As I said, it was surrounded by rolling hills. At the entrance to the farm, a few feet from the dirt road, stood two unpainted weather-beaten wooden silos near the shabby red barn, likewise coarsened and tanned from exposure to the weather. There were about thirty black and white Holstein cows in the barn. Attached to the barn, there was a small milk house, with an ice cream making room."

"They really made ice cream on the farm?" Alexia asks.

"Yes, Daddy made and sold ice cream on the farm. I still remember the big, handwritten sign posted on the outer door of the ice cream room: '*Carl's Premium Ice Cream: Produced by the Riley Farm Dairy*.' As a child, I loved living in the farmhouse near the creek and several yards back from the road. To me it seemed very large and grand. That is quite different from my present, adult perception. Actually, we had a modest house, considering our family size, and the fact that we had various relatives who came to stay with us from time to time. We only had three bedrooms, one for Marilyn and me, which my parents called the girls' room, one for my brothers, Floyd, Clifford, Donald and James, which was the boys' room, and my parents' room in the older part of the house. A living room, a kitchen and a screened porch made up the remainder of the house. My parents moved to Hamlet from Illinois in 1922. They converted most of the small house on the original property to those three bedrooms. The shed room, later my brothers' bedroom, had been a kitchen, a big walk-in closet and a pantry for previous residents. I always thought that closet to be an exciting place. It contained things that we didn't use all of the time. I loved to watch Mother get out the winter bedding from a large wooden chest which had been our family's kitchen wood box in Illinois. Sometimes I was allowed to get my older sister's beautiful china doll from the closet. There also was a strange looking musical instrument called a ukulele on one of the shelves. Mother and Daddy purchased it soon after my oldest brother Floyd died. They bought it for $14 from a traveling salesman and gave it to my brother Clifford, hoping it would cheer him up after the loss of his older brother. Cliff was never interested and he couldn't bring himself to touch that instrument. It was sad."

Grandma pauses again. "Remember, this all happened many, many years ago. The big closet and my brothers' bedroom were pretty much off-limits for me as a little girl."

Her mind still on the grandmother's brother who died young and on the brother who could never touch the ukulele, Alexia stares out the window, then her thoughts drift back to her grandmother.

"Not only did my brothers share this small room, but when we had male visitors they slept there, too. Even a hired hand occasionally occupied one of the beds." Grandmother smiles and touches Alexia's hand. "I remember Mother complained about Alfred Huxley, a hired man they called Fred. He was so huge and tall that he constantly pulled all the bed covers loose each night. Mr. Huxley's height reached six foot seven inches. He was the tallest person I remember when I was a child. His great stature left such an impression on me, I once remarked that I wanted to grow up to be as tall as Mr. Huxley and as slender and pretty as Cousin Sandy."

Alexia is now intrigued by the characters her grandmother described.

"Sandy was quite slender and very pretty as a young woman. She and her sister, Heather, were daughters of Mother's brother, William. They lived in Farmington, in Hamilton County and stayed with us a lot after their mother died. "From my brothers' bedroom," Grandmother continues, "there was a door into our parents' bedroom, which was rarely opened, and another door leading to the screened porch. Over that door to the porch, Alexia, as I mentioned the other day, were kept the family guns."

"Yes, I remember that," Alexia says smiling, and thinking about the dream she had a day or two earlier. She is still surprised that they would have guns on the farm. "What for, Grandma?"

"Family guns, dear," resumes Grandma calmly. "As I told you the other day, my brothers used the guns for hunting, or other necessary use around the farm. It was understood, dear, that those guns would never be touched, except for hunting. They were always loaded. One time I remember that rule being broken by a visitor in our home. A boyhood chum of my brother Donald, Tim Brooks, who had been in a mental institution for a time, found the rifle shells that had been hidden from him. Our family was asked to keep him during his rehabilitation because our farm was a less likely place for him to get into trouble than his parents' home in town. Well, somehow Tim found the loaded rifle and the shells, and he took the rifle out to the chicken yard where he started shooting at chickens' feet to watch them jump. Mother heard him and was frantic. She was afraid he would shoot her or Jimmy or me. Fortunately, she persuaded him to give her the gun, and the crisis ended. I don't believe I ever saw Mother shoot a gun, although I heard her talk about doing so in earlier years. Daddy didn't do any real hunting after I was big enough to remember," Grandmother sighs. "But as I may have told you yesterday, he did shoot rabbits that were damaging trees or shrubs around the place, or squirrels that were eating the corn crop." Grandma takes a deep breath. Then she continues.

"Our family ate a lot of rabbit and squirrel meat. We used the meat from such game even when we weren't actually depending on it. I really liked squirrel meat. I still remember the aroma of squirrel and dressing baking in the large oven heated by wood burning." The elderly woman looks out the window and sighs again. "That's why we had guns on the farm, my dear. My brother Floyd was the chief user of the guns and was the one who taught me and Jimmy about them. Cliff and Don didn't hunt as much. I vividly recall when and where we did this. It was a few feet behind our house, on a high bank overlooking the creek that he taught us to shoot a rifle using leatherback turtles as targets."

Alexia bites her lip and stares at her grandmother.

"I was especially fond of Floyd," the grandmother continues. "He was fifteen years older than me and thirteen years older than Jimmy and I delighted in the fact that he would take us hunting. I tagged along with him on night hunting trips to get possums and coons, with his dog, Skipper, at our heels and Jimmy and I carrying the gunny sack for the game. It seemed that we walked most of the night, through woods and fields. But I never was afraid because I was with Floyd. One night I remember wasn't so pleasant when Skipper tangled with a skunk."

"A skunk? Poor Skipper." Alexia is amused.

"Yes, Skipper stirred up the creature so that it sprayed the dog and us and the whole area around us with its offensive odor."

Alexia laughs with delight.

"When we got home we had to leave our clothing outside the house. Poor Skipper, for many days after the hunting trip he was boycotted by the whole Riley family. He really stunk for days. "On another hunting night," the grandmother resumes, "Skipper attacked a raccoon in the creek. My brothers and I watched helplessly. The raccoon nearly drowned Skipper. Floyd couldn't shoot the raccoon for fear of shooting Skipper. Finally Skipper maneuvered the coon to the bank of the creek and Floyd was able to shoot it."

Alexia squirms.

Grandma Rose-Anne pauses and glances at Alexia. Then she continues.

"I was very trusting of your great uncles as a young girl, but I wonder now how I could've been so trusting of my brother Donald, because he used to tease me unmercifully. Donald is nine years older than me. One dark cold night he took me snipe-hunting. He asked me if I would like to go and of course I wanted to go anywhere with him. We went out of the house and beyond the chicken coop. There he told me to hold the bag while he rounded up snipes. I stood still in the dark waiting patiently until I heard Don's voice and laughter back at the house. Suddenly, I realized I had been fooled by my big brother. That snipe-hunting was a joke, and he was inside laughing at me. It was so dark and I was so alone that I was afraid to move. After some time I got up the nerve to break loose and run for the house, crying all the way. Arriving at the house, I heard Mother's usual rebuke: 'Donald Riley,' she said sternly, 'you shouldn't do things like that to your younger sister.' Such teasing never made me unhappy for long. I idolized my brothers. I loved them very dearly."

Chapter 3

"I love your stories, Grandma, they're so interesting," Alexia tells her grandmother when she returns to her room that evening.

"I'm glad you do, my dear."

"It's great that you still remember all the details about your family and the Riley Farm."

"Yes, I remember a lot. That was the only life I knew. How did it go in school today, my dear?"

"School was great, Grandma. I love my English literature class. We're reading Jane Austin's novel, 'Sense and Sensibility,' and I have to write an essay about it."

"That's a great piece of literature, Alexia. I read it many, many years ago."

"Maybe you can read the essay I have to write about it and tell me what you think, Grandma. I have to submit it to Ms. Bates."

"I can, if you wish, my dear. Do you like your teacher?"

"I love her."

"That's good."

"Grandma, tell me more about your parents and about your brothers and about your life on the farm. Do you want me to ask Johnny to come in with us?"

"Johnny may be busy with more interesting things, my dear. Let's see, as I was saying, Alexia, my parents' room was the largest of three bedrooms. It often had two beds in it, to provide for visiting relatives. When I was three, I was promoted from the crib to share the girls' room with Marilyn. Thinking back, I now realize that Mother and Daddy had almost no privacy in that little house on the creek. But then, times were difficult. Even after I moved in with Marilyn I still had to go through my parents' bedroom to go to any other part of the house. And this central room of our home, my parents' bedroom, symbolized for me the security and love of the family I belonged to. My mother Juliana's faith was shown to me in many ways as a child, especially as I saw her kneel in prayer each night at her bedside. That was an important part of the security I felt as a young girl, Alexia. One of these days, when you are ready, I have something private I would like to share with you."

"That's sweet, Grandma."

"Thinking about the girls' room brings back many other memories of my childhood and youth. That room, Alexia, was quite small. I shared it with my sister until I was ten. The room had been Marilyn's, and in spite of her love for me, she must've resented giving up her privacy. She had to share her room and the things in it with me. As I said, Marilyn was nineteen years older than me, and therefore already a grown woman when I was born. To me, she was like a second mother, a wise, thoughtful and talented friend. During my early childhood, she was not well. She was often confined to her bed, or only managing to move about with crutches. I never knew the cause of her problem when I was young. Later, I learned that she had an accident when she was four. The family, then living in Illinois, was going to Grandpa and Grandma Riley's house when the horse shied. The buggy turned over and caught Marilyn's leg in a wheel as she was thrown to the ground. By the time she was twelve or thirteen years old, my parents noticed that she was not well and that her spine was developing a curve. After she graduated from the eighth grade in 1921, Mother and Daddy took her to Philadelphia, where she had an operation on her spine, after which the doctor said nothing was wrong with her spine, but with her hip. She had to spend a long time in a cast, then she had a brace and crutches. She took calcium to improve her bones. Over time she gradually improved, but she was still under doctor's care and had to stay in Illinois when the family moved from Illinois to New York in the fall of 1922. Marilyn did not see the house on the Creek until December of that year. That was very hard on my parents, but all of this happened three years before my birth in 1925," she sighs. "Do you want me to continue, my dear?"

"Yes, Grandma, I do."

"In spite of her affliction, Marilyn managed to complete high school in Hamlet and become a contributing member of the family. At times, her ailments confined her to bed, or at least to sedentary activities using her hands. I remember her teaching me embroidery before I was old enough to go to school, and my watching her doing beautiful needlework as I sat on the bed we shared. One quilt-top she made had embroidered feathers on it. I worked hard at trying to embroider too, but I constantly got knots in my thread and had to climb up onto our bed where she patiently untangled them. Although my stitches were far from perfect and beautiful like hers, I did learn how to do needle work. We had a double bed, a washstand and an intriguing dresser that was Marilyn's, which she took with her when she married. It had mirrors that would swing toward the center so that we could stand between them and see the back of our hair. Marilyn's hair was not as curly as mine. Poor Marilyn used to spend a lot of time keeping waves in her hair. In addition to pinning waves in while her hair was wet, she devised solutions to help secure the waves, one of which was a wave-set made by boiling flax seed. We raised the flax on our farm. One time Marilyn had some flax mixture sitting in a drinking glass ready to dip her comb in to set her hair. Don, my prankster older brother I told you about yesterday, came into the room. Thinking the solution was a glass of juice, he downed it before realizing what it was."

"It serves him right," Alexia giggles.

"It wasn't a disaster, but flax was a surefire laxative."

Alexia now laughs with delight.

"My sister used to share her bed with me. It was difficult in that double bed. I was a wiggly little girl and trying to lay still and not hurt my crippled sister was hard. But we had to sleep together. In the wintertime, we had feather beds, sort of like the English eiderdowns, except that we slept on them instead of using them for covers. When we got in bed we would sink down into the featherbed and it would keep us warm. One of my jobs was to help pick the down feathers off geese to make pillows and the feather beds. We would hold those poor geese upside down in our laps with their heads held under our arms while we picked off their feathers. The helpless birds squawked with each yank. I was so tender-hearted and used to cry when Mother told me to pluck, but she assured me that it didn't really hurt the geese."

"Did it?"

"Yes, I think so, my dear. At least it must've startled the poor creatures. In extremely cold weather, we would heat irons on the stove, the ones we also used for pressing clothes, and would wrap them in rags to put into the bed before going to bed. Sometimes the irons were still so hot when I went to bed that I couldn't put my feet against them. They did make the bed warmer in a room that had no heat. And we used to bathe in our room. The washstand, which had a rimmed top to hold a wash pan and a shelf with a water pitcher, was for bathing. As a child it represented the only method of bathing I knew. In the summer, I would take a bar of soap and a towel to the creek and bathe. After a hard, dirty workday in the fields, the men folk regularly used the creek as a bathtub in the summer. When I needed to do the same, I was required to wear a bathing suit. Of course, in the cold of winter, we were permitted to take our baths in the kitchen behind the wood stove with a wash pan of warm water. Each member of our family would take turns bathing behind the stove and the rest of the family would stay out of the kitchen. There was no heat in any of the bedrooms. In very severe weather, the water would turn to ice in the wash pan or pitcher if we forgot to empty them.

Water had to be carried to the room for bathing, and the dirty wash pan of water had to be carried outside and emptied by each one of us after we were clean and dressed. Baths, Alexia, weren't taken too often, usually just on Saturday nights, although I took more in the summertime. I always went barefoot in the summer. I was required to wash my feet each night in a tub kept at the well, which was the source of our water."

"It was a hard life, but an interesting one, Grandma."

"That's true, and you get used to it. Of course, people don't do that now, but who knows, some may still do it. Anyway, by the time I was ten, Marilyn was married, and the room was mine. It was on the north side of the house facing the creek, and had a window on that side. Even though the creek was normally far down from the high bank on which our house stood, occasionally rains upstream raised the creek high on the bank."

"It must've been scary."

"Yes, it was scary. One morning, Alexia, when I was a child, I woke up and looked out that window and there was nothing but water as far as I could see. Because the bank on the far side of the creek is not as high, the water had spread on that side clear across the field to the west pasture hill. I was terrified. I thought the end had come and that we would all be washed away. But then, like the many other times that the creek rose very high, it stopped short of coming over the bank around the house. I was very scared, I certainly was."

"I bet you were."

"Well, in thinking back about my room, I'm reminded of getting dressed in the morning for school and of all the clothing that I was required to wear. First, I had long underwear, either in two pieces or one-piece with a drop-seat. Next I wore long cotton stockings, which had to be pulled up over the long legs of the underwear. For a time, I had to wear a shoulder brace, which was sort of a vest pulled tight across my shoulders and down around my arms in front and laced tight to pull back my shoulders and make me stand straight. Next I wore a pair of homemade, knee-length bloomers. I then had to don a cotton petticoat and dress, both homemade, and put on high-top shoes and lace them up."

"Why did you have to do *all that*, Grandma?"

"Because the Northeast was very cold in the winter, my dear, and if the day was especially cold or snowy, my wraps before going outside for the two-mile walk to school included a two-piece snowsuit, boots, mittens and cap. Those were the days before the farm had electricity. We didn't have electricity, my dear. I didn't even use a lamp in my bedroom very much, because it stayed light late in the summer. In the winter, it was too cold to be in the bedroom unless I was in bed. If I needed a light, I usually carried a lamp from the kitchen. When I was little, Alexia, someone gave me a tiny kerosene lamp of blue metal, which I used sometimes. It didn't give me much light, but it was enough to dress by. Until I was in high school, nearly all of my dresses were made from sacks. Marilyn once told me that Mother made my first dress from a white flour sack, and Marilyn embroidered yellow ducks on it. During the depression, and even into the 1940's, sacks for chicken and other animal feed were printed so that they could be used for pretty dresses. Of course, one sack wasn't enough for an adult woman's dress. So, women traded sacks to get enough material with the same pattern. When we had neighborhood gatherings at the Hamlet Point School, the women would bring their sacks neatly washed and folded to trade."

Alexia was looking at her grandmother with awe.

"That was a very primitive existence by today's standards," the grandmother continues, "and the isolation on the farm was continually present. Our nearest neighbors were over a mile away from our home, and we rarely saw them, except at church services and meetings at the little country church when farm work was exchanged such as at threshing time. I, of course, was the only girl in the country school, except for short periods when some migrant farm workers were in the neighborhood, during harvest time for example. As a little farm girl, social life was essentially non-existent for me. My life basically was working on the farm and attending church on Sundays. Even though there were town children in the Sunday school, I was really an outsider who rarely had any interaction with them. I was a very bashful child, my dear, who preferred my own company. As I may have mentioned earlier, in the summers I never wore shoes, except to go to church. Knowing my primitive background, your grandfather, Chet Perry, bless his resting soul, who was a wonderful husband, Alexia, used to tease me that when it was time to attend school they had to lasso me and put me in a dress. I was terrified when my parents decided that my brother Jimmy and I should go to the town high school. The small country high school had little to offer and my parents wanted us to get a better education. It was four miles from Hamlet. And without school buses in those days, my parents arranged for a tiny apartment for us, where we lived during the week. Hamlet wasn't large. I had only twenty-five students in my class, but to me, a country girl, the town seemed like a metropolis. Daddy took us to town either on Monday mornings early, or late Sunday evenings. He came to town on Friday afternoons to do the trading. He brought farm produce and purchased his necessities and took us back to the farm. Because of this arrangement, my brother Jimmy and I were not in town for Friday night socials at the high school, and hardly any events took place on weeknights. This kept us from becoming part of groups or social happenings. And then the fact that country girls were not accepted very well by the town girls did nothing to build my confidence in social settings. My dresses were all homemade and still made mostly from feed sacks, and in many ways I was considered a hick from the sticks."

"Tell me about the fire on the farm, Grandma."

"You heard about that?" The elderly woman's eyes water.

"Yes, Mom told Johnny and me about it. I'm sorry if that upset you."

"I will tell you about it, Alexia."

"You don't have to, Grandma."

"I might as well," the grandmother sighs. "There was a fire pit only a few feet from the old barn, which was always burning trash."

"Are you all right, Grandma? You don't have to tell me about it."

"I'm all right, my dear, and you should also know this bit of family history. I remember two old tractors, which were deserted after my older brothers, Cliff and Don, went to war. The tractors were left unattended near the creek, which ran through the farm. There was a narrow, weathered bridge over the creek that divided the farm into two sections, one to the west, where the silos and the barn were, and the other to the east. Our family's small white house was on a hill in the eastern section of the farm. It was between two large maple trees, overlooking meadows and wooded lands. It was very pretty, but the farm was not prospering."

At first, Alexia hesitates. "Why, Grandma?" she then asks softly.

"Well, my darling, my brothers, Cliff, when he was twenty-nine, then Don, when he was twenty-five, were drafted into the Army and eventually they were shipped to Europe after several months of training during World War II. Daddy became depressed and couldn't operate the farm profitably. My brother Jimmy had an accident on the farm from which he later died and this tragedy changed my father. By himself, aging and demoralized, Dad seemed to give up. Impoverishment set in on the farm, my dear. Weeds and shrubs took over pastures, and the farm suffered from neglect. It was sad."

Alexia puts her head down.

Grandma Rose-Anne pauses, looks at Alexia momentarily then resumes. "With the farm yield continuing to fall, my dear, my parents no longer could make the monthly mortgage payments, and foreclosure loomed. They put an ad in the Stratford paper offering fields for rent." The elderly woman sighs again. "I remember a chill in the air that cold and windy morning in early December of 1942, when my parents went into the town of Stratford in search of work to save the farm. The cold winter wind blew and whistled menacingly. When they came back, I was standing helplessly near our home watching thick, dark smoke coming out of the barn. Our family didn't have insurance, we couldn't afford it. The barn was on fire. 'What's going on, Rose-Anne?' Mother screamed. When did this start?' 'Just started,' I screamed back.' 'I'll go tell the fire station?' Daddy shouted. 'Yes, hurry, Daddy,' I yelled back. 'Move back! Move back!' Mother hollered at me. Daddy, saying nothing, quickly rushed to the fire station. Mother Immediately grabbed a pail of water a few feet from the burning barn in a desperate effort to put the fire down, but the smoke was too much for her. She had to retreat toward the house, where I just stood helpless, unable to do anything.

The fire continued to move fast, eating up the bales of hay on its way. Trapped by the fire and the smoke, the dying cows moaned and cried like humans. Then something exploded inside the barn. The stench of the burning animals filled the air. It was hours before the Stratford Fire Department could bring the fire under control. There was severe damage to the barn. The milk house and the ice cream making machine were destroyed. The cows all succumbed to the flames. We all went inside our house stunned, not believing what had happened. Mother realized that moving from the farm was inevitable, even before Daddy could digest what had happened."

Feeling sad and hoping that her own tears won't upset Grandma, Alexia puts her head down.

"Several weeks later, Mother said to Daddy that he should resume looking for work in Stratford factories, which he did, but Daddy had worked as a farmer all his life, and he had no training for factory work. He was sick over the idea of leaving his farm, which he loved very dearly. As we prepared to move, Daddy began to look at the hills surrounding the charred rubble that had been our farm. 'No! No! He muttered under his breath,' shaking his head. 'Cain't take that!' 'What's the matter, Carl?' Mother said to Daddy, 'we can't look back.' 'Cain't take it no more, Julie; thought we'd manage 'til the boys came back; just didn't work; the fire done us in,' Daddy said. 'We can't be looking back, you did all you could, Carl,' Mother said to Daddy. 'Cain't take it no more, hate them factories, I ain't gonna work in no factory,' Daddy said. 'Poor Carl,' Mother murmured under her breath, hefting a dilapidated suitcase into our old Ford coupe. 'Julie,' Daddy shouted, 'cain't take it no more, don't wanna move to no Stratford, just won't.' I gazed at Daddy. I was scared out of my wits. Mother gazed at Daddy too. She was very grim. 'Cain't take it no more, Julie, not gonna work in no factory,' Daddy said. 'I know it ain't easy, Carl, but we got to tough it out, no choice, don't wanna lose the rest of the farm, do we?' Mother shouted back to Daddy. But Daddy just looked dazed. Mother and I were loading the car when Daddy went inside. I ran after him. I saw him put the shotgun in his mouth and die without making a sound. 'Daddy!! How could you!!' I screamed." The elderly woman closes her eyes. "Daddy's single shot often rings in my ears when I think about the hills and the meadows I haven't seen for so long."

"I'm sorry, that's so sad, Grandma."

"This is enough now, my dear. I'll tell you more a little later."

Chapter 4

"So, how's your grandmother?" Joan asks Alexia the next morning.

The two young friends are on their way to school on the Valley Town Senior High School bus.

"She's OK," Alexia replies grimly. Alexia is reluctant to share with her best friend the details that the grandmother had shared with Alexia the day before about the fire on her grandmother's family farm more than a half century ago, which led to the suicide of her great-grandfather. Alexia is still struggling to cope with the shock of that bit of tragic family history. Her grandmother's tears, when she was informing Alexia of her great grandfather's suicide, had torn Alexia's heart, and she continues to be tormented by it.

"Well, I finished my essay for Ms. Bates class," Joan says, subdued.

"I'm almost finished with mine. I should have it ready by tomorrow."

"Would you like to see mine?"

"Let's wait until I have mine done, then we can exchange them before we submit them. What do you think?"

"Good idea. I'm still recovering from the shock of my SAT's, Alexia."

"You shouldn't be, they're not bad."

"Compared to yours they are."

"I guess I'm just lucky."

"It's more than that, I'm sure. I'm really proud of you!"

"I'm a freak, Joan."

"Did you send your last application to Ivy University?"

"Not yet, I will after I finish Ms. Bates' essay."

"With your SAT's and grades you can go anywhere, but I wish we could go to the same School."

"We might still be able to."

"Not if Ivy University accepts you, or gets you a scholarship."

"That's a long shot."

"What made you think of Ivy University? It's so far away."

"My grandmother told me about it. She said it is one of the most distinguished universities in the Northeast."

"I'm sure it is, but it is so far away, and it is isolated, in a cold little Upstate New York town."

"That's true, and I also have heard that the little town, Byron, is very cold in the winter. Mom thinks I'm crazy to want go there. She wants me to go to Valley Town, with Johnny. It's way cheaper."

"Makes sense, what does your dad think?"

"He hasn't said much, but Johnny doesn't want me to be far away. He's been trying to convince me to go to Valley Town."

"I thought he might do that."

"What have you decided?"

"Well, while my grades are not bad, my SAT's being what they are, I guess Valley Town may have to be it, too. I would love to go with you to Ivy, but I know I can't get in, let alone get a scholarship there."

"Well, let's wait and see. I really don't know what I'm going to do, Joan. I really don't want to be far away from home and from my friends, and especially from you. I know that I'm going to miss you and Johnny a lot, but who knows? Ivy may not be interested in a young southern gal who's never been out of Virginia."

"I won't bet on that. I am sure you will get in, Alexia. Anyway, I need to get to calculus. See you later."

"Take it easy." Alexia too rushes to her government class, another one that she likes very much.

Chapter 5

"These are yesterday's flowers," Alexia says softly when she returns from school, walking into her grandmother's room and reaching for a vase of red and yellow roses she had previously placed on the windowsill. Alexia knows that her grandmother loves roses.

"They're lovely," Rose-Anne says in a low, weak voice.

"The arrangement isn't quite what I want though."

"They're quite pretty, my dear. Thank you."

"I hope they stay fresh."

"They will. Don't worry about them. Maybe they'll last longer if I water them every day, and when they wilt, I'll bring you more and different ones.

"Thank you, my dear. They really are a beautiful selection of roses, a very attractive selection. Come sit near me, Alexia. I want to tell you what happened after my father died. Would you like to know that?"

Alexia moves closer to her grandmother. "Yes, Grandma, I do."

"Of course you do, but I want you to keep what I tell you private, between you and me as long as I live.

Alexia looks at her ailing grandmother apprehensively. "Is this the private matter you've mentioned the other day, Grandma?

"Yes it is, are you surprised, my dear?"

"I guess I am a little, Grandma."

"Do you think that might be a heavy burden on you?"

"I don't think so, Grandma. Does Mom know?"

"No, she doesn't." The elderly woman pauses. "I don't want her to know, my dear."

"Why, Grandma?"

"It's a complicated matter, my dear, and I just would rather that she doesn't know, not now anyway. Maybe after I die she will know, or find out."

At first, Alexia hesitates, feeling a little frightened. Then she reaches for her grandmother's soft hand and rubs it gently. "How about Johnny, Grandma?"

"Johnny too will find out after I die, my dear. Do you prefer that we postpone this until you are ready? If you like, we can do that, Alexia."

Alexia thinks a little. She doesn't answer.

"Let us delay it, my dear. Take your time and think it over."

"No, Grandma, please don't delay it. I want to hear it now. I don't want to delay it."

"It's better for you to think it over, my dear. There's sadness in what I'll be saying, much sadness, Alexia. Just take more time to think it over. I also want to think it over myself, my dear. Maybe later would be better, maybe after you graduate from High School, my dear Alexia."

"No, Grandma, I'm ready now. Please go ahead, Grandma, you can tell me now. I'm ready, and I won't tell Mom, or Johnny, or anyone else, I promise."

"There's some sadness in what I'll be saying, my dear," the grandmother repeats.

Alexia's curiosity is rising as she looks intently at her troubled grandmother. "It's all right, Grandma, I want you to tell me. I'm ready."

The older woman pauses. "All right, my dear, I'll tell you."

"Great, Grandma." Alexia begins to listen attentively.

"After Daddy's death, Alexia, Mother worked in the Stratford Tractor Factory. I continued high school and kept house with Mother. Then I went to work as a cleaning girl in the home of a wealthy Stratford family. The man of the family was owner-manager of a cutlery factory. His wife stayed at home most of the time. Their son, an only child and football star in Stratford High School, was planning to enlist in the Army Air Force after his graduation. Whenever I worked at this large, stately mansion the son stayed home from school to flirt with me. His mother, who certainly noticed, paid little attention. Growing ever bolder, he began increasing his baiting and harassing of me. At first, I ignored his repeated references to my 'pretty face' and 'large bosom,' even feeling vaguely flattered. Eventually I resented him. I felt increasingly intimidated and frightened."

Alexia listens apprehensively, expecting something horrible is about to happen.

"One cold afternoon in early March of 1943, I was about to enter his room to clean it. I was surprised to find him lying in bed. 'Excuse me,' I said, moving to leave. 'You may stay, I'm leaving," he said. I stayed outside waiting. He got up, stood before a mirror framed in mother-of-pearl, which hung on one wall of his room, checked his image in the mirror, then combed his hair and started to whistle. 'You can come in,' he repeated, 'I'm leaving.' I didn't move. I stayed outside his room waiting for him to leave. 'What's the matter? Don't you want to come in? 'Come in, I don't mind,' he said. 'I'll wait,' I replied. 'Wait!! It may be a long wait!' he said. Suddenly, he rushed out, swerved toward me, reached for my breast and pinched me."

Blushing, Alexia is now frightened, but is waiting for more.

"I pushed him away, ran to the kitchen for his mother's protection, but didn't dare tell her."

"Why didn't you, Grandma?" Alexia asks.

"I was afraid of losing my job. Mother and I were struggling to make ends meet."

Alexia looks down at the floor, with sadness and fear.

"When he finally left, I went into his room, cleaned it hurriedly, took my pay for the day's work and left. When I returned to our newly rented apartment in Stratford, I did not tell the story to Mother, who was working overtime, often seven days a week. I was afraid of burdening her with my problems."

Alexia continues to listen and look down at the floor.

"Then on another cold, windy Saturday afternoon in late March of that year," the grandmother continues, "the woman of the house was out and I was sure that her son was out too, but I was uneasy when I entered his room to clean. He suddenly came out of nowhere, surprised me from behind, and forced his body against mine. 'Rose-Anne, are you going to let me or not?' he asked. 'Let you what!?' I shoved him, my whole body shaking. 'You know what,' he said, flipping up my skirt and pressing his hand between my legs. I shouted 'Get away from me! Stop it! No! No! Get away!' I began to scream.

Alexia closes her eyes, her heart pounding.

"'Don't scream!' he whispered. 'Stop it! Stop it!' He hissed, gripping me again violently from behind. I began to struggle with him. 'I'm telling you! No one's in the house,' he shouted. 'Stop it! Don't kick me,' he continued to shout and beat me. 'No! No! No!' I screamed. 'Let me go, let me go.' 'Don't fight me!' he began to scream and punch me. 'Stop it! Stop it, bitch! I'll kill you if you don't stop!' He continued hitting. I struggled with him for several minutes. I scratched his face and bit him."

Alexia is distraught and grieved. She only gapes at her grandmother with pained anticipation.

"He tore my blouse and panties, punched and kicked me again and again. He finally overpowered me and threw me on his bed. I kneed him in the chest, knocking him backwards. He came back in fury, more determined than ever. He punched me in the face and the ribs repeatedly. I was very exhausted. He forced me … he raped me."

"Oh, my God, Oh, my God," Grandma, Alexia exclaims. "How could anyone be that beastly?! What did you do? Where did he go?" Her voice quivering, she covers her face.

"I went home. I don't know where he went. Mother was working. It was night when she finally arrived at our rented apartment. My blood stains were on the steps of the terrace under the dimly lit lantern. The apartment inside was dark. I heard Mother turn on the light and exclaim: 'My goodness! More blood is splattered on the hall floor, why is the door to the downstairs bathroom wide open?! Where are you, Rosy?' Crying quietly in my bed upstairs, I could not answer. 'Are you home, Rose-Anne? Goodness sake, what is this? More blood on the kitchen floor!' I heard her say. 'I'm here in the bedroom, Mother,' I finally sobbed from my bed upstairs. 'Whatever is the matter, Rosy!?' Mother ran up the stairs. 'I was raped,' I sobbed. 'You were what?!' 'Their son, he raped me! He raped me!' I cried. 'How?! Where?!' she asked. 'In his room.' I said. 'What on earth were you doing in his room?' 'I was cleaning.' 'The swine!' Mother sobbed! 'I was cleaning his room, I was just trying to get my work done' I cried. 'The swine!! Mother repeated. 'He beat me bad, Mother!' I said. 'He did!?' Mother said. 'He raped me, Mother! He raped me! He did!' I said. 'He did!!? Where was his mother!?' Mother asked. 'She was out. She wasn't home,' I said. 'Oh, my God!!' Mother cried. My eyes were puffed and my face was swollen with cuts and bruises. 'The swine!!The swine!!' Mother continued to repeat. 'I don't know why he didn't kill me' I said. 'I'm sorry, honey. I'm so sorry, honey,' Mother continued to comfort me. 'He almost killed me, Mother! He almost did!' I said. 'I'm sorry, Rosy,' Mother continued to say. 'The swine! The swine!' 'I would've been better off if he had killed me, Mother!' I said. 'No, don't say that,' she said. 'He can't be allowed to do this to me or anyone else who works in his house. Please get the cops, please Mother!' I begged her. 'I will, honey,' she said. 'Get the cops! I think we have to get the cops, Mother, right now,' I pleaded with her. 'The swine!!' she murmured again and again. 'If only we had a phone, Mother!' I said. We couldn't afford a phone in those days, Alexia, we were very poor. 'Get the cops I cried again! I didn't ask for any of this and I don't deserve it, please, Mother!' I begged her again. 'Rose-Anne, listen!' Mother finally said, 'I'm afraid to call the cops, it could create a lot more trouble.' 'Go call the cops, Mother!' I screamed. 'Rose-Anne, please listen to me,' Mother said. 'What?!' I asked. 'Rose-Anne,' Mother said, looking at me directly, 'Rose-Anne, the man who owns that big mansion is a big shot.' 'I don't care! Call the cops!' I screamed. 'We must be careful, honey,' she said. 'Why? Why?' I continued to scream. 'Why? Why?' I repeated again and again. 'Please get the cops, Mother! I don't care how big a name that man has. Go get the cops, please, Mother.'"

Alexia is devastated. "Did the police come, Grandma?"

"No, they didn't because Mother never called them. She only said: 'Now just rest and we'll get some ice on your face. That will take care of the swelling.' Then she muttered: 'Oh, Lord God!! What have we done?!' And she began to cry again. 'Go get the cops now, Mother! Let them come and see what he did to me! Now, now, Mother!' I screamed. 'I will, I will,' she continued to cry. 'Oh, my God! Oh my God! What have we done to deserve all this? The swine! The swine!' Mother kept saying."

Alexia begins to cry.

Moving in her bed, the frail elderly woman clutches her granddaughter's hand.

"I am sorry, Alexia." She gazes helplessly. "That's right, Mother never called the police. Instead, she rushed to the mansion where I worked, and confronted his mother, and that woman came back with Mother to our apartment and offered to pay all my medical bills and to give me $5,000 for my humiliation, my pain and my suffering, as if money could heal the pain and buy my soul. The woman also offered to pay the $3,000 mortgage on our farm, so that Mother and I could go back to the farm and leave Stratford. In return, neither I nor Mother would say anything about what happened. Not to anyone, ever."

"Did you ever, Grandma?"

"I just couldn't bring myself to talk about it."

"Did you accept the money?"

"'I want him jailed,' I wailed after his mother left. 'I know you do' Mother said. 'I don't want their filthy money, Mother,' I screamed. 'I know you don't, honey,' she said. 'Don't do this to me, Mother, please, please don't. Do you understand?' I cried. 'I understand.' I cried and cried, Alexia. I felt awful."

Sad and still tearing, Alexia continues to look down at the floor.

"I just cried and cried my heart out. 'It's your decision, honey, not mine,' Mother then said. 'Then don't talk to me about it,' I told her. 'I won't,' she said. 'Thank you,' I begged her. Then she started again: 'Rose-Anne, all I'm saying is that his going to jail doesn't solve anything.' 'Why doesn't it?' I pleaded. 'The boy is crazy, Rose-Anne!' she said. 'Yes, the boy is crazy!!' I said. 'He is,' she said, 'he is a lunatic.' 'He could kill, Mother!!' I implored her. 'I know he could,' she said. 'So, should we let him get away with it?' I began to cry again. 'No, we shouldn't,' she said. 'Well?' I entreated her. 'The boy's dangerous,' she repeated. 'He's dangerous all right, and he should go to jail, Mother!' 'So he goes to jail, and it's the chair or twenty to thirty years for rape!' she said. 'Good! That's what he deserves!' I said. 'But why not let his parents pay for his mistake, Rose-Anne?' Mother said. 'What good is that!? I was raped, Mother!!' I began to cry again. 'I know, but we can't undo what was done' Mother answered. 'We can send him to jail, Mother!' I cried. 'All I'm saying is that his going to jail doesn't help us any,' she said. 'And you sure can use the money, honey.' 'What money?!' I cried. 'You're a pretty girl, Rose-Anne,' she said. 'What're you talking about, Mother?!' I asked her. 'You should go to college,' she said. 'What for?! I was raped, Mother!' I cried. 'You were in the top of your class, $5,000 is more than enough for four years in college,' she said. 'I don't want that, Mother! I want the bastard to go to jail!' I cried. 'Maybe you'll meet a nice young man there' she said. I was so mad that I just didn't answer her any more. 'Think about that, honey,' she said. 'You're a smart girl. That's all I'm saying. Get something for yourself out of this.' Then I just lost it. 'Castrate the son of a bitch! That's what I want,' I screamed. 'I know,' Mother said. 'I want to see him locked up for life!' I shouted. 'I understand, honey. I'd like that too,' she said. 'No, you don't understand!' I cried. 'But you know that man is a big shot in Stratford,' Mother repeated. 'So what!?' I cried. 'How do we know that he won't pay off the cops?' she asked. 'Pay off the cops!!' I cried. 'He has what it takes to do just that, you know,' she said. 'That's just it. The animal is trying to buy us off, isn't he!?' I screamed. 'Rose-Anne, listen,' she begged me. 'I won't let him! He's trying to buy us off!' I said. 'Yes, he is, but better we get the cash than the cops!' she said. 'Better us than the cops?!!' I shouted. We can save the farm, Rose-Anne,' she finally said. I was exhausted by then, Alexia. I put my head down and sobbed. 'Your poor father died heart-broken for it,' Mother cried. 'Those people are filthy rich,' I sobbed. 'Yes, they are,' she said. 'And can get away with murder,' I continued to sob. 'This is the way the world is,' Mother told me, Alexia. 'Sell myself for a farm!' I cried. 'And what's better, to go public, and have your scar exposed to the whole world, get nothing but disgrace, or to keep it private and get something for it?' Mother asked. 'I'm nothing!' I cried. With tears in her eyes, Mother then pleaded: 'Rose-Anne, you're everything, but your brothers are on my mind day and night. God only knows if they'll ever come home alive.' I finally relented. 'I know they are, Mother, I said. 'Your brothers shouldn't hear about this, on top of your brother's and father's deaths,' she begged. 'I know, Mother, I know,' I finally relented, 'do whatever you see fit,' I finally agreed."

"Your mother was a tough woman, Grandma."

"She was tough, but she was also a very good woman in many ways too, a really wonderful mother," Rose-Anne tells her granddaughter. "It's true that she was not very sophisticated, and may have seen the rape as an opportunity, to save the farm and to get me educated, but she had a good heart, Alexia." The grandmother pauses, she then looks at her astonished granddaughter and says: "That's enough for now, my dear. You need to get ready for school tomorrow. I'll tell you more a little later."

Chapter 6

The next morning, shortly before Alexia boards the school bus, her twin brother Johnny joins her. "Your eyes are puffed, and you've been crying. What's wrong, Alexia?"

"I'm behind in my homework. I'm nervous about it."

"Is that it?" Johnny seems skeptical. "Anything I can do, Alexia?"

"No, thanks, Johnny, I'll be fine. Please don't tell Mom anything."

At the next stop Alexia's friend Joan joins Alexia, sitting next to her as usual. "What's the matter?" Joan whispers, "Did you stay up all night last night writing your essay? Your eyes are blood shot. You look exhausted."

"Do I?"

"You look very tired. You should've gone back to bed. Have you finished your essay?"

"No, I haven't."

Joan pauses a little. "Is something wrong?" She finally asks.

"Yes," Alexia says, her eyes tearing.

"What is it, Alexia?" Joan whispers, beginning to tear a little herself.

"I will talk to you about it later, not now."

Alexia and Joan walk together to their English class, but Alexia waits outside the door for Ms. Bates. When she arrives, Alexia informs her that she is having family problems and hasn't finished her essay, but that she will have it ready the next day and will deliver it to Ms. Bates office directly.

"Are you all right, Alexia? Should you go see the nurse?"

"I'll be all right, Ms. Bates," Alexia responds, struggling to keep her composure.

"All right, then, you can turn in your essay tomorrow, but if you need more time, just let me know. You've been an outstanding student, Alexia. I'm sorry you're not feeling well. Take care of yourself."

"Thank you, Ms. Bates, I'll be all right."

"I hope so."

After their class, Alexia and Joan walk together to homeroom.

"Is your grandma OK?" Joan asks.

"She's just about the same," Alexia says, "and it isn't her health now, it's what she's been telling me about her life. It's as if I'm seeing a long movie of a tragic life. It's just devastating."

Joan remains quiet waiting for her friend to continue. She reaches for Alexia's hand and caresses it.

"I don't want to depress you or burden you with my troubles, Joan."

"It's OK. You won't trouble me, Alexia. Just remember I always want to stand by you!"

"I know you do. My poor grandmother witnessed the suicide of her father, can you believe that?"

"Wow! I can't imagine what that would be like. That's awful." Joan says.

"The other part of her tale is more devastating. She doesn't want me to share that with anyone while she is still alive, not even with Mom. I'm not sure I have the strength to share it with anyone anyway." Alexia sobs.

"Then don't. I'm sorry, I'm very sorry, Alexia," Joan says softly, tears now rolling down her cheek. She continues to hold Alexia's hand. "I'm always here for you, Alexia. I am really so sorry."

"Thank you, Joan. You're a good friend, and I appreciate it so much."

Alexia has just returned from school. It is an unusually rainy day. Lying in her bed, she listens to rain drumming on the tin roof outside her window. She loves that sound and begins to imagine herself standing in the rain, the water pelting her head, wetting her hair, running down from her shoulders and soaking her dress. She begins thinking again about her grandmother's revelations and continues to be troubled. Then she begins wondering about how comfortable her grandmother's room feels to her. She gets up, stretches, and goes to her grandmother's room, with its familiar scent. She begins to wonder why wherever her grandmother is, or goes, or sits, everything seems touched by that scent. Knowing that her grandmother never wears perfume, she is not sure why.

"Oh, Alexia!" the grandmother greets her granddaughter. "I heard you and Johnny come back from school."

As usual, Alexia sits by her grandmother and rubs her hand. "How are you feeling, Grandma? Are you ready for your pill?"

"I'm all right now, maybe in a little while I'll need the pill, dear."

"What happened, Grandma? Did you and your mother receive the payment?"

The elderly woman sighs. "Yes, we did."

"Did you then move back to the farm?" Alexia is unable to stop thinking about the revelation the grandmother has made and wants to know more.

"Not immediately," the grandmother says. "Mother and I had another disagreement. Then, after we did receive the money, I began to suspect that I was pregnant."

Stunned, Alexia begins to feel queasy.

"A few days after we received the money, I told Mother that I had missed two periods. I asked her if I could be pregnant. Mother said: 'No, Lord! Don't tell me!' At that point, I lost it again. I screamed: 'Yes, Lord! I'm telling you!' Mother then ran to the kitchen. 'Oh, my God.' she muttered. 'Don't run, Mother! You wanted a God damn, stupid settlement, so what do we do now!?' I screamed. 'I'm not running. You know that I don't run and I won't run. I just need to think, please!' 'Think!? Think what!?' Mother did not answer. 'Mother, I'm pregnant!' I shouted. Poor Mother put her head on the kitchen table and began to cry. 'I want to miscarry, Mother, get it?!' I shouted. 'Yes, yes I do, she choked. 'Hell, Mother, and I want to flush it down the toilet, I screamed. 'Yes, I understand, Rose-Anne,' she said. 'But, profanity!!?' she cried. 'Yes, profanity, Mother!!' I shouted. 'Don't, please don't talk that way it doesn't help us any,' Mother cried. 'Yeah, don't swear, it sounds like hell! My body for sale!! The whole big profane deal!! Profanity, my ass!!' I was out of my mind."

"I don't blame you, Grandma, did you miscarry?"

Rose-Anne looks out the window, visibly tormented. She does not answer her granddaughter's question.

"The next day," she continues, "the rapist's mother returned to our apartment. Mother angrily told her about my condition. 'We'll do all we can to be helpful,' she snapped at Mother, 'but stop screaming, and don't you dare scream at me again.' 'I'm sorry,' Mother said, 'but my daughter is - ah - to say the least, is very upset.' 'We're upset too, we all are upset and feel terrible,' the woman shouted at Mother again. 'My husband and I are sick over it. We want to pay for our son's horrible behavior.' 'My daughter is upstairs, and I'll certainly tell her what you've said, but she wants to miscarry.' Mother was intimidated. 'If that's what she wants, we'll meet the costs, whatever! We want to do what's right for her and for you. What else can I say?' the woman said calmly. 'I don't know how to go about it,' Mother said. 'I don't either,' the woman said. 'I'm terrified by the thought, and I don't know if anyone can help us here in Stratford. Who does abortions in Stratford?' Mother asked the woman. 'You can't have it done in Stratford, Mrs. Riley' the woman said. 'Not even in New York State?' Mother asked. "Not even in New York State, or in the United States,' the woman said. 'Where can we have it done then?' Mother asked. 'I don't know where myself,' the woman said. 'It's illegal. I need to discuss this with my husband. He may know.' 'Yes, please talk to him,' Mother pleaded. 'You and your daughter are very upset now,' the woman said. 'We certainly are,' Mother agreed. 'And my husband and I understand why,' the woman replied. 'Thank you for that,' Mother said. 'You two may want to think about it more,' the woman then said. 'Yes,' Mother said. 'As I told you,' the woman continued, 'we want to do the right thing for her and for you and for your family.' 'I know we should think about it,' Mother told her, 'but Rose-Anne is not herself now, Mrs. Arlington.' 'I'm sorry, Mrs. Riley,' the woman finally said. 'I'm not comfortable thinking about abortions,' Mother then responded. 'I agree, it is a distressing subject,' the woman said. 'Would it be dangerous for Rose-Anne? Would we go to jail for it? I just don't know the answers to any of these questions,' Mother said. 'I don't either,' Mrs. Arlington sighed. 'What are we to do?!' Mother asked. 'I'm sorry, Mrs. Riley. What our son did to Rose-Anne was horrible and inexcusable, but the baby? I just don't know what to say about that,' she replied. 'I don't know what to do,' Mother cried, 'but my daughter is determined. She is adamant, Mrs. Arlington. She doesn't want the baby.' 'I am very sorry, but I can understand how she feels,' the woman said. 'Can you?' Mother asked her. 'Yes, I certainly can,' the woman said, 'but who knows? Maybe she'll have a change of heart.' 'I hope so,' Mother continued to cry. 'I know these are difficult times for you and for your daughter, and for all of us, but whatever you want us to do to help her we will do it,' the woman promised. 'Let's hope that your daughter will soon recover from her trauma, but as long as it doesn't make things worse for everybody, we will pay any and all expenses for whatever your daughter decides to do.' Thank you,' Mother told the woman."

Grandma Rose-Anne sighs again and looks at Alexia.

"So, my dear, that's why I want you to be careful. I want you to be careful always. Do you understand now?"

"I do. Yes, I do, and I will be very careful, Grandma. You worry because there is reason to worry, but don't worry about me."

"Be careful, especially with young men that you don't know, won't you?"

"I will, I promise I will, Grandma," Alexia reassures her grandmother. She pauses and begins to observe the grandmother's pained face as the ailing woman reaches for her pill. Alexia agonizes about whether to ask again whether the grandmother had aborted the pregnancy.

She hesitates, but finally she asks again:

"Did you abort the pregnancy, Grandma?"

Appearing to be troubled and in severe pain, the grandmother says in a very low voice: "Can we talk about that later, my dear?"

"Yes, we can, Grandma," but Alexia finds it hard to move forward. She knows that not knowing would torment her, even in her dreams. "I'll go get you a glass of water," she finally says.

"Thank you, Alexia."

Chapter 7

"You look better than you did yesterday, much better, Alexia," Joan says to Alexia the next morning on the school bus.

"I feel much better, thank you, Joan, and I have news."

Joan looks at Alexia without asking.

"Do you want to know?" Alexia asks.

"Yes, of course."

"I received an early admissions acceptance from Ivy University. They granted me a full-ride, room and board, too."

"Fantastic," Joan says, beaming. "You can't beat that, Alexia. You have to accept it. As much as I wish we could stay together, you can't decline that. Have you told your parents?"

"Not yet, I only told my grandmother. She was in tears hearing it. I could see the joy on her face, Joan."

"All the more reason you should accept it. Have you told Johnny?"

"Not yet, but I will today. Poor Johnny, he has been dreading this."

"I am sure he will understand."

"Sure he will, and he wants the best for me. I am going to tell him before I tell Mom and Dad. I am sure Dad will be supportive. It's Mom who will try to pressure me to stay home, but even she will eventually accept it."

"I am so happy for you, Alexia. You've been under a lot of emotional strain. You really needed this bit of good news. That's just great, Alexia."

"Thank you, Joan, you are a great friend, and we'll talk on the phone every day."

"We will. Are you going to tell your parents today too?"

"Yes, then I'll tell the school and our friends. I am really excited, Joan, even more today than yesterday. It's just beginning to sink in."

"I can understand that. That's awesome."

After school, Alexia checks on her grandmother as usual. "Is that you, Alexia?"

"Yes, it is, Grandma."

"I am all right, dear, I'm still excited about your good news."

"I haven't told Johnny, or Mom, or Dad. I want to do that then come back."

"That's fine, my dear. Go inform the family, I'll wait for you. That's just marvelous."

First Alexia goes to her twin's room and knocks at his door. "Anybody home?"

"Yes!" Johnny replies in his bass voice.

Alexia goes in. She finds her brother lying on top of his bed uncovered. "I have news," she says, "I got accepted by Ivy University. They gave me a full-ride."

Johnny flips over and sits up on the edge of his bed to face his smiling twin. "That's great Alexia, congratulations!"

"Thanks!"

"Have you told Mom and Dad?"

"Not yet, but I will."

"I guess no one can argue against that. I hate to see you go so far away, but you can't decline something like this."

"I'm excited, seriously, really excited!"

"I don't blame you."

"Would you come with me when I tell them?"

"Of course I will. Why though?"

"I don't know, Dad will be all right, I just worry about Mom. She might try to talk me out of it."

"How can she? Who would decline something like this?"

"She has been concerned about its being too far away and cold, you know."

"That's nothing, Alexia. This is a once in a life time thing, you can't decline it. I'm sure Mom will be fine with it."

"I hope so."

Alexia sits with Johnny and her parents for dinner after Alexia delivered dinner to her grandmother in her bedroom.

"Guess what," she says matter-of-factly. "I received an acceptance from Ivy University today, with an offer included for a full ride!"

"That's great, Alexia," her father, Michael Hartley, says spontaneously. "That's great, sweetheart. Congratulations!" He gets up off his chair at the head of the table, and moves to his daughter's chair on his left and hugs and kisses her. "Isn't that wonderful?!"

"Thank you, Dad," Alexia blushes.

"I am happy for you," Alexia's mother, Carla, says. She too moves toward Alexia and kisses and hugs her. "Congratulations, Alexia. You certainly worked very hard. That is just wonderful, dear."

"I don't need to congratulate her or say anything," Johnny says. "Alexia gave me the news earlier. As much as I hate to see her go so far away, I think that this is something she can't decline."

"I agree," Michael Hartley says.

"Very good, Michael would you thank God for us?" Carla says.

"Certainly I will. Bless Oh Lord this food to our use, and us to your service. Bless our family, our children and have mercy on Grandma. May the good news Alexia received today be a good beginning for a new, healthy and prosperous life. May Alexia and Johnny succeed in their endeavors, may they always serve you, Oh Lord. May they also serve all humanity for the betterment of us all. Amen."

"Amen."

Chapter 8

The next day at school, Alexia informs her friends and teachers that she has been accepted at Ivy, and given a scholarship. Several of her classmates and many of her teachers congratulate her. She's elated.

A few days later, before she can tell her granddaughter what happened next, Rose-Anne lays dead. Alexia is very distraught over the death of her beloved grandmother, her friend and mentor. She is particularly disturbed over her grandmother's inability to tell her whether she had an abortion of that horrible rape pregnancy, which continues to torment her.

In fact, there was no abortion. Alexia's grandmother, Rose-Anne, and her mother, Juliana, had struggled with the issue of abortion for four months. At first Rose-Anne was adamant, insisting on aborting the pregnancy at any cost, even risking her own life. Her mother, Juliana, tried to comfort her, but for the most part remained neutral about the issue of abortion. Then one day Rose-Anne had second thoughts.

"Mother, I could feel it kicking!" Rose-Anne had said to her mother with excitement. "The baby is kicking, Mother! The baby is alive and it's kicking, Mother!! I'm not sure I want to lose it anymore!"

"Really!?" her mother exclaimed.

"I want to keep it, Mother!"

"It has to be your decision, honey. It's your baby."

"Is anything wrong with me!?"

"Nothing is wrong with you!"

"Am I crazy?"

"No, you're not crazy. It's natural that you would want to keep your baby."

"I just don't want the bastard to know about it, or ever see it."

"He won't."

"Ever, Mom?"

"Ever, Rosy."

"Or even to know that I'm going to keep it."

"No one has to know about your baby, Rose-Anne."

"I want to move out of Stratford and out of New York."

Juliana listened to Rose-Anne.

"I want to go far, far away, Mother!"

"I know you do, and I'll go with you."

"Wherever I go, Mom?"

"Wherever you go, Rose-Anne, I will go with you."

"Thank you, Mom, thank you. Maybe we'll go to California, maybe to Virginia, where no one would know who I am, and you will come with me, Mother!"

"Of course I will, and that's a good idea, Rose-Anne. Of course I'll come with you."

"Will you, Mother?"

"Yes, I would come with you to the end of the world, Rose-Anne."

"Great!! Thank you, Mother. We'll go to California!"

"Yes, we'll go to California! You can go to college in California and have your baby there."

After receiving a large payoff from the family for whom Rose-Anne had worked, Rose-Anne's mother, Juliana, leased the farm to neighbor Charlie Stahl, then moved with Rose-Anne to Salem, California, where Rose-Anne was admitted to Salem University at Salem under the name of Rose-Anne Riley Thornton. In her application to the University, Rose-Anne falsely stated that she was the widow of one Robert Thornton, who was killed in action in Europe, but she did not tell the University that she was five months pregnant. Her mother knew of the tale. At first, Rose-Anne's mother considered it sensible, harmless fiction, but she later had misgivings about it, and finally shared her doubts with Rose-Anne:

"Do you think the University could investigate the death of Robert Thornton of Areshvile, New York, or could they discover that you're five months pregnant?"

"No one ever cares, Mother! Besides, they'll never find Areshvile on the map. It doesn't exist. I invented it. And they'll never know I am pregnant. What would you have me tell them? That a filthy rich bastard from Stratford raped me!? What are you talking about, Mom?"

"No, honey, I didn't want you to tell them any such thing."

"Then?!"

"Nothing Rose-Anne. What you told them is fine. We just have to hope and pray that they'll never investigate or find out."

"They won't ever investigate or find out, Mother. Don't worry about that. As long as that awful family doesn't know where we are, we're safe."

"What about your brothers? Don't you think we should tell them why we moved and why we leased the farm to Stahl?" Mother asked.

"No, but we can tell them some of it."

"What will we tell them?"

"Easy: There are better jobs here."

Her mother looked at her suspiciously.

"Mother, why are you looking at me as though I have committed treason?"

"I just don't want you in any more trouble, Rose-Anne. That's all."

"I'll tell them that I had a shotgun marriage to Robert Thornton, who was killed in action, that I got pregnant before he left, that he left me some money, plus his $10,000 G. I. insurance, and that we leased out the farm to Charlie Stahl, then moved to California where I'm going to college, and you got a good job."

"Do you think your brothers would believe that?"

"Why not?!"

"But they mustn't write to their friends in Hamlet or in Stratford? Hamlet is a small village, and Stratford is not such a large town, you know. God knows what gossip may be circulating about us now."

"You don't think that his family is going around telling everyone that their bastard son raped me?"

"No, but their son is crazy. What if he bragged about it to his friends?"

"I didn't think of that. We've got to tell Cliff and Don something else, maybe what really happened. I hate to do that though, Mother, especially after Daddy's death."

"I'll write them, honey."

"Yes, do what you think is best, Mother."

On December 29, 1943, a few minutes after midnight, Rose-Anne woke up her mother.

"What is it?!" Rose-Anne's mother asked.

"Pain in my back! Do you think I could be in labor?"

"Could be. How does it feel?"

"Comes and goes."

"When did it start?"

"About two hours ago."

"We better get ready to go to the hospital. You should've gotten me up when you first started getting the pain."

"I didn't know what it was."

"Get dressed, honey. I'll call the taxi."

When Rose-Anne and her mother arrived at the hospital, Rose-Anne gave her name to the admissions attendant as Rose-Anne Riley Thornton. She stated that she was a widow, that her husband, Robert Edward Thornton, of Areshvile, New York, died in action in Europe seven months before and that her mother, Juliana Rooney Riley, who was with her, was her next of kin.

With tears in her eyes, her mother, holding Rose-Anne's hand, said nothing.

Her face white, Rose-Anne looked at her mother. "I love you, Mother," she said.

"I love you too," her mother said, dabbing at her eyes and waving to her. "You're going to be all right. I'm going to stay right here in the hospital."

Rose-Anne was then wheeled to the delivery room.

Still dabbing at her eyes, her mother walked to the waiting room.

At about five in the morning, Rose-Anne delivered a healthy, seven pound five ounce baby girl.

"She's adorable, Mrs. Thornton," the attending nurse said, placing the baby on Rose-Anne's tummy.

"Did you tell my mother?"

"Not yet, but I will soon."

"She's in the waiting room! Mrs. Riley is her name. Please tell her."

"We'll bring her to see you as soon as we can."

"Did you see the baby, Mother?" Rose-Anne had asked her mother when she arrived in the room.

"She's absolutely adorable."

"She looks like her father."

"She's beautiful, honey, and she looks like you."

"Does she?"

"Absolutely she looks like you, my dear."

"She looks like Robert Thornton. But I don't care who she looks like. I'm going to love her. I'm going to give her everything I've got."

"Of course you are. What if she looked like her father a little, she's still yours, all yours."

"I know that, Mother. You're so great. What would I have done without you, Mother?! I don't know."

"You're a strong young woman, Rose-Anne. You'll be a wonderful mother and a great student."

"I just hope I'll meet someone nice, so the baby will have a good father."

"In time, it's possible."

"Do you really think so, Mother?"

"Yes, I do."

"Now what should we name her?"

"Well, let's think."

"Carla! Carla Rose-Anne Thornton. I like that.

"So do I. You loved your father and I'm touched that you want to name her Carla. Your father was a good, hard- working man. It was the war, your brother Jimmy's tragic death, your other brothers' going away to war – and then the fire finally broke him. It was too much for him to handle."

"I know! I know!" Rose-Anne had said, touching her newborn daughter. "Daddy was a wonderful man!"

Several days after Rose-Anne delivered, she resumed attending classes at Salem University. Her mother stayed home and took care of baby Carla. When Rose-Anne returned, she played with her daughter then studied. For the most part, her mother took care of Carla.

A year went by faster than Rose-Anne and her mother could believe. When it was close to Carla's first birthday, Rose-Anne began to think of having a party for her.

"Who will we invite to Carla's birthday party?" Rose-Anne asked her mother one day, right after she came home from her classes.

"Who do you want to come?"

"Who, Carla?" Rose-Anne cooed to her baby. "Who? You tell me who?" She played with Carla. "Invite Chester? Shall we? Should we, Carla?"

"Her mother watched."

"I think I'm going to invite Chester, Mother. That'll be enough. The four of us will be just right."

"Whatever you think is fine with me."

"You never ask me about him, Mother."

"I figure when you're ready you'll tell me."

"Well, Chester Perry is an Arts and Sciences student. Remember, I told you we met in the library, where I was writing a term paper? We've been friendly since that first meeting. He's very nice. Handsome too!"

Her mother looked at her.

"Mother, Chet's real. I've been out with him several times."

"Well, well, has he met Carla?"

"No, he hasn't."

Her mother continued to look a little doubtful.

"Mother, I have not invented this one. Chet is real."

"Does he even know you have a one-year-old baby?"

"Yes, he does."

"Is that all he knows?"

"He only knows what he needs to know."

"Oh, Rose-Anne!"

"Mother, I can't bring myself to say that I was raped. I just can't. If this thing with Chet becomes serious, I'll have to say it to him, but I'm not ready now. I'm just not ready."

"I understand, honey. Do you know anything about his background, or his family?

"He comes from an old American family, Mother, and has one sister. I think that one of his grandmothers, the one on his mother's side, is a Navaho

Indian. I know his relations with his parents are good, and especially with his mother. His father is a lawyer, his mother a Fourth grade teacher. The ligaments in his left knee are torn. He was clipped playing football. That's why he hasn't been taken into the service."

"Have you met his folks, Rosy?"

"Oh, Mother!! Not yet, it's still too soon."

At the birthday party, the three adults sat in the tidy one-room, basement apartment. There was a tiny kitchenette in one corner, a hide-a-bed on a wall facing the kitchen, where Rose-Anne and her baby slept, and a small single bed in another corner, where Juliana slept. A small white metal table sat near the kitchen area with three white metal chairs.

Chester Perry seemed diffident, almost shy on meeting Juliana and Carla, but soon began playing with baby Carla who responded to him immediately. Rose-Anne's mother remained reserved, hardly speaking, but watched baby Carla's romance with the young man.

As the three sang Happy Birthday to Carla, Chet lifted the baby in his arms and looked into her glittering blue eyes. "She's a beautiful little girl, Rose-Anne! She's lovable!"

After the party, Rose-Anne and her mother Juliana had a discussion:

"Do you like Chet, Mother?" Rose-Anne had asked her mother.

"He's genuine, and he seems to like Carla."

"I have to muster the courage to level with him. Do you think I could?"

"Of course you could, honey."

"I have to, Mother."

"You'll do fine, just fine."

"How do I tell him?"

"Well, let me ask you first. Why do you feel that you have to say something now? Has he said anything to you?"

"Well, yes," Rose-Anne smiled. "He's wondered if I'm ready for another permanent relationship so soon after the death of my husband, Robert Thornton."

Her mother, folding her arms, just looked at her daughter.

"I could be getting myself into trouble, I know!"

"Oh, Rose-Anne, you won't, don't worry about that! You'll just have to tell him the truth. As simple as possible, relate what happened and why you invented the whole thing. That's all."

"Would he think the rape's an invention?"

"He won't, but if he does then you should stop right there. I'm sure he won't though, Rosy. He seems understanding."

"He is."

A few days later, Rose-Anne was on campus with Chet. The two were walking toward the cafeteria to have lunch together.

"Chet," Rose-Anne began, as they were about to enter. "I have something very personal I must tell you."

Gently smiling, Chet stopped. His tall frame, broad shoulders, and deep voice belied his kindly demeanor. His hand touching her shoulder lightly, he looked at her. "What is it, Rose-Anne?!"

"Chet," she said, her voice trembling.

"Yes, Rose-Anne, what's on your mind, my darling?"

Looking at his neatly combed, straight black hair, then staring at his piercing, dark brown eyes, at first she hesitated. Then responding to his reassuring touch, she put her head on his big chest. "Chet, I have a skeleton in my closet," she whispered. I need to tell you about it. The story I told you about Robert Thornton being my deceased husband was a lie. It isn't true. I invented it to protect Carla. I have never been married, and Carla is a child of rape who was born out of wedlock. I was raped about two years ago in the home of a well-to-do family in Stratford, New York, by an eighteen-year-old boy, the only child in that family. I worked for them as a cleaning girl."

"Did you inform the police?" Chet asked.

"No, I didn't. Terrified, the boy's family pleaded with my mother to settle and begged her not to report the crime to the police. Because my father had died a few months before, and because my two older brothers had gone to war, my mother felt helpless. So we accepted the settlement, which made my going to college possible, and we moved to Salem. I was ashamed of what happened, so I invented Robert Thornton and changed my name to create a new life. I feel I have to tell you this because of the serious discussion we've been having about marriage."

Chester looked bewildered. He said nothing for a long moment.

"I guess you must be concerned that Carla is the child of a rape," Carla said.

"What do you mean?" he asked softly

"I mean she was born out of wedlock."

Raising his head, he looked at Rose-Anne and hugged her. "That doesn't matter at all."

"Thank you, Chet, I love you."

A few months later, Rose-Anne and Chester were married in a small private wedding at the university chapel. Chester Perry's father, mother and sister, as well as his grandmother on his father's side, attended. On her side there were only her mother, Juliana, and Carla.

Two weeks after the wedding, Juliana said that she would be returning to the family farm in Hamlet. A few days after that, Rose-Anne drove her mother to the San Francisco railroad station.

"You've been great, Mother, and I will always be thankful that I have such a wonderful mom," Rose-Anne said to her mother as the two embraced and wept at the station.

"Take good care of yourself, honey, and Carla and Chet."

"I will, Mother. Chet's adopting Carla."

"That's wonderful news. I hoped he would. What about Carla's birth certificate?"

"After the adoption, we'll have it corrected and get her a new one, showing Chet as her father."

"Wonderful!! That's just wonderful, Rosy! I am very happy to hear that."

"I will write often, Mother," Rose-Anne promised her mother as they embraced again. "And when you hear from Cliff or Don, please write me."

"I will, honey, of course I will."

"When can you come to visit, Mother? Just come, and I'm hoping we'll have a bigger apartment soon."

"Sure I will."

They embraced again and cried as Juliana boarded the train to Philadelphia, *en route* to Stratford.

After World War II ended in 1945, Rose-Anne's two brothers, Clifford and Donald Riley, soldiers in Europe during the war, returned to the Riley family farm in Hamlet. They lived with their mother, Juliana, rebuilding, enlarging and modernizing the farm, with financial as well as moral support from Rose-Anne. The farm prospered. In 1951, Rose-Anne's mother, Juliana, died.

Chapter 9

When Rose-Anne dies on December 9, 1997, at the age of seventy-two, her granddaughter, Alexia, grieves very deeply for her. At the funeral, Alexia and her twin John stand solemnly and silently at the grandmother's fresh grave. Joan Atkinson, Alexia's best friend, as well as several other high school friends, are also in attendance.

Alexia then walks by herself closer to her grandmother's grave. Her eyes are tearing, as the grandmother's familiar voice begins to reverberate in her ears: ... *"The earliest event in my life that I can remember was being stung by a wasp in my crib ... So vivid was the impression made upon my mind that I still can close my eyes and see myself, a very little, blond-headed child screaming in my crib ..."*

Rose-Anne's Carla, at 54, is a beautiful and distinguished woman. With deep-set blue eyes and silver-streaked golden blond hair, she bears little resemblance to her uncles, Clifford and Donald. Neither does she look at all like her sisters or brother, all of whom have straight dark hair and brown eyes like their father, Chester Perry, who died five years earlier.

After the funeral, Alexia's best friend, Joan, as well as other high school friends embrace and kiss Alexia, and leave. Alexia's family then gathers at the home of Carla and Michael Hartley in Valley Town, Virginia, where Rose-Anne spent her last days. It is a comfortable unpretentious home.

Carla's husband Michael, a Virginian, is a professor of economics at Valley Town University. He is a quiet, scholarly academician. In contrast, Carla, an extrovert, is active in their community. In addition to her real estate business, she also directs some of her energy to civic, charitable and political activities. She has made a good name for herself. She serves as president of the Valley

Town Chamber of Commerce, teaches business and economics at Valley Town University as an adjunct professor, and is regarded as a potential candidate for United States Representative from the State of Virginia.

When the relatives arrive at the Hartleys' home, Carla and her husband lead them to their modest, tastefully furnished living room. Carla's sisters, Helen and Jane, also live in Valley Town. Carla's brother Henry is a successful lawyer. He and his family live in Southern California.

As the relatives gather, Carla gives special attention to her two uncles, Clifford and Donald Riley, and their families. Clifford Riley's wife Anita, at seventy-four, is an attractive, reserved woman. Donald Riley's wife, Norma, seventy-one, is a bit stout. She is hard of hearing and seems a little awkward and lacking the poise of Anita.

Although remaining quiet and reserved, Alexia begins to study her grandmother's brothers, searching for more of the mystery she believes surrounded her deceased grandmother's life. She has a deep-rooted and peculiarly intense desire to know more. She wants to know what her grandmother was unable to convey to her. That bit of history, which, as far as she knows, has not been revealed to anyone, not even to her mother, Carla. Motionless and spellbound, she finds herself irresistibly charmed by her great uncles. As she continues watching them, she can hear her Grandmother again. *"My brother Donald ... used to tease me unmercifully... I realized that ... snipe-hunting was a joke.... such teasing never made me unhappy for long with my idolized brothers, whom I loved very dearly..."*

"I remember seeing you only once," Carla says to her mother's two brothers. "I'm so sorry that we only see our relatives at funerals. I must've been seven or eight when Mom took me to Hamlet with her to attend Grandma Juliana's funeral. That would have been more than forty-five years ago. Mom was uneasy about the trip. She didn't want to drive through Stratford, and was even very nervous about going to Hamlet. I wasn't actually sure we would go, but I'm so glad we finally went. I could never understand her uneasiness about going. I thought Hamlet was a lovely little town, and I liked Stratford too."

Clifford Riley shakes his head. "Yeah, it is," he says. "And I do remember the time you came with Rosy. That visit was short, really short. So now you should all come and visit again."

"And Mom, bless her heart, couldn't wait to leave," Carla complains to her shy, reserved uncle Clifford, who appears slightly uncomfortable with the conversation. "I wanted to stay longer, but we left before I got a chance to meet my cousins, let alone play with them."

"Yeah," repeats Clifford Riley, "that visit was kind of short. Rose-Anne had a lot on her mind those days, her family and other responsibilities, and she wanted to go back to her work and family, my dear. We understood that."

"You should come and visit again," Donald Riley now says. "All of you should come. You can stay with us at the farm. We have plenty of space now, and we'll show you around Stratford."

Carla suddenly brightens. "I'd love to go and visit again, visit you folks and see the farm. And see where Mom grew up. I'd love to do that as an adult."

"We'd enjoy having you with us, my dear," Donald Riley says. "We'd enjoy having all of you come."

Carla pauses. "But I always wondered why Mom didn't like to visit? I always wondered if she had had an unhappy experience there when she was a young child."

There is a little silence and Alexia begins to feel sorry for her grandmother's brothers and their having to endure her mother's probing. She is embarrassed but takes comfort in thinking that the awkward silence now pervading the living room may prompt her mother to be quiet or to talk about something else.

"Yes," Clifford Riley finally says without responding to Carla's comment, "we would love to have all of you come and spend time with us."

"I'm so sorry Mom didn't exchange visits with her family in New York more often," Carla persists, "especially when we were young."

"It's because of the long distance between us, my dear," says Donald Riley. "We are so far away from Virginia, and you are so far away from New York. Now that air travel has made us closer to each other, we should make up for the past. We want you to come and visit us, all of you."

The room falls silent again.

Alexia's eyes sting. Her grandmother's soft voice rings in her ears again. *"I worked uneasily at this family's mansion ... I was wary when I entered the guy's room to clean ... He suddenly came out of nowhere, surprised me from behind, and held my body tightly against him. I shoved him, my whole body shaking ... I screamed ... I began to struggle...and continued to struggle for several minutes. I scratched his face and bit him ... He tore my blouse and panties, he punched and kicked me, Alexia ... He punched me in the face and the ribs ... I was overcome..."*

"Please don't misunderstand me, Mom always talked most fondly about you people and about the farm," Carla resumes, "and I didn't mean to imply any bad feeling, not at all."

"We know that," Clifford Riley says, rubbing his eyes. "She was a great sister."

Carla's sisters and brother appear to be uneasy listening to their sister's questions and watching Clifford and Donald Riley sit silently.

"Carla and I, and our children, as well as all of our families I am sure, will be honored to visit you all in New York," Carla's husband, Michael Hartley, finally says. "We are honored that you've come to us. I'm sorry these are unhappy circumstances. We hope your next visit will be a much happier one, and we would love to have you come again. This is your home and we are your family."

"And we would be honored to have all of you visit us," Clifford Riley says, his voice quavering.

"That's right. We want all of you to visit us," Donald Riley says. "All of you should consider visiting us in New York. You should come. We would like to extend an invitation, through Carla and Michael, to all of you."

"It is nearly impossible for all of us at once to get away," Carla says, "though it's always nice to talk about going and visiting. When it comes to doing it, it won't be easy."

"Those who can," Donald Riley says, "you're welcome to come any time. We're your kin and family, and Hamlet is your town. The farm is yours too. You should all come and visit."

"It's nice to contemplate but it won't be that easy," Carla says.

"Perhaps Carla and Michael, or Carla as a first explorer, if Michael can't make it, should be the first to come. Then all of you can follow," Donald Riley says.

"I don't know," Carla says, looking a little surprised.

"Distances are not as bad as they used to be," Donald repeats.

"I know that," Carla says softly, "and I do want to see the farm again after all these years." She pauses again. "Anyway, we'll think about it."

"Yes, please think about it," Donald says.

"Yeah, you should come then, and get acquainted," Clifford says in a wobbly, tentative, low voice,

"Make a plan to stay with us a few days," Donald says firmly. "We'll show you where Rosy grew up."

Alexia is mortified. Her mother has selfishly and blatantly secured herself an invitation to the family farm. Why does she want to go? Alexia asks herself. Does she have a clue about what happened to Grandma many years ago? Alexia is sure that her mother's uncles must know more about the grandmother's mysterious past than she, Alexia, does. Maybe the uncles know everything. Even if they do, Alexia wonders if they would ever share that knowledge with her mother. She feels that Clifford Riley wouldn't. Even Donald Riley, who seems more friendly and flexible, would not. She is sure he would not. She begins to contemplate what may happen at the farm, as her grandmother's voice begins to haunt her again: *"I was permitted to ... play on a strange musical instrument that was kept on a closet shelf ... a ukulele, which Mother and Dad bought and gave to my brother Clifford, hoping that it would cheer him up after the loss of his older brother, but Cliff was never interested. He never could touch that instrument..."*

Cliff is the stiff, shy older brother of her beloved grandmother. She begins to stare at him intently, feeling perhaps that she may absorb some of his shyness, his demeanor and his farmer's ways into herself. He does look like Grandma, she tells herself. He even seems to her to be another embodiment of her Grandmother. She begins to feel compelled to talk to him in person, to touch him and make sure that he is real. She yearns to ask him a few gentle questions, questions that would put him at ease, questions that would convey to him how close she had been to his departed sister. She wants to implore him not to say a word to her mother about what he knows of Grandma's tragic history. She wants that history to remain sacred and private, forever. She wants that history to be tucked away within her Grandma's bones. Yet, and paradoxically, she finds herself, more than ever before, wanting to know what happened to her grandmother's pregnancy. Maybe Grandma did not wish me to know that, she tells herself. Maybe that also should remain private and sacred, buried with Grandma's bones. Above all, she does not want her mother to ever know any of this history. She feels that her mother cannot and should not be entrusted with it.

Alexia now turns her eyes on Donald Riley, the brother who teased her Grandma when she was a little girl. He too fascinates her with his generous disposition and openness. He does not resemble her Grandmother as much as Clifford Riley does, and he does not look as old, or appear as stiff and shy as Clifford. He is probably easier to speak to, she thinks. What would possess a young man to tease and scare his younger sister out of her wits one pitch dark night, she asks herself. Yet her grandmother had forgiven him long, long ago, because she loved her brothers and idolized them. I should love and idolize them too, Alexia tells herself. I should do that out of respect for my Grandma.

Yet it is this brother, Donald Riley, with his generous and open heart that Alexia fears may divulge her grandmother's private past to his niece, her mother Carla. It is he who may be charmed by Mom, and who may relent and tell Mom what happened to Grandma, who, barely eighteen, was trying to make a living after the death of their father. The thought scares Alexia. Perhaps not, Alexia assures herself. Donald Riley is still my Grandma's brother, and he must love her very much. He wouldn't want to desecrate her memory for anyone, not even Mom, Grandma's daughter.

I hope not, she says to herself. I hope not, she repeats. I'm sure he wouldn't do it, she assures herself. He is a wise and decent man, just like Grandma was a wise and decent woman.

" One of these days, Uncle Donald," Carla says, "I may really take you people up on the invitation. I do want to see the farm where Mom grew up as well as the whole area around there."

Alexia winces.

At first, both of Carla's uncles are silent. Their sadness is obvious to Alexia, who shares the sadness. This confirms to her that the uncles really would not be comfortable with her mother's visit to the farm, despite their invitation and her mother's unabashed eagerness to visit. She wishes that her mother would notice the uncles' reluctance, and cease forcing herself upon them. Yet the uncles' silence doesn't deter Carla, nor does it seem to soften her insistence on visiting places that Alexia knows had haunted her grandmother for years.

"I hear that the winters are cold in New York," Carla says, once again breaking the lingering silence.

"That they are," Clifford says.

"The autumns are magnificent though," Donald now says. "Come see us in the fall, in September or in October, Carla. These are very nice months for sightseeing. The fall really is magnificent in Upstate New York."

Alexia now dreads looking at her grandmother's brother.

"You think I should?" Carla asks with visible delight.

"Yes, early September would be a perfect time," Donald Riley repeats.

"You really do want me to come?" Carla asks.

"Without a doubt," Donald says emphatically.

"Maybe I'll do just that, Uncle Donald," Carla finally agrees.

"Great! That's great, Carla!" Donald Riley says.

"I do want to see the farm and Stratford. I'll confirm when I'll arrive after I discuss our schedule with my husband."

"Great! That's great!" Donald repeats. He then turns to Carla's two half-sisters and half-brother. "Helen and Jane as well as Henry, and the children may come with you too, Carla. You're all welcome. You'll all like New York, and we love to have all of you visit."

"Carla should go by herself first, Uncle Don," Helen says.

"That's fine, whatever works out for all of you is all right with us," he says, "but we want all of you to come, if not now, later. We will make sure that all of you come and visit the farm. No doubt about it."

"Is that all right?" Carla asks her sister Jane, and brother Henry.

"Sure," they all say, giving approving nods.

Chapter 10

Two months have passed since the death of Grandma Rose-Anne. Alexia seems to be reconciling herself to the loss of her elderly grandmother for whom she was very devoted. She often thinks about her, and sometimes even dreams about her. Nevertheless, she continues to go to school regularly, interact with her friends and classmates and do very well in her studies. She has immersed herself in several humanitarian and *extra curricular* activities in honor of her grandmother.

She is also excited about going to college at Ivy University, as her grandmother had recommended. She often thinks and worries about moving to the Northeast, a part of the United States she is not familiar with. Yet she has convinced herself that moving away from home is part of growing up, and she is looking forward to that.

Instead of trying to become closer to her mother Carla, as a substitute to the departed grandmother, Alexia finds herself resenting her mother. She becomes ever closer to her twin brother John, for whom she has always had a special affection. Now she finds him a true and reliable friend, to whom she can confide some of her concerns. She also becomes much closer to her best friend, Joan, who has been her friend since they were in second grade. Despite the very busy life her father leads, she has also found herself becoming much closer to him than before. She discovers just how gentle a person he is, one who is willing to listen to her when she needs him. Unlike earlier impressions of him, she now finds him a sensitive man with a sense of humor who gives of himself and of his time to meet her and her brother's needs as seniors in high school preparing themselves to go to college.

When Alexia confides to her father, that on the basis of her academic achievements she seems destined to be the valedictorian of her class, and that her best friend Joan will likely be the salutatorian of the class, her father is delighted. He volunteers to read and critique the speech she is expected to deliver on graduation day and she agrees happily. Yet something is always missing in her life, her beloved mentor and friend, Grandma Rose-Anne. Nothing seems to replace the relationship Alexia has had with her.

One day when Alexia arrives home from school, she is summoned by Carla. "I want to speak with you, dear," her mother starts. "Do you have a minute?"

"Yes, of course, Mom," Alexia says.

"Let's sit in the den then."

"Sure," Alexia says nervously.

"Yes, let's sit there. It is more private," Carla walks to the den and Alexia follows her. "Sweetheart," Carla begins, "I know that you're proud of being accepted at Ivy University. We all are proud of you. I'm just wondering if you've thought of staying close to home. Your father teaches at Valley Town University and your brother has been accepted there. Many of your friends, including Joan, will be attending Valley Town, dear. Even if you apply at this late date, I'm confident that you'll be admitted. As you know, since your father is on the faculty of the university, we won't have to pay yours or Johnny's tuition. I know you've been granted a generous scholarship with room and board at Ivy University, but you and Johnny can be together at Valley Town University, my dear, and you don't have to be so far from home. Johnny will have you to lean on, and you'll have him to lean on, Alexia. The northeast and Ivy University are hundreds of miles away from us. We don't know anyone there, and neither do you. I just want you to think about it, Alexia."

Alexia is speechless.

"I hope I didn't upset you, dear."

Her eyes misting, Alexia at first does not answer. "I'll think about it," she finally says, "but I honestly kind of have my heart set on going to Ivy University, Mom."

"I was surprised when I heard you applied there. How did you find out about it?"

"I'll think about it, Mom. How does Dad feel about this whole thing?"

"I haven't discussed it with him, dear, but I'm sure he prefers that you stay close to home. As I said, think about your brother, Alexia. You need one another, dear."

"I'll think about it, Mom, but really it may be too late, and I'm excited about being admitted to Ivy University and going there. My teachers have encouraged me to go there too. They're proud that one of their students is accepted there."

"Well, my dear, think about it. I just want you to think about it."

"O.K, I will."

The next morning while Alexia and her twin John wait for the school bus, Alexia tells her brother of the conversation she had with their mother.

"I disagree with Mom," John says. "I wouldn't change a thing, if I were you."

"What about Dad?"

"I'm confident he wouldn't expect you to change your plans."

"I'm scared."

"Don't be silly. I'm sure when Mom thinks about what she said, she'll realize how wrong she is. I wouldn't worry about it."

"Thanks, Johnny."

When Joan joins Alexia in the school bus, Alexia asks her, "What if I decide to apply to Valley Town University to be close to you and to Johnny?"

"Alexia, are you crazy?"

"Why?"

"You're not serious!"

Her eyes moist, Alexia does not respond.

Chapter 11

On August 1, 1998, five weeks before Alexia and Johnny go to their respective colleges, Carla flies to Ashton, New York, which is twenty miles south of Stratford. Her uncles, Clifford and Donald Riley, meet her at the Ashton airport and drive her to the farm in Hamlet, fifteen or so miles south of Stratford.

The farm is neat and prosperous. The country dirt road leading to the farm has been paved and widened. It is in good repair. There are three large, shining silos near the entrance to the farm, flanking a large, red, modern barn which houses more than two hundred well-fed black and white Holstein cows as well as some calves. The barn was built after World War II, and has been expanded several times, the last time in 1990.

The creek which divides the farm into two sections has three small, and one large bridge serving several locations on the farm. Six well-maintained ninety-horsepower green tractors are lined up in a white garage a few feet from the main barn. Two other white buildings housing the ice cream station and the milk house with its eighteen milking stalls are behind the main barn. There are five black Labrador dogs on the farm.

The house where Rose-Anne grew up is now occupied by Clifford Riley and his family. It is still painted white and has red roof tiles, but it has been renovated and expanded. Donald Riley's house, which was built across the creek in the sixties, is also white, with green roof shingles. It is about a quarter of a mile from Clifford's. There are two flower gardens on the farm, one near the house where Clifford and Anita live, and the other near the Donald and Norma house. The houses, although built in different eras, are almost identical in size and design. Separated from Clifford's house by a hill several hundred yards to the south is another large, modern, red barn that houses several hundred chickens, a few hogs, and four white horses.

Uncles Cliff and Don show Carla around the farm.

"This is now a modern farm!" Carla exclaims. "I wouldn't have recognized it. I do remember the house where Mom used to live. I also remember the odor of the farm," she smiles. "I'm not used to that, but after a while it grows on you," she jests. "Anyway, this is a lovely setting. It's very beautiful all around."

Walking slowly, Uncle Clifford to her right, and Uncle Donald to her left, Carla suddenly stops. "Uncle Clifford, and Uncle Donald, this area is so magnificent, so calm and charming, so inviting that anyone connected with it would want to live in it, or near it, or at the very least visit it as frequently as possible. I'm frankly mystified. Why didn't Mom want to visit the farm? Was it because she witnessed the death of Grandpa, her father on the farm? Or, was there something else that happened to Mom when she was a young woman that kept her away from the area?"

Her Uncles remain quiet.

"Why didn't Mom want to drive through Stratford? And she couldn't wait to get out of the whole area."

The two older farmers remain silent.

"That's a mystery to me, and I always wonder," she sighs.

The uncles remain silent and do not respond.

"Where would you like to stay tonight, my dear?" Donald finally changes the subject.

"She'll stay with us a few nights," Clifford says.

"After that she'll stay with us," Donald decides out loud.

"Thank you both," Carla says, "it'll be wonderful to stay in your homes. That'll be very nice."

"We're delighted you came, and we want you to feel at home," Clifford says. "This is also your mother's farm. It's now yours and Helen's and Jane's and Henry's."

Seeming surprised, Carla winces. "I never thought of it that way, Uncle Clifford," Carla says, her face more serious. "Uncle Clifford," she then says, "the farm looks neat and beautiful. It's a wonderful farm, thanks to your and to Uncle Donald's very hard work. After all, were it not for you two, the farm would've been lost long, long ago. Don't worry about that now, Uncle Cliff. That's not why I wanted to come. I wanted to come and visit you folks, and visit the places where Mom grew up. I wanted to find out more about Mom and her family. That's all, Uncle Clifford."

"I know," Clifford hastens to apologize, "I didn't mean to imply that you came for any other purpose, my dear. I know why you came to visit, but the farm isn't all ours, it's also yours. The farm belonged to your grandparents, and Rose-Anne, bless her heart, helped us financially, she helped us expand

and modernize. The farm used to be about seventy-five acres of land when your grandfather died. Now it's more than four hundred acres. Your mother put a lot of money into the farm, my dear. We couldn't have done any of this without Rose-Anne's financial and moral help, sweetheart. You should all know that, and that's what I meant, my dear."

"I didn't know anything about that, or about what Mom did. Mom never mentioned that to us," Carla says. "As far as we're concerned, the farm is yours, Uncle Clifford, and Uncle Donald."

"Like I said, my dear, it's also yours. That's right, it's also yours," Clifford repeats.

Carla is overwhelmed. "I don't know anything about that," Carla says, "I just don't know anything about it."

Through the kitchen door, Carla, Clifford and Anita, enter the house where her mother grew up, and where Carla will spend her night at the Riley farm.

"The kitchen looks almost exactly the way it did when I saw it years ago," Carla comments.

"The central room of 'the Riley home on the creek' has always been the kitchen, and we didn't want to make any changes to it, we wanted to keep it the way it was, my dear," Clifford Riley tells his niece. "This room is part of the addition built after the family moved here from Illinois. Your late uncle Jimmy and Rose-Anne had not yet been born. The family then consisted of Mother, Dad, Marilyn, who was fifteen, Floyd, who was thirteen, me, I was seven, and Donald, who was two. My brother Floyd was not destined to enjoy middle age because he died in the summer of 1935. Marilyn died a year later and poor Jimmy died in a tragic accident two years after Marilyn. He was too young. Jimmy's death and the fire that followed devastated your grandfather Carl, it broke his heart."

"I know," she says, "that was awful."

"The family lived in the three rooms during the winter of 1923-24 while this kitchen, the living room and the screened porch were being built. Like I said, that was before Jimmy and your mother were born."

"I understand, and where was Mom's room?"

Clifford takes her to her mother's childhood room. "This was called the girls' room, because for a while your late aunt Marilyn shared it with Rose-Anne."

"Is this then where I'm going to sleep tonight?"

"Yes, if you like, my dear, you can stay in your Mom's old room."

"Yes, I'd like that so much. I do want to stay in my mothers' old room."

"This is the same bed where Rose-Anne and Marilyn slept."

"Mother spoke often and very affectionately of her older sister."

"That's right, they really loved each other."

"Yes, I heard a lot about Aunt Marilyn. I can imagine Mom as a child waking up and looking out this window at this view of the water and green meadows. What a magnificent sight, Uncle Clifford!"

"Well, Carla, it's even more magnificent with you around us! We're so happy you're finally here."

"Thank you, Uncle Clifford," she smiles then looks at a small dresser next to the double bed. "I can also imagine Mom getting dressed for school in this little room."

"That's right. The whole family lived in the three rooms. Great Uncle Howard had promised Dad and Mother that he would build on to the house at the time that he persuaded them to move to New York to farm his land for him, and he quickly kept his promise. He hired local men to build the rooms, and a Mr. McClure made the kitchen cabinets to Mother's specifications."

"I can't believe how low the bread board is placed!"

"Mother was only five feet tall, and to make the work space right for her to use, she had specified an incredibly low level."

"Even so, I can still imagine Mom as a child standing on a stool to be able to work with Grandma Juliana at this board."

"Rose-Anne loved to bake biscuits for the family."

"I am amazed that Grandma Juliana had so little work space in her kitchen."

"Except for this folding-down board and the small shelf on the end of the stove, your grandmother had no place to work except for the table, and the bread board was made especially for the regular chore of making bread. About every two or three days, Mother baked several loaves using starter yeast. At that time most farm families made all of their own bread using that kind of yeast."

"And is this the white with rust kitchen stove they used?"

"Yes, it is. In those days, before electricity, perhaps the most significant item in the kitchen was the stove, because it was so important to everyday life. This used to be a large wood-burning stove with warming closets above the cooking surface and with two metal shelves extending from the fire end and a water reservoir at the end beyond the oven. The first thing each morning Mother started a fire in the stove to prepare breakfast while Dad and us boys did the chores. There was always wood nearby on the porch which Mother and Rose-Anne brought in as part of their evening chores. After putting wood in the stove, Mother poured on kerosene before lighting the fire in order to get a hot fire quickly. The fire was kept going all day in the winter and until after the noon meal in the summer. Not only did it give warmth, there was an aura of security about it, my dear. It provided a place to thaw out our frozen fingers or toes after working outside on a wintry day. And usually there was something cooking on the stove, even if Mother wasn't preparing the next meal."

Folding her arms, Carla listens attentively to her uncle's descriptions.

"There might've been a big kettle of cottage cheese on the stove," Clifford Riley continues. "Or perhaps the oven was full of bread baking, or maybe a big kettle of hominy simmering. Your Grandma Juliana loved to make the hominy, and it was a long process. The hard corn kernels were cooked with lye and then rinsed and rinsed to remove the hard outside of the corn and all trace of the lye. Then the white insides of the corn kernels were cooked some more until they were soft and puffed up. Hominy was not one of Rosy's favorite foods," he smiles.

"I know," Carla agrees.

"As you can see, there's about two feet of space between the stove and the wall behind it. This is where we had racks to dry towels. It was also in this space behind the stove that we took baths in the winter and dressed for bed when it was very cold. The water stored next to the stove gave us a constant supply of warm water, if Mother and Rosy remembered to keep it filled. We loved the aroma of delicious things cooking through the day.

"Thank you, Uncle Cliff, for the tour. It's really precious, hearing all the stories. The Riley house is still so charming and beautiful."

"You're most welcome, Sweetheart. You've had a long day. Why don't you go wash and rest a little. Don and Norma will join us for dinner."

"Splendid, I will, and thank you for everything, Uncle Clifford."

Chapter 12

The next morning, Carla goes to the Donald Riley kitchen, where Uncle Donald's wife, Aunt Norma prepares eggs. "Come on in," Aunt Norma says, "I'm fixing eggs for breakfast. Do you like them scrambled?"

"Yes," Carla replies. "Can I help, Aunt Norma?"

"I'm a bit hard of hearing," the seventy-one-year-old Norma says. "Raise your voice a little, dear."

"Can I help, Aunt Norma?" Carla raises her voice

"No, just sit down so we can talk while I get breakfast ready. Anita went to the field to pick some tomatoes; she'll be back soon. Cliff and Don are in the milking parlor. They get up at five every morning, you know, but they'll be back soon too. We're so glad you're visiting. I remember you as a dear little girl, a pretty, little blond Alice in Wonderland. Maybe you were seven or eight. You're still very pretty, my dear, and you look a lot like your father."

"Did you see a lot of my father?"

"Eh! What's that?" Norma asks, "I couldn't hear what you said, my dear."

"When was the last time you saw father?" Carla asks raising her voice again.

"I never met him, my dear, but he was a very prominent Stratford minister for many years. He's now the bishop in the Diocese in Northern New York, lives in Lake Charles, not too far from here. He's a very well-to-do and highly respected man now. He was an only child and inherited a lot of money from his father, who died a few years ago."

"I'm sorry, Aunt Norma, I'm not sure how that could be. My father has been dead for many years, so maybe you're a little confused about him?"

"I'm not talking about Chet. My goodness, is it possible you didn't know that Chet was your adoptive father, dear, not your real father? Of course I knew Chet. I knew him very well, a very sweet and kind man. Chet was your adoptive father. Your real father is the bishop I'm telling you about.

Carla is speechless. Her face turns white. She sits down. Opening her mouth wide, with a deep inward breath, she gapes at her uncle's wife.

"Are you alright, my dear?" Norma asks, walking toward Carla. "I just never dreamed that you wouldn't know any of that."

"Know what?" Carla answers sharply, but in a weak and distant voice.

"I'm so sorry!" Norma walks back to the stove.

"For what, Aunt Norma? Don't be sorry." Carla is exhausted.

"I feel so badly for upsetting you. Let's sit down, and you can recover a little."

"Thank you, Aunt Norma. You're right; I do just need to recover a little. I suspected something all along, but I didn't know what."

"I'm so very sorry. What have I done? Oh, my God! What have I done?!"

"Please don't worry about it, Aunt Norma," Carla mumbles in a very low voice. "Please don't. So that's what that going to court with my mother and father in Salem, when I was barely four, was all about. I had no idea what was going on, Aunt Norma. All I can remember is an elderly dignified man with curly white hair and a black robe sitting behind a big, elevated bench. I sat in my father's lap staring at the old man."

"What are you saying Carla?"

"I'm saying that you're right, Chester Perry was my loving father, Aunt Norma," Carla mumbles again. "He was the only father I ever had or knew."

"How's that?"

"So, what are you talking about, Aunt Norma?" Carla continues to mumble as she goes back to her mother's childhood room, shaken.

"I blew it, Don, I blew it," Norma says to her husband when he returns from the cow barn for breakfast at Cliff's house. Cliff and Anita had not come back.

"Blew what?" Donald asks in bewilderment.

"I made a fool of myself!"

"What happened?"

"Your niece didn't know anything about her real father. The poor woman! What an idiot I am!"

"Oh, Norma! Cliff and I warned Anita and you about that!"

"I must've not heard it!"

"For God's sake what happened? What did you say? Where is she? Where did she go?"

"She must've gone back to her room. She's really distraught. She's very upset, very upset, Don. What a fool I am! Oh, my God! What have I done?! What have I done?!"

"Good Lord," he says, leaning against the wall and staring out the window, trying to sort out what has happened. "Maybe it's all right, Hon," he finally says coming back to his wife. "It's just as well it happened this way. After all, she came here to find out."

"How do you know she came here to find out? How do you know that?"

"Well, Cliff and I discussed that at length before she came. We both think that she suspected something, but she didn't know exactly what information she needed from us.

"I shouldn't have said anything to her. I shouldn't have been the one to tell her."

"It's all right, my dear, it doesn't matter who tells her. That'll make it easier for Cliff and me to tell her the whole story."

"Oh, my God, what a fool I am!"

"Don't say that about yourself, my dear. It is going to be all right. I am sure it will be, and let's not raise our voices."

"She can't hear us, she went to Cliff's house. Did you say you want to tell her everything?"

"Yes, everything."

"You mean also, the rape and what happened after?"

"Yes, we'll have to tell her the truth. That means the whole truth, everything."

"That might be rough on her, Don. Oh, my God, what a tough situation!"

"Yes, it may be rough, but if we're going to level with her, we've got to tell her all of it. She wants to know anyway, and I have never been comfortable keeping this a sacred family secret. It shouldn't be kept from her. She wants to know and she should know."

"I would be very careful telling her every detail. Maybe some things should remain unsaid. Those things should possibly remain private, just between you and your brother."

"I'm not so sure of that. Nothing should be kept from her. Rose-Anne is gone, and Carla is her daughter. She should know. It's her story too."

"I'm not saying it should be kept from Carla, I am saying that you and your brother have to be careful. There may be a few details that should not be said, my dear. I agree that keeping what happened to Rose-Anne from Carla cannot be sustained any more, but it also could be very destructive if it is not told in a thoughtful and sensitive way."

"She's an adult woman, and she's very bright."

"I know that, but does she have to know that her mother was raped and that she is the child from that rape?"

"Yes, we need to tell her about the whole sad event, it's the right thing to do. If she wants to keep some of it private, that's her decision. It is no longer up to us to decide what she should or should not know, my dear."

"Talk it over with your brother, you and your brother know best."

"I will."

"That you should do, but I'm surprised Rose-Anne never mentioned anything about it to any of her children."

"We don't know that."

"It is a horrible situation, but in her older years, she should have mentioned it, if not to Carla, then to someone else in her immediate family. That is what I think."

"You may be right, but Rose-Anne was a hurt woman, my dear. She never recovered from that awful event, which faced her so early in her life."

"And she could not reconcile reality with privacy."

"I am not surprised she didn't tell her daughter any part of the tale, but I will be surprised if she hasn't told some other member of the family about it."

"Who would she tell?"

"I don't know, but I am willing to bet that someone in her immediate family she cared for and trusted must have been told about it. I know my sister."

"Who could that be?"

"I don't know, my dear. But someone other than Carla knows, my dear. I know Rose-Anne."

"Anyway, Carla shouldn't have found out about it the way she did, from a fuzzy old woman like your wife."

"Don't worry about that, my dear. Carla came to find out, and she has. Now it has fallen on Cliff and me to explain it. That's what brothers are for, I guess."

"You're right, that's what brothers are for, my dear. Poor Rose-Anne!"

"How're we going to do it?"

"Get Cliff involved."

"I've got to. He knows more about it."

"But the two of you should talk to her."

"Cliff has more details about what happened. Oh, my God! Life is so cruel," he says pacing the kitchen floor. "Please call Cliff and Anita, tell them breakfast is ready."

When Clifford and his wife Anita join Donald and his wife Norma, Carla is still in her mother's room.

"Where's Carla?" Clifford asks his brother.

"In Rose-Anne's room, she's upset, Cliff. Norma spilled the beans."

"What happened?"

"I don't know exactly how it happened. I just know what Norma – "

"Listen: I was in the kitchen preparing breakfast, and Carla came in offering to help me. One thing led to another and I remarked how Carla looks like her real father, the bishop."

"My God!!"

"It's all right, Cliff. It's just as well it happened. She is curious. You remember when you and I discussed how we thought she suspected something. The way she talked after Rose-Anne's funeral, how she came with Rose-Anne to Mother's funeral, how Rose-Anne didn't want to come in the first place and how Rose-Anne couldn't wait to go back, and so on. You remember that?"

"I do remember," Clifford says, "and you may be right, but what do we tell her now?"

"Well, everything."

"How do we do that?"

"It will be easier now."

"Because she has an idea?"

"That's right."

"I don't know, Don."

"If we're going to level with her, this is the time to tell her."

Cliff reflects.

"Now is the time to tell her, Cliff. Keeping this from her now could disrupt the whole family."

"I agree."

Later that morning, after breakfast, the two brothers and their wives sit with Carla.

Clifford Riley addresses his niece first.

"Carla," he starts, "you came here, curious about your mother's past. I guess that you had a feeling there was something hidden from you, something that you wanted very badly to know, and I can't say that I blame you. If I were in your shoes, I would want to know that too. So here it is: When your mother was eighteen, Carla, she was raped by Philip Arlington, the child of a rich Stratford family, where your mother worked. She became pregnant as a result of the rape. Horrified, the Arlington family begged your grandmother Juliana and your mother to accept a payment. Your mother finally relented, accepted the payment and moved to California, went to college, delivered a little girl named Carla, named for your grandfather who died only a few months earlier. Rosy met Chester Perry, married him and he adopted Carla. Chet and Rose-Anne had three more children, Helen, Jane and Henry."

Carla covers her face with her hands and cries quietly.

"I am sorry, sweetheart," Clifford Riley says to his niece.

"So I am a child of rape," Carla chokes, still covering her face.

"You are a child of God, my dear," Clifford Riley says emphatically.

"And Philip Arlington is a bishop of God!" Carla exclaims bitterly.

"After the incident," Clifford Riley continues, "Philip Arlington enlisted in the service. When he returned to Stratford after the War, he was a different man. He went into the ministry. He was recently elected Bishop of the Diocese of Northern New York. He's married and has two married daughters. As far as we know, he never knew that your mother delivered his child. That's because your mother wanted it that way. The Arlington family always believed, and as far as we know still believes, that your mother had an abortion or a miscarriage."

Chapter 13

The following day the family's emotions are more under control and Carla expresses continued interest in the family home and furnishings. "This must be a very old table, Uncle Clifford," Carla says, as she, her uncle Clifford, and his wife, Anita, enter the modest living room of the old Riley house.

"This is the library table, my dear. It has been in our living room for a long time. It always represented learning, because it provided a place to do lessons for school. Marilyn, Floyd, Don and I all used it, as did your mother and Jimmy. What papers or magazines Dad and Mother acquired, were usually kept on the shelf you see beneath the table, awaiting time for family members to read. In those days, they did not get periodicals delivered to the farm, but whenever Dad or Mother went to town, they would bring back with them a paper or a magazine. We took only the weekly Stratford Star, but there were usually some other things to read, such as church literature, Bibles and the Montgomery Ward catalog. The catalog was our wish book, although we did occasionally order some clothing from the catalog. When a new "Monkey Ward" catalog came, the old one was taken to the outhouse to be used for toilet paper. It was a primitive existence we had in those days!"

In the corner of the living room, near the kitchen door, Carla spots a built-in bookcase containing a collection of old books. She goes to the bookcase and bends to look at the titles.

"Quite a treasure," she says, "Jack London's *Call of the Wild*."

"For lack of other books to read, your mother, used to read these books over and over during her childhood. Here are some Wild West tales by Zane Grey, Jane Eyre, *The Last Days of Pompeii*, *Pinocchio*, *East Lynne*, Tennyson's *Idylls of the King*. *Idylls of the King* is the only book I never finished," Clifford Riley says.

"*Peter Pan*," Carla resumes reading from the collection."

"Here are several Horatio Alger books and some little moral books. These moral books were put out by the London Sunday School Union. Rose-Anne liked the Horatio Alger books. She read them so many times, Carla, that she practically had them memorized."

"Here are some school books, Uncle Clifford."

"These belonged to Marilyn, to me, to my brothers and to your mother, my dear."

"Here is some good literature," Carla says.

"*Pride and Prejudice* by Jane Austin, Shakespeare's *Hamlet*. Many of the books belonged to Mother and Dad."

"What's on the bottom shelf?"

"In the bottom part of the bookcase, Carla, your mother stored her scrap books from high school. There is one on ancient Greece. That's a very interesting collection, Carla. You may like to take that one out to look at. You should see all of the pictures that she clipped from papers and magazines about ruins from ancient times. I looked at them once a few years back, and they are like an enchanting fairy tale. I never realized that these pictures and stories depicted real things."

"I am not surprised that Mom read so much."

"One reason we all read a lot was because we never had a radio. Mother and Dad always said that listening to the radio would take up time that should be spent working. Your grandmother Juliana used to tell us that people who spend a lot of time listening to the radio are lazy. Your grandfather, Carl, was a strong Democrat living in an area of the country that was almost totally Republican. He liked to listen to President Roosevelt speak. He would drive about six miles to the Huntleys, the closest Democrats that he knew, to listen to Roosevelt on the radio. Just before I went into the service, Dad purchased a radio. After I finished my chores in the summer of 1940, I would allow myself time to listen to the program 'The Greatest Story Ever Told.' I remember that I could hardly wait to hear the next episode of the story of Jacob and the many years he worked to get Rachel for his wife."

After Clifford finishes his tour, Carla and Anita remain in the Riley's living room by themselves. Carla sits on an old leather Davenport, facing her Uncle's wife, and two pictures hanging on the wall. "I have always been intrigued by these two pictures, Aunt Anita. I remember them from my first visit here, when I was a little girl. The pictures are of the famous "Blue Boy, and an elaborately framed rendering of the Capitol building in Washington. The frame's inlay of mother-of-pearl catches the morning light."

"I understand that these pictures have been in the Riley family for many years," Anita says.

"And these pictures have remained with me from that first time I saw them as a child, when Grandma Juliana died. I never thought of the Capitol as being a real building. I first went to Washington at the age of eighteen, after I graduated from high school. It was like an old memory coming alive to see the building that looked like the picture I remembered seeing in Grandma Juliana's living room. I also remember that there was a child-size rocking chair in this living room that I sat on when I was young. That rocking chair first belonged to Aunt Marilyn, then it belonged to Mom, I was told. I really liked to sit in it when I was little. It usually had a fragile china doll sitting in it. My first experience with a ventriloquist was connected with that chair. It was a Sunday morning, and I was sitting in the chair when two families came to visit. One family had a little girl who wanted to pick up Aunt Marilyn's doll. The man from the other family solved the problem by having the doll say, 'I don't wish to be played with.' The little girl just looked at the doll apprehensively and left it alone after that."

"The ventriloquist was their minister, Edward Osborn. I remember him clearly. He was a very interesting man."

"There was a piano in the living room too," Carla continues.

"That piano was considered your Mom's, dear. I understand that no one in the family played the piano in those years. Your mother took piano lessons from a Mrs. Auert, who lived in Hamlet."

"Mom told me about that, she said that she really was interested in learning to play the piano, but because lessons were expensive for her family's limited income in those days, she didn't take them for very long. I think that she managed to play a little though, Aunt Anita. Mom once said that when she was ten years old, there was a man staying with them, who apparently was an accomplished pianist. He wanted to teach Mom to play like he played. Sometimes when Grandma Juliana wasn't looking, or wasn't nearby, he would make Mom sit down at the piano and keep practicing. If she stopped, he would hit her fingers with a stick. She used to be terrified of that man."

"Awful! Some people are awful."

"That's right, Aunt Anita, that's right," Carla sighs.

The room falls silent. Carla, her torment becoming visible, pauses and turns to look out the window.

"I know, Aunt Anita," she then resumes, and sighs again. "Some people are really horrible. And I don't know which is better, to have known about all these horrible things Uncle Clifford told me about myself and about Mom when she was young, or to find out now when I'm a grown up woman."

"I don't know either, my dear. There's never a right time for these tragic happenings to be known. I am very sorry you had that shock yesterday."

"Well, I brought it upon myself, I wanted to know. I can't blame it on Aunt Norma."

"I want to assure you that Norma is a good person, a very good person, Carla, and believe me, she is sad, and feels terrible about upsetting you with the whole horrible episode."

"I have no doubt that she is a very kind person, and she shouldn't feel badly about anything," Carla says. "I wanted to know. I always suspected something, and I should know. I want to see Aunt Norma again before I leave, to tell her myself that she shouldn't feel badly."

"You will see her before you leave, I am sure, and I am glad you feel this way, my dear Carla. Norma is truly a very kind hearted, wonderful woman. She and Don have been discussing your question with us, with me and with Cliff, about whether you should have been informed of this when you were younger. We discussed it at length. We all feel that Rose-Anne's intentions were to protect you, Carla. It was a horrible thing she had to endure all these years, and it would have been very painful and difficult for her to inflict her pain and agony on her beloved daughter, but I'm glad you don't blame Norma. She'll feel better knowing that."

"Of course I don't blame Aunt Norma. Why should I? How could I? I wanted to know. Yes, poor Mother! My poor, loving Mother! She wanted to shield me, yet I have always suspected something, I suspected that something very sad must've happened to her when she was a young woman, but I didn't know what. Should she have told me? Could she have told me? We all know now that, emotionally, it would have been very, very hard, and the question of whether she should have told me becomes moot and perhaps irrelevant. Yet, as ugly as this whole incident is, it is still a part of me, a part of my family and a part of my children. My first impulse is like Mom's, to protect and shield my children from knowing anything about it, but as I reflect on it more and more, I begin to think that would be a mistake. I have to muster the courage and the wit to share it with my own family and with my own children in particular. I am in a better position now than Mom was when she went through her painful experience. I have not experienced the intensity of the pain and the suffering that she experienced, and I am now an older and more mature woman learning about it than she was when she experienced it. She was barely eighteen when this happened to her."

"I admire you, my dear Carla, and I agree with every word you've said. As Don and Norma said, and we agree with them, your mother probably considered the tragic event a private matter, her own private matter. She most likely felt that way."

"I agree that it was a private matter, but unwittingly perhaps it became a sacred family secret, and I feel obligated to myself and to my children not to continue it as a sacred family secret. I fear for my children, and I fear that keeping it a sacred secret could be destructive to my family, and especially to my children."

"You're right, but I am sure Rose-Anne never intended it to be a sacred secret, although it seemed that way, and that was unfortunate. Both Cliff and Don think and say that knowing their sister, your mother, and recognizing that she could not have shared the tragic tale with you, Carla, she most likely would have shared it with another trusted member of the family, in order to prevent it from becoming a sacred family secret."

"Who would she share it with?" Carla snaps, her demeanor changing unexpectedly.

"They don't know. They just speculate that she may have. That's all there is to it, Carla," Anita says. "I didn't mean to add to your anxiety, my dear."

"You don't add to my anxiety, Aunt Anita, and they may be right," Carla responds in a faint and distant voice, as if something has startled her. She walks to the window and looks at the green meadows outside. "My Uncles may be right," she repeats to herself in a low voice, "but who would Mom share this with? Alexia," she mutters under her breath.

"Perhaps she didn't, my dear, no one knows, and we certainly don't know," Anita tries to reassure Carla.

"One day, I would like to meet Philip Arlington," Carla says abruptly. She seems more troubled than before, now a different woman from the woman who spoke thoughtfully a few minutes before.

Anita looks at Carla with surprise, not saying a word.

"I want to think about how to go about meeting and speaking with Bishop Arlington," Carla says softly.

"What would be accomplished by that, my dear?"

"Maybe nothing, Aunt Anita, but I need to see him," she continues to speak in a low and pained voice. Poor Mom! So that's why she wouldn't come to Stratford. That's why she always had that empty look whenever I asked her about the farm and about you folks. That's why I don't look like Dad, bless his heart. So, my natural father is a rapist and a bishop. That's just great."

"Please don't torture yourself, Carla."

"I don't want to torture myself, Aunt Anita," Carla continues to say in a low and distant voice. "These are the facts of life." But the devil in me wants to torture the bishop by informing him of my existence, Aunt Anita, she muses. Wouldn't that be dandy!

"You don't want to embarrass yourself or your family, my dear."

"No, I don't," she says, as though she is in a trance, "but I still want to embarrass the beast who raped Mom, the horrible beast responsible for my existence, she continues to speak in a very low and soft voice, "by making him know that I exist. That would teach the rapist turned bishop a thing or two!"

"But why write him, Carla? You don't really want to see, or meet the man who caused your mother so much pain, do you?"

Carla seems to regain her composure. "Why wouldn't I, Aunt Anita?" she asks. "I just want to see my natural father. I have a great urge to see him. I want to see what he looks like. Is there something wrong with me for wanting to see that man?"

"I am not saying that. I do understand why you want to see him, but I wonder if any good can come of it. And do you think your mother would feel comfortable if she thought you were going to see the man who was very hurtful to her? It's your decision, dear. You are an educated woman. Whatever you decide to do will be the right thing, I'm sure. You know best.

Her eyes moist, Carla begins to muse again, feeling insecure, shaky and distant and imagining herself addressing her deceased mother:

So, Mom, I now know much more about you and about the torment and humiliation you endured, things that you never wanted to share with me, or perhaps inflict on me. I always suspected that you had a profound sadness, a deep-seated pain inside you. Even as a very young child I sensed that there was something hidden from me. I didn't know just why, no one ever told me anything about what happened to you in Stratford when you were young. Yet I knew that you had a hidden scar you never wanted me to see. Now I know the scar is me. She chokes. I was born of violence done to you in Stratford. You never wanted to go back to Stratford, but I will. I will go and face the man who inflicted that pain on you, Mom. I want to face the man whose violence forced you to give birth to me. I want to see the man whose violence was responsible for my coming to life. I want him to see me and know I exist. He should know I'm the daughter you were afraid to have, the daughter he never intended to father.

Weeping, Anita gets up, reaches for a box of tissues and comes closer to Carla. "I wish I could be of more help, Carla." She sits next to Carla and tries to comfort her. "I know everything will work out for the best for you and for your family, my dear. You are a very strong and good person."

"Thank you. I hope so, Aunt Anita." Carla continues to cry. "You've all been wonderful. Thank you for all your concern. I wish I never knew any of this. Why did I want to know this? I don't know."

"I wish I could do more, my dear, but it'll all work out."

"I hope so. Thank you for everything, Aunt Anita."

The night before her return to Valley Town, Carla sits by herself in the bedroom that used to be her mother's. She reaches for her pen and writes:

"August 2, 1998

Dear Bishop Arlington:

I feel uneasy writing you this letter, because I do not know what kind of a reaction you will have. I believe that I am your daughter and would like very much to meet you. If, however, this would embarrass you, or cause you any difficulty with your family, and you prefer we not meet, I will understand.

I am fifty-four, the daughter of the late Rose-Anne Riley, who worked in your parents' Stratford home during World War II.

If you decide you can meet me, I will be glad to come to Lake Charles. If on the other hand you prefer to come to Virginia, I will be happy to meet you in Valley Town, where my family and I live.

Sincerely,

Carla Rose-Anne Perry Hartley"

Before leaving her uncles' farm in upstate New York, Carla mails her letter. The next day she flies back to Valley Town in Virginia.

Chapter 14

"Mom went to New York for a few days," Alexia informs her best friend Joan. The two friends are at a small coffee shop near Alexia's home.

"What's in New York?"

"Well, after Grandma's funeral, Mom got herself invited by Grandma's brothers to their farm near Hamlet. It's the farm where Grandma grew up."

"What's the attraction at the farm?"

"Grandma's brothers."

"What about them?"

"Mom wants to find out from them private things about Grandma. That really burns me up. Remember, I mentioned to you a few months ago that Grandma shared with me private things she did not want me to share with anyone else?"

"I do."

"That's what Mom is after."

"Do they know?"

"Probably."

"Would they tell her?"

"I doubt it, but you never know."

"Does it matter to you?"

"It does. Unfortunately I don't trust Mom. I don't trust her judgment. Besides, Grandma did not want Mom to know. I asked Grandma specifically if I should share what she told me with Mom, and she emphatically said she didn't want Mom to know."

"Does your Mom know that you know?"

"No, she doesn't."

"Does Johnny?"

"No, no one knows what I know."

Joan looks at Alexia with awe. "Your Grandmother must have trusted you a lot."

Her eyes watering, Alexia pauses. "Yes, she did," she rubs her eyes.

"When is your mom coming back?"

"Today or tomorrow."

"I guess you'll know what happened."

"I guess so."

"See what happens, Alexia. It'll be O. K. Get your mind on getting ready to go to Ivy. You have a lot of preparation ahead of you. Who's taking you?"

"Dad is, he's been very sweet and helpful. He has really amazed me after Grandma's death. He realizes how much I miss her, and he has been encouraging me a lot. He knows how anxious I get sometimes. Having to get ready for college, and coping with Mom's unreasonable demands can be depressing, Joan. Dad told Mom to get off my back when she began to tell me again that I should give up Ivy for Johnny's sake and enroll in Valley Town instead."

"Incredible! What did he say?"

"'That's already settled,' he told her. 'I don't want to hear any more of that, Carla. And neither does Johnny'. She really quieted down, and did not bring it up again."

"That's good."

"But the atmosphere at home is poisoned and depressing, Joan. I can't wait to go far away."

"I am very sorry, I know how difficult it has been for you."

"I'm going to call you regularly."

"I hope so, and so will I. Don't worry about your Mom. She loves you, I am sure. Even if she should come with some information from New York, don't let it upset you."

"I won't."

"Take it as it comes, Alexia, it won't be the end of the world."

"I know, Joan. Thank you ever so much. You're a real friend. I just wish you could go with me."

"I wish I could," Joan says, hugging her friend. "I'll see you soon."

"For sure."

"Hi there," Carla's husband, Michael, greets his wife. He is waiting at Valley Town's airport when she arrives.

"Sweetheart!" she greets her husband, smiling.

Even as she says "sweetheart," and smiles, her tone betrays her. "Carla! Ah - was the trip bumpy?" Michael asks. "Is anything wrong?"

"Yes, but let's wait until we're home. Please go get the car. I'll wait here and get the luggage."

While driving home, Carla informs her husband about the uncles' revelations about her mother and about herself.

"I'm very sorry, Carla," Michael commiserates with his wife.

"I must face the children with this, and my sisters and brother."

"Don't worry about that now."

"I feel awful."

"It isn't your fault."

"The children are my main worry."

"The children will understand, as will your sisters and brother, I'm sure."

"I'm upset to learn that I'm the child of a rape, Mike. I am particularly concerned about possible problems for me and for our children."

"Don't worry about that, my dear. You're a good person, and so are our children."

"I can't help thinking of and worrying about our children."

"They're wonderful children. Don't fret about any of that now."

"But how do we present something like this to kids in their teens? Our kids have had a sheltered upbringing all their lives, and may God help us if the local papers should get wind of this."

"So what if the local papers should find out? This is old stuff. I'm confident they'll never find out about it."

"The world is cruel, my dear."

"This has nothing to do with your person, or with your character. You didn't even know about it, for God's sake."

"I know that, but no matter what, it would affect me and my career."

"Why should it?"

"This is how the world is, my dear."

"I think that you underestimate the fairness of people. No fair-minded person would hold something like this against you personally, or against our children. You had nothing to do with what happened to your mother more than a half century ago."

"I hope you're right, and that's what the relatives on the farm kept saying."

"They're right. Did you mention any of your concerns to any of them?"

"I didn't, but I was very distraught and shocked, and they saw me get upset."

"That's natural."

"They were all very sweet to me. I still fear that this may threaten my potential, and may even affect our children, as well as us."

"Why should it? This is old stuff," he repeats.

"I just have all kinds of fears, Mike. I can't help agonizing about it."

"But we shouldn't let it overwhelm us."

"I'm unsure of myself, and I don't know how to break the news to my sisters and brother."

"Take a little time to think about it, we don't need to rush, but we mustn't let it destroy our lives, my darling. This happened many, many years ago."

"I know it did, but this is not the way people will look at it, I'm afraid."

"We don't know how people will look at it, and we shouldn't make it seem worse than it is."

"Let's go home. I am very tired and nervous."

"Yes, let's. Relax a little my dear, and let's go out for dinner. We'll find a way to deal with this. Think about the good things, our children, our careers and our accomplishments."

"I'll try, I'll try," she cries. "Thank you for your support, Mike."

"Oh, Carla, I am sorry!" He rubs her hand gently. "I wish there was something else I could do."

"Don't worry about me. I'll be fine."

After dinner, Carla and Michael sit by themselves in a restaurant near their home, quietly sipping coffee. The subject of Carla's new discovery comes up again.

"Why tell the children now?!" Michael asks his wife. "Let's wait a little. Then we can decide what to do, and how to do it."

"I don't want to keep it from them, the way Mom kept it from me, and I don't want our children to hear about it accidentally, the way I did."

"I agree with that, but do we need to do it immediately?!"

"I think so."

"Let's at least give ourselves a day or two, to mull it in our own minds, and to think what we should do and how to divulge it."

"No, we don't need to mull it in our minds. That would be too painful, and I shouldn't take any chances. I need to tell the children soon."

"Why do we need to rush, Carla?!"

"They're grown-up children, my dear."

"They're teenagers, Carla, and Alexia is going away. We shouldn't upset her. Let's wait, Carla, please let us wait."

"They'll handle it. Alexia will handle it."

"But why do we need to rush?"

"I just don't feel comfortable waiting, Mike, and they will begin asking me questions about my visit. They'll read the anguish on my face instantly, the way you did. I don't want to take any chances."

"We ..."

"I do wish Mom had prepared me for this many years ago by at least hinting something."

"The poor soul, how could she? Anyway, I just don't feel that our children should be shocked somehow. We need to prepare them first, by gently explaining the meaning of what happened to their grandmother."

"Yes, I'll do that, but the sooner the better, tonight would be good."

"No, we shouldn't do anything tonight, not tonight, Carla!?"

"Why not tonight, Mike. As you just said, Alexia will be leaving soon. I want her to know about it before she leaves. I want to be open about it. We should be open about it."

"We shouldn't be compulsive about it."

"If they say, 'Mom, did you like it at the farm?' I don't want to lie. Our children are smart, so I'll level with them at once."

"I think this is too soon. We should reflect on it ourselves before we say anything about it to them. We need to try to digest it ourselves first."

"What's there to digest?"

He exhales.

"It's not easy, but gossip spreads fast. Let them hear about it from us, from me."

"Of course they will hear about it from you."

"They'll hear at once."

"Whatever you say," he finally says.

They sit silently, not saying anything to each other for quite a while.

"I guess we better go home," he finally says.

"Yes," she hesitates. "Mike, I didn't tell you one more thing."

"What?"

"I sent a letter to Bishop Arlington from Stratford."

"You what?!"

"I sent Bishop Arlington a short letter."

"What did you say to him?!"

"I said, I am the late Rose-Anne Riley's daughter, that I believe I am his daughter, and want to meet him."

"Oh, my God!! Oh, my God!! Why did you do that?"

"Because I want to torture him, that's why," she smiles.

"Are you serious?"

"Half serious, Mike, but I want to meet the man who raped my Mom, and have him see me, his daughter. That's why."

"Good Lord!"

"What's the matter?"

"It could create problems. It could raise difficulties."

"Well, that's what I did"

"I guess so."

"Let's go home."

"All right," he says wearily.

Chapter 15

At about 9:00 that evening, they arrive at their home. Their twins are waiting.

"Oh, Mom!" John embraces his mother. "We knew you were back when we saw your suitcase in the hall, he smiles.

Carla asks: "Where's Alexia?"

"In her room, upstairs." Johnny then calls for his sister.

"What took you so long?" Alexia embraces her mother.

"I did stay a few days, didn't I?"

"How did it go?"

"I have so much to tell you both."

"Great!"

"I want to hear about the farm and relatives in New York. Is it a big farm?" Johnny asks.

"It isn't a very, very big farm, only about four hundred acres. It's nothing like great Texas ranches."

"Big enough," Johnny says.

"Did you find out how the farm was acquired by Grandma's family, Mom?" Alexia asks.

"I gathered from my uncles that the Riley family originally settled in New York because Grandma Rose-Anne's father, Carl Riley, was willed land in Kansas by his Uncle Charles Riley. Grandpa Carl Riley sold the Kansas land and moved east, first to Illinois, then to New York, where he bought the Riley farm."

"Why would Charles Riley will his land to his nephew?"

"I guess because he didn't have children of his own. He never married. I was told by my uncles that Great Uncle Charles, Great Uncle Henry and Great Grandpa Bradley were the three sons of the Reverend Malcolm Wood

Riley, a former Baptist minister in Virginia who had gone west to Illinois in the 1840's to work for railroads. Malcolm Wood Riley, after leaving the Baptist church in Virginia, went to Philadelphia in the 1840s, where the Illinois Central Railroad had just opened a line down to the south of Illinois. He was paid by the railroad as a Colporteur to distribute religious pamphlets and Bibles and to preach--and marry couples who were new settlers in the growing migration west."

"So, our ancestors were Baptists," Johnny jests.

"In 1860, Malcolm Wood Riley was instructed by the Episcopal bishop in Philadelphia to continue his work along the line of the railroad but to add organizing Episcopal congregations. His reports back to the bishop until his retirement in 1872, list towns in Illinois where he started Episcopal congregations. Some of these were: Centralia, Mattoon, Salem, Tuscola, Arcola, Bement, Chatsworth, and Effigham. As young men, soon after the Civil War, the three young sons of Malcolm Wood Riley went to different parts of the west, Henry as a minister for a time in Illinois, and Charles and Bradley, Great Grandpa Bradley Riley that is, went to New Mexico territory to raise sheep."

"How do they know all this?" Johnny asks.

"Uncle Clifford showed me some of the letters back to their father telling him about their experiences out there. Some comments from their letters were that 'this land has never been surveyed' and 'this part of the plains is the best sheep grazing ground there is in the world.' They wrote that 'sheep men like us in this country live very much as they did in Bible times,' that is in tents and moving about from place to place. They also wrote about returning from a buffalo hunt, where they had killed a bull, how they saw a band of mustangs, describing that as 'a very pretty sight.' When they needed supplies or wanted to mail a letter they apparently had to cross into the states, which was the southern border of Virginia. In 1880, Great Uncle Charles and Great Grandpa Bradley decided to leave the migrant life and settle down. Great Grandpa Bradley bought a farm in Illinois, where he married and raised his family. Great Uncle Charles took his brother Henry's suggestion to homestead land in Kansas. Later, Great Uncle Charles, who was never married and who had no children, invited his nephew, Grandpa Carl, to work with him, to whom he eventually willed his land. When Great Uncle Charles died, Grandpa Carl sold the land and moved first to Illinois, then east to New York, where he bought the farm."

"Did your uncles say anything about the original Kansas farm?" Johnny asks.

"Only that Great Uncle Charles built a shoddy house on that land, near where he later had a shed for grinding corn for cattle, in order to meet the requirements of the Homestead Act of those days. With the help of his brother Henry, he purchased more land adjacent to his property until he owned a total of about seventy-five acres. Then he sold all that and moved to Illinois, and from Illinois he moved to New York. This is the way I understood it, as I said."

"That must've been very small then," Johnny says.

"Yes, it was. As I said, Great Uncle Charles never married, and as he got older, he no longer could farm his land. He tried to rent it, but he had trouble getting good leasers. I think it was about 1921, when he persuaded Grandpa Carl Riley to move his family from Illinois and go to New York to farm the land with the promise that Grandpa Carl would inherit it. Grandpa Carl moved his family's belongings to New York on an immigrant train, which meant that he rented a whole train car where he loaded their furniture at one end and the livestock that his father allowed him to take at the other end. Grandpa Carl rode in the train to feed the animals and look after everything. In addition to household items and farm tools, according to Uncle Clifford, they had five cows, five horses, crates of chickens, turkeys, geese and a dog. Grandma Juliana, my late Uncle Floyd, Uncle Clifford and Uncle Donald went on a passenger train a few days later. They arrived in New York before Grandpa Carl because he was sidetracked several days in Philadelphia before he could get a train to New York. Neither Grandma Rose-Anne, nor her late brother Jimmy had been born yet. Great Uncle Charles took Grandma Juliana and the boys out to the farm to await Grandpa Carl's arrival and have the first view of their new home."

"All that was before Great Grandpa Carl moved to New York, Mom?" Alexia asks.

"That's right. Your Grandma Rose-Anne wasn't born then." Carla says. "She was born in New York."

"Why were you so eager to go, Mom?" Johnny asks.

Carla looks at seventeen-year-old Johnny. "Why was I so eager to go?" she repeats her son's question. "Well, I wanted to see where my mother grew up. I wanted to find out more about her."

"Find out what?"

"Well, dear, from the time I was a very young girl, I always thought there was something mysterious about Grandma Rose-Anne. Now I have something very interesting to tell, which I discovered during my visit."

Alexia winces.

"Really? What is it?" Johnny asks.

"You see, Johnny, for some reason I can't explain, I always thought that Grandmother Rose-Anne had a very painful experience when she was a young woman living in upstate New York. I just sensed it. She never told me and I never asked her, I just felt it. There was something within me that kept nagging me to find out what that terrible experience was.

Alexia, her head down, folds her arms. Until now she has not suspected that her mother had any inkling of what she, Alexia, already knows. Compressing her lips, and displaying no emotion she remains silent.

"What did you discover, Mom?" Johnny repeats.

"I'm going to tell you all about it," Carla hesitates. "Before I do, though, I want you and Alexia to remember that the terrible thing which happened to Grandma Rose-Anne happened a very, very long time ago. Grandma is now in Heaven. Out of respect for her, we should be careful first to keep it private, and second, we should realize that it happened, as I said, many years ago, and we shouldn't let it upset us or make us unduly sad. It's just important that we recognize it as part of us and part of our family history."

The children sit quietly.

"You see," Carla continues, "when Grandma Rose-Anne was eighteen years old, she was raped by a young man in Stratford."

Stunned, Alexia remains quiet, not saying a word, but trying to keep her composure and not show any emotion.

"What are you saying?!!" Johnny exclaims?

"I'm going to tell you how, but remember what I just said, that this happened a long time ago, and we have to be careful not to let it upset us too much. It's something out of the past."

"I know," Johnny says, "but it really happened to Grandma!?"

"That's right, but we can't do anything about it now, dear."

Alexia listens to her mother, saying nothing, but continuing to stare at the floor. She thinks of her grandmother, tall, slender, gentle and elderly. An image of Grandma Rose-Anne dressed in light green, drifts into her mind. She gazes up and remembers holding her grandmother's waist, helping her upstairs. She wants to stop her mother, but doesn't know how.

Looking at Alexia, Carla pauses.

"Mom, what happened to the guy who raped Grandma?" Johnny asks looking at his mother. "Why did you stop?"

"Well," Carla continues, "his family paid Grandma and her mother compensation for their suffering and humiliation."

There is another long pause, as Carla puts her head down quietly.

Oh, my God!! Alexia says to herself. She found that out, too. She begins to look down at the floor again herself. Suddenly, her grandmother's words begin to reverberate in her ears: *"No, Alexia, Mother did not call the cops. Instead, she rushed to the mansion where I worked, and confronted his mother ... and that woman came back with Mother to our apartment and offered to pay all my medical bills and to give me $5,000 for my humiliation and suffering ... The woman also offered to pay the $3,000 mortgage on our farm ... I want him to go to jail ... I don't want their filthy money ... Don't do this to me, Mother ... you know that man is a big shot in Stratford ... How do we know that he won't pay off the cops ... The animal is trying to buy us out!*

Isn't he ... 'Yes, he is, but better us than the cops, honey ...Your poor father died heart-broken ... Those wicked people are filthy rich ... And can get away with murder ... This is the way the world is ... And what's better, to go public, and have your scar exposed to the whole world, get nothing but disgrace, or to keep it private and get something for it ... I finally relented, Alexia ... Don't run, Mother! You wanted a stinking settlement, so what do we do now!? ...Mother, I'm pregnant! ... I want to miscarry ... and flush it down the toilet ... So, my dear, that's why I want you to be careful. I want you to be careful always..."

"Are you all right, Alexia," Carla asks.

"Yes, Mom, I am."

"What happened to the guy?" Johnny asks.

"He enlisted in the service."

"I would've had him castrated. I'd have him put in jail for life and thrown away the keys." Johnny places his hands over his face. "What a horrible thing!!"

"Remember what I said before, Johnny, this happened a long time ago."

"So what?! It still happened to Grandma!"

"I am sorry, Johnny, but yes, it was dreadful."

"Where's the guy now?" Johnny asks.

Carla does not answer at once.

"What happened to the guy, Mom?" Johnny repeats.

"After the War, he returned to Stratford a changed man, apparently repented and went to a seminary. He became a minister and now he's a bishop."

"What?!" Johnny cries. "A rapist and a criminal psychopathic monster becomes a bishop?! Grandma got a raw deal. She shouldn't have agreed to any compensation. She should've insisted on the guy's going to jail. What if she had become pregnant?"

Carla hesitates. "Grandma did become pregnant."

"I was afraid of that!" Johnny says. "What happened?"

Carla hesitates again, looks down and sighs.

"Did she have an abortion?" Johnny asks.

"Did she, Mom?" Alexia asks.

Carla's eyes tearing, she still does not respond.

"Don't tell me!" Johnny says. "She didn't have a miscarriage, and the child lives on the farm. Is that it?"

"She didn't have a miscarriage, you're right about that, Johnny, but the child doesn't live on the farm, the child lives here in Valley Town," she chokes.

"Lives here in Valley Town?!" Johnny exclaims.

"Wait a minute, Johnny," Alexia now says with surprise, as she looks at her mother's grieved eyes. "The child lives here in Valley Town! Oh my God, Mom!! Oh my God!!"

"That's right, Alexia," says Carla, tears rolling down her cheeks.

Chapter 16

"You did the right thing after all," Michael says to his wife as they retreat to their bedroom.

"I don't know. I could not help wondering whether I was doing it right. It sounded like a soap opera. I wanted to stop at the rape and carry on some other time, but Johnny kept me going."

"It worked out better that way."

"I have to tell you, I was surprised at Alexia and her reaction."

"In what way?"

"Her silence at the outset, she hardly said anything until the end, and I got a sense that she may have known something about this."

"How could she?"

"I don't know, dear. She and Mom were very close. Closer than either one of us thought and even closer than Alexia or Mom has been to me."

"She loved her grandmother, that's true, but how would she know about this?"

"Alexia always looked up to Grandma more than she has to me. Mom could have said something about her history to Alexia."

"She may have been fond of Grandma, but why would Grandma say anything to Alexia about something so private?"

"Mom trusted Alexia, and also worried about her, and she must have given her a hint of the incident, if not the details. I feel sure she must have. The relatives at the farm all think that Grandma, the smart woman she was must have shared her experience with a close member of the family. When they said that, I immediately thought of Alexia. That thought really startled me, and made me dizzy. I almost fainted. On the basis of her reaction tonight, I am sure she must have known about the rape from Mom, but not the pregnancy."

"Alexia would've said something about it to one of us."

"Not if Mom asked her not to, and Alexia can be very tight lipped."

"Why would she be?"

"I don't know, my dear," she murmurs. "Alexia's reaction to what I was saying was strange, very strange."

"How?"

"It was muted. She wasn't as shocked as Johnny was. Didn't you notice?"

"Anyway, I'm glad that now they both can face it, and it's done with."

"I don't think Alexia knew that I was a rape child, though."

"How do we know what she knows or doesn't know?"

"She knew about the rape, but from the way she behaved, when I said, 'the child of the rape pregnancy lives here in Valley Town,' I've concluded that she didn't know I was that child."

"You may be right."

"I think I am right, I know I'm right and I just hope this doesn't create problems for Alexia."

"How about Johnny?" Michael asks.

"Johnny will get over it. My main worry is Alexia. She was very close to Mom."

"She'll get over it too."

"I hope so, I hope it works out that way but I am very concerned."

"I want to ask you about the letter you sent to 'that guy,' to use Johnny's words. Why on earth did you do that? Do you truly want the man who raped your mother to become part of your life, our lives?"

"I don't want him to be, he is."

"He doesn't have to be part of your and your family's lives, even if he's your natural father."

"You don't understand. I have the need to see him."

"But why?! Why?!"

"I would like to know more about him, and I want him to know that I exist, that he did not get away with what he did to Mom. I am not kidding about that, I want him to know that he did not get away with what he inflicted on Mom, the pain, the humiliation and the suffering. I want him to get a taste of that."

"Then what?!"

"Then I'll decide what to do next, as we go along, whether he should or shouldn't have any further role in my life and my family's lives."

"You think that won't create more problems?"

"We'll see, but it shouldn't create any problems."

"You're dreaming. Of course it will. I fear it will create a lot of problems. I just hope it doesn't, but if it creates more problems, things will become worse, much worse."

"I'm sorry, but I don't care if it creates more problems. I need to confront him. I guess I am very hurt, and because of the hurt I haven't been able to comprehend it all."

"That's all the more reason why we need to reflect and think before we jump into any action, my dear. Of course you are hurt, but we have to be careful not to make things worse for us and for our children."

"Maybe I just don't know what I'm doing."

"I am not saying that. I guess there may be no harm in meeting him." Mike looks down, "but we must be very careful from now on."

"Maybe he'll decide he doesn't want to see me, or perhaps he'll deny it or just ignore my letter."

"You think you were hurt and shocked?! Wait until he gets your letter!!"

"I'm sure he'll be surprised."

"He'll be surprised?! That's an understatement if I ever heard one. He'll be dumbfounded!! He'll be floored!! The man is a bishop. He may even have a heart attack!! He committed this atrocious act some fifty-five years or more ago, when he was a crazy, spoiled brat, and now he's seventy-two. He's a man of the cloth now, a bishop!! He's probably convinced himself that this terrible thing he did in his brash youth is long past and that he and his family bought off the girl and that it's forgotten."

"You're right, but I still needed to write him."

"You were upset."

"That's right, but most importantly, I needed to let him know that he and his family didn't get away with it. I know you think that I shouldn't have written him, that I blundered and that I should've thought it over, but I disagree."

"As you say, he may choose to ignore it."

"And if he does?"

"That should be the end of it, for your children's sake and for your own peace of mind."

"How could I have any peace of mind if he completely disregards my letter?" She looks at the floor, her head between her hands.

"But he won't ignore it. He can't ignore it, I'm afraid," Mike says.

Her face brightens. "If he doesn't respond, you're right, that'll be the end of it. Nothing else I can do."

"I wish he would not pay any attention to it, but I don't think that will be the case."

"We'll just have to wait and see."

They pause again, not saying a thing for quite a while. Then Carla resumes. "Aunt Norma said that the bishop is a very wealthy man. He was an only child and he inherited a lot of wealth from his father. He got about $50 million dollars."

"That's not why you wrote him, I hope. That's not why you want to see him, I hope."

"Not at all, although if he has all this wealth and he raped my mom, and I am truly his daughter, why shouldn't this be a consideration for me?"

"I don't know. It just seems wrong."

"Why?"

"It demeans you."

"It what?"

"It demeans you and it demeans your family. It demeans all of us."

"Why should it? You are not impressed then."

"Not in the least."

"Mike, the man who raped Mom, who is responsible for my existence is one of the wealthiest people in the state of New York."

"So what if he is? He also has a horrible criminal history in his closet."

"If I am his daughter, and he raped my mom, I should be entitled to some of his wealth, shouldn't I?"

Her husband looks down again. He does not respond.

"Shouldn't I? Answer me."

"If I were you, I wouldn't think about that, and I wouldn't bring it up."

"Why not?"

"I don't know!" He shouts with anger. "This just doesn't sound right. If I were you, I wouldn't bring it up," he repeats.

"Why not?"

"Because it just doesn't sound right, it is not appropriate," he shouts again.

"It doesn't sound right! It is not appropriate! Even if he is my natural father, and he raped my mom?"

"Carla, this is in very poor taste, trust me. It is not appropriate."

"All right, I won't bring it up now."

"Not now or later, we should direct our attention to how this whole tragedy will impact our children."

"Of course we will."

"You don't want our children, or any one, to think that your motives are just about his fortune."

"My motives are not completely about his fortune, but if I am his daughter, and he raped my mom, why shouldn't I inherit from him?"

"I don't know whether you should inherit from him or not, I am not a lawyer. All I am saying is that, if our children, or anyone else for that matter, should come to the conclusion that you want to find the man who raped your mom in order to inherit from him, it won't look good for you or for your family, that's all."

"I didn't know he even existed, for God's sake. How could I have wanted to find him? Please try to understand: If it turns out that he is truly my natural father, why shouldn't I receive a share of his estate?"

"Regardless of how he became your natural father?"

"Not regardless of how he became, but because of how he became my natural father!"

"I have no idea. Maybe you should, but if I were you …"

"Of course I should."

"I don't know. I just don't know. Do as you please."

Chapter 17

The next day, Carla invites her two half-sisters, Helen and Jane, for tea at her home. Helen is four years younger than Carla. She is petite, has straight black hair, and dark brown eyes, like Chester Perry, her father. Jane is six years younger than Carla. She is a little taller than Helen, but like Helen, has straight black hair and dark brown eyes. Neither of the two younger sisters looks like Carla, who is tall and blond.

Carla tells the two younger half-sisters what she learned about their mother Rose-Anne, and about her visit to the farm. The three sisters sit in silence after Carla concludes.

"Did you have any indication, any clue that there was something like this, Carla?" Helen finally asks.

"Only that I always sensed that there was something sad in Mom's past, but I didn't have the slightest hint of anything like this."

"We all had the impression of a great sadness about her at times," Jane says, "but I always attributed that to the way Grandpa Carl died when Mom was a teenager. I thought Mom never got over that suicide."

"Yes, of course that," Carla says, "but I also felt that there was something else, which was more personal."

"I never had that feeling," Helen admits.

"Neither did I," Jane says.

"I guess it's because I'm the oldest child, and as Uncle Clifford was telling me all this, I suddenly remembered something from early childhood, before either of you was born. I guess I must've been three or four. Mom dressed me up. As she combed my hair, Dad excitedly asked Mom to hurry. Then they rushed me to the car and took me to a big building with huge columns, which I now know must've been the Court House. Dad carried me. Then Dad slipped on the marble floor and we both fell. I cried, but Mom comforted me and told me it was all right. Dad carried me into a huge room with a lot of chairs and he held me in his lap. An old man with curly white hair wearing a black robe came and sat behind a large bench. I stared at him. We sat for a long time and finally we all went home."

"That must've been the adoption proceeding," Helen says.

"Yes," Carla says. "You know something? I always remembered that, but I never associated it with adoption. Even as an adult I recall how I cried when Dad and I fell."

"That's something a child would remember!" Helen says.

"I never forgot the old man with the white curly hair in the black robe," Carla says.

"Children remember the strangest things," Helen says. "So anyway, the kid who raped our mom became a bishop."

"That's right," Carla says.

"I can't believe my ears," Jane says.

"That's the tale Uncle Clifford told me at the farm," Carla says, tearing.

"It's like a lifetime movie," Helen says. "Anyway, I think we should keep this to ourselves."

"We all have to," Jane says, "but what about Henry?"

"I don't feel up to saying anything to Henry now, Jane. Would you mind writing him?" Carla asks. "I know he'll want to talk to me about it eventually, but for now would you do that for me?"

"Yes, of course," Jane says.

"We'll both write him," Helen agrees. "He'll be coming to Valley Town soon, then all four of us can talk again."

Chapter 18

On August 4, 1998, at about noon, Bishop Philip Arlington receives Carla Hartley's letter of August 2 at his spacious mansion in Lake Charles, New York. He reads it intently twice. Mortified and bewildered, he immediately rushes upstairs, where his ninety-four-year-old mother has a special apartment. He knocks at his mother's door gently.

"Is that you, Grace," the elderly woman says softly, thinking that the bishop's wife is coming to check on her.

"No, it's me, Mother, Philip." His face white and holding Carla's letter in his trembling hand, the bishop could hardly speak. "I got this a few minutes ago, Mother."

"What is it? You are shaking."

"It's a letter from the daughter of that young woman I assaulted more than fifty years ago, Mother."

"Which woman, what are you talking about?"

"The farm girl, Mother, the cleaning girl who worked at our home whom I assaulted sexually, remember?"

"Yes, of course I remember her, she died recently."

"The letter is from her daughter, Mother."

"What does it say? Take it easy, my dear. Hand me my glasses."

The bishop reaches for his mother's glasses, sits next to her on the edge of her bed and hands her the letter. His head down, clutched between his hands, he stares at the floor and says nothing.

The elderly woman reads Carla Hartley's letter, puts it down on her bed and contemplates momentarily. "Has your wife seen it?"

"No, Grace hasn't."

"Don't say anything about it to her or to anyone else now."

"What do we do?" he asks. He seems to calm down a little.

"Well, I don't know. The girl and her mother moved to California and I was sure she had an abortion there. We paid for it."

"Where in California, Mother, do you remember?"

"Yes, I am sure they moved to Salem, California."

"And that's where you think she aborted the pregnancy?"

"Yes, that is what her mother, Mrs. Riley, told me they wanted to do before they left."

"And that's how many years ago?"

"Well, let's see, you were eighteen years old, so it has to be fifty-five years ago."

"That's right."

"What are you thinking?"

"I will hire an investigator to look into the abortion issue in Salem, California, some fifty-five years ago. What was the name of the girl, do you remember, Mother?"

"Yes, her name was Rose-Anne Riley, and the mother's name was Juliana Riley. Both are dead now. I remember reading their obituaries in the Stratford Journal."

Philip Arlington reflects. "That was a horrible thing I did, Mother. It was a very horrible thing."

"You were young, my dear, and we tried our best to do the right thing for the girl and for her family. Don't blame yourself for that sad event. It happened more than fifty-five years ago. You are now a solid respectable citizen. You have a lovely wife, two very fine professional daughters and five beautiful grandchildren. You have done many good things during your life. Don't blame yourself. What happened was an aberration. You are a man of the cloth now. God is merciful. He is forgiving, Philip."

"Yes, He is, but I need to do more, Mother."

"Go see your Dad's lawyer. Mr. Hudson is a wise and smart man."

"I don't want to do that, Mother. I want to respond to the letter I received."

"What's the name of the girl who wrote you?"

"Carla Hartley."

"She's named after Carl Riley, Rose-Anne's father. He committed suicide after their farm was burned down."

The Bishop listens, not saying a word, his perspiring face is grim.

"Take it easy on yourself. I'm sure it'll be resolved. There must be a misunderstanding here. I am sure the girl aborted the baby, Philip."

"What if she hadn't?"

"Well, I don't know what to say. God acts in mysterious ways."

"Yes, He does. I think I am going to write Carla Hartley and tell her that I will meet with her. In the meantime, I will hire an investigating firm in California and see what they come up with."

"Whatever you do, don't upset Grace or the girls."

"Sooner or later they have to know, even the grandchildren have to know, I'm afraid."

"You know best, my dear. God is merciful, I know He is."

"Yes, He is, Mother."

"Wait until you know more before you say anything to Grace, or to the girls."

"I will wait, Mother, but sooner or later, they all have to know."

"Yes, I know that."

"I'll go down now. I'll keep you posted."

"Yes, do that."

A week later, Bishop Arlington receives a report from the investigating firm he hired saying that there was no record of an abortion involving Rose-Anne Riley, or any such name. However, the firm found that Rose-Anne Riley Thornton was admitted to the hospital in Salem, California, on December 29, 1943, and delivered a baby girl named Carla Rose-Anne Thornton, fathered by Robert Edward Thornton, of Areshvile, New York, who was killed in action during World War Two, a few months before the birth of his child Carla Rose-Anne. After receiving the report, Bishop Arlington writes Carla Hartley the following letter:

"August 18, 1998

Dear Mrs. Hartley:

I have your letter of August 2, 1998. I can meet you as you requested on August 25, 1998, at the Valley Town Hotel, Valley Town, Virginia, at 12 Noon. I hope this is convenient for you.

Faithfully,

Philip Arlington, Bishop

Of Northern Lakes Region

Lake Charles, New York"

Chapter 19

Two weeks go by after Carla's return from her uncles' farm. She and her husband sit in their bedroom speculating as to why she has not received a response from Bishop Arlington.

"I'm restless, Mike," she confides to her husband. "If the man is a bishop, and is as respectable as my uncles have indicated, why doesn't he respond?"

"Well, dear, the subject of your letter is a very delicate matter. It must be torturing him, as you wanted it to do. What do we know? He may be wondering how to answer. Perhaps he's consulting his family or a lawyer or someone higher than he is in the Church. What do we know?"

"Yes, you're right it must be giving him trouble, and I must admit, I do feel badly for him now, as I think more about it. The poor man is sweating it out. The crime he committed was some fifty-five or more years ago, now he's a bishop. What he did is something in the past, which his parents paid for. God has forgiven him and his offense should be forgotten because it belongs to a different person in another era."

"Now you begin to make sense, Carla. Now you're right."

"But I have to confess, Mike, I am still conflicted. I still have a strong urge to humiliate the S.O.B., and I also want to meet him, not because he's wealthy, or because I only want to embarrass and humiliate him with my existence now, but because he's my real father."

"I can understand that, but we have to wonder if it's wise, or in the interest of our family."

"I wouldn't even mention what happened fifty or more years ago."

"You don't have to."

"I know, and Mom is now in Heaven and God must have forgiven the bastard, or should I say Bishop Arlington."

"You think so? That's good, but you're still bitter, which I understand."

"I do sincerely believe, Mike, that God must've forgiven him. And sooner or later, he has to acknowledge my letter. When he does, and agrees to see me, I'll show him the respect appropriate for a father and a bishop."

Her husband listens.

Carla continues to speak of her conflicting thoughts. "But I am truly torn, Mike. Father or not, bishop or not, he still raped Mom. Who knows? Maybe he's hiding behind religion now or is still a dangerous psychopath. How can I ever respect him, anyway? How can I ever respect a man who escaped justice with bribery? Can God ever forgive a criminal rapist, even if it all happened more than fifty years ago, even if his family paid a lot of money to Mom and Grandma Juliana for his crime? He was and still is, just the same, a violent rapist, who made Mom pregnant. I'm afraid of him, and I don't think I can meet him, even if he agrees to meet me."

"I think I do understand your predicament," Mike says to his wife. "My own mind, like yours, often zigzags in frustration and futility."

"So, what should we do?"

"What would you like to do, and how do you really want to proceed?"

"A part of me wants to forget it, but I really don't want to forget it."

"Let's wait and see what'll happen."

"We have no other choice."

Chapter 20

"Mom," Alexia calls on the morning of August 20, 1998, as she cleans her room and prepares herself for the trip to Ivy University, "you have a letter from a Philip Arlington."

"Where is it!?" Carla blushes in excitement.

"I put it on the dining room table. Wow, Mom! Why are you so excited? Who is he?"

"Please bring the letter here," Carla says. "Never mind," she then says. "I'll go get it."

"Who is he? What's the matter, Mom?"

"I'll tell you later, sweetheart."

Oh, my God! Alexia mutters as she watches her excited mother dash out to the dining room, pick up the letter, and go to her bedroom upstairs, closing the door behind her.

Carla, her hands trembling, opens the letter. It is brief:

"August 18, 1998

Dear Mrs. Hartley:

I have your letter of August 2, 1998. I can meet you as you requested on August 25, 1998, at the Valley Town Hotel, Valley Town, Virginia, at 12 Noon. I hope this is convenient for you.

Faithfully,

Philip Arlington, Bishop

Of The Northern Lakes Region

Lake Charles, New York"

Carla reads the letter a second time, folds it, puts it in her purse and goes back downstairs to the kitchen.

"Who's Philip Arlington, Mom?" Alexia asks again.

"Alexia," Carla says with some irritation, "I said I'll tell you later."

"Why are you agitated, Mom? Is anything wrong?"

"Nothing is wrong, dear."

"I hope not," Alexia says, walking away. I wonder what's this all about, and what's the matter with Mom, she muses, and goes upstairs to finish cleaning her room.

Carla then calls her husband at the University. "I got a letter from the devil this morning."

"You mean from Bishop Arlington?!"

"Yes."

"What does he say?"

"It's very brief. He'll be glad to meet me and he'll come to Valley Town this month if I like."

Her husband says not a word for quite a while.

"Are you there?"

"Yes, I'm thinking. Can you come to the office? I think it's better to talk about it face-to-face."

"I'll be there in a little while."

When Carla arrives at her husband's office, they read and reread Bishop Arlington's brief letter in an effort to glean from it something other than the written words.

"You seem troubled," Michael says.

"To say the least! I'm really puzzled."

"There's nothing to be puzzled about. He's willing to come to meet you here in Valley Town."

"His letter is short. I am baffled by it, and I don't know why. I just have this strange feeling that the son of a bitch is too confident."

"He's confident about what?"

"I don't think he believes I'm his daughter."

"How do you know that?"

"The brevity of the letter, his addressing me as 'Mrs. Hartley,' and his readiness to come here all tell me that the son of a bitch is confident that I'm not his daughter."

"Don't jump to that conclusion. In your letter, what was your salutation?

"It was 'Dear Bishop Arlington.'"

"There you are."

"But that's different."

"How is it different?"

She pauses. "His letter is so short," she finally says.

"So what if it is? What do you expect the man to say? You don't expect him to say, 'I'm sorry, my dear Mrs. Carla Hartley, I committed this atrocious thing against your deceased mother fifty-five years ago, please forgive me.'"

"Please cut the sarcasm, and don't talk to me like that, Mike, I'm beside myself. Do you understand?"

"I do, but the man is probably going crazy himself. Put yourself in his shoes."

"Serves him right, and I can't put myself in his shoes."

"Look, here's a seventy-three-year-old bishop, who committed this horrible thing when he was a youngster, and probably feels that he got away with it. Out of the blue, he receives a letter from a fifty-four-year-old woman who says to him: 'Guess what? You're my daddy!'"

"I'm astonished the bastard answered my letter."

"But he did, and frankly, I always thought that he would. He couldn't have ignored it, but now that the man has responded graciously, you have to decide if you want to meet him."

"I can't decide by myself. I need you to help me. What do you think we should do?"

He takes a deep breath and gazes at his wife. "I'm not sure. Let's think about it. It took him two weeks to answer you. Take your time and reflect on the whole affair. Where would it all lead? What will be the implications for you and for our family? If it were me, I would drop it."

"But I'm not going to drop it. You know that, Mike. I can't drop it. I want to meet him, and I want you to come with me when I meet him."

"Why?"

"Because I need you, and you're my husband."

He takes a deep breath again. "If that's what you want, of course I'll come with you, Carla"

"I appreciate it, I really appreciate that. Thank you, Mike."

"I'll be with you through it all, of course I will."

Chapter 21

"You wanted to know about the letter I received this morning, Alexia?" Carla asks her daughter when she returns from her husband's office. "That letter came from the awful man who hurt Grandma."

"Really, Mom, you mean the man who raped Grandma!?"

"Yes," Carla says.

"How did he know our address?"

"I wrote him from New York, before leaving the farm."

"You wrote to him?! Alexia is stunned and anguished. Why did you, Mom?!"

"I want to meet him."

"You want what, Mom?!"

"I want to see him and meet him, and humiliate him with my existence, Alexia."

"Why, Mom? He's a rapist, Mom! The guy's a rapist, Mom! He raped Grandma. Does Dad know you've written him?!"

"Yes, he knows."

"What does Dad think?

Carla turns away and does not answer.

"What does Dad think, Mom?!!" She is frantic.

"Dad too doesn't think it's a good idea, but he'll be with me when I meet him."

"That's good, but is he coming to our house?! Will you be bringing him to our house?"

"No, we're not. We'll meet him in a restaurant in the Valley Town Hotel. Your Dad will stay by my side."

Whew! At least she has that part right, she thinks, still fuming. "If you don't mind, Mom, I don't want, ever, to see or have anything to do with him. I hope you understand, Mom!"

"I do, Alexia, and I don't know whether I want to have anything to do with him. I just want to see him and meet him, and let him realize that I exist. That's all, Alexia."

Unhappy, she looks at her mother with suspicion.

"I do know how you feel, sweetheart, but don't worry about anything now. I have some of that feeling myself."

Vexed, distrustful and seething with anger and suspicion, she begins to cry. Don't sweetheart me, she says to herself. You should know how I feel! Why did you write him?

"I want you to be calm and take it easy, Alexia."

"Why did you write him, Mom?" Alexia now says, still crying.

"Alexia, calm down, dear. I wrote him because he assaulted Grandma Rose-Anne, and because he's my real father. A part of me wants to humiliate him with my existence, and I want to see what he looks like and hear him speak. I'll then decide what kind of relationship, if any, I may or may not want to have with him. I'm curious about him. Can't you see the turmoil I'm in, Alexia?"

"Yes, I can, and I sympathize with that, but we're all in turmoil, Mom, and what's there to be curious about? He's a rapist, who raped Grandma Rose-Anne." Still crying, she turns away from her mother and her Grandmother's voice begins to ring in her ears: *Don't fight me! he began to say and punch me ... Stop it! Stop it, bitch! I'll kill you if you don't stop! ... he continued to beat on me ..."*

Herself now crying, Carla turns to her daughter. "I want to see him, Alexia. I want to humiliate him, but I also want to forgive and love him, if I can. I want him to see me. Maybe when he sees me, he'll realize I'm his daughter. I wish, Alexia, that it would be possible for you to know the emotional turmoil I feel about finding out that I am a child of rape. Maybe the man responsible will know how brokenhearted I am. Perhaps the shock of discovering that the child he thought was aborted still exists and now claims him as her father will have an impact on him. Perhaps it will force him to get within my soul, will make him feel just as brokenhearted."

"But what will that accomplish, Mom? Why would we want to have anything to do with a man who raped Grandma Rose-Anne?"

"I need to see him."

"He raped Grandma Rose-Anne! He raped Grandma Rose-Anne, Mom!" Alexia is anguished.

"I'm his daughter! I want and need to see him. I want him to see me, and to know that I am his daughter." Carla begins to cry.

"But how can you stand to meet the man who raped your mom?"

"I'll muster the courage to do it, because I'm his daughter, and he's my real father, and I want to see him and meet him."

"Where will all this lead? We don't know where all this will lead," Alexia says trying to regain her composure, "and we don't want our family to get hurt."

"No, we don't want our family to get hurt, sweetheart," Carla says, trying to reach for her daughter's hand.

Extending her hand to her mother, Alexia has a fixed look. Her grandmother's familiar, hoarse voice continues to reverberate in her ears. She gazes at the floor, again remembering her grandmother, distinct, real, and wrinkled, dressed in a light yellow dress. She remembers how Grandma Rose-Anne always sat on a special chair in their family room, to be where Alexia and Johnny were. She remembers her scent, her searching eyes, which continue to haunt her. She wishes she could reach for her grandmother's hand and touch it, but she knows her grandmother, mentor and friend is gone. Then she begins to hear her voice again: *"For many years I had a pet bantam hen which was quite spoiled and loved to come to the house, especially for laying her eggs. ... I would open the door to let the hen in.... The hen would slip into the dirty clothes basket, lay her egg ..."*

"Are you all right Alexia?" Carla asks her daughter.

"I'm all right, Mom, but I think I'll just go upstairs to lie down."

"Yes, do that, sweetheart."

Chapter 22

Bishop Arlington is a very distinguished looking man, tall and broad shouldered. He has wavy white hair and deep-set dark blue eyes. His ruddy, clean-shaven face is kindly and almost child-like. He looks to be in his fifties, rather than his early seventies. He smiles cordially as he approaches the Hartleys in the hotel lobby.

Carla, standing tall and beautiful, is dressed in a light pink suit and a white silk blouse. She has pulled her wavy blond hair into a bun. With her imposing frame, deep-set dark blue eyes and fair complexion, the resemblance between her and the bishop is striking. It is eerie, anyone can see it, but Carla does not seem to notice it. Her husband at her side, she walks with unease toward the poised looking bishop and extends her hand to greet him. "You must be Bishop Arlington," she says, her voice reflecting discomfort and apprehension, but she maintains a dignified appearance.

"Yes," the bishop says looking at her intently, his amiable smile gradually fading.

"I am Carla Hartley," she says, "and this is my husband, Professor Michael Hartley."

"How do you do," the blushing bishop greets her, shaking her extended hand and examining her closely. He then turns to her husband and shakes his hand. "It's very nice to meet you, Professor Hartley."

"I'm happy to meet you, Bishop."

"Shall we go into the restaurant?" Carla asks.

"Yes, of course," the bishop says, his voice a bit unsteady. He appears bewildered. His smile has now vanished completely. He is visibly troubled.

They walk from the hotel lobby into the adjoining empty restaurant and are promptly seated in a secluded booth.

"Would you like something to drink?" the waitress asks.

"May we order you something to drink, sir?" Carla asks the bishop.

"Just water for now," he says.

Carla asks the waitress to bring them the menu.

"I hope you had a pleasant flight to Valley Town," Carla says.

"Yes, it was quite pleasant," the bishop says, his ruddy face now perspiring. "Actually, I arrived last night."

"Is this your first trip to Valley Town?"

"No, I was here in Valley Town about three years ago to attend a bishops' convention, which was held here in this hotel."

"It's a cheerful place," she says.

"Yes, it is," the bishop replies. He looks at her momentarily then turns away. "Valley Town is a very nice city, I liked it and the people are kind and friendly."

"I'm glad you feel that way about Valley Town," she says lightheartedly. "Michael is a native of Valley Town. I was born in Salem, California."

"I know," the bishop says, avoiding eye contact with her and wiping the sweat from his flushed cheeks and brow.

"I'm sorry about the heat," she says.

He continues to wipe the sweat from his face, not responding immediately to her remark and not making eye contact with her. He then says, "Well, this weather is really something for us from New York to adjust to! How long did you live in Salem, Mrs. Hartley?" Bishop Arlington asks Carla.

She exchanges looks with her husband, as though surprised that the bishop would know that she was born and had lived in Salem. "I think I was nearly six when my parents moved to Valley Town, sir. I recall how hot it was compared to Salem."

"Those of us who grew up in the Northeast," the bishop resumes, now struggling to appear at ease, "immediately notice the heat and humidity here in Virginia. It's much cooler in upstate New York this time of year."

"I know, it's gorgeous there now," she says, trying to help him relax. "I just came back from a short visit to Hamlet. It's beautiful there this time of year," she says, trying to make eye contact with him, to no avail.

"It is magnificent," he says, looking away.

"I've been to New York City many times," Michael says, "but I've never been upstate. I would love to visit upstate one of these days."

"Many people think New York is only New York City," the bishop says, addressing Michael. The bishop seems a little more comfortable looking at Carla's husband. "Upstate New York, especially in the northern area where we live, is agrarian and poor for the most part, but it is quite scenic, with lots of beautiful grassland and rolling hills, if one likes that sort of thing."

"It's heavenly," Carla says. "I have the fondest memories of gardens filled with colorful blossoms that made a magnificent display during the spring and summer in upstate New York. My late grandmother used to take especially good care of her roses and they were very lovely."

"Yes, our spring is quite spectacular," the bishop says, with only a fleeting glance in Carla's direction.

"I loved those large shade trees growing in New York," Carla continues.

"Our maple trees are splendid," the bishop says, still avoiding eye contact with her.

"Shall we order?" she says, addressing her husband and ignoring the bishop's reluctance to face her squarely.

"Good idea," Michael says.

"You two go ahead. I am having a little discomfort. Maybe it's the late breakfast I had, or it could be that what I ate didn't agree with me, but I'll have a cup of tea with you."

"I'm sorry," she says. "Anything we can do?"

"I'll be all right," the bishop replies. "We can have a little chat. You two go ahead and order something to eat."

"We can wait," Michael says.

"I am sorry I didn't respond to your letter sooner, Mrs. Hartley," the bishop says, at last looking at Carla. "I have to admit that I was surprised by it, and I confess that I am stumped because of the resemblance you have to my older daughter Christine, who everyone says looks a great deal like me." The bishop blushes again and focuses on Carla. "You could even be her twin."

Now Carla herself blushes.

"The information I have though, Mrs. Hartley," the bishop resumes, "is confusing. I understood that your late mother did have an abortion after that regrettable incident. After that, she moved to Areshvile, New York, with her mother, and married a gentleman by the name of Robert Edward Thornton and became pregnant again. My understanding is that Robert Thornton was killed in Europe, during the War, while your mother was still pregnant by him. She and her mother then moved to Salem, where you were born. So, if this is true, which I am frank to say seems doubtful to me now, your natural father would be Mr. Thornton. A year or so after you were born, Mrs. Hartley, so I am told, your mother met the late Chester Perry, to whom she was married, and who, as you undoubtedly know, later adopted you." The bishop, his reddening face now perspiring profusely, pauses, wipes his flushed face and clears his throat. "This is the information I have. Frankly, I am astonished at the remarkable likeness you bear to Christine."

Remaining quiet, Carla and her husband only exchange fleeting looks.

"Did you have any idea that your mother was, or could have been married to a Mr. Thornton before she married Mr. Perry, Mrs. Hartley?" the bishop asks Carla very gently.

"I never heard of Mr. Thornton, sir," she truthfully replies.

"Really, that surprises me."

"No one ever mentioned that name to me."

"This is strange and perplexing I must say. Robert Thornton's name appears on your birth certificate as your natural father."

"Actually, my birth certificate shows Chester Perry as my father." She is visibly shaken and appears troubled.

Reaching for his pocket and appearing uneasy, at first he hesitates, but he then shows her a copy of her original birth certificate. "You clearly have never had an occasion to see or examine this document." He hands Carla her original birth certificate.

Carla and Michael pour over the document the bishop produced. "I have never seen this before, sir," she says. "I didn't even know this one existed. As I said, the only birth certificate I have ever seen shows Chester Perry as my father." Appearing vexed and helpless, her face turns white. She continues to exchange quick looks with her husband. "Oh, my God," she murmurs.

"Take it easy, my dear," Michael whispers to Carla.

"I think that I'm also mystified by the information I have about Mr. Thornton," the bishop hastens to say.

"Where did you get this data, Bishop Arlington, may I ask?" Michael Hartley says.

"After receiving Mrs. Hartley's letter of August 2, I was frankly very surprised and disturbed by it. So I shared the letter with my mother. She is ninety-four. Mother of course knew about the incident and was involved in the settlement that was made with your late mother and grandmother. Mother seemed to think that Rose-Anne Riley had an abortion, but she was frank to say that she didn't know that for sure, because your mother, Rose-Anne, and Rose-Anne's mother, Juliana, left the area. We are speaking about facts dating back some fifty-five years or more. I therefore engaged an investigator when I received your letter in order to verify whether Rose-Anne did or did not have an abortion. Of course that also would've been about fifty-five years ago, and the investigator couldn't produce anything to confirm it or not, but he came up with this information about Robert Thornton and the birth certificate which I felt I should show you, Mrs. Hartley." He turns to Carla. "I am sorry, Mrs. Hartley. I didn't want to do this to you, I assure you. Anyway, there must be something wrong with the certificate if you've never heard of Mr. Thornton."

"I agree, there must be," she says.

Looking at Carla again with a faint smile, "You even sound like my daughter Christine." He shakes his head.

"We need to find out who Robert Thornton is," Michael whispers to Carla again. "Don't you think?"

"Maybe my uncles didn't have it all straight," she whispers back.

"I don't believe it really matters," the bishop says. "I think I need to be honest with myself too. You do look incredibly like Christine. You could very well be sisters."

"I need to speak to my uncles," Carla again whispers to her husband, not paying attention to what the bishop said about her resemblance to his daughter.

"These past few days have been very hard on our family, Bishop Arlington, and we need to know who Robert Thornton is before we proceed any further," Michael Hartley says.

"We also don't want to cause you and your family any problems," Carla adds.

"I know, you mentioned that in your letter, Mrs. Hartley. Your being my daughter won't cause me, or my family, any difficulties, I assure you. My family will be gratified, and I will be fulfilled if I am reunited with a daughter I didn't know I had. Our Lord would look at it with delight."

Carla eyes the bishop.

"You didn't invent yourself or bring yourself into being. Neither did I do that, even if I am your father. I could not name or control the hour of your conception, or the gender of your being, or its exact nature. I did not even know you existed, Mrs. Hartley. God is your creator and maker. He is the creator of all things. Most importantly, He created you in His own image, and gave you His life for the sake of your joy and His, and for the sake of humanity. Because you are created in God's image, you belong to no one, not to me, not to your mother, not even to yourself, you only belong to Him, Who made you and gave you His life."

Carla appears moved, but she does not utter a word. She only looks at the bishop with awe.

"These are moving words, Bishop Arlington," Michael says. "We appreciate them very much, sir. Thank you."

Saying nothing, Carla continues to contemplate the bishop.

"Are you concerned about Robert Thornton, Mrs. Hartley?" the bishop asks her gently.

"Yes, I am, Bishop Arlington. My husband and I need to find out who he is."

"I understand that you do, but, really, it doesn't matter. This isn't important anymore."

"We don't want or need more surprises, Bishop Arlington," Michael Hartley says.

"I would like to talk to my uncles again," Carla says. "They were in Europe during the War when the incident occurred. Their information is second-hand and could be wrong. I want to talk to them."

"I was in Europe too, after the incident, but I understand what you are saying, and you should discuss this with your uncles again. However, I am now quite sure that you are a member of my family, Mrs. Hartley. I am ready to concede that you are my daughter. Maybe, having recognized that you are the image of Christine, I shouldn't have brought up the subject of Robert Thornton, but I had to. I am sorry now that I mentioned him."

"I am glad you mentioned him, Bishop Arlington. I am not upset about that," Carla says.

"And we need to know who he is," Michael adds.

"Thank you for your kind words Bishop Arlington," Carla says, "I will be speaking with my uncles."

"We want to be careful," Michael adds.

"Can we meet again after you converse with your relatives?" the Bishop asks.

"I will call you after I talk to them," Carla assures the Bishop.

Chapter 23

"What do you make of him?" Carla asks her husband as they drive back to their home.

"I don't know what to make of him. He seems like a nice and devout man, and he is ready to concede that you're his daughter, but I also know that he raped Grandma Rose-Anne. That instinctively makes me cautious."

"Isn't it wonderful that he has conceded that I am his daughter?"

"It's a good start, but you still need to be cautious. My advice is that you keep your guard, maintain your poise, Carla, and don't lose your dignity. Above all, don't rush into anything."

"I have changed my mind about him. I now regret every bad word I said about him, and I feel wretched for having put the gentle, elderly soul in this uncomfortable position. I now find myself wanting to love him, wanting to cheer and comfort him, Mike. I even want to embrace him. He doesn't sound like a rapist to me. Do you think I am out of my mind to change so fast? Is something wrong with me?"

"Not so fast, Carla, and I don't know if he does or doesn't sound like a rapist, but he has to be one, and you should never forget that."

"Didn't you like him? Didn't you wonder if it's the same man?"

"Life can be deceptive. He is the same man. He admitted to the rape."

"But he must have changed a lot. He's an older man now, Mike. I was truly moved by his dignity and by his words, I must admit. He's very sweet. I loved him. I couldn't help it."

"Well, I was moved by his words too, I must admit, but that is not enough. How would we know if he has truly changed or not? All I am saying is that we have to be careful, very careful, Carla. Believe me appearances can be deceptive, especially in this case."

"Who is Robert Thornton, I wonder."

"He sure surprised us with that information."

"Yes, but he had to. That's a puzzle, isn't it?"

"To say the least, and after seeing you and immediately recognizing that you must be his daughter, he didn't have to spring that on us. You're right, his words are moving, and he does sound sincere; nevertheless, I feel that we must be on guard. As you said when you first found out about all this we don't know, but the guy may even be psychopathic. We need to see more of him and know more about his adult life.

"I'm now sorry I ever used that word, and I'm sure now that he's not that at all. I know we have to be careful, but he's not psychopathic. I'm quite sure he isn't that."

"We don't know, Carla."

"And what about the Robert Thornton issue? Who do you think he is?"

"I have no idea."

"That really startled me."

"I know it did."

"It really stumped me and shook me up, Mike."

"What are you going to do about it?"

"I'll have to ask my uncles."

"Good."

"Do you think we should invite him to our house tonight?"

"Absolutely we should not."

"Why shouldn't we?"

"We don't know him for God's sake!"

"I really want to invite him, Mike."

"Why do we have to rush?"

"Mike, he's ready to concede that I'm his daughter, and he traveled from New York to meet us. We have to invite him to our home. It's the only decent thing to do."

"But we can't invite him to our house now."

"Why? He admitted it, didn't he?"

"Admitting it has nothing to do with inviting him to our house. I don't feel easy about bringing him into our home, at least not on this trip. The kids are apprehensive about the whole affair. Alexia in particular doesn't want him near the house. She made it clear she didn't want ever to see or meet him. You heard her say that. You don't want to upset her, especially now, when she's about to leave."

"That'll change. When she sees him, she'll change her mind, just like I did. I'm sure of it."

"You're dreaming. She'll never change, you should know that."

"Besides, we don't want Alexia to decide for us whom we socialize with, do we?"

"We don't want to upset or lose our children either, do we?"

"No, we don't, but I want him to visit our home. I really loved him. I really did. I don't know what happened to me, but I really and truly was taken by him, and I think that he is real and sincere."

"I wonder also what that business about Robert Thornton is about."

"I have no idea. Maybe Mom was married to him before she married Dad."

"Robert Thornton couldn't possibly be your father, unless he's a twin of the bishop."

She smiles. "Mom was young and must've been very distressed when it all happened. She was ashamed of the whole thing and couldn't wait to marry someone so that I'd have a father. I think she could have married Robert Thornton, who went to war and got killed. When I was born, she must've put his name on my birth certificate as my natural father. What else could it be?"

"Yes, it could've happened that way, but we really don't know that yet. Let's wait and see what your uncles may say."

"If the bishop thought for a minute that I was Robert Thornton's daughter, do you think he'd ever say that I look like his daughter, or entertain the idea that I'm his real daughter?"

"No, he wouldn't."

"Then as soon as I speak with Uncle Clifford and find out who Robert Thornton was, I want to call the bishop and tell him what I learned. Then let us invite him to the house."

"You are tiring me out, Carla. It's too soon I said, and the kids are not ready."

Carla pauses, not saying a word for a long moment. "We'll see," she finally says.

Chapter 24

On arriving home, Carla and her husband find their twins are waiting for them.

"You look worried, Mom," Johnny says to his mother.

"Do I? I guess I'm a little worried. I need to speak to Uncle Clifford."

"Why?" Johnny asks. "What happened?"

"I'll tell you after I speak with Uncle Clifford."

"Tell us now, Mom? Did he deny it?"

Carla ignores her son's question as she tries to find her uncles' phone number.

"Did he deny it?" Alexia asks.

"No, no, he didn't."

"What happened then?" Johnny asks.

"Let me first speak with Uncle Clifford, darling, then I'll tell you both what happened."

Carla calls Clifford. Her husband and two children sit quietly in the living room and listen. "Uncle Clifford," she begins, "Mike and I just had a lengthy meeting with Bishop Arlington."

"Great, how did it go, sweetheart?"

"It went very well, Uncle Clifford. He was nervous at the beginning, but he opened up and became very gracious."

"Did you like him?"

"Yes, I loved him, Uncle Clifford, but Mike is more cautious about him, and wants me to proceed slowly. I got the impression that the man is sincere and honest. He's very thoughtful and kind. I felt comfortable with him."

"That's good."

"What comes across to me from this first meeting is that the man is very devout."

"Yes, he's deeply religious and pious."

"I have to admit that his gentle demeanor forced me to change my earlier perception of him. I found him lovable, Uncle Clifford, but I want to give myself more time to know him."

"Good. In time you'll get to know him better."

Alexia suddenly feels pained. The voice of her Grandmother Rose-Anne begins again to ring in her ears: *"I want to see him go to jail, Mother! ...So he can't do this to anyone else! ... Lock him up for life! ..."*

"I do want to get to know him better, Uncle Clifford, but I have a question I want to ask you."

"Shoot."

"Who is Robert Thornton?"

"Oh, God, how did you hear about him?!" Clifford chuckles.

"The Bishop brought his name up, Uncle Clifford."

"How on earth did he hear about him?"

"He said that he hired an investigator to look into the supposed abortion who couldn't find anything about that, but the investigator produced my original birth certificate, which the Bishop showed to us. The birth certificate names Robert Thornton, of Areshvile, New York, as my natural father."

Uncle Clifford is quiet.

"Do you know anything about that?"

"Did the bishop use this to deny that he's your natural father?"

"No, he didn't use that to deny that I am his daughter, not at all."

"He didn't deny that."

"No, he didn't deny the incident, or that I could be his daughter, Uncle Clifford. To the contrary, he in fact stressed repeatedly that I look like one of his daughters. He said that he's ready to concede that I'm his daughter and that he would be fulfilled to have me as his daughter."

"That's wonderful, Carla. That's what you want, isn't it?"

"And he was very honest about conceding what happened. He was very kind and very gentle, and he spoke very kindly about Mom, Uncle Clifford. Even when he showed me the birth certificate he was uneasy doing that. He's willing to concede that I'm his daughter, but Mike and I want to know who Robert Thornton is before we talk to him again."

"Robert Thornton, Carla, did not and does not exist. He was an invention."

"He was what?"

"He was an invention."

"He was an invention? What does that mean, Uncle Clifford?"

"He was an invention, Carla. That means that your mother invented him. She created him out of thin air, in order to show that you had a father. She made him up. Then she told the hospital in Salem that Robert Thornton died in the War, which was obviously also an invention. Your grandmother Juliana was scared for Rose-Anne when Rose-Anne made up this tale."

"Oh, my God, why did Mom do that?"

"Your Mom was stressed out after what happened to her, Carla. She was demoralized and ashamed of what had happened to her and she made up all that. She didn't want to tell the hospital that she was raped, she was ashamed to do that, Carla."

"Oh, my God, oh, my poor mom, poor Mom!"

"And Areshvile was also an invention. There is no such village or town or city in New York State. Rose-Anne invented that out of thin air also, so that no one could trace who Robert Thornton is, or so she thought at that time."

"Oh, my God, Uncle Clifford, I didn't think Mom could do such a thing. So Grandma Juliana knew that Robert Thornton wasn't real, and that Mom made up the whole tale?"

"Yes, she did, and she's the one who told us all this. Your Grandmother Juliana was scared for your mom, she was afraid that someone would find all that out, and Rose-Anne would get in more trouble, but Rose-Anne was adamant."

"This is incredible!"

"Remember, my dear, Rosy was only eighteen when all this happened, and she was very angry and very ashamed of what happened to her, and she was very scared."

"How sad, Uncle Clifford! Did Dad know about the Robert Thornton tale?"

"Rose-Anne leveled with him about all this before they got married. So, yes, Chet knew, and was very sympathetic with Rose-Anne. He loved her very dearly and always treated your mother very kindly. So Chet knew everything, and as soon as he and Rose-Anne got married, he volunteered to adopt you and to correct the birth certificate. Chet always felt for your mother, my dear. He was always very nice and kind to Rose-Anne."

"I know that. Dad was a saint."

"He certainly was."

"I appreciate your telling me all this, Uncle Clifford. I need to know it."

"How did you leave it with the bishop?"

"That we'll call him after we speak with you."

"This is the story, my dear."

"I'll call the bishop, and level with him. I hope he'll understand."

"He should understand, my dear. He should."

"I am sure he will. I really loved him, Uncle Cliff, and I want to invite him to the house for dinner tonight. What do you think?"

"Talk it over with your husband, my dear, and see how your family feels about it."

"But do you think that it would be appropriate to invite him, Uncle Clifford?"

Clifford Riley pauses. "Yes, I do, but see how it goes, and see how you and your husband and your family feel about inviting him."

"You agree that it would be appropriate to invite him?"

"I see no harm in doing that, if he'd accept, that is. As I said, discuss it with your husband. See how your family feels about it. The bishop is very reserved, but a real gentleman. I hope you, your husband and the children will get to know him better."

"I hope so."

"I'm glad you had a good start, and it all went well. Let us know more when you can. We're all anxious for your news, my dear."

"I'll surely keep in touch, Uncle Clifford. Thank you so much for explaining the mystery to me. I feel a lot better knowing about it."

"You're welcome, my dear."

"I suspected something like that," Michael Hartley tells Carla after she hangs up the phone and relates to her family what her uncle told her. "I had a feeling that Robert Thornton wasn't real."

"Poor Grandma," Johnny says.

"Your poor mother," Michael says to Carla.

Alexia remains quiet.

"I never suspected it, I must say," Carla says. "I'm wondering what I should say to the bishop."

"There's nothing to wonder about. Say exactly what your uncle said, that there was no Robert Thornton."

"I agree, and I'll tell him that. Then I want to invite him to our home."

Michael Hartley stares at his wife but he says nothing.

"You want what, Mom?" Johnny asks.

"Wait, Johnny," she says.

"What do you mean, wait, Mom?"

"I said wait!"

"Are we going to invite the man who raped Grandma to our house, Dad?" Johnny asks his father.

Michael does not answer.

"Shouldn't we have some regard for Grandma Rose-Anne, who brought Alexia and me up, who took care of Alexia and me, while you and Mom, Dad, were pursuing your careers and other interests? What's going on, Dad?"

Alexia remains silent.

"How can the man who raped Grandma, be lovable, Dad?" Johnny asks.

His face grim and his head down, Michael does not respond.

"What's going on, Mom? What's happening, Dad? The guy rapes Grandma, then after Grandma dies all is forgiven and forgotten! I can't believe it. What is this?! Someone should stand up for Grandma! I promise you, Mom, that if he comes to our home, I'll stand up for Grandma. I'll walk to the son of a bitch and tell him that he's not a bishop, he is a rapist."

Carla is jolted. She stares at her son, fire in her eyes. "Johnny," she says sternly, "I dare you to do exactly that, go ahead, just try and do exactly that."

"What will you do if I did?" Johnny asks in response to his mother's threat.

Alexia sits, shaking her head in silence, and visibly very upset.

"All right," Michael Hartley intercedes. "That's enough for now, let's all take a deep breath. Mom and I will talk it over. Johnny, please go help Alexia get ready for her trip, son. Please go upstairs. Please go help Alexia in her room. We'll talk to you both in a little while."

Alexia motions to her twin, and the two go up to Alexia's room. "She's a bitch," she whispers to her brother.

"Hush, Alexia."

"She'll never dare do a thing to you, and she knows that."

"We don't want a confrontation, Alexia."

"She's asking for one, can't you see her? She depresses me, Johnny, she does. I can't wait to get out of here."

"Take it easy, we don't want things to get out of control. Let's see what they'll decide."

"She's going to pressure Dad, or threaten him."

"Dad will handle her."

"How could he? She will cry and rant and insist, and Dad will go along with her, just watch."

"Dad's heart is in the right place though. I'm sure he will be firm, but let's not make it difficult for him."

"I know that Dad's heart is in the right place, but he won't be as firm as you hope."

"He'll be firm, I know he will be, but he has to live with Mom, and we're leaving."

"I can't wait to get out of here," she repeats.

"Take it easy."

"I wish you could come with me."

"If only I had better grades."

"I truly wish you could go with me, Johnny," her eyes water again. "Let's see what happens. She depresses me so much, Johnny, that I don't want to look at her."

"Take it easy."

When the parents go to their room, Carla tosses herself on their bed and stares at the ceiling.

Michael sits on the chair and remains quiet.

"What should we do?" Carla finally asks.

"It seems to me that we should not react that violently," Michael softly tells her.

"Johnny was being provocative. Didn't you hear what he said?"

"Yes, I did, but we should try to help our children understand how people can mature and change."

"That's fine, and I will try to do that, but I also want them especially to understand how it feels to want to be able to know and love a long lost father."

"That's all right too, but can we do it gently, and without anger?"

"I'll try."

"Will you do your best?"

"Of course I will."

"Let's go back then."

"Let's," she says.

"Alexia," Michael Hartley calls, "is Johnny still with you?"

"Yes, Dad, he is."

"Come on down, I want to talk to both of you."

Alexia and her twin go down. "What happened? Do we have to have him in our house, Dad?" she resumes softly.

"No, we don't," her father says, "but we are going to, sweetheart. Your mother feels that it is the right and decent thing to do. She wants to invite him. She feels that the man came all the way from New York to see her, and that he conceded that Mom is his daughter. She wants to invite him."

"What do you think, Dad?" Johnny asks.

"I think we should wait, but if Mom wants this to happen, I want us all to calm down, and let Mom invite him. It won't be the end of the world, and it won't change how any of us feel about it. I will call Mom to join us, and let us all be civilized in the way we talk to each other. Is this all right with you?"

"Yes, Dad, it's all right," says Johnny.

"And is it all right with you, Alexia?"

"Yes, it's all right, Dad."

"Thank you. I love you both. I'll call Mom now?"

"Go ahead, Dad," Johnny says.

"Carla," Michael calls his wife.

Carla comes down and sits next to her husband, facing her twins. "I just want to say that I felt better about everything after speaking with Uncle Clifford," Carla starts after a few moments of quiet. "Even he thought it would be appropriate to invite him, but I feel badly making my family miserable," she says. "I feel horrible making you two miserable," she says. "I must say that I know how you feel, because this is how I felt from the beginning, but something happened to me after I saw the man. I changed, and I don't know what happened to me, or how to describe it. I found myself wanting to comfort and protect the elderly man, far from my original desire to humiliate and embarrass him by my actual existence. I found myself trying to convince myself that the incident happened more than fifty-five years ago, and that the tormented man facing me is my real father. I feel that my family should be sympathetic with what happened to me. My family, I feel, should look at my own turmoil with a little understanding. If I need and want to know him better, my family should allow me to decide what to do in this situation. I am not saying that you two don't count at all, you do. But I should be the one who makes the final decision. This is the only way I can get to know him better." Her eyes tearing, Carla speaks very calmly.

"I agree," Michael says.

"He's truly an honest and sweet man, Alexia. He is a good and gentle man, Johnny." Carla pleads with her children.

"Do we also have to see him?" Johnny asks.

"No, Johnny," Carla says, "you don't have to see him, if you don't want to, but it would be nice if you will consider it. I would appreciate it if you would agree to meet him."

"I'm not sure I can. I don't feel comfortable meeting him."

"And you, Alexia?"

"I too feel uncomfortable meeting him."

"Maybe you'll meet him later?" Carla appeals to her children.

"I'll talk to you about it later, Mom." Johnny goes upstairs.

"I understand, dear."

"I'll see you all later." Alexia too goes upstairs.

"What do you make of that?" Carla asks her husband.

"It went better than I expected. You made a frank and honest opening statement, Carla, but the kids were very close to their grandmother, and we should be very careful. We too have to be sympathetic with how they feel."

"I agree, and I can't say I didn't expect their response. It all went well on the whole. I'm glad it did. Thank you for interceding."

"They obviously feel very strongly about it. Young people are like that, and we have to continue to be careful. We can't push them too hard. I supported you because I felt I should. Although I supported you, I truly think it's better if we take him out this time. That'll be a very kind gesture to our children. They'll be leaving soon, Carla. Let's take him out someplace, my dear. We don't have to bring him to the house on this trip."

She remains silent.

"The kids' nerves are still raw about the whole affair. Let's take him to a nice place."

"I really want to invite him to the house, Mike. I'm sorry."

"Let's not pressure the children to meet him then. Let them have time to digest all this. It isn't easy. Maybe you want to think it over again. Maybe we could still find a way to take him out for dinner without having to have him come to the house this time. Please think about that."

"I thought about it, and I don't want to do that. It would be a mistake for me to agree to take him out, because I can't let the children dictate to me, not in this delicate situation. They need to know that I've decided to acknowledge the man as my father, and treat him as such. They have to accept that."

"I don't want us to lose our children in the process."

"We won't lose our children."

"They're horrified by the whole affair."

"I know they are, but they're going to be all right, and they'll eventually come to know and like him, just as I did. He's a man of the cloth. He's very thoughtful and holy. I can't insult him by failing to invite him to my home, especially after conceding that I'm his daughter."

Remaining silent, Michael only looks down at the floor.

Chapter 25

Carla and Michael are now in their bedroom, getting ready to go bring the Bishop to their home for dinner. They inadvertently leave their bedroom door wide open. Alexia is by herself in her room on the same floor. She can hear her parents discuss the first meeting they had with Bishop Arlington.

"I was surprised at my feelings," Alexia hears her mother begin the conversation, "how quickly I became involved, and how I liked and respected Bishop Arlington immediately."

"What do you think was the triggering point?" Michael asks.

"Well," Carla says, "I can't put my finger on any one thing exactly, but when he began to talk about how I didn't invent myself or bring myself into being, how, even if he were my father, he was not responsible for my coming into existence, or some such thing, because he couldn't name or control the hour of my conception, or the gender of my being, or its exact nature, that really moved me."

"I must say that also moved me," Michael says, "but he still is responsible for your coming into existence. Were it not for his atrocious deed, you wouldn't be here today. That's the irony and the tragedy of it all."

She pauses not saying a word for a long moment. "But he said other touching things, which I don't recall exactly, about not knowing that I even existed."

"I remember those also, and I agree that they were remarkable words, but you have to be careful about remarkable words, and about people who use them, and how they use them. You have to be careful about those who invoke the name of God at the drop of a hat, especially when they talk about God our creator and maker, who created us for his joy, and in his own image. I think these are the words the bishop used. What do they mean?"

"He said more than that. He said that God created us for the sake of humanity also, that we don't belong to ourselves, or to our parents, but only to God who gave us His life."

"Whatever words he used, what do these words mean? How do they impact what he, the bishop, did to Grandma Rose-Anne? These beautiful and remarkable words are a distraction, my dear. Don't be taken by them."

"I don't think they're a distraction, and I must say that I was very impressed with them. I think he's a good man."

"He's a charming man. He's trained to be that."

"He's not only a charming man. I think he's truly a good person. Uncle Clifford even says so."

"I hope that he's truly a good person, not only for your own sake, but also for the sake of our family and our children, yet we also need to be careful. That's all I am saying."

"I don't disagree, and I'll try to be careful, but I also want to be forgiving. I want to forgive him for an act, regardless of how mean it was, which he committed when he was young and immature. As you said earlier, I should find a way to convey that to our children, but I need your help. And I also want and need to know him better, and that's why I'm inviting him for dinner at our home. Yes, we need to be careful, but how else can we know him better?"

"That's fine, and I don't have any quarrel with your noble desire to forgive. I admire that."

"How else do I, do we, get to know him better, if I'm going to accept him as my father."

"I don't know. I just hoped there was another way, other than bringing him to our home so soon."

"If he's willing to accept that I'm his daughter, then I must begin to show him respect, don't I?"

"I suppose."

"If I don't, I would have no chance of having a father-daughter relationship."

"You really want that relationship? You feel that you need it?"

"I do."

"But I don't feel that you need it."

"What do you mean I don't need it, for God's sake? If he's willing to concede that I'm his daughter, and I accept him as my father, then I'm a part of his family, a member of his family."

Michael just stared at Carla, saying nothing.

"Why do you look at me, as if I committed treason? I'm truly his daughter, aren't I? Then I should be considered as a member of his family."

"You're not thinking about the inheritance issue again, I hope."

"Yes, I am. Why shouldn't I? What's wrong with that?"

"Carla, when you speak about forgiving him for an act he committed as a youth, I admire you, but when you begin to speak about creating a father-daughter relationship with him, in order to inherit from his extraordinary wealth, you lose me, and I lose confidence in what you're doing. I also lose respect for you."

"Why do you lose me?" Carla shouts at the top of her lungs, "and why do you lose confidence in what I am doing? You also lose respect for me! And why is that? Why? Why?"

"Because you demean yourself and you demean your family and I find that disgusting."

"You're the one demeaning me," she cries. "You're not very nice. I don't understand you."

"Right, you don't." He turns away.

"Why shouldn't I? Why are you turning away from me? If he concedes that I'm his daughter, and I accept him as my father, I should be entitled to inherit from his estate, as a member of his family, like his other children, shouldn't I?"

Her husband does not answer her.

"Answer me! Shouldn't I?" She is very angry.

Dejected and flustered, he leaves the bedroom. "I'll wait for you downstairs," he says.

Following him, Carla goes downstairs and into the hall. She reaches for the phone and starts to dial the hotel where the bishop is staying to inform him that she and her husband will be on their way to pick him up. She is surprised when Alexia starts down the stairs. "Oh, Alexia," she says, stopping midway through her dialing. "I didn't see you."

"I'm sorry if I startled you," Alexia says to her mother calmly. "I couldn't help hearing your heated discussion with Dad. How could a rapist become worthy of so much respect so soon? Do you really want to claim the man who raped your mother as a father? Think about that, Mom."

"I don't know, sweetheart," Carla says, her lips trembling, "but he truly is a good person, and very devout. He's a very kind man."

"How would we know all that already? We don't even know him, and he raped Grandma Rose-Anne."

"But I want to forgive him."

"And as Dad says, that is noble, if you have the strength to sincerely forgive him, but should we bring the man who raped Grandma Rose-Anne to our home? Should we do all that in order to claim him as a father so as to inherit from his filthy rich estate?"

"But he's my father."

"No, he isn't, Mom. Chester Perry was and should always be your father. He and Grandma Rose-Anne were and should always be your parents. It is they who brought you up and took care of you. This man didn't do that. He and his family would have preferred that you didn't exist. Think about that, Mom. If you want to invite the person who raped Grandma Rose-Anne to your home, that's your business, Mom, I can't do anything about it."

Carla only listens, staring at her daughter.

"But you want to do this in order to inherit from the man who raped Grandma Rose-Anne. That's not right, Mom. I'm very sad."

"Alexia, dear ..."

"I'm very sad." Alexia goes upstairs.

Chapter 26

Carla is visibly disturbed after her encounter with Alexia. She asks her husband if he could pick up the bishop by himself, to give her time to recover, and her husband agrees. A few minutes later, Michael arrives with the bishop at the Hartley home.

"Welcome, welcome to our home," Carla greets Bishop Arlington.

"Thank you for having me," the bishop says with marked reserve. "I'm also grateful to your husband for coming to pick me up."

"We thought that would make it easier for you, but I'm sorry I couldn't come with him."

"There's no need for the two of you to trouble yourselves. Thank you so much."

She leads him to the living room. "This way please, Bishop Arlington."

"You have a lovely home."

"Thank you, Sir, we like our home." She seats him in a part of the Hartleys' living room which is always reserved for special guests.

"This is a very comfortable chair!" He sits down and quickly surveys the tastefully furnished room.

"Can I offer you something to drink?" Carla says.

He raises his head, looks at Carla and hesitates. "I think I'll just have a glass of water."

"We also have wine."

"Well, I can have a glass of wine, a dry wine if you have it."

"Would you prefer white wine or red wine? We have both."

"Either will be fine. I'm a light drinker."

Michael comes in carrying a tray that has glasses of water and glasses of wine, which he offers to the bishop.

The bishop stands up and reaches for a glass of red wine. "Thank you so much, thank you. It's an honor and a pleasure being in your lovely home."

"We are delighted to have you, Sir," Michael responds. He picks up a glass of red wine and sits next to the bishop.

"Thank you very much," the bishop says. "These past few days have not been easy. I'm sure they haven't been easy for your family."

"They have been hard on everyone," Michael says.

"I'm glad the subject of Robert Thornton is resolved now."

"We are too."

"These matters, tragic though they may be, have a way of resolving themselves."

"True."

"We have to keep our faith in Him and pray that He will guide all of us to do what is right."

"That's right," Michael says.

"I believe all will be well."

"I agree."

Carla returns carrying another small tray with one glass of red wine, and some hors d'oeuvres.

The bishop and Michael stand up. Michael then walks toward his wife, and gently takes from her the silver tray. He lets her pick up the lone glass of red wine, and offers the bishop the hors d'oeuvres, which she has brought to the living room.

Carla now reaches for her glass of wine. "May we again welcome Your Eminence to our home," she nervously says, toasting the bishop.

"Thank you." The bishop looks at Carla and raises his wine glass. "Let me also make a toast to this discovery you made, that it will become a manifestation of God's loving nature, so that we can nourish and support and forgive and love one another as members of God's family."

"Hear! Hear!" Carla says.

Michael raises his glass.

Carla walks toward the bishop and embraces him. "These are comforting words, Bishop Arlington," she says. "Thank you."

"Philip," the bishop says. "You and your husband, please call me Philip."

"Yes," she hesitates. "And I am Carla. Call me Carla, please."

"And I am Michael."

"I would like to arrange for you to meet the rest of my family, your family," the bishop says.

"We would like that very much."

"We'll arrange it soon."

"And, and, ah, we would like you to meet the rest of our family, too," she hesitates.

"That'll be very nice."

"Will you excuse me," she says, about to return to the kitchen. "I'll let you and Michael entertain each other and become more acquainted while I work on dinner."

"I'm a very light eater, especially at night. Please don't overburden yourself."

"It's not a burden at all. We are honored. It's a privilege to have you visit our home." She walks to the kitchen.

Carla produces a very light meal. When it is ready, she and her husband lead the bishop to their dining room. She invites the bishop to sit to her right, her husband to her left facing him, and she seats herself at the head of the table.

"Thank you," the bishop says.

"Would you care to say grace?" Carla asks the bishop.

"Yes, of course," he says, his face reddening again. "Bless, Oh Lord, this food to our use, and us to Thy service. Make us ever aware of the needs of others. Bless the home of Carla and Michael. Bless their family. May the love, which is your heavenly nature, be freshened in us through your food, Lord, God. May it cleanse us, so that we go from here to nourish, support, cheer, love and forgive, Amen."

"Amen," Carla and Michael say.

"That was very nice," Carla says. "Thank you so much."

"Yes, thank you," Michael says.

"Please help yourself," Carla says. "I've kept it very simple."

"It really smells good," the bishop says, helping himself to a small piece of baked chicken. "Chicken is my favorite meat, and I love mashed potatoes."

"That's good. I played it safe!"

"I would like all of you to come to our home in Lake Charles, and meet the rest of the family," the bishop resumes.

"That would be nice. I know one of your daughters is Christine the one who looks like me."

"Actually, both look and sound like you, but Christine's resemblance to you is more remarkable than Elizabeth's. It is actually striking. You do also sound very much like Christine."

"So, the other daughter's name is Elizabeth?"

"That's right. We named the younger of the two girls, Elizabeth, for my mother. Mother is ninety-four now, will be ninety-five soon, but she's alert and in good health, God bless her. I hope that you'll meet her soon."

"I would like to meet her."

"She'll be very happy to meet you."

"Will she really!?"

"Yes, she always had a feeling of guilt about the supposed abortion. She'll be relieved to know that it never happened."

"Wonderful!"

"Father died about ten years ago. He was eighty-four. I am an only child, my dear, but Christine has two boys. Ronald, who is named for my father, is 18, and Dean, who is named for Christine's husband, is 15."

"These are very nice names."

"Elizabeth has twins, a son and a daughter. Bryan, named for his father, and Jennifer, named for Elizabeth's mother-in-law. They're 14."

"That's very interesting."

"Do I understand that you have two children?" Bishop Arlington asks gently."

"Yes, that's right. We have a son and a daughter, but I don't remember if we said that they are twins. Alexia is one hour older than Johnny. They are 17. They'll soon be 18. Alexia has been accepted at Ivy University in New York State. She's getting herself ready, and we are excited for her. Johnny will attend Valley Town University, where Michael is a professor."

"Our grandson, Ron, Christine's boy, was accepted at Ivy University. That's marvelous, and you have selected very nice names for your children. Did you name them after any members of your families?"

"We didn't name either for any of our family members."

"And they are twins," she repeats.

"Yes, that's interesting," he says. "What an unusual coincidence!"

"And, as you know, I have two sisters and a brother."

"And now you have four sisters. I will be fulfilled when you meet your other two sisters, and it'll be nice when the cousins meet," the bishop says as he continues to nibble at his food.

"Wouldn't it?!" Carla exclaims.

Following dinner, Carla and Michael lead the bishop to the living room. After they have coffee, Carla takes leave and goes upstairs to talk to her children again. She speaks very gently to Alexia first, pleading with her to come down and meet Bishop Arlington.

"I don't feel comfortable seeing or meeting him, Mom, I am sorry," Alexia says to her mother.

"Okay, perhaps you will meet him later."

Alexia turns away from her mother.

"And you, Johnny, would you like to come down and meet him for a few minutes?"

"Yes, I'll come down and meet him," Johnny says.

"That's wonderful, thank you, Johnny. Thank you so much."

Alexia is startled.

"I'll just put on a decent shirt and come down."

"Great, thank you, Johnny, I'll see you downstairs." Carla turns to Alexia again. "I respect your feelings, Alexia, but I do hope that the day will come when you will feel comfortable meeting Bishop Arlington. He's an elderly man now, and a different man, not the brash eighteen-year-old youngster who assaulted Grandma Rose-Anne."

Her head down, Alexia does not respond. Please, please, she muses, get off my back! You've conned Johnny into going down to meet your beloved bishop, the monster who raped and humiliated Grandma Rose-Anne, but that won't work with me, ever, Mom!

Chapter 27

"This is Johnny, one of the twins," Carla introduces her son to the bishop.

"Hello, Johnny," the bishop rises from his chair. His rosy face beaming, he walks toward the young man, and extends his hand to him.

"Hello, sir," Johnny shakes the bishop's hand nervously. For a moment he looks around awkwardly, then moves and seats himself next to his father.

"You will soon have new cousins to meet," the bishop says cheerfully. "Some of them are twins like you and Alexia."

"Oh," Johnny says, visibly nervous.

"Would you like to meet your new cousins?" the bishop smiles.

"Yes," John hesitates. "Do they know about us?"

"They will soon know about you and Alexia."

"Do they know about what happened?"

The bishop's face reddens. "I am going to tell them what happened soon. How about you, do you know about what happened?"

"I know a little, in a general sort of way." John looks at his mother.

"Would you like to hear from me about what happened?"

Appearing to be surprised, Carla and Michael exchange glances.

"I would," Johnny says timidly.

Visibly uneasy, Carla begins to shift restlessly in her chair. She exchanges glances with her husband Michael again, who does not seem as perturbed as she.

"About fifty-five or so years ago, Johnny," the bishop begins.

"Really," Carla interrupts, "this is not necessary. I did not expect this to happen, I assure you. Johnny has an idea of what happened. That's all he needs to know now. You don't need to trouble yourself. I'm sorry, I'm very sorry."

"It's all right. There's nothing to be sorry about. As long as this is on the young man's mind, and he wants to hear it from me, I don't mind relating to him what I remember happened."

Her face grim, she looks at her husband again, who seems intrigued.

"You see, Johnny," the bishop resumes, "when I was barely eighteen, your late grandmother Rose-Anne was a very lovely and attractive young woman, about my age, working at our home. During that time, I became very attracted to her, but I committed a very horrible act, which I have regretted all my life. I assaulted her sexually. I don't know why it happened, and I certainly don't know, don't remember how it happened, or how to describe it even." His voice is unsteady and beads of sweat have appeared on his forehead. The elderly bishop hesitates. "In any event, there was no excuse for what I did. It was a horrible crime I committed against her and against God. I just don't know why I did it," he stammers again. "It was inexcusable. I will always regret it as long as I live, and wish I could undo what I did."

"Did you see Grandma after that?" Johnny asks in a low, unsteady voice, his own face blushing.

"No, I didn't see her. I wish I could have seen her. I would have apologized to her personally. I would have asked for her forgiveness. I would have asked and pleaded with her to forgive me in person. Your grandmother was a good and honest person, working at our home and trying to make a living. I violated that sacred trust, but she is now in Heaven, in the company of God, whose forgiveness I seek daily."

Clearly uncomfortable, her husband at her side, Carla rubs her eyes. She seems helpless, unable to stop the bishop and remains silent, as does Michael, who himself seems moved now.

"Obtaining your grandmother's personal forgiveness before her death," the bishop continues, "would have been most rewarding, and most comforting to me." Shifting from side to side in his chair, the bishop sighs. "I'm sorry I never saw your grandmother as an adult, after that horrible incident. I'm sorry I could never apologize to her, or ask for her personal forgiveness directly. And you have no idea of the extent of the feelings of guilt I have had over the years for what I did to her in my brash youth, for that horrible deed which I committed against her and against God. Had I been able to attain her forgiveness in person, before her death, God's forgiveness, if granted, would be more meaningful, Johnny. This is because God's forgiveness is the ultimate forgiveness, which all of us always seek. If in His wisdom God grants it, on the basis of our subsequent deeds and actions, it supersedes human forgiveness."

"How's that?"

"Johnny!" Carla pleads. "That's enough, dear!"

"I'm not offended by his questions, my dear. I don't mind pursuing his questions, if you and Michael don't object. They're reasonable questions. As long as they're on his mind, I'd like to make every effort to address them."

"We just don't want the discussion to upset you," Carla rubs her eyes again.

"We won't let the discussion upset any one," the bishop smiles, "will we, Johnny?"

Clearly engrossed and mystified, Johnny does not answer. He only eyes the bishop silently.

"Johnny is a very thoughtful and intelligent young man. He's raising thoughtful questions. You see, Johnny, as I said earlier, when one commits a sin against another, one also commits that same sin against God. When as a youth I assaulted your late grandmother, I also assaulted God. In order to compensate your grandmother for her hurt and injury, resulting from my horrible and reckless deed, and in order to obtain her earthly forgiveness, my horrified parents paid her and her family substantial monetary compensation for the humiliation and suffering I caused, or, to use a legal terminology, my family paid damages. In a sense, by accepting these, and my mother's deep regrets and apologies, I, in my youth and naïveté, assumed that your grandmother had forgiven me. The reality, however, is that one may not think so now, but we don't really know."

Michael, the sympathetic expression on his countenance now changing, wiggles a little in his chair and looks out the window. He then leans his head on his hand, looking down.

"My family," the bishop continues, "certainly assumed that she had. That notwithstanding, I still need and seek hers and God's heavenly forgiveness every day of my life, and I have been trying to earn that by being a good person and a true believer in God's wisdom and mercy. Because your Grandmother was very hurt by my horrible deed, when she discovered that my offense against her and against God made her pregnant, she understandably wanted to end that pregnancy through an abortion. The invisible, holy and mighty hand of God intervened and prevented another horrific and ghastly sin."

"But why didn't the hand of God intervene earlier, to prevent what happened to Grandma?" Johnny asks the bishop.

His face reddening again, and noticeably restless, the bishop at first does not answer. "I don't have an answer for that, Johnny. I don't know why," the bishop says, stuttering. "Perhaps, but we don't know, ah, perhaps, perhaps, so that, we don't know, but perhaps, in His Heavenly Wisdom, ah, God would bring your mother into life, and, ah, and so that, perhaps, she and your father would perhaps have the divine joy of having you, and your sister Alexia come into this wondrous, perhaps, flawed world."

Obviously disquieted and disturbed, Johnny locks his fingers nervously. "Really?" he mutters quietly.

Chapter 28

Moments after the Bishop leaves, Alexia joins her brother in the family room. Flopping down on a pillow, Johnny is wrung out. "Johnny," Alexia greets her brother, "tonight was one of your finest moments. You put that religious nut in his place. Perhaps, perhaps. The invisible, holy and mighty hand of God intervened, my invisible, holy ass!"

"So, you heard everything?"

"I couldn't help hearing his preachy voice."

"That's good, but I didn't realize that you would hear us. That's why actually I wanted to go down to meet him. I wish you could've come down to meet him too. You would've asked him much better questions."

"I couldn't come down."

"You have delicate ears."

"Delicate stomach too. I couldn't stand him pontificating, even if I had shut my door I would've heard him, but you were at your best, Johnny. You were magnificent."

"He does have a roaring voice, but, hey, he really isn't a bad guy."

"Are you serious?"

"I am very serious, Alexia, he isn't a bad guy. His sincere repentance moved me. I can see why he appealed to Mom."

"You've changed then?"

"After seeing him and listening to him I have changed."

"What happened?"

"He's human, Alexia, he stutters, he even blushes."

"So what if he stutters and blushes, does that make him a good person?"

"When you see a person face-to-face, you observe closely the expressions on his face and watch him and listen to him struggle to express an idea, whether you agree with him or not, you get a different perspective. My present impression of him is that although he may be flawed, he is not the evil person I portrayed him to be before meeting him and listening to him. I am sure this is the way Mom felt about him after her first meeting with him, and I understand now why she wants to know him better."

"I can't wait to hear Dad's reaction."

"I would like to hear that too. Maybe we can both talk to Dad later. My feeling really is that, while he may be flawed, he's not a bad person. You should've seen him sweat over the whole thing. Maybe what Mom says about him is true."

"Which part of what she said?" Alexia asks, feeling miserable.

"That he is an older man now, that when he assaulted Grandma Rose-Anne he was a brash eighteen-year-old, but he has now matured and become a decent human being. In my opinion, he has changed."

"If he's not a bad person, Johnny, why doesn't he give plain answers?"

"About what?"

"About what he did to Grandma, he's had fifty-five years to think about it."

"What more answers do we want from the guy?"

"He should be able to give true answers about why he did it and what it all means, not only to him and to God, but to Grandma and to her family."

"Maybe there aren't good answers."

"What do you mean there aren't good answers?"

"I mean there are no good answers."

"Johnny, the guy raped Grandma. He committed a rape! He raped Grandma when she was eighteen, when she was destitute and helpless, and in the security of his own family home!"

"I know all that."

"All he does is to invoke the invisible, holy and mighty hand of God. The invisible, holy and mighty hand of God intervened."

"I agree with you, that part is not persuasive. I didn't like that part."

"It's a farce. Don't you see that?"

"Yes, I agree with you."

"Don't you see how he spouted the name of God whenever you asked him something important? Can't you see what's happening? The guy raped Grandma, and just because his family was rich, he got away with it. Now he's a bishop. Instead of taking full responsibility for his action, he's hiding behind the invisible, holy and mighty hand of God. All he says is holy this and heavenly that. He thinks we are stupid."

"He says more than that."

"Oh sure, endless talk of God's loving nature and God's human family."

"I don't see anything wrong with that."

"What does it all mean? What about Grandma's misery carried for a lifetime and then to her grave? He has the gall to talk about the money his filthy rich family paid to Grandma."

"I know that was lousy, and I didn't like it, but he only mentioned it to show that he wanted to make up for his awful deed."

"But he also said that when Grandma Rose-Anne accepted the money, he could assume she would forgive him. That's rubbish!"

"We can't say that, because we don't really know what went on, or what was said."

"Money was a way out for both sides, Johnny. It's true we don't know all the facts, whether Grandma's mother accepted the bishop's mother's money and apologies with forgiveness."

"Right, we don't."

"But can you imagine Grandma being pregnant with a child she never wanted, a child she knew was a rape child, then loving, caring for, nourishing and encouraging that child the rest of her life?"

"It couldn't have been easy, I know it wasn't easy and we agree on that."

"All the money in the world would not compensate for Grandma's suffering. I can't bear seeing Mom deserting Grandma, her mother. I just hope that his flowery and misleading words will not persuade you or Dad to agree with what Mom is doing. That would be devastating to me."

"Dad and I would never desert Grandma."

Worried and frustrated, she looks down. "Why then did you and Dad sit with him? Why did Dad socialize with him?"

"Be reasonable, Alexia. Sitting with him, or socializing with him does not mean we desert Grandma."

"I'm amazed at Mom falling for the guy's flowery words and wealth!"

"I would never desert Grandma. You know that! Neither would Dad. Dad is in a very difficult position, and he's trying to be reasonable and polite to the man, who after all is a guest at our home. During my conversation with the Bishop, Dad didn't say a word, but I knew from the expression on his face where he stood. Let's try to be reasonable, Alexia. Like you, I disagree with what Mom is doing. I wish that, after seeing the bishop, speaking with him, listening to his remorse and sorrow, which I believe to be sincere, and satisfying her curiosity, she would stop what she is doing and come back to her family. But neither Mom, nor Dad, nor I have deserted Grandma, and you should stop saying that, because you only weaken your argument. You know how much we all love Grandma."

"Then how can you listen to the garbage this guy dishes up?"

"But he's sorry, and I could even see and feel his sorrow."

"He's a rapist and a criminal with flowery words. That's what he is, and his sorrow is fake and insincere."

"I'm sorry, but you may be wrong on that. Believe me, he is very sorry, and he is very convincing. I feel very strongly, after meeting the guy that his sorrow is genuine and sincere."

"But it isn't. If you listen to what he says carefully, you will realize that his repentance isn't sincere."

"I disagree. He made a mistake when he was young and now he feels rotten about it."

"No, he doesn't."

"What should we do? Ruin him! We could! What would that accomplish? You're right about Grandma's misery. No amount of money would ever pay for that."

"So why did he bring it up?"

"To defend himself and show that he and his family tried to right a wrong and sort of paid for it."

"I don't buy that."

"What was done was done. We can't undo that. Do we have to go through life correcting the misdeeds of humanity? We can't. We can't, Alexia. The best you and I can do is to live our lives, do the best we can, and at the same time respect the way Mom feels about her own life."

"I can't respect what Mom's doing, I'm sorry, I can't. I did not want to tell you this about Mom, fearing that it would shock and disappoint you."

"Then don't, and I don't want to hear it."

"I won't, but you should know it."

"Why?"

"Because it would give you a better perspective on this tragic saga, and would make you appreciate better what is happening."

Perplexed and anxious, Johnny looks at his sister. "Then tell me," he says tersely.

"Mom doesn't only want to satisfy her curiosity about this man and then come back to her family. Mom is after his wealth."

"I don't believe that."

"Mom wants to be recognized by this man as his daughter, and she wants to become close to him and to his family in order to inherit from his estate upon his death. Mom wants to inherit from the man who raped her Mom, our Grandma Rose-Anne. Dad knows this and he's disgusted. I'm disgusted too."

"How do you know this?"

"I overheard Mom and Dad arguing about it. After that, I confronted Mom and told her that's not right, and that I'm very sad."

"What did she say?"

"She stuttered and stammered and I went upstairs."

Johnny reflects quietly.

"So it isn't that Mom has reconciled herself to a difficult situation, and that if she wants to establish a relationship with this man, you and I should not interfere, it's that Mom is selfish. She's putting money above her family, above what happened to her mother. So, as far as her relations with the rapist bishop go, we, her children, or Dad, her husband, don't count. What counts is that she wants to scheme to inherit from the man who raped her mom."

"Listen, this is very disturbing, it's upsetting, and I can see how disappointed you and Dad are. I'm sort of disappointed myself, but if that's the way she is, and the way she feels, you and I should keep out of it. After all, the man is her father."

"You keep saying that, but he isn't. He's a rapist, and we shouldn't have anything to do with him."

"We shouldn't, but if Mom wants to have something to do with him, it is her choice, not yours or mine. Mom's the one who found him."

"And she should stop the relationship right now, if she cares for her family."

"He didn't look for her, or even know she existed."

"She's out of her mind to be pursuing this horrible rapist, who raped her mother! She should stop it now, if her family means anything to her."

"He's a thoughtful man. You say he's hiding behind God? I don't think so."

"The guy's a cheese. He's a poser. He's a religious nut, I'm telling you."

"I don't think so. He admits his crime and he's sorry. He doesn't deny it, and I'm sure he wishes it never happened."

"No, he doesn't wish it never happened."

"You don't know that! How can you say that?"

"I don't think he wishes it never happened. And it's driving me crazy. When you asked him why the invisible, holy and mighty hand of God didn't intervene to prevent the rape, first he said that he didn't know. Then he said it must have been so that Mom would come into being, or some such idiotic thing, and have the heavenly joy of having us come into this wonderful world. He is full of crap."

"I remember when he said that. You're right. It wasn't a good answer."

"That should tell you what kind of person he is."

"I said I didn't like that answer, but it doesn't change my mind. I still feel that he is sorry for what he did years ago."

"Well?"

"I said I didn't like that answer, what more do you want!"

"Listen to me, Johnny, please listen. How can God be behind such a horrible and mean deed?!"

"I'm not speaking about that, I am saying that seeing him, looking him in the eye, listening to him, he seems very sincere to me."

"He's a rapist!"

"I could believe that he might have been out of his mind, mentally deranged, or sick when he did that. Maybe his mental condition or sickness had something to do with what he did to Grandma. But now he's a different man. He's been rehabilitated. He's reformed."

"Come off it! That's a crock! This is just another alibi. I don't buy any of it. Now he is suddenly sick! What kind of sickness are you talking about? How did he get sick? You just made him sick in order to excuse the horrible crime he committed against Grandma. You depress me when you defend him like that. I can't believe you're defending him. "

"I didn't make him sick, how could I?"

"You just did, but if you didn't make him sick, then who did?"

"Who did? If we believe in God, and that He is behind all our actions and so on, then maybe his sickness was God's responsibility."

"Oh, God! So, the rape is all God's responsibility!"

"Wait a minute. If so, then yes the rape has to be, in some way or other, also God's responsibility."

"I can't believe what I'm hearing. What about free choice? What about individual responsibility? What about all the murders, the kidnappings and the genocides? Are they all God's responsibility? All preordained?"

"In a way, sure they must be."

"Oh, Johnny, come off it!"

"If we believe that God is the Creator of all things and that He is all powerful, then what people do, good or bad must be due to God's will."

"That's the bishop's God. The bishop's God is almighty, all-powerful and therefore responsible for all the horrible deeds of humanity. He's also loving and forgiving. So, the bishop's God created the rapist bishop, let him rape Grandma, then forgave him and loved him. Further, the bishop's God, through an act of rape, wanted Mom to come into this wonderful world in order to have the joy of having you and me. Don't you see the contradiction, Johnny? Do you believe that?"

"No, I don't, and I can see the contradiction, but…"

"Of course you don't. The rapist bishop wants you to believe that God creates people to do His dirty work for Him. Then He loves and forgives them. What a joke!!"

"Oh, I don't know. You confuse me, Alexia, but he was convincing and sincere. That was enough for me to accept him. Who knows what I will think when I learn more."

"For a start, keep God out of it."

"Why?"

"The bishop dissembles."

"He what?"

"He dissembles. He's using God to excuse being horrible. Individuals should be responsible for their deeds. If blaming God excuses murder, the bishop's rape of Grandma and so forth, we'll be in a mess."

"What does that have to do with whether the bishop's repentance is sincere or not? I'm saying that I think that it is, but I may agree with you that we should be accountable for our deeds. That has nothing to do with whether God created us or not, and whether our imperfections are also God's creations and therefore His responsibilities. Are you saying you don't believe in a God?"

"All I'm saying is that if we give a role to God in these criminal activities, then we would have anarchy and individuals would not be responsible for their actions."

"And I am saying that individuals should be responsible for their actions, but that responsibility has nothing to do with whether there is a God or not. Are you saying there's no God?"

"No, I'm not. Try to understand."

"I am desperately trying to. In your opinion, did God create the world?"

"I haven't the slightest idea."

"You don't know?"

"I don't know, and I don't care. Don't corner me," Alexia says.

"I have no intention of cornering you. I just want to know if you believe in God."

"I like to think of God as a loving but helpless God, who has no control over our actions and deeds, or over what happens in the world. That makes him a good God. If you want to think of Him as an all-powerful creator, that is your choice, but to be a good God, he would then have to prevent all the disasters, the earthquakes, the floods, the rapes, the wars and the crimes against humanity. I would like to believe that God's nature is loving and is forgiving, but he doesn't have the power to prevent evil, or to forgive anyone."

"So, the God you believe in is weak," Johnny says.

"He certainly isn't like the bishop's God. I am saying that I would like to imagine God to be loving, wise, and forgiving if you wish, but without the power to make forgiving meaningful. Mainly, I imagine Him to be helpless. He has no control over our lives or over the world. Otherwise, the world would have been a better world, and we would have been better people."

"Really! I don't agree that God is a helpless God, a kind of observer who is out there, loving us to death and wishing to help and forgive us but unable to do a thing about our lives. It's a scary idea. I don't like it."

"I know it's scary, and I don't like it either, but what else could He be, with all that we see happening around us?" Alexia says.

"You can think whatever you want, to me God is loving, wise, forgiving and also mighty, who created everything and who can help to make us better people if we can earn that."

Smiling, she is amused. She reaches for her brother and touches his hand. "I didn't know we were going to have this discussion. I guess we haven't resolved anything. I love you Johnny."

"I guess not. Anyway, nothing we say matters. I love you too," Johnny says.

"Yes it does matter. You were taken in by his admission of guilt, but that admission is too little. He should resign and enter a monastery and donate most of his fortune to charity if he has really repented. Mom is ready to forgive him without his doing penance adequate to do justice to Grandma. Mom's forgiveness is tainted because her motive isn't noble.

"He will never resign or enter a monastery or donate his fortune to charity Alexia."

"I know he'll never do that, and that is why I think he is insincere. You say that sickness may have been behind his awful behavior. Maybe it is, and if so, what guarantee do we have that he hasn't repeated this, or won't repeat it?"

"I don't know."

"It's possible."

"I guess anything is possible."

Chapter 29

When the bishop returns to Lake Charles, he sits with his mother to report to her about his trip to Valley Town.

"How was your trip, my dear, did you see the girl?"

"My trip was very troubling to me, Mother, and yes, I saw her. She is no longer a young girl, Mother, she is a woman."

"So, what did you think of her?"

"She's a lovely and attractive woman. I was touched by her. I want to keep in contact with her, and have her come and meet you. I want her to meet our two daughters and their children. I want her to become a member of our family, Mother. She is truly my daughter, pure and simple, and I want to treat her as my daughter. That is what our Lord expects of me."

"Be careful, my dear. I can understand how troubling the whole thing must have been to you, but take it easy and don't rush into anything. You need to be careful."

"I know I need to be careful, but seeing this lovely woman, meeting her husband, visiting her modest but attractive home and especially speaking with her bright, handsome seventeen or eighteen-year-old son, all this opened for me the memories of an old wound, a tragic and vicious crime which I committed in my brash youth against an innocent young woman, Rose-Anne Riley, and against God."

"You shouldn't feel that way, my dear. Your family paid for what you did in your youth many, many years ago. I am sorry you had to make this trip. What on earth possessed this young woman to write you after all these years?"

"My family may have paid for what I did, but I haven't paid a penny, Mother. This experience of the past few days has reminded me that I haven't addressed this dormant problem, a problem that has haunted me for a long,

long time, Mother, and now I must. The good Lord expects that of me, He is calling me to pay my share, Mother and I must."

"What do you have in mind, my dear?"

"First, I want to integrate the daughter I just discovered I have into my own family. I want to love her, love her family and children the way I love Christine and Elizabeth and their families. I want to make sure that she is included in my will. Second, Dad, may the Lord's mercies be on his soul, left for me half of his estate as my share of the inheritance, and left for you the other half. My share amounted to about twenty-five million dollars, which has now more than tripled. I will be speaking to Dad's lawyer, Mr. Hudson, about revising my will. I am thinking of putting aside one fourth of my estate to be distributed between my wife Grace and the three daughters. The rest of my estate, I would like to donate to charity, my dear. I want to obey the Lord."

His mother is stunned. Her mouth half open, her eyes disbelieving, she is unable to speak. "Philip, my dear," she finally says, "you're tired and upset. I beg you. I implore you to be careful and to not do anything rash or hasty. Please, Philip, please, my dear, promise me that you will not, at least not now, say anything to Grace or to the girls about this. You promise me?"

"Mother dear, I may be tired, I may be upset, but I have thought about this for a long, long time. Even before discovering that I have a daughter I did not know I had, I have always felt that the wealth the Lord has granted me is a trust. It is not mine, Mother, it is the Lord's. I am now a seventy-three-year-old bishop who is expected to do what Christ wants and expects of me: Feed the hungry, shelter the homeless, care for the elderly, help the sick and educate the young. That's my true calling, Mother. The wealth entrusted to me is sitting idle and is multiplying. None of it is being used to meet the obligations of a true Christian, Mother. There are millions of people here and elsewhere that Christ would want me to help. I must, Mother, I must. I promise you I will not discuss this with Grace or with our two girls now, but I would like to ask you to do the same. But I will not change my mind about sharing my wealth, the Lord's trust, with the needy among us."

"What happened, dear? Did something happen while you were in Virginia?"

"A lot of things happened when I was in Virginia, Mother, but what happened in Virginia has nothing to do with what I want to do with the wealth entrusted to me by the Lord."

"Did anyone say anything about your family, about your father, about your wealth and your family's wealth, dear?"

"No one, Mother, not a word was mentioned about my father or about money, nothing whatsoever, Mother. Only the Lord did. Only the Lord did, Mother."

The elderly woman only sighs. "Now tell me about the people you met, about the girl, her husband, her children and how you got along with them. Tell me first about Carla."

"Carla, Mother, is my daughter. She's a duplication of Christine, as though they are twins."

"Really?!"

"Really and truly, Mother, and I want to get to know her better. I want to treat her as I treat Christine and Elizabeth, no difference. This is what God expects of me. She is my daughter, no question about it."

"But I think you should move slowly, my dear, very slowly. You should be careful."

"There's nothing to be careful about, she is my daughter, pure and simple. She is a sweet woman, Mother. She treated me with utmost genuine respect. She invited me to her home for dinner, treated me as a daughter would treat her elderly father. I was touched, and I need to reciprocate the generosity shown to me. One way of showing it is to repent, not by words only, but by deeds, by honoring the memory of the young woman I assaulted and injured without mercy, without remorse. I inflicted injury on that helpless and defenseless young woman. She was an innocent child of God. I inflicted injury on her family, on her children and on her grandchildren. What is horrible about my deed, Mother, is that I thought I could get away with it. The Lord decided to wake me up, to tell me that I did not get away with it, that I must attend to and atone for a wrong that I fled from, and I will, I want to build schools, hospitals, housing for orphans, and housing for the homeless and the elderly. I want to dedicate all that to the memory of one innocent child of God, Rose-Anne Riley. The Lord has entrusted me with a huge fortune. It is then and only then, that our Lord will, or should, forgive me."

The older woman only stares at her son. She is clearly distressed.

"Did you also meet her husband and her children?"

"I did meet her husband Michael. He's a professor of Economics at Valley Town University. He's a tall and distinguished looking youthful native of Virginia, fair complexion, very reserved, kind and thoughtful. He was very cordial to me, but did not converse with me much."

"Are they church people, do they go to church?"

"I am not sure, but that doesn't matter, Mother. I am sure I can lead them in that direction. At dinner, Carla invited me to say grace. They bowed their heads and were very respectful. I suspect that they may be more secular in their lives than we may desire, in that the Church is not a dominant part of their activities, but that doesn't matter. I sensed that they are good and decent people."

"How about their children, did you meet them?"

"They have two children, twins, a boy and a girl. I didn't meet the girl. I only met the boy, who's very handsome. He looks a lot like our grandson,

Ronald. Like his father, he is tall, taller than I am, maybe six feet four. He's blond, has blue eyes like Carla, and broad shoulders like me. He was very, very polite, but I could tell that the injury I inflicted on his departed grandmother upsets him greatly, and who can blame him? At first, he was uncomfortable sitting with me, looked at me as though I was a vicious criminal who shouldn't be sitting in their living room, but after a while he relaxed, and we had a good conversation. He's very bright."

"You didn't meet his sister?"

"No, I didn't. She too was most likely intimidated. By the way, I understood from Carla that their daughter, her name is Alexia I believe, was accepted at Ivy University. She'll start there this fall. I mentioned to Carla that Christine's son, Ronald, will also be attending Ivy."

"Isn't that interesting?"

"Like her brother, after all, to her mind I'm probably that awful monster who assaulted her beloved grandmother. I don't blame her if she doesn't want to meet me, or have anything to do with me. I was frankly surprised that her brother came down to meet me."

"I'll bet that his mother put him up to it, if he was uncomfortable there. She must have twisted his arm."

"If she did, I'm glad she did. Put yourself in the shoes of that poor family, Mother. Here they are, living quietly and peacefully in a small town in Virginia. Suddenly and without warning, they discover, that fifty-five years ago, their beloved grandmother was sexually assaulted by a cruel, evil young man who has now become a bishop. They discover that their grandmother became pregnant as a result of that criminal sexual assault. They further discover that their own mother was also a victim of that assault, being the child of that rape pregnancy, and was born out of wedlock. How do you think they feel?"

"I'm sure it isn't easy, my dear."

"And that is why the Lord has called me to address the wrong I perpetrated on that innocent young woman and on her entire family. That is why the good Lord wants me to make adequate penance. He wants me to honor the memory of the young woman I assaulted by making these donations, and to do justice to her daughter and my daughter, Carla, by integrating her in my own family. Only then could I possibly deserve His forgiveness."

A week after his meeting with his mother, the Lake Charles Chronicle has a major front page article with a big headline: BISHOP PHILIP ARLINGTON DONATES NINETY PERCENT OF HIS ESTATE TO CHARITY. HE WILL RETIRE.

Bishop Philip Arlington of the Diocese of The Northern Lakes Region has announced that he will retire. He with his wife and his mother Elizabeth Arlington plan to move to Ashton where they will reside in a monastery.

Chapter 30

The next day, Carla, Michael and the twins sit at their kitchen table for dinner as usual. Alexia and John are unusually quiet.

"Who will say grace tonight?" Carla asks.

Alexia scowls, and John remains silent.

"I will," Michael says quickly. "Bless us, O Lord, and bless this food we are about to eat, and bless our children and family. Guide us always to say and do what is both the right and wise in your sight. Amen."

"Amen," they all say.

"Well," Carla says, "I'm glad the last few days turned out better than we feared."

"That's right," her husband says.

"That was a relief," she continues.

They all then eat in silence.

Alexia's eyes glaze as her mind wanders, and she begins to hear her Grandmother's voice echoing in her ear: *"On Sunday afternoons, my dear Alexia, or evenings in winter after the chores around the farm were done and supper over, our family would sit around the living room ... Usually Jimmy and I, being the only young children, would play by ourselves ... but occasionally Daddy would play dominoes with us ... Sometimes Daddy would get out his harmonica, and he would entertain us with songs like Turkey in the Straw, Ole Dan Tucker, and my favorite, Red Wing ..."*

"Well," Carla interrupts the silence, "I guess we're going on a trip."

"Where?" Johnny asks.

"We are all invited to Lake Charles for Thanksgiving," she says.

"We have lots of time to talk about that," Michael says.

"What's in Lake Charles," Johnny asks.

"The Bishop invited us, all of us," Carla says, "to meet his mother, wife, two daughters and their families."

"So we're all invited?" Johnny asks.

"Yes, if we all want to go," Carla answers.

"We have lots of time to talk about that," Michael repeats.

"Would you like to go, Johnny," Carla asks.

"Yes, I'll go."

Alexia glowers.

"We don't have to decide who goes and who doesn't now, we have plenty of time," Michael says.

"I know," Carla says, "but he needs time to acquaint his family with the developments of the last few months, and to prepare them for our visit. What did you think of the Bishop, Johnny?"

"He may be O. K."

"You were a little rough on him," Carla says.

"I gathered from Alexia that I was, but I didn't actually mean to be. I just wanted some answers to some questions."

"Oh, did you hear the whole discussion, Alexia?"

"Yes, I did. As I said to Johnny, his booming voice was all over our house. I couldn't help hearing the discussion, and I was curious about how he would answer Johnny's questions."

"Yes, it was a lively discussion, and his voice was a little loud."

"What did you think of Johnny's questions, dear? What did you think of the discussion?" Carla asks.

Alexia reflects, looks at her brother and squints. "Johnny and I disagree a little about that, but I was honestly uncomfortable with some of what he said."

"We all were," Michael says, "Mom and I were somewhat uncomfortable with some of what he said."

"That's right," Carla says, "But I was touched by his sincere grief and sorrow for what he did when he was a young man."

"That's right," Michael says.

"How did you feel about that, Alexia, his remorse for what he did?" Carla asks.

"I guess I'm in the minority about that," she says. "I didn't feel that his remorse was genuine. I know that Johnny disagrees with me on that."

"I felt that his remorse and sorrow were genuine and sincere," Michael says, "but the part that made me uncomfortable is when he began to speak of what he called the damages his family paid to Grandma Rose-Anne and to her mother."

"Yes, that part made me uncomfortable too," Carla says, "but, while taking full responsibility for his actions, he said it perhaps to show the extent to which his family went in trying to redress the wrong done. He said to show that his family wanted to express further grief. And he wanted to show by making payments that he wished the offense never happened."

"I don't see it that way," Alexia says, with clear irritation, "I don't think that he wishes it never happened. When Johnny asked him why the invisible hand of God, whatever that is, did not intervene to prevent the horrible rape, he said: So that your mom and you and your sister Alexia would come to this wonderful world, or some horrible thing like that."

"I agree with Alexia, and I told her I didn't like that," Johnny says.

Carla remains silent.

"That part made me cringe," Michael says.

"I was horrified by that," Alexia says, "and frankly that confirms for me his insincerity."

"It shouldn't," Carla says, "it shouldn't cast doubt on his sincerity."

Alexia does not say anything.

"Alexia," Michael tries to address his daughter.

"Dad, I don't feel that Grandma's terrible ordeal was properly treated in the discussion, and I'm not up to discussing it any further. It really drains me. I wish that he didn't discuss Grandma. He should've been told that."

"How could he not discuss Grandma?" Carla asks. "Johnny wanted Grandma discussed, didn't you Johnny? Besides, the man was a guest in our house. We couldn't tell him to stop talking about Grandma, when he wanted to."

"Maybe he shouldn't have been a guest in our house," Alexia says with feeling. "Maybe that desecrates Grandma."

Carla winces.

"Was there anything else that bothered you, Alexia?" Michael asks.

"Everything bothered me. His being in our house bothered me, because it demonstrated to him that Grandma's family does not grieve for Grandma in her ordeal. That saddens me, Dad. It saddens me because by insisting on inviting this horrible man to her house, Carla Hatley has now dishonored her mother."

Jolted, Carla cries out: "I have not dishonored my mother. I have not." She is visibly shaken. "I don't want to hear any more of this. You should have more sympathy with your mother and your family and stop saying these things. I don't understand you."

"Mom has not dishonored Grandma, Alexia! What are you talking about?" Michael says.

"Dad, I said I didn't want to discuss this. So, please I want to be left alone."

"What are you saying to me then?"

"I'm saying that by embracing the man who raped Grandma, and inviting him to your home, you have dishonored Grandma Rose-Anne. That's what I'm saying."

"Then you shouldn't be sitting at this table with me." Carla is furious.

"That sorrowful event happened fifty-five years ago," Michael says.

"I don't care if it happened a thousand years ago," Alexia cries.

"I guess we just have to stop this discussion," Carla says, completely flustered.

"We just have to disagree," Michael says.

"Yes, we have to disagree," Alexia continues to cry. "Tell Grandma you have to disagree."

"Tell Grandma what?" Carla's voice is subdued now.

"Tell her nothing!" Alexia is sobbing.

"What do you want me to do, Alexia? What?" Carla is distraught.

"Mom, I want you to imagine Grandma Rose-Anne sitting here with us, and imagine yourself saying to her: 'Mom, we now know that when you were eighteen, working to make ends meet after your father's death, one Philip Arlington raped you and made you pregnant. Your pain led you and your mother to leave town and move to Salem, California. We know they paid you off. Still feeling the shame and humiliation of the rape pregnancy, we know you invented a husband named Bob Thornton, killed in the war, and we know that I was truly born out of wedlock. We know you married Chester Perry, who was my adoptive father. You carried the pain, the anguish and the humiliation of what happened to you to your grave, you never shared it with any of your children. Now, Mom, guess what? After your death, we decided to dig up the man who raped you. We've met him and have invited him to our home. You know what, Mom? He's such a nice guy! He's a holy man! He's lovable! He's sweet! He's inspiring! He's so inspiring that we, your loving family, are about to go and spend Thanksgiving at his home. Now, Mom, you don't mind any of that, do you?' What do you think Grandma Rose-Anne would say?"

"You left out something very important," Carla says.

"What did I leave out?"

Carla pauses.

"Well?"

"What about your mother's life? What about your and Johnny's lives? Then look at the life of the bishop himself. Look at our family, at yours and at Johnny's. Isn't this good from evil, hope from horror?"

"Oh, God, Mom!" Alexia makes a pained face.

"OK, you want to know what Grandma would think of all this? Carla resumes. "Grandma's life, as you know, was wrapped up in her children and in her grandchildren, especially in you and in Johnny. Not only was Grandma a loving person, she was first and foremost a forgiving person. I think that you would agree with that."

"I agree with that, but she never forgot or forgave the rape."

"How do you know?" Carla asks. "Did she ever say anything to you about it?"

Alexia does not answer.

"Did she?" Carla repeats. "Did she? Did she? I want to know, Alexia."

Alexia, her eyes stinging, does not answer her mother.

"I firmly believe," Carla then says, "that from where she is now, somewhere in Heaven, she has forgiven Philip Arlington. She has forgiven him because she sees us getting acquainted with him, hears him sincerely and devoutly expressing his deep sorrow for the horrible thing he did to her and to her family in his brash youth. She sees that he is continuously seeking God's forgiveness and hers. She knows that he has, without hesitation, accepted as his own daughter the person who came into being as a result of that tragic incident. She knows that he has not only embraced me as his own, but has also embraced my husband and is willing to embrace my children as members of his own family. Why wouldn't she forgive him? Why wouldn't she, Alexia?" Carla asks.

"Because he stole her pride and innocence, and hurt her deeply and indelibly. That's why."

"Oh, Alexia!" Carla exclaims.

"He humiliated her, and made her pregnant against her will," Alexia is crying. "Because of that, I'm going to stand by Grandma Rose-Anne as long as I live." She pushes her plate away from her gently and stands up. "I can't understand it," she continues to cry. "What is this?" Then she begins to remember again. She remembers her grandmother, dressed in a light brown cotton dress, waving at her and smiling as the school bus in which Alexia was riding drove away. "I don't understand what's happening," she continues to weep. "You have not said one word that makes sense to me! Not one! Mom, you depress me so much, so much that I can't stand it. I can't, Mom."

"I'm sorry," Carla says to her husband, "I shouldn't have let it go so far. "I'm sorry, Alexia, I really understand your pain, dear. I'm very sorry." She turns to her husband again, who has remained silent throughout the entire argument. "I shouldn't expect that she'll ever agree to meet the Bishop."

Alexia looks at her mother, fire in her eyes. "That's right, Mom. You got that right, Mom. Don't expect that I'll ever agree to meet him. I'll die before I do that.

After dinner, Carla and her husband sit by themselves in the living room. "I truly feel for Alexia," Michael says to his wife.

"I just worry that she may become so obsessed with this tragedy that she becomes bitter and unhappy the rest of her life."

"Well, she was very close to Grandma Rose-Anne. She empathizes with what happened to her, and we shouldn't be rough on our daughter."

"She's rough on me, on all of us."

"She is young and emotional now. Time will take care of this, let's try to help her get over it and be careful not to make things worse."

"It's my fault. I underestimated the degree to which Alexia's whole being would be shaped by her closeness to Mom."

"We both should've been more tuned to that."

"I am now convinced that Grandma Rose-Anne must have discussed her tragedy with Alexia, but why would she?"

"She loved and cared a lot about Alexia."

"Yes, Mom worried about her, and obviously she talked a great deal about her life on the farm with Alexia."

"Including her tragic encounter with the bishop, I think."

"I agree, Mom must've discussed that with her."

"That's why our reaction to the bishop's remorse is different from Alexia's. We were spared learning the graphic details directly from Grandma Rose-Anne."

"We don't know how much of the violence and brutality of the assault was recounted directly to Alexia."

"Remember too, she's at an impressionable age, my dear, and her grief for her grandmother is different from ours."

"For sure," Carla says. "Oh, Mom," she then exclaims, addressing her deceased mother, "why did you do that to Alexia?"

"That's why we have to be careful," Michael says to his wife.

"Can she ever get over it?"

"Let's hope that she will in time."

"But why would Mom share so private a matter with my daughter, and not with me? She makes me jealous of my own daughter."

"But you mustn't alienate her further."

"I don't want to alienate Alexia further, because I know it's all my fault, Mike, it's all my fault. I should've been more of a mother to our children. I failed to meet my responsibilities as a mother, and this is the price I am paying now for that. Yes, I did, I failed to meet my responsibilities," she repeats in a distant voice. "I failed to meet my responsibilities, and I'm suddenly recalling what Mom told me about my grandfather, Carl, who committed suicide, and I was named after him. I just feel a sharp pain in my back. I should say something reassuring to Alexia. I don't want her to think that I don't love Mom, or don't love her, Alexia. I don't want her to feel isolated from me. What do you think?"

"It wouldn't hurt to tell her you love her."

"She's angry with me, very angry. She wants me to reverse course, which I can't do, and won't do."

Chapter 31

In Lake Charles, two days after Bishop Arlington spoke with his elderly mother about his Virginia trip, Bishop Arlington's wife, Grace, knocks at the door of the elderly mother.

"Who is it?"

"It's me, Mother, Grace, may I come in?"

"Yes, you may, dear. I didn't see you yesterday, and I worried about you. Have you spoken with Philip since his return from Virginia?"

"Yes, Mother, I have," the attractive tall woman says, her eyes tearing, and this is why I came to speak with you.

"I'm sorry, my dear, please don't be upset, Grace, what did he tell you?"

"He told me about what happened fifty-five years ago, and what he wants to do. It's so sad, Mother, it's very sad, not only for me to find out about it, but for him, to see him so devastated. The poor man, he's upset with himself for the hurt he's bringing to me and to our daughters, and to our grandchildren. The woman he went to see in Virginia tore his heart. Apparently he also spoke with one of Carla's children. That's what I think he said her name is, and that also overwhelmed him. He recognizes that she's his daughter, and he wants to add her to our family, which is perfectly all right with me. I told him I'll stand by him, and do whatever he wishes. He cried like a baby when I told him that, and that saddened me to see him so shattered by all this. He's a very good and gentle person, with a big heart. I'm sure it'll be all right with our girls if he wants to include Carla in the family. I'll stand by him and support him on that. That part is all right, but that's not all he wants to do, Mother. He wants to do penance by donating ninety percent of his wealth to charity. At first he thought he would donate seventy-five percent, but he now thinks that leaving for me and for the girls, including Carla, twenty-five percent is too much. He is adamant, but he should wait. He's now too upset to make such a momentous final decision. What do you think? Did he mention any of this when he spoke with you? That's why I came to see you. That is the part I want to discuss with you, Mother."

"Yes, he did, but as you mentioned, he said that he wanted to donate seventy-five percent of his wealth. I didn't know he raised it to ninety percent."

"I think that he figures that his estate is in the neighborhood of a hundred and ten million dollars, and twenty-five percent of that will be in the millions, much too much for our needs. He wants to build hospitals, schools, shelters for orphans, homes for the victims of rape, housing for the elderly and the poor in New York State and in other states, as well as in Mexico and Africa. All of this sounds noble but is he in the frame of mind after his Virginia trip to make such an important decision? Or is he too upset for that. That's what I wanted to speak with you about."

The elderly woman listens, at first saying nothing. She finally reaches for Grace's hand, looks her in the eye and says: "Grace, my dear, you are a wonderful woman. My son is blessed to have you as his wife and partner and friend. I share your concern, every bit of it. Yes, Philip isn't himself now. He shouldn't be making these very important decisions. He's not mentally or emotionally ready to make them. I know how hard this must be on you, my dear. You're a very good woman, Grace. Thank you for standing by Philip's side through all of this. Thank you, my dear, you're a wonderful person."

"Then you feel like I do, that he shouldn't be making these huge commitments now, because he's too distressed?"

"I do, and I have spoken with the family lawyer, Mr. Hudson, about it. He told me that Ronald Arlington, Philip's father, you know, would be shaking in his grave if he knew his son was disposing of the Arlington family's wealth so abruptly."

"Did you then ask him to do anything about it?"

"Well, yes, I asked him to file papers in court challenging Philip's capacity to manage his financial affairs, in order to prevent this from going forward. If Philip wants to help that woman, Carla, that is understandable, but to give away ninety percent of his estate to charity! That's crazy. It's preposterous, my dear. Who would do such a thing, except an emotionally disturbed man? He is my son, and I love him, but to give practically all his wealth away like this is insane."

"I haven't discussed this with the girls, have you?"

"Yes, I have. Elizabeth was livid."

"Are they going to join in on the legal papers?"

"Elizabeth is, but Christine wants time to think it over. How about you, my dear?"

"I am like Christine, Mother, I would like a day or two to think it over."

Grace then moves from the edge of the elderly woman's bed and sits on a rocking chair facing her mother-in-law. "Don't you think there may be another way to handle this, Mother? Do you think going public with this may embarrass our family?"

"Of course it may, but how else can we stop him from going ahead with his scheme?"

Grace looks at the elderly woman and remains silent.

"Charity! What charity?" the elderly woman asks with indignation. "'This is not mine, it belongs to the Lord!' That is just crazy. Who ever heard of such nonsense?"

"I understand your frustration, Mother, but could you wait until I have a chance to speak with Philip again. I just don't want our family to be embroiled in legal fights. This will take years, Mother. The lawyers will make a lot of money, and we will be hanging our laundry in public. Can we wait a day or two, Mother?"

"He's adamant, my dear. I spoke with him, until I was blue in the face, but he is determined. He keeps saying that this is what the Lord expects of me."

"I know, he says the same thing to me, but we should be careful, Mother. I really want to wait a few days, can we?"

The elderly woman looks disturbed. "I think it may be too late, my dear, but let me speak to Mr. Hudson, and I will let you know what he says."

"Thank you, Mother." With her eyes swollen, her face grim, Grace leaves her mother-in-law's room and rushes back downstairs.

Chapter 32

Back in Valley Town, Carla and her husband are downstairs worrying about Alexia. Alexia and John are upstairs. An hour or so after the heated discussion between Alexia and her parents, John goes to his twin sister's room and knocks at her door.

"Well?"

"It's me, Alexia."

"What's up?"

"Alexia, do you remember that antique box in the attic Dad got from his grandmother?"

"What about it?"

"Dad wants to dismantle it and use the wood for a bookcase. Can you believe that he would do that?"

"I can believe anything in this family."

"Are you still brooding!?"

"I can't like what she's doing, Johnny."

"Alexia! Mom wants to be close to her natural father. That's her business."

"I don't want to talk about it."

"Why?"

"Because I can't take it! I can't take it anymore!"

"Why get excited and upset Alexia? Take it easy, please."

"Can't you see what's happening?"

"Alexia! Take it easy! Please calm down!"

"I heard her ask Dad again if she can inherit from the son of a bitch."

He pauses. "I bet Mom's just curious about a possible inheritance."

"That's not true."

"I don't think her motives are anything like that."

"I say that's not true. These are her main motives, believe me."

"I think she really wants to know her natural father and be close to him."

"That's not the whole story, and I told you that before. Don't you remember?"

"Anyway, it's none of our business."

"You keep saying that, but it is our business! Our grandmother was raped and Mom is not being fair to her."

"You yourself don't have to be close to him."

"She wants us to become close to him, because of his wealth."

"You keep saying that."

"That's right, because he's rich."

"I don't think that has anything to do with it, but so what? What's the big deal?"

"It has everything to do with it."

"Well, you don't have to be close to him."

"And I won't."

"No one is forcing you."

"How about you?"

"I'd like to get to know him better. I liked the guy, for one thing, and I think his remorse is real. You don't agree with that, and that's your business."

"How about what he did to Grandma?"

"Well..."

"Shouldn't we have any regard for her?"

"We all do."

"By paying homage to the criminal who raped her!?"

"Alexia! You're upset again."

"What is this?! What is happening to my family?!"

"Alexia!!"

"I don't think I can take this anymore."

"Alexia, you're making it worse. You want to make us all feel guilty."

"Sorry, this is the way I feel. I can't help it."

"I guess there's no sense in talking to you," he says and starts to walk out of her room.

"Johnny, please Johnny," she pleads. "Don't go. Please don't leave me, stay with me."

Shaken and surprised, he turns back. "What is it?" Johnny looks at his distraught sister. "What would you like me to do?" His voice is tender and loving.

In agony and tormented, she begins to cry. Her brother tries to comfort her to no avail. Then very quickly she wipes her tears and stops crying.

"What do you want me to do, Alexia?" John asks her softly. "What do you want me to do? I won't go with them, if you don't want me to go, I won't go."

"It's all right," she continues to cry, "you can go with them if you want, Johnny."

"I won't go. OK? I won't go, I mean it, I won't go."

"Don't worry about me, Johnny. I'll be OK."

"I won't go, I really won't.

Embarrassed and unhappy with herself, Alexia remains silent and pensive. Then she begins to hear her grandmother's voice reverberating in her ear again: *"... My snack on arriving home after the two mile walk from school in the afternoons was an apple from the cellar ... The house and the yard were my world when I was very young ... By the time I was school age, I began to help with the work about the farm ...*

Chapter 33

The next day, Johnny goes to his father's University office.

"What a great surprise." Michael Hartley greets his seventeen-year-old son. "What's on your mind? You seem anxious."

"Dad, we need to talk about Alexia."

"What about Alexia?"

"She hates the bishop. She's furious about our family becoming close to him."

"I know that, and it worries me very much, Johnny, but I don't know what to do."

"I don't think that either you or Mom realize how depressed she is, and how strongly she feels. She's very depressed, Dad. She's depressed. I mean she could do something foolish, something, eh, I don't know, Dad."

"Like what?"

"She's very depressed, and I'm scared for her."

"I don't think she'll do anything foolish."

"Dad, don't say that! Alexia is very depressed and distraught. She's very upset, desperate even. She's depressed, Dad."

"I don't want you to alarm your mother. Don't say anything like this to her. I don't want to get her upset."

"What about Alexia? Mom should know that Alexia is very depressed and very upset with her. Alexia is very distraught and frustrated, Dad."

"I hear you, and I said I'm worried."

"You should be worried, but that's not enough."

"What can I do? I have your mother to live with too, Johnny. Your mother is determined. She's made up her mind. She wants to be close to the Bishop. Heaven and earth won't change her mind. Your mother and I have discussed this whole thing many times and at length. I don't exactly agree with what she is doing, but we need to see where this will take us.

"Then tell Alexia that you don't agree with what Mom is doing, Dad."

"She knows. We discussed it at length."

"That will relieve her a little, but she feels isolated and has become very bitter and angry, Dad."

"Your mother and I have had a bad fight over this, and we are not discussing the subject anymore."

"I don't know how else I can say it, Dad. Alexia is seriously upset. She may do something foolish."

"Your mother's upset too. And so am I! We're all foolish!"

"Well?"

"Well, let me think about it more. In the meantime, let them both think about it, and if Alexia still decides she doesn't want to go, it won't be the end of the world."

"Alexia won't go, Dad, and that's not why I'm here. Alexia is upset because Mom is determined to get close to the man who raped Grandma Rose-Anne, and because our family is considering making a visit to his home. That's what's upsetting Alexia. Do you think, Dad, that Mom's sole interest in cultivating the Bishop is his wealth?"

"What do you mean by that?"

"So that Mom would inherit from him?"

"Why do you ask?"

"Am just wondering."

"Well, that's not the main reason, I don't think, but if the man is your mother's natural father, and he has conceded that he is, why shouldn't she have a share from his estate? What's the big deal, and what does that have to do with Alexia?"

John does not answer.

"What does that have to do with Alexia, Johnny?"

"Alexia is upset that Mom would be like that."

"Like what?"

"Would put inheriting from the bishop above all else."

"Well, let's see how it works out. We all -even the bishop- need time to think about the meaning for us of this discovery your mom has made."

"But is it all right if I don't go with you guys when you go to visit the bishop's home, Dad?"

"Right now I personally prefer that you don't go. If I can find a way, I may too not go, either."

"Then tell Alexia."

"She knows it."

"But I told Mom that I would go."

"Well, you changed your mind. Anyway, I am not going to worry about that now."

"I don't know what to do. I don't want to hurt Mom, but I'm very worried about Alexia. Nothing I do is going to make me feel comfortable, or exactly good. One more thing, are you ready for this one? I looked the bishop's name up on the Internet. Alexia suggested it, but I haven't told her what I found. The bishop is donating ninety percent of his wealth to charity. The Stratford Chronicle announced it on their front page. His mother and one of his daughters are challenging this move in court, on the ground of the bishop's mental competence."

"Oh my God!"

"Please don't tell Mom, or Alexia."

"I won't."

"Carla," Michael says to his wife as the two of them retire to their bedroom, "Johnny came to see me in the office this afternoon."

"What's on his mind?"

"Alexia, and I'm more concerned now than ever before, Carla. Johnny doesn't want to upset Alexia by going with us to the bishop's house on Thanksgiving, or upset you by not going. He's very concerned about his sister, and says that she is depressed and demoralized. He thinks she is a very disturbed and sick girl."

"How is she sick?"

"Depression, Carla."

"That can be dangerous," she says. "Should we suggest treating her?"

"She won't hear of it, not now, and she's getting ready to go to college. She'll think we're trying to delay her going to Ivy."

"Especially after the conversation I had with her about it."

"Johnny is also wondering if your interest in the bishop is due to the bishop's fortune."

"What did he say about that?"

"He's wondering if by wanting to become close to the bishop, your motive is solely material, the inheritance issue you've been discussing with me. He wasn't as concerned or upset about that as he was about Alexia."

"He's been talking to Alexia about it. She herself spoke to me and rebuked me about it. She overheard us discuss it. I hope you told Johnny that the inheritance issue isn't my sole interest in the bishop. I also want to know him. He's my real father, but what of it? What if I think I'm entitled to inherit from him if he's my real father? I don't understand Alexia. I don't. What did you tell Johnny?"

"Pretty much what you just said, although I'm pretty sure you agree that the inheritance issue shouldn't be raised with the bishop by you and that would be inappropriate so early in your relationship. I think we know that it would give the wrong impression about your motives, especially in view of the tragic background of this new relationship. So if the bishop, on his own initiative should decide that you should inherit from him, that'll be a different story."

"You know something, this is the first time that I find what you're saying about this issue making sense. Maybe I should never have brought it up."

"It's never too late to explain yourself a little."

"How is that?"

"Let the kids know what you just said, that you thought it over, and after the bishop's visit, you decided that you don't want to think about your right of inheritance, that you were naturally curious about it, that you recognize that pursuing it is inappropriate, in view of the tragedy of Grandma Rose-Anne, and that in any event that it isn't your decision to make. If the bishop decides to include you in his will, as one of his heirs, that's his business."

"You think that'll make Alexia feel better about me?"

"I know it will. Of course it will."

"But I wouldn't know how to do it now. She's become so alienated from me that she doesn't want to look at me or speak to me."

"Would you like me to say something like that to both of them, to Alexia and Johnny together?"

"Yes. Just don't make it appear that you want to meet with them especial-ly for the purpose of giving them this new information. Look for an opportu-nity to say it so that it'll be natural."

"I'll see what I can do."

"You know, Mike, I really don't mind if Johnny doesn't go with us to Lake Charles."

"I agree, he shouldn't, but this is something you have to tell him."

"Yes, let him stay with Alexia, just like we said the other day. I don't want her to feel isolated. I'll speak to Johnny about that."

"Let them sort it out."

"About Alexia, Mike, I agree with Johnny. Alexia is sick, very sick, and I don't know how to make her agree to get treated." Carla is visibly concerned.

"Johnny really shook me up. I think that he's worried that she may do something foolish to herself."

"Like what?" Carla's face turns white. "When did he say that?"

"He said it after I spoke about your right to inherit."

"What were you saying?"

"I was saying to Johnny that the bishop is your mother's natural father, why shouldn't she inherit from him, just like his other children?"

"Maybe I'm entitled to inherit, but I was stupid to bring it up, or to let Alexia hear me bring it up. That really shook her up. I know it must've. That's why she's disgusted with me. That's why she's depressed. It's all my fault."

Her husband looks anxious and uncomfortable for having upset his wife. He turns his face away from her, as if to hide his anxiety. "I'm sorry, Carla," he says, "I was only trying to explain to Johnny your thinking about it all." He pauses, then he resumes. "Something else keeps bothering me my dear. Remember when you first came back from the farm and you said you were concerned that the bishop may have some flaws?"

"I do."

"Do you think we should look into that?"

"But I wasn't concerned about the bishop when I raised that point, I was more concerned about our children, but that's something we don't need to worry about now."

Many days pass. It is now early September. Neither Carla nor her husband nor the twins talk about the bishop or the proposed visit to his house. Alexia and John are now busy with their preparation for entering the colleges they will be attending in the fall. They have been going to parties with their high school friends. Johnny is all set to go to Valley Town University. He has had several helpful conversations with his father about what to expect. Knowing that his father will be there to help him, he does not seem to be too intimidated by the challenges facing him. Alexia, on the other hand is visibly anxious. In addition to her anger over Bishop Arlington's visit to their home, and the ensuing conflicts she had with her mother, and disagreements she had with her twin brother over the bishop's visit, she is worried about the new challenges facing her at Ivy University. Yet she can't wait to get there, to be away from home, a place she now associates with conflict and tragedy. She has seen and spoken with her best friend Joan several times, but has not shared with her any of the strains she is feeling. She feels that Joan must herself be busy with her own preparations for starting at Valley Town University.

The day before leaving for Ivy, Alexia opens the subject of the bishop with her twin, who wonders if she has packed everything she will need. She has been busy and absorbed in making a decision as to how much clothing to take, and though she has vacillated between taking all her clothes, or just some, and buying more when she arrives, she has now made up her mind that she will take all she can and discard most of what is left behind. That took several days of constant and careful consideration. Johnny tells her that he has decided to take very little of his own clothing to Valley Town University because he will not be too far from home. He still hopes that after a term or two, Alexia will decide to come back and go to Valley Town University where she could enroll in the College of Arts and Sciences.

"What are you up to?" he asks his sister.

"I'm all ready. I'm finally packed. I had a rough time making up my mind how much of my clothes to take with me," she says. "I hate it when I'm like that, when I can't make up my mind."

"That doesn't sound like you."

"You don't know me. I've finally decided to take everything with me."

"Why do that?"

"I'll be too far from home, and I think I may want to settle in the Northeast."

"Don't you dread the cold winters up there?"

"I'll get used to that, but I'll need to buy more winter clothes when I get there. Dad said he will give me some money for that."

"I was hoping that you would consider coming back to Valley Town after a year or two at Ivy so that we could be together again, Alexia. Joan and I discussed this as a possibility, and she also hopes that you may consider that."

"I don't want to come back to Valley Town, Johnny. I've thought about that, and I really want to try to finish at Ivy. I want to try and get a job in the Northeast after I graduate. Anyway, that's too far off, and we have plenty of time to think about it, but I don't want to come back to Valley Town, or attend Valley Town University. That's too close for comfort."

"Ivy is too far, Alexia, come back and stay closer. We'll be together. Joan even says so. Think about it, Alexia."

"Anyway, have you heard any more about Mom's and Dad's Thanksgiving trip?"

John squints. "I haven't heard anything in a long while. Have you heard anything?"

"They never discuss any of that with me anymore. You know that. Did you tell them you weren't going?"

"I did, but I have to tell you that I might change my mind."

"You mean you might still go?"

"Yes, but I'm not sure. I'll be thinking about it, and we'll see what comes up."

Alexia is silent, but she is unhappy.

"You were right though, Mom was interested in inheriting from the bishop, but Dad says that after the bishop's visit, she changed her mind."

"Yes, Dad told me the same thing, but I don't believe her. Has Mom spoken to you about the trip?"

"No, she hasn't, but Dad said that Mom wouldn't mind if I did not go. We both know how she feels though."

"Well?"

"I don't know, Alexia."

"What?"

"I wish I could make you and Mom happy. I really don't know what I'm going to do. I'm not sure about going."

"Well, you just said you were going to go. So, go!"

"I don't have to decide on anything now I said."

Disappointed, her pained voice showing it, she avoids making eye contact with her brother.

"Are you mad?"

"No, I'm not mad. Why should I be mad?"

"Anyway, we'll discuss it later."

"What's there to discuss?"

"You're angry."

"I said I'm not. Why should I be? You're a free man."

"It isn't easy, Alexia."

"Don't worry about me! Go with them!"

"You don't mean it."

"Why do you say that?!" she raises her voice.

"Because I know you're angry, that's all."

"No, you don't, and I don't want to talk about it anymore."

Chapter 34

That same day, and during the time that Alexia and Johnny were having their spirited conversation, Carla and Michael sit in their living room discussing plans for taking their children to their campuses. Carla agrees to drive with Johnny to his dorm at Valley Town University, only a few miles from home. Michael agrees to fly with Alexia to Byron, New York, where she will enter the College of Arts and Sciences at Ivy University.

"How did your shopping with Alexia go yesterday?" Michael asks his wife.

"She didn't buy a single thing. She was polite and formal, and barely said a word to me, and she hardly said anything about going to Ivy, or leaving home. I couldn't tell how she was feeling about anything. I took her to several nice women's stores, but she wasn't interested in looking at anything or buying anything. She just went through the motions."

"That's too bad; did she show any excitement or apprehension about leaving?"

"I couldn't tell, I didn't notice anything, but Johnny's excited."

"He's a little concerned about living in the university dorm, and he's sad. He told me that Alexia told him she wants to settle in the Northeast, and does not want to come back to Valley Town. Well, such is life," Michael says, rubbing his eyes.

"Johnny dislikes leaving home, and he fears being so far away from Alexia. I have to admit that I hate to see them both leave, Mike."

His face anguished, he looks down. "Yes, I know," he finally says in a low voice. "I guess we'll get used to it."

"It's all happening so fast. I don't know if I can get used to it."

"Yes, you will."

"Poor Johnny, he's more dependent on Alexia than she's on him."

"You'll be surprised. She's just as dependent on him as he's on her," Michael says, "but she tries not to show it."

"She's too proud to show it."

"But it's good for them to go to different schools," Michael says.

"Anyway, sooner or later they have to go their separate ways," she sighs. "Did Alexia say anything to you about leaving tomorrow, or about being away from home?"

"She only thanked me for agreeing to go with her, but she didn't really say much else. She has a lot on her mind, but I'm sure she'll be all right," he says.

Carla looks out the window at the empty lawn, once a play yard. "It wasn't so long ago that I played with toddling twins in that empty space over there. It's difficult seeing them leave, isn't it. I feel like a part of me is being taken away. I'm just not ready to see them leave at the same time."

"They'll be all right, my dear, they'll be O.K."

Chapter 35

On their trip to Byron, Michael and Alexia sit together in the economy section of a flight from Valley Town to John F. Kennedy Airport, in New York, where they will catch a connecting flight to Byron, New York. Alexia is anxious, but she does not share that with her father. Then her father begins to speak to her gently, and she listens attentively. He informs her that the new experience she will have at Ivy - one of the most distinguished universities in the world, he stresses - will change her life forever. "You have a good head on your shoulders, my dear," he says to Alexia. There is a glistening of his blue eyes. "I am confident, my love, that you'll do well in this magnificent institution. You'll meet some of the brightest kids in America, and possibly in the world. You'll be taught by some of the best professors anywhere. The breadth of the education available there is unmatched in other schools. But you have to be prepared for the difference between high school education and college education, my dear. You're going to become independent. You're pretty much on your own, and the competition is tough. Try not to get behind in your work. Go meet your professors privately whenever you can. Introduce yourself to them and don't spend too much time at first. These are very busy people, but I'm sure they'll give you the time you need."

Alexia listens to her father with emotion. "Thank you, Dad, I love you," she says.

Her father himself becomes emotional. "You're very welcome, sweetheart." He reaches for her hand and rubs it gently. "I'm sorry, dear, I'm getting a little emotional, realizing how far away you'll be. Anyway, my dear, I know you're interested in English Literature. But you'll find so many other fascinating fields of study available to you. That's what a liberal arts education is all about. So dive in! Along the way you'll be developing more confidence about what you want to do with your life."

"Thank you, Dad. I would love to take a course in music. Grandma Rose-Anne even encouraged me to consider that."

"Bless her heart," Michael Hartley says. "Was she the one who encouraged you to apply to Ivy, sweetheart?"

"Yes, she was, Dad, but please don't tell that to Mom."

"I won't. Bless her heart."

"And Grandma Rose-Anne did tell me about her sad experience. I knew about that before Mom did, but please don't tell Mom."

Her father is speechless.

"Are you upset, Dad, that I told you this?"

"No, I'm not, sweetheart. I'm glad you are telling me this, and I won't tell Mom. I know Mom asked you about this before, but you never said yes, or no."

"Grandma Rose-Anne asked me not to tell Mom."

"Did she say she'd like to tell you something but don't tell Mom?"

"No, that's not how it happened. I was asking her about her life on the farm, and she became emotional, then after a while she said she had something special, or private I think she may have said, that she wanted to tell me, but she said she didn't want me to tell anyone about it. I asked her how about Mom? Grandma Rose-Anne emphatically said that she didn't want Mom to know. Then I asked her if I could mention it to Johnny. She hesitated, then she said something to the effect that Johnny may not be ready for it. I was scared and I hesitated. She then asked me if I preferred that she not tell me, and I said no, I would like to hear it. Maybe she began to have second thoughts about telling me, and I was afraid that she may have changed her mind about telling me, so I begged her and begged her to tell me, and she did." Alexia becomes very emotional. "She broke my heart, Dad. She broke my heart. I can't stand seeing Mom wanting to become close to the monster who raped Grandma Rose-Anne."

"I know, sweetheart, I know, I know how you feel, darling," he rubs his eyes. "I'm sure Mom now knows more than she did, Alexia, and she's thinking more and more about what she's doing. It'll take time, but I feel that she's reconsidering her relationship with the bishop. You already know that she has changed her mind about wanting to inherit from him."

"I don't believe her, Dad, I don't. I'm very sorry to say that, Dad, but I'm sure she'll never change her mind about him."

"I know you said that before, my dear, but I really feel that she means it. I wouldn't say that if I didn't have some indications of it. Perhaps you and I may have time to talk about that later, and before I go back to Valley Town."

"Mom depresses me, Dad, she does," Alexia continues to cry.

"Anyway, my dear, you'll be meeting very nice people at Ivy, and you'll make life-time friends. College friends can become life-time friends. Some of my very best friends, sweetheart, are the ones I met in college."

Alexia listens to her father, trying to regain her composure and remaining mostly quiet now. "I love you, Dad, but I wish I could say the same about Mom," she tells her father, then turns and looks through the airplane window at the emptiness extending into the distance.

"I love you, too, Alexia, and I'm sure, very sure that Mom loves you as much as I do, even more if that's possible."

Alexia's father then begins to warn Alexia of the severe winters of the Northeast. He encourages her to get some new warm clothes for the winter and to eat well in order to remain healthy. "Please use the additional cash I gave you for some warm winter clothes. Will you do that, Alexia?"

"I will, Dad."

"Buy yourself a heavy overcoat. The winter will soon be upon us, and it's very, very cold in the Northeast."

"I will, Dad," she nods her head, but seems distant, as distant as the grave, as she again hears her grandmother's words; they come as if to haunt her: *"And this central room of the house, my parents' bedroom, symbolized for me the security and love of that family, to which as a child I belonged."*

Her father asks her if there is anything on her mind she wants to bring up or talk with him about.

"Not now, Dad," she says in a weak voice, shaking her head. "Maybe a little later."

He then asks her to call him or write him if she needs anything, or wants to discuss her courses further with him, and to be sure to let him know how he can be helpful.

"Thank you, I will," she nods her head again. "I love you, Dad," she repeats.

"I love you too, sweetheart."

Alexia then turns away and looks down at the motionless clouds in the distance. She again begins to remember her grandmother, dressed in a blue cotton dress, motioning to her to follow her. Alexia locks her thin fingers together, as the Grandmother's voice begins to come to her again. *"The West pasture which lay across the creek north of the house was predominantly a large hill ... Around the hillside of the West pasture grew blackberry briars ... Jimmy and I knew the West pasture best because we walked across it on our way to school, although Mother and Daddy preferred that we walk by the road ... I loved riding horses and often would ride over to the pasture, tie the horse to a tree, and just sit and daydream all by myself ..."*

"Are you OK Alexia?" her anxious father asks.

"I'm all right, Dad. I'm all right, don't worry about me."

"Is anything bothering you now, sweetheart?"

"No, nothing," she unlocks her fingers and rubs her face briskly, as if awakening from a momentary dream. "I'm all right, Dad. I'll be all right. Don't worry about me."

Chapter 36

On arriving in Byron, Michael rents a car and takes Alexia to her dormitory. Her roommate has arrived with her parents a few hours before Alexia and her father.

"I'm Michael Hartley, and this is my daughter Alexia," Michael says, introducing himself and his daughter to a couple in their mid-forties who are accompanying their daughter.

"I'm Bill Falvo, and this is my wife Maureen and our daughter Anna-Marie," the easygoing man says.

"How do you do, I am very pleased to meet you, sir," Michael says. "I guess our girls will be sharing the room."

"It looks that way." Bill Falvo smiles as the accumulation of boxes around them grows. He is a short, stocky man with a thick dark mustache and a light complexion. He has an upstate New York accent and seems pleasant and relaxed.

"Are you folks from out of state?"

"Yes, we're from Valley Town, Virginia."

"That's quite a distance from here."

"Yes, it is, and you folks?"

"We're from Green Meadow, just east of Syracuse, only a few miles from here, I think just about sixty miles."

Alexia, folding her arms, walks across the room to join her new roommate.

"What do you do, Mike?" Bill Falvo asks.

"I teach at Valley Town University."

"Oh, what do you teach?"

"I teach economics," Michael answers. "How about you, Bill?"

"I'm an electrical engineer. I work in Syracuse. Would you and Alexia like to join our family for dinner tonight?"

"Yes, that would be very nice. Alexia, is it all right with you if we go out for dinner with Mr. and Mrs. Falvo and Anna-Marie?" Michael speaks to his daughter from across the room.

"Yes, that sounds good, Dad," she says.

"That's great. So let's let the girls get acquainted and arrange their room," Mr. Falvo responds.

"Good idea."

"Should we meet downstairs in the hall at 6:30 this evening?"

"Super, that's great. I'll go for a little walk, Alexia, while you and Anna-Marie start sorting out your things."

The contrast between Alexia Hartley and Anna-Marie Falvo is striking. Alexia, tall and slender, with long, blond, curly hair and blue eyes is diffident, even shy. Anna-Marie, petite, with beautiful, big, brown eyes and long, dark, curly hair, is very open and friendly. The two girls, each in her own way, are very attractive. Despite having such different personalities, they hit it off from the beginning.

"Which college will you be in?" Anna-Marie asks Alexia.

"Arts and Sciences, and you?"

"Human Ecology."

"Oh? My grandmother taught that after she finished college," Alexia says. "They used to call it Home Economics in those days. My grandmother died a little less than a year ago."

"I'm sorry to hear that, you must miss her."

"Yes, I do, very much. She was my maternal grandmother, and she grew up on an upstate New York farm. She used to tell me a lot about the farm, and about her life back then."

"There are a lot of nice, big dairy farms there."

"My father's mother is sort of a southern belle."

"She must be very nice, and I can tell that you like her."

"Yes, I do, very much, but I was much closer to my maternal Grandma Rose-Anne, she was cool and very smart. She was the one who encouraged me to come to the Northeast and to apply to here. I loved her very dearly, and I miss her a lot."

"I bet you do, I'm very close to my maternal grandma too. Do you know what you're going to major in?"

"I haven't decided, although I am interested in literature and music and languages."

"Do you speak another language?"

"I took Spanish in High School, but I'm not fluent in it. I would love to take French. Do you know another language?"

"I know Italian, from speaking with my grandparents. They were born in Italy, but my Italian isn't too good, just enough to get by."

"That's so cool!"

"You have a beautiful southern accent."

"Thanks," she smiles.

"I like it, it's different."

"Your accent is like Mom's uncles, they live here in the Northeast."

"I don't notice my accent."

"I like the way people speak around here."

"The way people speak around here is a little different from the way they speak in New York City. In which part of the state do your uncles live?"

"They're my mom's uncles, they live on a dairy farm upstate, near Hamlet, that's where my grandma grew up. They're nice, but I don't know them very well. I only met them once, when my Grandma Rose-Anne passed away."

"Where in upstate is Hamlet? I never heard of it."

"It's a tiny little village of less than a thousand people, north of Stratford, I think. I've never been there."

"I know where Stratford is, it's very pretty up there."

"That's what everyone says. My grandma used to tell me a lot about the farm she lived on and how pretty it was. I dream about going to see it sometime."

"You'll love it. It's a truly majestic and beautiful area. The whole Adirondack region is breath taking! You should go and visit your Mom's uncles, you'll love it there."

"I'd love to go see that area. Maybe after settling down a little here, I'll try to go and visit the farm."

"You said you're interested in literature, the English Department here is one of the best in the country, you should keep that in mind."

"Yes, I've heard that the English Department is excellent. Ms. Bates, my high school English teacher, oh, I loved her, she told me that. She also encouraged me to apply here and to major in English."

"You must've been a very good student in high school."

"Not too bad, but I had to care for my Grandma Rose-Anne after school, and missed out on extra curriculars."

"It was nice that you could do that, you must've been very close to your grandmother.

"Yes, I was," Alexia sighs, "and I really miss her, but I'm glad I had the opportunity to care for her. She has influenced me and my thinking about a lot of things very greatly."

"That's very sweet," Anna-Marie says. "So do you think you're going to study English Literature?"

"Yes, I might, but I'm not really decided yet. I'll be taking different courses during my first semester, to have a feel for college and to see how it goes. That's what my Dad recommended on our way here, and I'm going to try to do that, I'm hoping that'll help me decide. My dad also suggested that I take some music, psychology, history and political science courses, but I'm not sure I want to do all that. I'm very interested in music, though, and I wish I could become fluent in another language too."

"You can. Anyone can learn. Is your mom at home?"

"Yes she is. She took my brother to Valley Town University, where he'll be studying chemical engineering. I'm very close to my brother, Johnny. I'll miss him. Do you have brothers and sisters?"

"I have a younger brother who's fourteen, and a sister who's six. I adore my little sister, and I'll miss her."

"Do you like your brother?"

"I like him, but he's spoiled. My dad lets him get away with murder. I guess he's all right."

"I like my brother, he's my twin. We're very close and we think alike, most of the time, that is."

"I'll bet it's neat to have a twin."

"It makes you very close to one another, and even dependent on one another. You'll know how the other one feels and thinks, almost always, and often instantly."

"That must be fascinating."

"And you become almost telepathic. Even when he's far away, I'll have a sense if he's sad, or if he's hurting. It's hard to describe."

"Isn't that remarkable?"

"Do you get along with your mom and dad?"

"Yes, but I'm closer to my mom, and you?"

"I'm closer to my dad. My dad is very understanding. Does your mom work?"

"She's a school teacher, and your mom?"

"She's in real estate. She's a managing partner in a real estate office in Valley Town."

"Cool! I think we better get ready, your dad will be back soon, and I hear my parents chatting in the hall."

"Yes, and I need to wash a little before we go out. See you in a little while."

Anna-Marie joins her parents.

Chapter 37

Carla and Johnny are traveling from their home to Valley Town University. Johnny is driving. "If I had worked a little harder in high school," he says to his mother, "I would've been with Alexia at Ivy University now. I wish I had."

"You worked very hard, Johnny," Carla assures her son, "you did your best and did very well. You made a great choice. Valley Town is a very good university. Their engineering college is among the best in the United States. You have nothing to be ashamed of, dear."

"I know that, Mom" he says, "but it isn't like Ivy, I can't kid myself."

"It is an outstanding university, Johnny."

"I know it is, but I still wish I had better grades. If I had better grades, Mom, I could've been with Alexia."

"I know you miss her, we all do, but life is like that, my dear, and we'll adjust to all of this. She'll miss you too. I know she will."

"I think so," he sighs.

"Of course she will."

"We got in an argument the day before she left. I wish we hadn't."

"What was it about?"

"It was about going to Lake Charles on Thanksgiving."

Carla pauses. "That was bound to come up, wasn't it? Did she bring it up?"

He does not answer.

"Well, I have to tell you, Johnny, that I feel very badly that Alexia is upset. I know it's my fault."

"Why is it your fault, Mom?" He looks at his mother, surprised that she would acknowledge that it is her fault. "How is it your fault?"

"Well, my dear, I mishandled it from the beginning. I wasn't prepared for it, Johnny. It was very difficult for me to discover, then accept, being a child of rape, and to cope with the fact that I was born out of wedlock. Instead of seeking help, I began to behave irrationally, and even selfishly, without much concern for my husband or my children."

Still visibly surprised that his mom is admitting to this, Johnny continues to drive, listening attentively and not saying a word.

"I also misread Alexia, and could not understand her violent reaction to the bishop. I didn't realize that Grandma Rose-Anne had told Alexia about the rape."

"Had she really Mom?"

"I'm sure that she had. I'm very sure, even certain that she had."

"On what do you base that?"

"It's very complicated, Johnny, and I can't get into the details now, maybe later, but Dad and I have concluded that Grandma Rose-Anne must have discussed the rape with Alexia, but we both also believe that Alexia didn't know that I was a child of that rape."

"That is amazing, that's incredible, and you may be right, come to think of it." Johnny slows the car down, pulls off the narrow road to the right, and stops just a few miles from Valley Town University."

"What's the matter?" Carla asks.

"I just want to rest a little. Continue, Mom."

"Do you want me to drive?"

"No, let's just stop here a little, we have plenty of time. So Alexia knew about the rape. That makes sense, a lot of sense. And Dad also agrees with that, I mean that Alexia must have known."

"Yes, Dad agrees with me on that. We both believe that she knew about the incident from Grandma. We believe that Grandma Rose-Anne spoke to Alexia about the incident before she died, but we don't know whether she gave Alexia much detail, or any detail. We don't know if Grandma described her struggle with her young attacker, now the bishop, the young man who raped her, for example."

"Oh, my God," Johnny exclaims. "I bet you that Grandma did give Alexia some details. That's why the bishop, in Alexia's eyes, is the embodiment of evil. That's why she cannot forgive him, or stand to meet him, or even see him."

"And that's why you're more willing to meet him, speak with him and accept that his remorse and sorrow now, as a seventy-three-year-old man of the cloth, is genuine."

"I'm sure that it is. I didn't tell you this, Mom, I mentioned it to Dad. I saw on the internet that Bishop Arlington has donated ninety percent of his wealth of over one hundred million dollars to charity."

"When did he do that?"

"I think that he did that shortly after he returned to Lake Charles from his visit to Valley Town."

"Why didn't Dad tell me?"

"I just felt, Mom, that it would be better if I gave you the information myself. I knew we would be driving to Valley Town University together."

"Are you going to tell Alexia?"

"Not now, Mom, and please let me tell her, I know how to do it and when."

"That's a good idea, and I won't say anything to her about that."

"So, Alexia knew about the rape from Grandma Rose-Anne herself, before she died. That's why after school, shortly before Grandma died, Alexia always used to go into Grandma's room, close the door behind her and stay with Grandma for hours on end. Sometimes she'd come out shaken up and crying. I thought that was because Alexia knew that Grandma was terminally ill. I now know there was more to it, but why wouldn't Alexia share this with me, or share it with you and Dad?"

"We think that Grandma Rose-Anne must've asked Alexia not to share it with any of us."

"Why would Grandma ask her not to share it with any of us?"

"We don't really know why, Johnny. We think that Grandma didn't want me to know that I'm a child of rape, that is probably why, but we can't really know for sure."

Somewhat more relaxed, Johnny resumes driving.

Chapter 38

While Michael and Carla deliver their twins to their respective universities, Bishop Arlington, his wife Grace and their two daughters, Christine Arlington Barton and Elizabeth Arlington Robinson, meet at the bishop's spacious office in the Arlington mansion in Lake Charles.

"Before we embark on any discussion, let's seek our Lord's guidance with a few moments of meditation, then a prayer," the bishop suggests. "Is that all right with you?"

"That's a good idea," says Christine.

"Grace? Elizabeth?"

The two nod approvingly.

The bishop, his wife and his two daughters bow their heads, for a brief moment of silence. Then the bishop breaks the silence and prays: "Our Lord God, we seek your guidance. We want to know how best we can serve you. Guide us, Lord, with your mercy, wisdom and love. Give us the vision to recognize our weaknesses, our vulnerabilities and our need for one another. Show us that as long as many of our brothers and sisters, members of your own family, whether here or abroad, are hungry, homeless, sick or uneducated, then all of us are challenged. Give us the strength and the humility to share the wealth you have given us with those who are in need. Forgive us our sins, our pride and our indifference. Amen."

"Amen," they all say.

"That's beautiful, Philip," Grace says, "I want you to know, my love, that I agree with you wholeheartedly, that I support everything you wish to do and that I'll stand by you, until I die. I also want to say to our beloved daughters, that the wealth that God has given you, He gave for a reason, and to you personally. He did not give it to me, or to Christine or to Elizabeth. He entrusted you personally with that wealth to manage with His guidance. I don't feel that it's for me to say to you how you should use it, or how you should share it. I just want you to understand this, at the very beginning, but I also want to ask you, if you see fit, my dear Philip, to tell our daughters what you told me a few days ago, when your returned from your trip to Virginia. Our daughters should know. They're our flesh and blood. Our pain is theirs also, and we need them now, more than ever. God will look at that with favor. He knows how difficult these few days have been for you. I'm confident that He will help you through these difficult times. I'm also sure that Christine and Elizabeth will be with us as well.

"Is something the matter, Grace?" Christine asks anxiously.

"What is it?" Elizabeth asks.

"The reason for this family meeting, Christine and Elizabeth, is to share with you some new developments that have arisen during the past few days, but first, thank you my dearest Grace, thank you. I agree with every word you've spoken, and I intend to share with our daughters what I've shared with you. I will also share with our grandchildren what I'm about to tell you. They too need to know." There is sweat on the bishop's brow and his face reddens as he bows his head in prayer for a few minutes.

The two daughters exchange looks, and are visibly both anxious and perplexed.

Grace's eyes moisten.

"My dear Christine and my dear Elizabeth: For many years, I have had a very big skeleton hidden in my closet. It has not only been hidden in my closet, it has in fact been sitting heavily on my heart." The bishop's voice quivers and his face reddens again as he continues: "During World War Two, and before I married your mother, when I was seventeen years old, almost eighteen, I committed a great sin against God, against our Lord, and against a young woman my age who was working in our family home in Stratford. I violently assaulted her sexually against her will, and made her pregnant."

The two daughters cover their faces and begin to cry.

Grace, sitting between them, extends one hand to Christine and the other to Elizabeth.

"Shocked and horrified by my crime, my parents, especially my mother, pleaded with the girl's destitute mother to accept two payments for my offense, one to be given to the mother, to help her with her then increased financial problems, and one to be given to the daughter for her pain and suffering. The two of them left town and we understood that the young victim would have the baby aborted."

Christine withdraws her hand from her mother and covers her face. Elizabeth only stares down at the floor.

"As far as we knew," the bishop continues, "the mother and her daughter moved to California and the pregnancy was aborted." The bishop pauses again. "Early last month," he continues, "on August 4th, to be exact, I received a letter from a fifty-four-year-old woman, Carla Hartley, of Valley Town, Virginia, advising me that she is the daughter of Rose-Anne Riley Perry, the young woman I assaulted, advising me that she believes that she is my daughter and expressing interest in meeting me, if that would not cause me any difficulty or embarrassment with my family. Shocked and disbeliev- ing, I immediately showed the letter to your grandmother. She too was in shock and disbelief, saying that she was sure that the pregnancy was aborted since our family paid for that procedure. I then consulted our family lawyer, Mr. Hudson, who recommended that we engage a reputable firm in Califor- nia to investigate whether the pregnancy was aborted or not. The investigator could not confirm the abortion of the pregnancy, but could confirm that a Rose-Anne Riley Thornton was admitted to the hospital in Salem, California, on December 29, 1943, almost exactly nine months after my sexual assault on Rose-Anne Riley, and delivered a baby girl, Carla Rose-Anne Thornton. She was named after Rose-Anne's father, Carl Riley. Shortly after receiving this report, and armed with the birth certificate showing one Robert Edward Thornton as Carla's father, I wrote to Carla Hartley informing her that I would go to meet her in Valley Town, Virginia, and I did.

When I met Carla Hartley and her husband Michael Hartley, I could not believe my eyes. It was as if you, Christine, were sitting in front of me, looking at me and speaking to me. I was stunned. At first, I could not even look at my daughter Christine's double, then the Lord gave me the courage and the integrity to realize that Carla Hartley is indeed another innocent victim of my criminal assault, and is indeed my daughter, whom I never knew existed. So I immediately acknowledged to Carla that she must be my daughter and I confirmed to her and to her husband, who sat restlessly with her, my willingness to recognize her as such. After more discussion and consultation within their family, Carla and her husband invited me to their modest home. Carla is a very attractive and dignified woman. She is highly educated. She is a graduate of Salem University in California, has an MBA and a Ph. D. and is the senior partner in a leading real estate agency in Valley Town, Virginia. Her husband is a professor of economics at Valley Town University. They have two children, seventeen-year-old twins, Alexia, who has been admitted to Ivy in Byron, this fall, and Johnny, who has been admitted to the college of chemical engineering at Valley Town University. I only met Johnny, who looks very much like Christine's son, Ronald. He is tall, very handsome and very bright. I was told that Alexia graduated as valedictorian of her high school class. I did not meet her." The bishop, now perspiring profusely, looks at his two daughters momentarily. His blue eyes glistening, he continues.

"This is what I discovered, and what I shared with your grandmother and your mother, and now I am sharing with you. On my way back to Lake Charles, I had long hours of flying and of reflecting and praying, after which

I came to the inescapable conclusion that our Lord has decided, in my own interest, to remind me of my sin, which has weighed on my heart for all these years, but which I have refused to attend to. I decided that the Lord is calling on me to do penance for my grave offense against an innocent, defenseless young woman, Rose-Anne Riley, whom I overpowered and assaulted sexually. She died at the age of seventy-two from terminal cancer, just a few months ago, and undoubtedly carried the scar of my horrible offense against her and against our Lord to her grave. Yet, she did not have the heart to share her tragedy with her daughter Carla. Carla discovered it by accident. She was shocked and horrified when she discovered that she is a rape child who was actually born out of wedlock. Carla's husband, children and family were all shocked."

"Philip," says Christine, "I want you to know that I will stand by you, support you and do everything in my power to help you during these difficult times."

"And so will I," says Elizabeth. "I did not know this was happening. Grandma Elizabeth didn't tell me any of this. I am very sorry I went along with the lawsuit. I will withdraw from it. You can rest assured that I will, and I too will stand by you and will do everything I can to support you. I am sorry, very sorry."

"So this is what I would like to do," the bishop continues, "and I shared this with your grandmother first, then with your mother. I want Carla to join our family as my own daughter, and therefore as Christine's and Elizabeth's sister. I want her to inherit from my estate equally with my other two daughters. I want to do penance to the Lord, for my sin against Him and against Rose-Anne Riley. I want to give ninety per cent of my wealth, which the Lord gave me, back to the Lord, by building schools, hospitals, housing for orphans, housing for the elderly, the poor and the homeless and infirmaries to care for the victims of rape. When Dad, your grandfather, died, he left an estate of one hundred million dollars, fifty million was left to me, and fifty million to Mother, your grandmother. My share has grown to about two hundred and fifteen million dollars, and possibly more. We don't need all that money. What do we need it for?"

"Philip," asks Christine, "How did Grandpa accumulate so much wealth?"

"He accumulated it during World War Two, my dear. Dad owned a modest cutlery business, but he landed a few major government contracts during the war, supplying cutlery to the US Armed Forces. So Dad expanded his business dramatically during the war. He used very cheap female laborers, who patriotically worked long hours with very modest compensation as part of the war effort, but Dad made a lot of money. He didn't have to pay overtime, or health benefits in those days, as is done today, or had to contribute toward their retirement, and he made huge profits. That's how your grandfather accumulated his wealth. That's how he made his millions. Truthfully, I was never interested in all that, but because I was an only child, I inherited half of it. As a young man, I used to think that I could, literally, get away with murder, certain that my very wealthy, influential and powerful father could come and rescue me no matter what I did. Now, considering the crime I committed in my youth, I've at last been prompted to return my wealth to the Lord by helping His children, especially the poor, the weak and the defenseless victims of rape."

"Amazing, that is truly amazing," says Christine. "I can't understand how Grandma Elizabeth would object. That doesn't affect any of her estate."

"No, that does not affect any of what Mother inherited, which is the other half of Dad's estate. And when I return ninety percent of what I have inherited to the Lord, there will be more than ten million dollars left for Grace, Christine, Elizabeth and Carla. I know that Mother, God love her, is unhappy about that. Elizabeth was unhappy too, but she is not now, thank God for his mercy. You all know that Mr. Hudson was instructed to challenge my action on the ground of mental incapacity, and mental incompetence. I regret that, and pray that this action will be discontinued."

"It will be discontinued, Philip," Elizabeth says. "I promise you it will be discontinued."

"I thank the Lord, and thank you, my dear Elizabeth," the bishop says with feeling.

"Is there anything else we can do?" Christine asks.

"Maybe you and Elizabeth and I can speak with Grandma Elizabeth again," the bishop's wife Grace says in a very low voice.

"Mother, sooner or later, will realize that I can legally do whatever I want, with what I inherited from Dad. It will not hurt though, if you three spoke to her kindly and gently, if you wish. Mother now realizes that if and when I inherit the share she inherited from Dad, I'll do with that whatever I want. That's her concern. She mentioned that concern to me when I returned from Virginia. You may wish to alleviate her concern by letting her know that I'll be contented and if she bequeaths her estate to all three of you. It would be too much to expect her to include your sister Carla in that. You three can then do with what you inherit as your hearts dictate."

"Let me speak to Grandma Elizabeth by myself first," Elizabeth suggests.

"I think that's a good idea," Grace agrees.

"That's all right with me," Christine says, "then, all three of us should speak to her. I really would like to speak to Grandma Elizabeth about all this."

"Whatever you three decide is fine with me," the bishop says. "God bless all of you."

"Amen," they all say.

The Bishop's younger daughter Elizabeth goes into her grandmother's suite. "May I sit with you for a few minutes, Grandma," the young Elizabeth says, speaking softly in a very low voice.

"Yes, you may, my dear, of course you may."

"Grandma, I've had a change of heart about bringing a legal action against Philip, and I'd like to speak to you about that, if I may."

"Of course you may, what happened, my dear? What brought that change, dear? Who have you been speaking with?"

"I've been speaking with Philip and Grace and Christine, Grandma. I heard Philip describe what he did when he was a young man. That shocked me, Grandma, and made me feel horrible, very horrible, Grandma."

"I knew it would, my dear."

"I don't have the heart to bring further agony to Philip, Grandma, he's my dad, and I love him."

"He's my son, and I love him too, but he's out of his mind, dear."

"No, he isn't Grandma. He definitely isn't. I think pursuing this lawsuit would be a disaster, not only to Philip, but to our whole family. We cannot afford to hang our dirty linen in public, not now, Grandma, and not in the context of the tragic tale Philip shared with Grace, Christine and me. I'm therefore here to beg you, to plead with you that we must discontinue this madness. I don't want my name to remain on the legal papers, and you shouldn't have yours there either, Grandma."

"But Philip is going to do the same thing when he inherits my estate, and he will sooner or later."

"No, he won't. He discussed that with us. He's willing to have you bequeath your estate to Grace, Christine and me, Grandma, and to the newly discovered sister, if you wish."

"Ah! Why would I leave anything for her?"

"Whatever you want to do, Grandma, but let's not continue the legal action, please, Grandma. It's unseemly, it's wrong, Grandma."

"If Philip agrees to what you say in writing, yes, I will discontinue the legal action. Yes, I will do that, but I need to have that in writing and notarized in court as part of discontinuing the lawsuit, but I have no intention of leaving anything for the woman in Virginia. I was assured by the girl's mother, Mrs. Riley, that the girl would have an abortion, and we paid for that, but she didn't. They cheated us."

"I am sure he'll agree. We discussed it, and he said he would do that, Grandma."

"Where's Grace? And where's Christine? Where did they go?"

"I'll go get them, Grandma."

When Grace and Christine enter, the grandmother greets them warmly. "My dear Christine, I haven't seen you for ages, why don't you come to see me, my dear? I miss you, my child, I do."

"Her eyes bloodshot and puffed, Christine reaches for a tissue to wipe her tears. "I miss you too, Grandma."

"You've been crying, I know you have, and I also know how difficult this is. It's very sad, but we'll all get over it. Elizabeth has been reporting to me about your meeting with Philip. And yes, I agree that we should discontinue the legal action, as long as Philip agrees that I can bequeath my estate directly to you three, just as he should if I were to bequeath it to him, but I know that he's out of his mind and he wouldn't."

"He is not out of his mind, Grandma," Christine says, "please don't say that."

"My dear Christine, I know that Philip is your father and you love him very much, but he's also my son, and I love him more than life itself, but he's out of his mind, he's crazy, my dear. What sane man would do what he's doing, giving away ninety percent of what his father left for him? Who would do that, please tell me. His father, your grandfather Ron, worked all his life, day and night, to earn that money. And here comes his son, his only son, and throws it all away, to the wolves! Who ever heard of such a thing? Tell me. Of course he's out of his mind, crazy, my dear."

Grace and the two girls remain silent.

"Where did he go? I haven't seen him in four days."

"I am sure he'll come and see you before long, Mother," Grace says.

"He'd better come! You can help him, Grace, more than any of us can. You're his wife, and he loves you and trusts you, he told me that many times. He'll listen to you. He trusts you with his life. Speak to him, Grace, maybe you can reason with him, or convince him to get treated. Maybe you can help him see a psychiatrist. What do you think, Grace."

Grace and the two daughters listen politely and remain quiet.

"I wish there was a way I could communicate with him again," the elderly woman sighs. "He always used to listen to me, he doesn't anymore. He doesn't listen to me anymore. Oh, Philip, what happened to you?"

Chapter 39

"How was the trip to Ivy?" Carla asks her husband when he returns home from Byron, New York, having helped Alexia settle in her dormitory.

"It went very well, Carla, much better than I expected."

"That's great, tell me all about it. How did Alexia like Byron and Ivy University? Did you meet her roommate?"

"She seemed to like the little town and the University, and she has a nice roommate from upstate New York."

"Did Alexia like her?"

"I think she did, they seemed to hit it off. After we met the roommate and her parents, they took us out for dinner. They're very nice country people from upstate New York. They are middle class, working people like us."

"That's nice. Did you have any conversation with Alexia before you left?"

"I did, and she got a little emotional and cried. I did too. She tore my heart, Carla, looking at me the way she did. It was very strange the way she looked at me. I didn't expect that, and didn't expect my reaction to be so strong, but I hugged her and kissed her and told her how much I love her. She seemed to be reassured and came back and hugged me again. She appreciated that."

"I wish I had been there with you to comfort her and tell her how much I love her too," Carla becomes emotional and rubs her eyes. "Did you talk a lot on the plane?"

"We did."

"Tell me."

Michael hesitates.

"Tell me, Mike, please tell me."

"I'll tell you, but I also want to be careful, Carla. Alexia is still hurt by the entire affair. She has spoken to me in confidence about some of her feelings, and I don't want to violate that confidence, but I know that you want to know, and you should know. That's why I hesitated. I feel that I should share with you as much as I can without violating her request to keep what she told me as a private father-daughter conversation. I hope you understand, Carla."

"I do understand, Mike, and I'm glad she was able to confide in you. It's very important that she can confide in one of us. I know she's upset with me, very upset with me, and I understand that now, more than I was able to earlier on when I first made those discoveries. So, please tell me as much as you can feel comfortable telling me."

"First, Carla, I think that the death of Grandma Rose-Anne still haunts Alexia."

"How?"

"I think that Alexia keeps thinking and remembering her grandmother from time to time. It may even be that she senses Grandma Rose-Anne's presence with her constantly. It seems as though Grandma is with Alexia all the time, Carla. Alexia looks at Grandma Rose-Anne, she talks to her, she is intimately involved with her, I don't know, but Grandma continues to haunt her. In the plane, she would stare, looking at the clouds, clasping her hands and intertwining her fingers, as though she is in another world, in a trance, then she would come back as if she has awakened from a dream. She did that two or three times during the trip, and that really caught my attention and upset me."

"This is very strange," says Carla, "and scary."

"Then she would begin to mention some of her own recollections about Grandma to me, how Grandma helped her in her school work, how she encouraged her to appreciate music and literature and how Grandma encouraged her in many ways."

"That's very sweet, and I thought that Mom may have encouraged Alexia to apply to Ivy University. Alexia didn't know much about Ivy before," Carla says.

"She and Grandma were very intimate, there's no question about that."

"I'm sure of it, and I'm sure now that Grandma must've told Alexia about what the bishop did to her many years ago."

Michael pauses. "She was very close to Grandma. You know, after I took Alexia to her dorm, I had a walk around the campus. What a beautiful campus! It has these magnificent gorges with bridges over them. They're breathtaking, and a great engineering feat. When I came back to go out for dinner, I could hear Alexia and her roommate talking. They were enjoying each other."

"What's the girl's name?"

"Her name is Anna-Marie, Anna-Marie Falvo. I think that she's going to be a good companion for Alexia. You know, something shocking and tragic happened the day before we arrived on the Campus which shook up the whole university community. A distraught, young student jumped off one of those bridges on the Campus into a ravine some two or three hundred feet deep, killing himself. The Ivy Daily, the student newspaper, wrote about the tragedy. That suicide really shocked and saddened me very much, my dear. It scared me." He pauses again for a moment, thinking. "How did you and Johnny manage?" Michael then asks his wife, changing the subject.

"Well, Johnny and I had a very pleasant drive to the University. We talked about many things too, but mostly about his concern for Alexia and how much he is going to miss her. Apparently, the day before you and Alexia left, Alexia and Johnny had a heated disagreement about the invitation we had from the bishop to visit Lake Charles, and Johnny is concerned about that. It seems that he told Alexia that he wants to go to Lake Charles with us, and that led to the argument and the disagreement. He then told me what he already told you, that the bishop has donated ninety percent of his wealth to charity. I couldn't believe my ears. It is as though the bishop has been listening to Alexia's repeated refrains, that the bishop should do penance by donating all his wealth to the poor, and moving to live the life of a monk in a monastery. Maybe the bishop will do exactly that."

"Who knows? Maybe he will."

"And I didn't tell you, when I came back from the University, I got a call from the bishop. He thanked me most graciously for our hospitality, in-formed me that he has shared the events of the past few days with his family and said that he informed his mother, wife and daughters that from this point on, I am a full member of the family, their family, in all respects, and will inherit from his estate as a daughter, like Christine and Elizabeth. He said that he told Christine that Alexia is a student at Ivy University, and Christine suggested that Ronald, her son, who is also a freshman at Ivy, should try to meet Alexia and invite her to meet Christine's family in Ashton. Christine is going to encourage Ron to do that, to try to meet Alexia."

"Oh, boy," Michael cringes, "and what did you say to that?"

"I said that would be wonderful, what else could I say, Mike? I couldn't say, no, please don't let him try to do that, that would be most inappropriate, don't you agree?"

"Yes, I agree, but do you think this could really happen?"

"I don't know, and it may even be fortuitous. It won't hurt."

"I just don't want to upset Alexia, Carla, her nerves are still raw, very raw, and it may not be the time to do something like that now."

"Would Christine's son even know how to find Alexia, Mike?"

"If he's determined, I'm sure he could, it's not very difficult. All he has to do is to look in the Student Directory. The bishop knows her name."

"If you think this would really upset Alexia, you might want to warn her, and if she still feels uncomfortable meeting the young man, tell her to do whatever she thinks is best for her."

"Even that won't be easy, but I don't know what else we can do," Mike finally concludes. "What else happened, did you meet Johnny's roommate?" He then asks Carla.

"Yes, I did. Johnny's roommate seems shy and very reserved. He's tall and good-looking like Johnny. He's quiet. Johnny liked him, but he didn't say much after Johnny introduced me to him."

"As you say, he's probably shy, but they'll get along."

"Johnny's easy to live with," Carla says.

Chapter 40

A month passes during which Alexia calls her best friend Joan several times. She also exchanges several letters with her father, brother, and Joan, but she does not write to her mother. Alexia only speaks with her mother when Carla calls, and when that happens, Alexia is polite but brief. She does not say anything to Carla about her new experiences at Ivy, nor does she ask her mother for any assistance or guidance, as she does when her father calls. Yet Alexia is happy with her new friend and roommate at Ivy, Anna-Marie, who has helped Alexia adjust to a new and different life. Alexia is also happy with her new academic work, although she is often distracted by the haunting memories of her grandmother. However, she becomes close to her roommate, and considers going out with her roommate on double dates. But she always changes her mind at the last minute, stands up the boys, and neither she nor her roommate goes out.

One day, Anna-Marie tells Alexia that a Ronald Barton has left a message for her, with his phone number, asking her to call him. "Who is he?" Anna Marie asks Alexia.

"I haven't the slightest idea," Alexia responds.

"Maybe you have a secret admirer," Anna Marie teases her roommate and new friend.

"Do you think so?" Alexia says. "There is nothing to admire about me now."

"Don't say that, Alexia, you're beautiful, you're stunning. Didn't you know that?"

Alexia blushes. "Thanks, Anna-Marie."

"Alexia," Anna-Marie resumes, "there's this guy in my chemistry lab. He asked me again to go out for coffee this coming Thursday, what do you think?"

"You should go out with him."

"I don't want to go alone. Why don't you go with us? I even told the guy about you. He can fix you up with someone he knows, Alexia."

"Who?"

"He has a very close friend who's freshman at a nearby small college."

Alexia is bewildered. She moves slowly to a chair in the corner of their small room, sits down and faces her roommate.

"It's been five weeks since we've arrived at Ivy, and neither one of us has gone on a date even once," says Anna-Marie. "We've had several invitations, and I really would like to date, but I don't want to go without you, I don't want to go alone."

"You said he's a freshman?"

"Yes, at Byron College, he studies music."

"Where's that?"

"On the other side of town, Alexia, it's a nice small college, not many people from out of state know about it. It's mainly a music and drama college. It also has a good journalism department and a good physical education program."

Alexia is intrigued. "I never heard of it, but it sounds interesting. Let me think about it a little." Alexia, her head down, stares at the floor. She begins to remember her grandmother's dignified presence, then her grandmother's words reverberate in her ear again: *"...At first I was afraid to go out when I was in high school ... Only during my last year in high school did I have friends who called me ... Only then did I become comfortable even talking to my friends on the phone ...*

"Alexia, listen to me, this guy, Lloyd's friend, is studying music, and Lloyd has known him for a long time. Byron has a wonderful music program. It's one of the best in New York, and maybe in the country. I know you love music. Wouldn't you like to try and go out with this guy? You'll enjoy it. We both will."

"Maybe, maybe I'll go," she hesitates.

"Let's try it, he's really a nice guy, Lloyd says so."

Her head between her hands, Alexia begins to think again.

"What are you worried about? I know we'll have fun. It's not good for us to be cooped up in this dinky little room all the time."

"I know we shouldn't stay here all the time, but I don't know the guys. I'm kind of shy, and am scared to go out with someone I don't know."

"We'll all be together, and he's very nice. Please don't worry about it, and you don't need to be scared, I'll be with you all the time."

"Have you ever met the guy who goes to Byron College?"

"I haven't met him, but I saw him once. He's from Hyden, about an hour from Byron."

"What does he look like?"

"He's tall, broad shoulders, curly blond hair and blue eyes. He's good looking. Honest, he's very good looking. I'm not kidding, and he's very musical. Lloyd says he's a nice guy and comes from a good family."

"When is it again?"

"This Thursday, 3:00 in the afternoon, we'll all go to Sam's Hot Grill."

"OK, I'll go with you."

"Great! Great Alexia! You'll like him, I'm sure you will. He's very good looking."

"What's your date's name again?"

"Lloyd Williams. They're both from Hyden."

"What's the other guy's name, the one I'll be dating?"

"Douglas, but Lloyd calls him Doug."

Feeling nervous, Alexia hesitates again.

"What are you thinking about?" Anna-Marie asks.

"Nothing, I'm fine, I'll go with you."

"As I said, they were classmates in high school. But I don't know Doug's last name."

"That's O.K."

"He's Douglas something, but Lloyd says that he likes to be called Doug. Don't worry about it, you'll be all right."

"I dated very little when I was in high school. My friend Joan and I used to go out with two guys we knew very well, but I never dated anyone I didn't know."

"This will be interesting."

"What should I wear?"

"Casual. Very casual, I'm wearing jeans."

"Good, I'll wear jeans too."

"I don't blame you for not wanting to go alone, Alexia. I wouldn't go alone if my life depended on it, until I know the guy, that is."

"That's right."

"Lloyd seems nice though. And he's smart. Lloyd's father is a surgeon at the hospital of the University of Hyden, and I trust him. He said that his friend Doug is a good guy he's known for a long, long time. They grew up together, and they're best friends."

"That's good." Alexia looks out the window again. She again sees her elderly grandmother, slight but tall, sitting in a chair by a reading lamp. Alexia is instantly absorbed visualizing her grandmother, her aging face, her creases, her hopelessness, her silent pain, and yet her smile: Then the grandmother's words ring in Alexia's ear: *"... Be careful with young men, won't you, dear ... I will, Grandma. Of course I will. Don't worry about me, Grandma ... Rhubarb came each year along the west end of the garden ... Several herbs which we used, such as sage and horehounds, grew along the garden fence ... The garden was very important for our livelihood so we tended it well ..."*

"You're miles away again, Alexia. Is something bothering you?"

"What did you say?"

"I said you're miles away."

"I am daydreaming, I always do."

"I do that too."

Alexia and Anna-Marie's Thursday date is pleasant, though brief. The two young men are well behaved. The conversation is mostly about the new experience away from home. It seems that Alexia is the farthest from home. Her date, Douglas Wheeler, as Anna-Marie said, is from Hyden, New York. He is in fact good looking, intelligent and very interested in classical music, more so than either Anna-Marie, or Lloyd Williams, but not much more than Alexia, who finds herself attracted to the young man. She is mystified by her feelings. This curious feeling scares her, as if she shouldn't have it.

In the conversation Anna-Marie discloses that Alexia has agreed to go home with her for Thanksgiving.

Lloyd mentions that he and his family are going to spend Thanksgiving at the home of his grandparents, along with cousins and other relatives.

Alexia and Doug remain mostly quiet that evening.

Then the two young men escort Alexia and Anna-Marie back to their dorm.

"How did you like your date, Alexia?" Anna-Marie asks when the two girls return to their room.

"He's a quiet guy. I liked him. Actually they're both nice and interesting."

"Doug is good looking, isn't he?"

"Yes, he's very good looking."

"Maybe all four of us will go out again, what do you think?"

"I still don't know the guy, and I'm not sure I want another date so soon."

"He liked you, let's try going out with them again! Doug's all right, and he liked you, and Lloyd likes me. I want us to go out with them again, let's try it. Don't be afraid, I'll always be with you."

"We'll see."

Chapter 41

One afternoon, a few days after Anna-Marie and Alexia double date, Anna-Marie arrives at her and Alexia's dorm after her classes. She overhears a student asking the girl behind the desk in the hall about Alexia Hartley. "I'm her roommate," Anna-Marie volunteers, do you want me to give her a message?"

"Yes, please, my name is Ronald Barton. I'm related to Alexia, but we've never met." The young man hesitates. "Please tell her that I'm Christine Arlington Barton's son. She'll know who I am. Thank you so much."

"I'll tell her, I am sure she'll come down shortly."

"Thank you, I'll wait for her here."

Anna-Marie goes up to her room and immediately advises Alexia that there's a young man down in the hall who wants to meet her.

"What does he want?" Alexia asks nervously. "Who is he?"

"His name is Ronald Barton," Anna-Marie says casually. "He said that his mother is Christine Arlington Barton, and that you would recognize the name."

Alexia's face turns white. She is speechless.

"What's the matter, Alexia?"

Covering her face, Alexia does not answer.

"Is anything the matter?"

"Yes, but I'll tell you later. I don't want to meet him, I can't Anna-Marie, I can't. I really can't."

"He seems very nice, and he looks like you, very much. He could even be your brother, I'm not kidding. Who is he? Why don't you want to meet him?"

"It's complicated."

"Are you afraid to go by yourself? I can come with you if you like, but you shouldn't keep him waiting. He seems very nice and polite. I'll come with you if you want."

Alexia thinks. "Let me put on some decent clothes, and I will go down."

"Do you want me to come with you?"

Alexia hesitates. "No, I'll be right back."

Alexia walks by herself in the hall of her dorm, wearing her sweater and jeans, the same she wore for the date she went on with Anna-Marie a few days before. She sees Ronald Barton from a distance. He is standing by the dorm's desk facing the outer door, and did not seem to notice her walking toward him. He is tall, blond and very handsome. The resemblance between him and her twin, Johnny, is striking. She notices that immediately, and finds herself a little more relaxed. Yet she approaches him with considerable discomfort, her heart pounding. Finally she gets closer to him.

He turns and sees her approaching. Smiling, he walks toward her, seeming to be comfortable as he examines her face. "I'm Ronald Barton, Ron, I'm Christine's son, Christine Arlington Barton's son."

"Hello," she says in a low and soft voice, extending her trembling hand. "I'm Alexia."

"Thank you for coming down," he greets her. "It's really nice to meet you," he continues to smile.

She finds herself a little more comfortable. "Thank you for coming to meet me," she smiles back.

"Of course," he says. "Would you like to walk to the coffee shop down the hill? It's just a few steps from here."

He begins to sound like Johnny. She hesitates. "There's a music room right here on this floor, why don't we go sit there? I'm sorry I can't stay very long. I have a lot of homework for tomorrow."

"That'll be fine," he says, blushing. "I'm sorry if I interrupted your homework.

"It's O.K."

As the two walk to the music room, she finds herself attracted to the young man walking by her side and intrigued by his resemblance to her twin. She is touched by his polite shyness. She even finds herself curious about him, wishing to spend more time speaking and listening to him speak, but she is conflicted. What does he want from me, and why has he come to see me? Does he know how much I despise the grandfather he and I share? Probably not, and I need to be as polite as he has been. But who may have urged him to come and see me, or twisted his arm to come and see me? Is that why he is shy and blushes when he speaks to me? Yet he doesn't only look like Johnny, he even sounds and acts like him, and I want to hear him speak more until I can figure him out. Maybe he's very nice after all. He's not like the monster bishop."

"I hope you're enjoying Ivy," he says.

"I'm trying to get used to it," she says, sensing a warm feeling settling within her. She is surprised by the warmth of his friendliness. She feels comforted by it, but at the same time a little frightened by it.

"I'm sure you will get used to it soon," he says.

"I hope so," she says looking at him closely again, mystified by his resemblance to Johnny, "I am swamped with my homework, I can't stay very long this time, but can we try to meet again later, maybe Friday afternoon? Would you like to come again? Maybe I can have you meet my roommate Anna-Marie again. The three of us could walk to the coffee shop down the hill."

"Yes, that could work," he says. "I could invite my roommate too."

"Cool," she says. "Let's go sit over there for a few minutes." What's the matter with me? Am I losing my senses? Alexia asks herself. Why am I doing this? I hardly know him. What if he looks and sounds like Johnny? I should be more careful, yet he does seem gentle and nice, and I must be careful not to blame him for what the bishop did to Grandma Rose-Anne.

"Please thank your roommate for me. I'm sure you'll both like my room-mate. He's a great guy."

"How did you know about me?" Alexia smiles, "and how did you know I live in this dorm?"

"My mother wanted me to come and meet you, and invite you to our home in Ashton, which is not too far from here, so I looked you up in the student directory."

"That's nice, and I appreciate it," she says. "I haven't seen the student directory yet. I'm glad you did that."

"Mom thinks that maybe we can take a day or two on a weekend and go visit my family."

She is startled, and does not respond.

"You can invite your roommate to come too, if you like. It's beautiful where our family lives."

"Thank you so much," she says. "I'll tell Anna-Marie."

"I know you're very busy, and I don't want to take more of your time."

"Should we meet again on Friday?" she repeats.

"Yes, that would be good," he says. "Can I give you my phone number?"

"Of course, and you already have mine, right?"

"Yes, I do," he says. "You can call me anytime," he says, handing her his phone number. "I'd like to be like a brother to you while you're away from home."

"Thank you, thank you so much, that's very sweet of you. I appreciate it very much," she is visibly touched. "I'm glad you came, and I'm looking forward to seeing you again on Friday."

Ronald Barton stands, shakes her hand warmly, and leaves.

What am I doing? Alexia asks herself again. Am I out of my mind? Do I really want to do this?

I guess you do, pure and simple.

What about Grandma Rose-Anne, have I forgotten about her?

No, you haven't. This young man is innocent, and you can't blame him for the horrible crime of Bishop Arlington.

But he's still Bishop Arlington's grandson, and his mother is Bishop Arlington's daughter.

You too are Bishop Arlington's granddaughter, and your mother is also Bishop Arlington's daughter. You can't blame yourself or your mother for Bishop Arlington's sins.

So what has struck me?

His likeness to Johnny hypnotized you, his shyness and warmth disarmed you. His unexpected visit quieted your anxiety and comforted you in your loneliness. And this is what has smitten you.

Shaken and excited, Alexia runs up her dorms stairs and into her room.

Anna-Marie is waiting for her. "You stayed longer than I expected," Anna-Marie greets Alexia. "How did it go?"

"It was amazing, Anna-Marie, very amazing, and it went extremely well, much better than I ever expected."

"You're excited."

"I'm surprised and shaken by my own reaction to him. He's a considerate and sweet guy, Anna-Marie. He wants to meet you again. Can you join us this coming Friday at 4:00 in the afternoon, in the music room, downstairs?"

"Of course I can, I would love to do that. Tell me, what happened? Who is he?"

"I'll tell you, but let's go sit down."

"Take it easy. What happened? Tell me. You're very excited."

"Am I? I want to tell you, but I want first to tell you something private about myself and about my family. That may give you an idea about why I hesitated to go down."

"What's his name? Who is he?"

"His name is Ronald Barton, and he goes by Ron. His mom and my mom are sisters, sort of. I really didn't want to go down to meet him, but I felt I had to. I almost fainted when I saw him. He's my twin Johnny's double, looks like Johnny and sounds like Johnny. He's the spitting image of Johnny. As much as I tried to cut the conversation short, I couldn't, I just couldn't. My heart got the best of me, and I couldn't do it. I had the urge to be with him and to listen to his sweet and gentle voice. I wanted to hear him speak, so I stayed with him longer than I thought I would. You know something, I'm glad I stayed with him as long as I did. It would've been horrible if I had cut his visit short, and I would've felt horrible, more horrible than I already feel about other unhappy things in my life. As much as I thought I would give him short shrift when I first went down, I just couldn't do it." Alexia looks down, perplexed. "I just couldn't."

"You did the right thing, I'm sure you did the right thing."

"I hope so."

"You said you want to tell me why you were reluctant to go meet him."

"Yes, I did say that," Alexia hesitates. "I can speak to you freely, Anna-Marie, because I feel comfortable with you, and I trust you." She hesitates again.

"If you don't want to tell me, I understand."

"No, I want to, just give me a minute to calm my nerves."

"There's no rush. Take your time. If you think it'll help you. And if I can help you, I'll be glad to do whatever I can."

"Yes," Alexia repeats. "I want to tell you about this, and I know that you're my friend, and that I can trust you, but I'm scared and embarrassed."

"About telling me?"

"Yes, but it's not because of you, it's because I'm ashamed of the whole thing, and I'm scared, but I still want to speak with you about it."

Anna-Marie looks at her roommate. She says nothing.

"Do you understand?"

"Yes, I do, but what is it?"

"I have a private secret, a private family secret."

Anna-Marie looks at Alexia again, still saying nothing.

"Can I tell you about it?"

"Of course you can."

"I want to ask you to keep it private and confidential," Alexia repeats. "Do you think you would mind doing that?"

"Of course not, if you want me to keep it private and confidential, I will. Of course I will."

"I'm sorry," Alexia fidgets. "I'm constantly worried."

"What are you worried about, Alexia?"

"Anna-Marie, I think I'm insane."

"Why do you say that?"

"Because I'm sure I am."

"You seem normal to me."

"I'm not normal. I'm crazy, scared and confused. I just don't feel safe or right, especially at night."

"Why, what happens at night?"

"I feel sick, unsettled and depressed."

"Does your mom know?"

"I haven't told anyone. You're the only one I've ever said this to."

"What makes you think you're crazy? You should tell your mom, Alexia, or you should speak with the dorm's nurse. Maybe you should talk to the university doctor about it."

"I don't want to do any of that now, I want to wait. I really don't want to say anything about it to my mom either. I don't feel comfortable doing that now."

"I really think you should speak to your mom about it, the sooner the better for you."

"I don't want to tell my mom, not now anyway."

"How about telling your dad, he seems like a very nice man."

"My dad is a wonderful man, and I love him with all my heart, but he's very busy. I might tell him later, but not now."

"That's good, but why not now? You should tell your dad now. I think that'll be better for you."

"Well, it's a complicated story."

"What is it? Tell me about it."

"It's a long story, Anna-Marie."

"But why do you think you're sick? Why are you frightened? What frightens you Alexia?"

"It's difficult for me to say why. I can tell you what's behind all this, but you must promise me to keep it very private, something you'd never tell a soul, not to your mom, or to your dad, or to anyone."

"I promise. I promise I'll never say a word to anyone, not to my father or mother or anyone, unless you say that I can."

"Thank you. You see, there's a bishop in Northern New York. He's a very prominent man. He's highly respected. Well, the private thing I want to tell you is about him and about my family. This bishop is a rapist. When he was a young man, about our age now, he raped my grandmother, the one who just died, you know? The one I told you I was very close to? He raped her and got her pregnant. And my mom, the child of that pregnancy and of that rape, was born out of wedlock. Mom found out about it about a few months ago, about the same time Grandma died. She told my dad and us about it. When my mom found out what I just told you, she wrote the bishop and said that she believes that he's her real father and asked to meet him. The bishop came to Valley Town and met my mom and dad. He admitted everything I told you. And my mom and dad and brother might be going to the bishop's home on Thanksgiving to meet his family. Ron, the guy who came to see me, is the grandson of this bishop and Ron's mom, one of the bishop's daughters, is therefore my mom's half-sister from the bishop."

"What a story!! I can't believe it. That would make anyone crazy, but why aren't you going with them?"

"I just don't want to see or meet the man who raped my grandma. My grandma always hinted to me that she had a terrible experience when she was a young girl, but she didn't tell me all the details of her rape until I was 17. It took her several days to tell me the whole painful story, when she was dying. She wanted me to be careful with guys, you know. She always worried about me. She warned me to be careful. Just before she died, she took hold of my arm, looked at me and said: 'I want you to be always careful, my dear, and don't forget that I was raped, Alexia, and be very, very careful, always very careful, my dear, won't you?' As soon as she said that, and I said, 'I will, Grandma,' she withdrew her hand slowly and died. This is my private secret, and it's driving me out of my mind. I live with it. I sleep with it. I wake up with it. I eat with it. I don't know what to do. I can't concentrate on anything because of it. I'm afraid to go out with nice young guys because of it. I'm always afraid to disappoint my grandma because of it. Even after we went out with Lloyd and Doug, I kept thinking that I may have disappointed Grandma. This is why I didn't want to go down to meet that nice kid, Ron, who came to the dorm to meet me, but I'm glad I did. I feel good about going down to meet him, Anna-Marie, but that makes me feel guilty and confused. Something about him touched me. Maybe it's his resemblance to Johnny. Maybe it's because he speaks and sounds like Johnny. Maybe it's something else, I don't know."

"Your brother Johnny must be very good looking."

"But it doesn't matter why, he made me feel comfortable. Yet I'm still feeling guilty and confused. I don't know why I should be confused. Even though I felt comfortable with him, I keep blaming myself for that, even trying to convince myself that I shouldn't like him. That's why I think I'm crazy, and out of my mind. I don't know what to do with my life."

"Now I understand why you didn't want to date. I kept asking you to go out. I'm sorry. I shouldn't have kept pushing you."

"You didn't push me, and you didn't know. How would you know?"

"You shouldn't feel guilty about seeing or meeting nice guys though, Alexia. It isn't your fault what happened to your grandma. Why should you punish yourself for that? That's not right, but I understand how conflicted you must be. Remember, what happened to your grandma happened so long ago, before you or I were born. I truly believe that you need counseling. You should speak to a professional person, who can help you. I'm glad you spoke to me about it, but you really need to speak to your dad about it, if you're uncomfortable speaking with your mom, and if you're uncomfortable look-ing for, or trying to look for a good counselor, maybe I can help you find one. What do you think?"

"Thank you, Anna-Marie," Alexia's eyes mist. "I know I should speak to my dad about it, and I almost did on the plane, but then I didn't. I'll write him about it, but not now."

"That's a good start, Alexia, the sooner the better for you. I agree that you shouldn't feel guilty about meeting Ron, and I'm so glad you met him and liked him. I'm also glad we'll see him again Friday and meet his roommate."

"I'll tell you, Anna-Marie, I'm excited about that too, and I never used to be."

"That's wonderful. Maybe by meeting other guys and going out you'll become more comfortable and that'll help you relax, but you really should speak with your dad soon, Alexia.

"I know I should."

"So you knew about the rape before your mom found out about it. You weren't surprised when your mom came home from her visit to the uncles and told you about your grandma's rape?"

"No, I wasn't surprised that the uncles told her about the rape, but I could never describe the shock of learning that my mom was born out of wedlock and was a rape child. That was dreadful, and the constant nagging knowledge that my brother and I are grandchildren of a rapist is more than I can take. That really kills me. It demoralizes me and depresses my spirit. I keep thinking of my grandma, Anna-Marie. Knowing that she went through horrible anguish throughout her life drives me mad. I could hear her whisper softly, yet passionately, her fragile hand gripping my arm, then falling, and her ashen face so sad. 'Be careful, Alexia, won't you?' How could I ever meet the man who raped her?"

"You can't! You can't! I understand that. That would drive anyone out of their mind. I do understand how you feel. I'm sorry, I'm so sorry for you and for your family."

"And as it becomes more and more clear to me what my mom's doing, I become so depressed that my whole life turns to total misery. That's very painful. Now I'm in more of a mess! Oh, I'm in a bigger mess! I can't study, I can't concentrate on what the professors say when they lecture, and I'm going to bust out of Ivy."

"No, you're not going to bust out of Ivy, Alexia. Don't say that, and please take it easy. You'll find a way to handle all this. You're very strong. I know you are."

"Not anymore," Alexia cries.

"You'll overcome it, I know you will."

"How can I overcome such a horrible thing? It's wearing me down, and I don't know what I'm going to do!"

"Oh, Alexia, I'm so sorry." Anna-Marie pauses, looks at her roommate and then sighs. "What a terrible thing to happen to any family!!"

"It's awful, Anna-Marie, just awful."

"You must have strong disagreements with your family over this, don't you?"

"Not with my whole family, just with Mom, I don't want to have anything to do with her. My dad's very understanding and very sweet, but sometimes he feels that he has to stand by Mom. My brother Johnny's confused. Sometimes he agrees that we shouldn't have anything to do with the bishop out of respect for Grandma, and other times he agrees with Mom, that this thing happened fifty odd years ago, when the bishop was young, that, after all, the bishop's still my mom's real father and that he, the bishop, has been transformed, has become a holy man, and what have you. That makes me so angry that I lose my senses. I'm losing my senses, and I'm becoming crazy. I don't know what to do with my life any more. I'm going out of my mind."

"Calm down, Alexia. We'll find a way, and I'll stand by you. I'll do everything I can to stand by you, but you must speak to your father, the sooner the better. You promise that you will?

"I'll speak to my dad, I will, Anna-Marie."

"What's the name of the bishop who did that awful thing to your grandma?"

"His name is Arlington, Bishop Arlington. He lives in Lake Charles, New York."

"Oh, my God, Alexia! Oh, my God! Bishop Arlington's a very distinguished and highly respected person in the State of New York. He's a very generous and kind man. He's a philanthropist."

"He's what?"

"He's a philanthropist. He's one of the wealthiest people in New York State, worth more than half a billion dollars. His name has been in the news all over New York because he just donated ninety percent of his wealth to charity, to build hospitals, schools, housing for the homeless and the poor, and other charitable and noble deeds. He's even planning on donating his ten-million-dollar mansion in Lake Charles to 'Homes for The Elderly,' an organization that takes care of elderly people who have no one to care for them. He and his wife are planning to move into a convent, near Lake Charles, and to live the rest of their lives modestly, while continuing to help the sick, the poor and the elderly. His very old mother, and one of his daughters, I think his daughter's name is Elizabeth, were mentioned in the press article as having challenged the bishop's donation on the ground of mental incompetence, but the bishop ultimately prevailed. I believe that he finally settled the matter with his mother and daughter out of court and the donation will stand."

Alexia is speechless.

"What about Ron? Why did he come to see you?"

Alexia does not answer.

"Why did Ron come to see you, Alexia?"

"I think he just wanted to meet me," she says, still digesting what she has just heard from her roommate about the bishop's donations.

"That's very nice of him. I now remember that he asked me to tell you that he's the son of Christine Arlington Barton, so Ron's mother is not the daughter who sued her father. I didn't actually make the connection, when he said his mom's name, but I can see now why you at first hesitated to go down to meet him. I'll tell you, Alexia, Bishop Arlington is very highly thought of throughout New York. If it weren't you who's telling me this about him, I wouldn't have believed it. I can fully understand now why you want me to keep it private, and I will."

"I know you will," Alexia says, "thank you, Anna-Marie."

"You're welcome."

Alexia looks through their bedroom window into the distance, reflecting, and begins to debate with herself.

I wonder if Ron would ever come to meet me if he knew how much I loathe his grandfather.

You mean your grandfather also?

I wish he wasn't my grandfather also.

But if he weren't, then Ron, whom you were smitten by, wouldn't have come to see you.

I am crazy, troubled and confused.

You should listen to Anna-Marie's advice and go to the counseling center. Or you could at least tell your dad about your problems, you love him so much.

But how could I tell Dad that I met with the grandson of the bishop who raped my beloved Grandmother Rose-Anne.

Yet you can't wait to see the grandson of the bishop again, the bishop who raped your beloved Grandmother Rose-Anne.

But I shouldn't feel that way.

Yes, you should. He's nice, kind, handsome, and he looks and sounds like Johnny. You were truly smitten by him.

"You're miles away, Alexia."

"I'm daydreaming."

"I told you that I always do that myself. I just hope that one day, for your own sake, you'll be able to get over what the bishop did to your grandma, and I'm not belittling what he did."

I too hope that I can, Alexia says to herself.

"For your own sake and for the sake of your own family, I hope that you'll get it behind you. What do you think, Alexia? What should it take for society to forgive a heinous crime, like the one committed by Bishop Arlington, and which was committed more than a half century ago?"

I have no idea, Anna-Marie, Alexia muses. And what does it mean to forgive? She continues to look at her roommate but not answering her.

"What does a perpetrator of a horrible crime have to do to be forgiven by us for his crime, Alexia?"

Alexia remains silent. She only muses with herself. I don't know, Anna-Marie, I don't know.

"In my estimation, Bishop Arlington has done a lot, as a step toward giving him that forgiveness," Anna-Marie continues.

Who are you, and who am I to be sure about that, Anna-Marie? Alexia continues to muse.

"Yet, who's anyone to judge?" Anna-Marie asks.

"I don't know," Alexia now answers, tears rolling down her cheeks as she continues to stare at her roommate. "You're a very good thoughtful person, Anna-Marie. You're a much better and stronger person than me."

"No, I'm not better or stronger than you," Anna-Marie says emphatically. "Please don't say that. Who am I to say if or when the bishop should be forgiven?"

"I don't know, Anna-Marie," Alexia continues to tear.

"If it were my grandma who was raped by the bishop, or if it were me who had to face what you face, I'm not sure that I would have the courage, or the strength, to love and forgive him. I'm only concerned about you, Alexia. I didn't mean to upset you. I'm sorry if I did."

"You didn't upset me, Anna-Marie, you didn't. I should be thinking seriously about what you say. It's very sweet of you to share my anguish about it all. I wish I could have the courage and the strength to love and forgive Bishop Arlington."

"I'm sure that you can. I'm sure that one day you can, and will. You're a very good person, Alexia."

Chapter 42

Alexia's cousin, Ron, calls her to confirm that the arrangement they made to meet again in the hall of her dorm on Friday still stands. He also wants to know if Alexia's roommate will join her so that he can encourage his roommate to come along. She confirms the arrangement, and tells him that her roommate is indeed joining her.

On Friday afternoon, Alexia and Anna-Marie wait in the hall of their dorm. A few minutes later, Ron arrives, accompanied by his roommate, Bradley Burgess. Ron introduces his roommate to the girls, referring to Alexia as his cousin, and to Anna-Marie, without mentioning her by name, as Alexia's roommate.

Alexia then introduces her: "This is Anna-Marie."

The four students exchange a few pleasantries, then they walk down the hill together to the coffee shop a little distance from the dorm.

Chatting, smiling, enjoying the get-together, they reach the coffee shop, seat themselves in a booth in a corner and begin to exchange information about themselves and about their courses at Ivy.

Alexia and Anna-Marie sit together facing Ron and Brad.

"So, you two are in the college of engineering?" Anna-Marie starts the conversation.

"Yes, we're both in chemical engineering," Ron says.

"Wow," exclaims Anna-Marie. "We're in the company of geniuses."

"I'm not so sure," says Brad, "the geniuses are in business and finance these days. Ron says you're from Virginia, Alexia?"

"Yes, I am, and you? I know that Ron's from Ashton."

"I'm from Philadelphia," Brad says, "and you, Anna-Marie?"

"I'm from near here, from Green Meadow, just a few miles from here. I'm the closest to home."

"I guess I'm the second farthest from home, after Alexia," Brad says. "Are you both in Arts and Sciences then?" he continues, addressing Alexia.

"No, Anna-Marie's in Human Ecology," Alexia says, "I'm in Arts and Sciences."

"That's because I'm the laziest of the four of us," Anna-Marie jests.

"That's not true," Alexia says emphatically. "Anna-Marie's a real worker and the smartest person I've ever met. I'm lucky to have her as my room-mate."

Anna-Marie blushes. "Thanks, Alexia."

"Alexia is not to be underrated," Ron says. "I've heard she was the valedictorian of her class of more than nine hundred, graduated with the highest honors and she has a full-tuition scholarship with room and board. I don't think any of us can claim full rides like that."

"Oh! Alexia!" Anna-Marie exclaims. "You never told me any of that, that's really remarkable, really great."

"What're you going to major in?" Brad asks Alexia.

"I haven't really decided yet, I'm taking a few different courses to help me decide. I'm taking English literature, music, history and psychology."

"Those are all really hard courses," Brad says.

"Yes, they are very demanding," Alexia concedes. "Next semester I take a class in economics, or government. My dad suggested I should. My twin Johnny is like you two, he's taking chemical engineering. He goes to Valley Town University in Virginia. It's near where I'm from. I just wonder what the first year of chemical engineering is like. What do you guys take?" Alexia asks her cousin.

"Well, Brad and I are taking Freshman English, calculus, Physics, Chemistry and Engineering Drawing. All engineering students take the same courses during the first term, and those courses are continued in the spring term."

"That's very interesting," Alexia says.

"How about you, what courses are you taking?" Ron asks Anna Marie.

"I'm taking the chemistry and physics courses you guys are taking, plus English 101 and Human Ecology 101. Now that we've resolved all this, what are you guys doing for Thanksgiving? I've invited Alexia to my house for Thanksgiving. What are you doing Brad? Since you're the next farthest from home, maybe you'd like to join Alexia and me in Green Meadow? It's only sixty miles from here. We plan on taking the bus."

"I wish I could," Brad says, "but Ron beat you to it."

"Alexia," Ron says, "I thought you and your family are all coming to Grandma and Grandpa's house in Lake Charles for Thanksgiving. Am I wrong about that? Mom said she could drive to Byron, to pick us all up."

Alexia is stunned, her face turns purple. She is speechless.

"I think I may have invited her before she knew of that," Anna-Marie says, trying to rescue her roommate.

"How about coming with us, Anna-Marie? It would be fun for all four of us to go together."

"I need to talk it over with my parents," Anna-Marie says. "I want to see what arrangements they've made. My parents might've invited other people to come to meet Alexia, and they're already expecting us. I told them about Alexia coming home for Thanksgiving with me a while ago, and they're excited about it. My parents met Alexia and her dad on our first day here. They loved her. It would be great for all four of us to be together for Thanksgiving though, Ron, but let me talk to them first, and we'll let you know. What do you think, Alexia? It's also your decision. What would you like to do?"

Recovering now from her shock, and awed by her roommate's tactful response, Alexia has relaxed. "I'd love for all four of us to be together on Thanksgiving. Let's think it over while Anna-Marie checks with her parents, Ron." But Alexia is still perplexed, despite what she said to Ron. She even finds herself, much to her surprise, amenable to considering the unthinkable, going to Lake Charles in order to be with Ron again, even though that might force her to meet that monster of all monsters, Bishop Arlington.

"Sure, we want this to work for the parents too. Talk it over then," Ron says. Turning to Alexia, he pleads: "Alexia, if it turns out that you and Anna-Marie can't come for Thanksgiving dinner, maybe you two can join us on Friday after Thanksgiving. I could come to Green Meadow to pick you two up."

Touched by his appeal, Alexia at first is unable to speak. Then she stumbles: "I'll talk it over with Anna-Marie, and call you later, Ron." Oh, my God, what's happening to me? What's happening to me? Alexia asks herself.

The four new friends are ready to say their good byes.

"It was nice to meet you," Ron says, giving Anna-Marie a hug. "Thanks for being so sweet and protective of Alexia."

"Thank you," Anna-Marie says, as she gives Ron a hug back. "You guys are great, and thanks for inviting me for Thanksgiving. I'll talk it over with my parents and with Alexia."

"It was nice to meet you," Brad hugs Alexia. "I hope we can get together again soon."

"Thanks, Brad, I had fun too."

Ron then turns to his newly discovered cousin, Alexia, opening both his arms. "Take care, Alexia," he says hugging her warmly. "I hope you catch up with your studies, and please try to join us in Lake Charles. Please do your best, Alexia."

"I will, Ron," she says, her eyes moist, "I promise, I will."

Chapter 43

"What did you think of Ron and Brad?" Anna-Marie asks Alexia when they go back to their room.

"I loved them. They're nice guys."

"Yeah, they're nice guys."

"I'm sure they are."

"They come from nice homes and good people."

"Yes, they do," Alexia concedes.

"What do you think about Thanksgiving?"

"I don't know, Anna-Marie."

"Do you feel like going?"

"I'm still unsettled. I'd like to go, but I'm still scared of going, and I wouldn't know what to do there, if I begin to feel depressed and unhinged. Would you go with me, if I could muster the courage to go?"

"Of course I'd go with you, but then I have to speak to my parents about it."

"I know, you do."

"I need to explain to them why I won't spend Thanksgiving with them. To explain to my mom why I won't be spending Thanksgiving at home, I might have to tell her some of the things you shared with me. Mom's a schoolteacher, she's very understanding, and I trust her with my life. I'm sure that she wouldn't tell anyone, especially when I explain to her how sensitive you are about it, and how confidential you want it to be."

"How about your dad, do you think she would tell your dad?"

"Not if I ask her not to, she won't."

"I don't mind if you tell your mom. I won't even mind if she shares it with your dad. Your parents are very good people."

"Thank you. I'm sure they'll let me go with you, and they won't let you down."

"I'm sure of it. So, if they say it's all right for you to go, I'll call Ron, and let him know that we'll both go with him and Brad to Lake Charles. I'll also have to tell Mom and Dad and Johnny. I feel much better doing it that way."

"This is the right way."

"I know it is. When do you think we'll go?"

"Ask Ron. When you speak with him, ask him. Ask him if his Mom's car will have enough room for all four of us. If not, maybe Mom can drive us to Lake Charles on Wednesday. It isn't that far from here. Or maybe we can all just take the bus."

"How far is it?"

"It's about a hundred and fifty miles from Byron to Ashton, and about forty-five or so miles from Ashton to Lake Charles."

"It's not too far."

"No, it isn't. I think I'll call my mom and ask her to come and pick me up, or I'll take the bus to Green Meadow. I'd rather speak to Mom in person about all this. What do you think?"

"I agree. It's much better that way. Then when you come back after you talk to your Mom, and if she lets you go with me, I'll call Ron and tell him that we can both go."

"That's right. I'm sure Mom will understand. I'm sure she won't mind if I go with you."

"I hope so."

Anna-Marie returns from Green Meadow, having secured her parents approval to let her accompany Alexia to Lake Charles. Alexia then calls Ron and tells him that she and Anna-Marie accept his and his family's kind invitation to join him and his roommate Brad for Thanksgiving at Lake Charles. Ron is delighted and tells Alexia that he will so tell his mom. Alexia then sits in her room and writes to her family:

"November 2, 1998

Dear Mom and Dad, and Johnny:

I am sorry I have not written you much lately. After the several short letters I have written, many interesting things have happened here at Ivy. First, I have been able to catch up with all my work for my courses. I have also been able to adjust to life in this fascinating place. My roommate, Anna-Marie, whom Dad met, has been wonderful. She has helped me in many difficult moments of uncertainty and adjustment. She is truly a very good and sensible person, exactly what I needed to reassure me when I needed assurance. I hope, Mom and Johnny, that you will meet Anna-Marie soon. She had graciously invited me to go home with her for Thanksgiving, and I accepted, but something unusual happened that made her and me change our plans. I had an unexpected visitor come to my dorm asking about me and wanting to meet me, it was Ron Barton. So I met him in the Music Room, on the first floor of the Dorm. I almost fell off my chair when I first saw him. The resemblance between him and Johnny was so striking that I could even have thought he was Johnny. He is the son of Christine Arlington Barton, the elder daughter of Bishop Arlington. Ron was so kind and so proper that I found myself taken by him. I could not spend much time with him, the first time I met him, but he agreed to come back a couple of days later, so that he could also meet Anna-Marie. As it happened, he had encountered Anna-Marie in the hall of the dorm, when he first came looking for me. She overheard him ask the fellow behind the desk about me, so Anna-Marie went to him and spoke with him, and she volunteered to give me any message from him. He asked her to tell me that he is a cousin, the son of Christine Arlington Barton and is waiting for me by the student desk and that he came in order to meet me. At first I hesitated about going down to meet him, but after Anna-Marie and I discussed it a little, I decided to go down to meet him. I am glad I did. The next time he came to our dorm, he brought his roommate with him, so Anna-Marie and I went out with them for coffee. It was a good experience for me to meet Ron and his roommate Brad. They're both study-ing Chemical Engineering like Johnny.

Shortly before we were about to leave, he invited me to join him and his family for Thanksgiving in Lake Charles. I almost fainted, but then Anna-Marie came to my rescue. She explained to him that she had invited me to her home several weeks before, that her parents were expecting us and that they would be disappointed if we did not go. Ron then made a very sweet appeal to Anna-Marie and to me to see if her parents would allow her to join me in going with him and his roommate to Lake Charles for Thanksgiving. After Anna-Marie spoke with her parents, she and I accepted Ron's invita-tion. I know that this will sound incredible to all of you, knowing how strongly opposed I have been to spending Thanksgiving at the home of Bishop Arlington. Yet, it seems that the experiences of the past few weeks have mellowed me a little. I have had several discussions with Anna-Marie, in one of which I have confided our family's tragic history. Anna-Marie has helped me cope with the issue of forgiveness, and has encouraged me to ask myself how long it should take for a sinner to be forgiven for a sin he committed more than half a century ago.

I know you all have been trying to help me with that difficult question. After Anna-Marie told me that Bishop Arlington has donated ninety percent of his wealth to the poor, the homeless, the elderly and the sick, I began to think that maybe his repentance is sincere after all. Yet I must confess that I am still troubled by my decision to go to Lake Charles. I find myself feeling guilty for deciding to go. The tragedy of Grandma Rose-Anne continues to haunt me, and I am not out of the woods, far from it. Yet I want to go, and I want to see Bishop Arlington face to face. Maybe that will help me overcome my grief for Grandma Rose-Anne. I still hear her voice detailing her struggle and her anguish over the beastly attack she suffered as a young woman. I hear her constantly speaking of her pain, and I see her day and night. Anna-Marie has counseled me to share that with all of you. Anna-Marie keeps encouraging me to seek professional help, Dad and Mom. I want to consider that. Perhaps when we meet in Lake Charles we can discuss that. I would like to get treated for my depression. Its pain is horrible, but I am so thankful for the comfort and reassurance Anna-Marie gives me. I cannot wait for you to meet her.

So, this is my news. I hope to write you again before Thanksgiving. I'm sorry for the turmoil I caused the family when Mom returned from her trip to our uncles' farm. The shock of learning about Grandma Rose-Anne's pregnancy after she was raped, which Grandma had already told me about, and of knowing that this resulted in Mom's birth -- all this was more than I could bear. I still struggle with it, but I am hopeful that the coming days will help me get over it.

I love and miss all of you with all my heart.

Alexia"

Chapter 44

Painfully confused and depressed after sending the letter to her family, Alexia sits in her room waiting for her roommate to return. Ron unexpectedly calls Alexia. They chat for several minutes and she is delighted. "I'm so glad you called me, Ron," she says.

"I'm also glad we were able to connect, and I want to tell you how happy Mom is that you and Anna-Marie will be coming to Lake Charles. Did you tell your family?"

"Yes, I just did, I wrote them a long letter about how we met, and how excited I am to go."

"Great, we're all looking forward to getting together. I'm really eager to meet Johnny, my double."

"Johnny is too."

"Brad was very happy to meet you and Anna-Marie. You seem to have a wonderful new loyal friend. She's so good-hearted. It shows in everything she says and does. I'm sure you must like her."

"I love her. Wait until you and Brad get to know her better. She's the best any one can hope for in a roommate. She's so thoughtful and generous. She'd do anything for a friend. Being a total stranger when I first arrived, I wouldn't have known what to do without her. I just want to tell you how much I appreciated your coming to my dorm to look for me. That has meant a lot to me. I want you to know that. I'm sure my family will also appreciate it as much as I have. Thank you very much, Ron. I'll never forget what you have done."

"You're welcome, Alexia. I'm glad you can come to Lake Charles. The whole family is delighted that you can come. They're especially grateful that you were able to change your earlier plans in order to join us. Maybe we can stop at our home in Ashton for a little rest before we go on to Lake Charles.

225

If Mom is unable to come and pick us up the day before Thanksgiving, maybe we can all take the bus to Ashton. Then I could drive all of us to Lake Charles from Ashton. By the way, Brad and I both enjoyed our get-together with you and Anna-Marie – maybe we can plan another one after Thanksgiving. Would you too like that?"

"I'd love to do that – and I'm sure Anna-Marie feels the same way, so we'll look forward to it."

"That's great. Anyhow, it's getting late now. Let's say Good Night, and I'll see you soon."

"Yes, it's getting late. Good Night, Ron. Thanks again, I really appreciate your call."

"Good Night, Alexia."

Alexia finds herself elated after her conversation with Ron. Yet her anguish over her Grandmother Rose-Anne continues to disrupt her peace of mind over and over again. She does not know how to cope with it. She is especially demoralized by her continuing depression. She waits for Anna-Marie, hoping that she can at least distract her from her ongoing distress. Torn between the joy she derives from talking with Ron, and the misery of always hearing her beloved Grandmother's voice in her ear, Alexia decides to lie down in bed to wait for Anna-Marie. Soon she hears the door open, then the familiar sound of Anna-Marie's footsteps, to which she has become attuned.

When Anna-Marie returns, Alexia instantly tells her that Ron has called. With delight she tells her roommate about the conversation she had with Ron, about the travel plan, and in particular about his suggestion that they get together again after Thanksgiving.

"That's awesome," Anna-Marie exclaims. "Of course we'd like that. I knew that they liked us. I liked them too. They seemed to be really nice, and I had fun last time. I'm so happy."

"I think it's awesome too that when we come back from Lake Charles, they'd like to take us out again. I'm very happy also, more than I can say."

"By the way, Alexia, when you were out, Doug Wheeler called. He wondered if you and I would like to go out with him and Lloyd. He said he'll call you again later. Then Lloyd called me a few minutes after that and asked if we wanted to go out with him and Doug. I told him you were still out. What do you think? Would you like to go out with these guys again?"

"I guess when it rains it pours. I really don't think I want to go out tonight, Anna-Marie. Let's see how this new relationship with Ron and Brad will develop. What do you think?"

Anna-Marie thinks. "I see your point, I really do, but I also like Lloyd and Doug very much. I especially like Doug. He's quiet and very nice. These two relationships are new, and we don't have to stop seeing Lloyd and Doug, not yet anyway. Let's tell them that we'll go out with them this time. We can decide if we want to continue later, after we know Ron and Brad better. What do you think?"

"I'm still trying to cope with too many things, Anna-Marie, and I'd like to simplify my life. I don't mind it if you'd like to go out with Lloyd tonight, but I want to stay in the dorm, listen to some music downstairs, study a little and go to bed. Is that all right?"

"That's all right. I'll go out briefly by myself with Lloyd tonight."

"I'm sorry."

"Don't worry about it. I understand exactly how you feel. It's that I already told Lloyd that I'll go out with him tonight, and I also told Doug that I'll speak to you about going out together, but I understand that you're not up to it tonight, and it may be too much anyway. If it weren't for the fact that I made the commitment to Lloyd, I wouldn't go, believe me I wouldn't."

"I'll return Doug's call, and tell him that I can't go tonight. Do you mind?"

"Of course I don't."

"I wish I felt like going out, but I'm tired. I'm sorry, Anna-Marie."

"Don't worry about it. I understand, Alexia, I really do."

Alexia calls Doug and tells him that she is very tired, and prefers to stay home, but hopes to see him again another time, when it would be suitable for him and for Lloyd, but that Anna-Marie could go out with Lloyd tonight. Doug tries to persuade her to agree on a date for two nights later. She apologizes and says that she cannot commit herself for that now. She then goes down to the hall of the dorm on her way to the Music Room. Walking by herself in the hall, and wearing her usual sweater and jeans, she is surprised to see Lloyd Williams so dressed up.

"Hey Alexia," is Lloyd's warm greeting. "Anna-Marie and I are going out for coffee. Come along and I'll call Doug so he can join us."

"Where are you going?"

"To the same grill we went the last time."

"Oh."

"Come on."

"I have too much homework," she says. Then she adds, "I just want to relax a little in the Music Room. I'm really tired and I need to study a little then go to bed early tonight. I just spoke with Doug and apologized to him. Thanks anyway."

"So, I can't twist your arm?" Lloyd persists in jest.

"No, sorry, I'm going to stay in my room tonight, thanks." She moves on.

"Do I need to go change my jeans?" Anna-Marie says when she meets Lloyd in the hall of her dorm minutes after his encounter with Alexia.

"No, you don't. I'll just take off my necktie."

"I just thought it would be informal, like last time."

"Where would you like us to go?"

"Let's just go where we went last time."

"OK."

"May I take you to dinner some time?"

"Yeah, sure."

"Maybe Alexia and Doug would go with us."

"Maybe."

He drives her to the grill in College Town again. "I don't think Alexia is comfortable with guys."

"She's reserved," Anna-Marie says. "I've never been in a pickup truck before!" she changes the subject.

"Haven't you? It isn't mine. I borrowed it from one of the guys in our dorm for the evening and I have to take it back to him tonight." Then he parks on the street next to the grill.

At the restaurant, they sit in a booth.

"Where's Alexia from?"

"She's from Valley Town, Virginia."

"So far from home, isn't she?"

"Yes, and she's trying to get adjusted to the new life away from home."

"She's really beautiful, but she must feel a little awkward with guys," he says. "I can understand that. Young and away from home, she's probably homesick."

"I'm sorry Alexia couldn't make it tonight. Where did Doug go?"

"He stayed at his dorm. I urged him to call Alexia again, but she said no again. We could've gone out together, but she really didn't want to go out. She told him she needed to study tonight."

"Alexia's worried about her courses. I didn't know that he called her twice. In fact, I took one of his calls, and told Alexia."

"I spoke to her too, in the hall here. She was on her way to the Music Room, after she told Doug she didn't want to go. I tried to encourage her to go."

"What did she say?"

"She said the same thing."

"I know she's tired tonight, and she's busy with her courses."

"I think she has a problem."

"What problem?"

"I don't know."

"She's just shy, and is trying to feel her way in a new place. That's all."

"I think she has complexes about guys."

"No, I don't think she does. She's just shy."

"I just sort of feel that she has a problem."

"What gives you that feeling? You can't really say that she has a problem, when you don't know her, can you?"

"Didn't you notice how quiet she was last time?"

"Well, if you were a total stranger in a place like Ivy, and as far away from home as she is, I bet you'd be quiet too."

"I guess I might."

"She's not used to this area."

"The winter can be really cold, and she might be worried about that."

"She actually told me that she's looking forward to the snow, but she worries about the cold."

"Anyone who comes up north has to have a warm wardrobe, but she wasn't wearing anything warm enough and was shivering. Did you notice that?"

"I guess she'll have to buy some winter clothes. I'm going to take her to a nice store near Byron which isn't too expensive."

"Do you think money's a problem?"

"I don't think so. And you know, she's very smart. She was valedictorian of her graduating class of more than nine hundred students, so she has a full-tuition scholarship from Ivy, with room and board."

"That's amazing. Tell her there're nice and inexpensive stores in Byron, not too far from the Campus. I can show you where they are if you want. Tell her it'll be very cold soon in Byron, and she really should buy winter clothes pretty soon."

"Thanks, Lloyd, but if you don't stop talking about Alexia, I am leaving!"

"I'm sorry."

After a little while Lloyd takes Anna-Marie back to her dorm.

Chapter 45

Alexia is in her room by herself, waiting for Anna-Marie to return. She's just back from the Music Room. She begins to hear again the last song she listened to there. Alone and melancholy, she begins to sing that song softly under her breath. Then she remembers:

"...I have something private I would like to share with you."

She stops, stares out the window into the darkness and begins to imagine herself with her newly found cousin, Ron. She imagines herself looking into his deep-set eyes with devotion. She imagines herself touching his lips with hers gently, then passionately. She imagines him gently holding her close. She imagines herself walking with him on the sands of Lake Byron, both of them barefoot, both in bathing suits. They are all alone. She imagines him holding her hand. Should we go in for a swim? Heat rising through her body, and blushing, she nods her head approvingly. They begin to swim in the warm water of Byron Lake. The lake is all theirs. Touching and caressing each other sweetly and gently, they finally embrace fully. The intensity of her joy overpowers her even as she relaxes again in contentment.

Embarrassed, she recovers from her daydreaming. She begins to reflect on her attraction to her cousin Ron. What is it? She asks herself. Perhaps it is his unexpected and cheering visit at the very moment I needed a visit and some good cheer. Perhaps it is his surprising and uncanny resemblance to Johnny. Perhaps it is that he is unbelievably handsome. Perhaps, but it is his warmth that has meant the most to me.

Then she remembers:

"... I was a very bashful child, my dear, who preferred my own company. As I may have mentioned earlier, in the summers I never wore shoes, except to go to church."

She begins to sing softly again, then she turns to a poem she had composed the night before and begins to sing it to herself softly.

Finally, Anna-Marie arrives. She finds Alexia waiting for her.

"I'm glad you're back," Alexia greets Anna- Marie. "I couldn't go to sleep, so I decided to go down to the Music Room for a little while, and come back to wait for you. How was your date?"

"It wasn't too bad, but I like Ron and Brad a lot more."

"What happened?"

"Nothing special, but I think that Ron and Brad are more fun. I find myself more comfortable with them. Anyhow - when do you want to go and get yourself some winter clothes, Alexia? You'll need them sooner than you think."

"Soon, but sometime you and I should also go see Byron College, how far is it?"

"Just about four or five miles drive from here, it's a nice small college. I'm sure you would be impressed with it. That's great that you want to see it, we can take the bus there. Would you like me to tell Doug about that? He can meet us and show us around. Does that sound good?"

"No, not yet, let's just you and I go for now. Actually I never heard of it until you told me about it."

"You haven't heard about it because you're from out of state. Even some New Yorkers think Byron College is associated with Ivy. Are you sure you don't want Doug to go with us? He's really very nice. He says Byron is a good school, I am sure he'd love to show us around."

"I'm sure it's a good school, I've been reading about it. Some programs there sound really great. It's much smaller than Ivy though. Please let's go by ourselves for now. I'd feel better about it that way. And when do you think you can go with me to buy some winter clothes? You're right, it's getting cold, and I need to buy something warm. That'll also be a good distraction for me."

"We can go tomorrow, if you like."

"Yes, let's do it tomorrow, then we can go see Byron College quickly. I want to visit their music department."

"OK, cool. As I said, Doug said they have a really good music program."

"I'm sure of it, they do."

"What makes you think of Byron College, Alexia?"

"I like music. It calms my nerves, and distracts me from my depression. My Grandma, the one I was telling you about? She loved music too. She always thought I was very musical. Maybe I should take a course or two in music at Byron. I want to think about that. It's something different and exciting, but it might not be practical, since I don't have a car, and I can't be sure if the bus would work to get me there and back without my missing any of my courses at Ivy."

"If it's just one course a term, you can take that here at Ivy, but if you want to switch to music as a major, then maybe you would want to consider Byron College. I think Ivy is much better for you, and you have a scholarship."

"I'm not thinking at all of transferring to Byron College, Anna-Marie. That's not why I want to visit. I would just want to take one course a term there, but I'm sure it may be difficult because of the transportation problem."

"That might be hard on you too, Alexia."

"Yes, it might be." Alexia sighs.

"My mother went to that school and loved it though. She and Dad were married in Byron and I was born here in Byron, where Dad had his first job. My parents urged me to apply to Byron College as a second choice, but when I was accepted at Ivy, it was my first choice."

"Oh, well. I'm not really sure I want to take another course at another college now, but I just want to take a look."

"It doesn't hurt to take a look, but you like it here at Ivy, don't you?"

"I do, very much, but it's very hard work, and I'm not sure of myself. I'm still apprehensive and restless. I feel lonely and nervous most of the time, Anna-Marie. I felt that loneliness after I wrote my mom and dad and Johnny. I also feel guilty seeing guys. As much as I look forward to seeing Ron and Brad, I feel guilty about feeling that way. Even when Ron calls, and I am delighted with his call, it doesn't seem right to be feeling so good after I speak with him."

"That's so sad. I feel for you from the bottom of my heart, Alexia, but I'm glad you wrote your family. Did you tell them you think you need professional help?"

"I did, and I also wrote them about you, and about how helpful you've been to me."

"I'll do anything for you, Alexia. I know you're homesick, and I'm so sorry you're homesick. I wish so much that I could convince you that you have nothing to feel guilty about. You shouldn't feel guilty seeing nice guys. It isn't your fault what happened to your grandma. Why should you punish yourself for that? That's not right. I'm glad you wrote your family about needing professional help."

"I'm too."

"And you told your family that you knew about the rape before your mom found out, and that you weren't surprised when your mom told you about your grandmother's rape?"

"Yes, I did. But I'll tell you, Anna-Marie, I could never describe the shock of learning that my mom was born out of wedlock and was a rape child. That was dreadful, and the constant nagging knowledge that my brother and I are indirect products of rape is more than I can take. I keep thinking of my grandmother. Knowing that she went through horrible anguish throughout her life drives me mad. I continue to hear her whisper softly, yet passionately, her fragile hand gripping my arm, then falling. Now I'm about to meet the man who raped her. How could I ever meet the man who raped Grandma Rose-Anne? Yet I have decided to do exactly that. I'm so conflicted over that, and it makes me very sad and unhappy with myself. That's why I'm always in agony, and have this strong feeling of guilt, Anna-Marie. If I can convince myself that seeing the bishop isn't so bad, I'll feel much better about our going with Ron and Brad."

"I'm sure that your Grandma meant well when she told you of her rape and of the details of her tragic experience, but I'm willing to bet that if she knew how horrific and traumatic that has been for you, she would never have told you."

"In fairness to her, Anna-Marie, she asked me if I wanted to know, and she hesitated at first about telling me, but I insisted. I brought it upon myself, Anna-Marie."

"No, Alexia, you didn't. She must've started it, otherwise how would you know anything about it. Even though she hesitated, and even though you insisted, if she knew how difficult this would be on you, I'm almost certain that she wouldn't have told you anything of what she did. Look at it this way, the grandmother who loved you, and whom you loved so dearly, has unwittingly brought this pain and suffering and anguish and depression to you, her beloved granddaughter. Think about it, and maybe this should make you reconsider your feeling of guilt. No loving parent or grandparent would ever think of inflicting such pain on someone he or she loves. I'm sure if she knew of your pain, she'd be the one to feel guilty, not you the innocent and vulnerable child, Alexia."

Alexia is startled. "Grandma Rose-Anne didn't mean to hurt me. She didn't want to tell me, but I begged her to. I mentioned that to you before, Anna-Marie. So there's no way I can blame Grandma Rose-Anne. That's not right. It's the bishop who's to blame for what he did, and for all this, not Grandma Rose-Anne. Grandma was the victim, Anna-Marie."

"I know," Anna-Marie says, "but you shouldn't feel so guilty."

"I know that I shouldn't feel guilty, but as it becomes clearer and clearer to me what I'm doing, wanting to be closer and closer to Ron, and in order to be closer to Ron, I'm willing to meet Bishop Arlington at his home, I become very depressed when I realize what I'm doing. And when I'm depressed, I can't study. I can't concentrate on what the professors say and begin to worry again about busting out of Ivy and losing my scholarship."

"You're not going to bust out of Ivy ever, Alexia. You're too smart for that. Take it easy. You'll find a way to handle all this. You're very strong. I know you are."

"I'm not strong anymore, Anna-Marie. I'm not." Alexia cries. "I love my mom, and I don't want to argue with her, even if I'm angry over what she did. My dad told me that Mom changed her mind over the inheritance. I hope that's true, and if it is, then I don't have any issue with Mom any more. I don't want to fight with her, or with anyone. I love my mom, and I love my dad, and I love Johnny. Dad's a wonderful man. I love Johnny with all my heart, but he's confused, like I said before. Sometimes he agrees that we shouldn't have anything to do with the bishop out of respect for Grandma, and other times he agrees with Mom, that this thing happened a long time ago, when the bishop was young, that, after all, the bishop is still my mom's real father and that he has been transformed, has become a holy man, and what have you. That drives me crazy." Alexia begins to cry again.

Anna-Marie listens, looking very sad and broken hearted.

Finally, Alexia calms down. "Thank you, Anna-Marie, thank you. I keep you worried about me and I shouldn't. How did you like going out with Lloyd again?"

"I liked it. He's a nice guy, considerate, not pushy, but he's too inquisitive."

"About what?"

"About a lot of things, don't worry about it, but as I said before, I liked Ron and Brad more, and I was nervous after you told me about the bishop, but the minute I said I wanted to go back to the dorm he brought me right back."

"That's good. Are you glad you went then?"

"I am, but I may not going out with him again."

"Why?"

"I agree that we should concentrate on Ron and Brad. I like Doug, though, and he likes you too. Maybe you should go out with Doug by yourself sometime. He'd love to see you again, I'm sure, and it would distract you from some of the things that are on your mind. You may not have that feeling of guilt, if you went out with Doug, what do you think?"

"We'll see."

"You should try to see people, different people, and you should speak with your family, especially with your dad and with your brother, a lot. You shouldn't isolate yourself."

"I know."

"I was saying, the minute I said to Lloyd I want to go home, he just brought me back. Doug would do the same, I'm sure."

"I'm sure he would."

"You wouldn't be nervous with Doug, he's nice and considerate, and you wouldn't feel guilty going out with him maybe? He keeps asking me about you."

"What does he say?"

"He's politely curious about you, about your accent, I guess. He knows you're far from home. He knows you're a good person and you're very pretty."

"He doesn't know how crazy I am."

"You're not crazy, Alexia. Please don't keep saying that you're crazy. You're not!

"I'm a mess."

"Doug wants to take you out again. Maybe you'll go to a movie with him. Please try, and don't be nervous. He's a nice kid. I'll come with you. I'll never leave you for a minute."

"I know that, and he's a good kid, I'm sure, but I'm not good company now, and I'm still confused—conflicted." And I'm smitten by my own cousin Ron, the bishop's real grandson, she says to herself. She then begins to hear the words of Grandma Rose-Anne reverberate in her ears again:

"... We had a piano in the living room ...It was considered mine because no one in the family played the piano and I was being given lessons ... I really wasn't very interested in learning to play ... Because the lessons were expensive for our family's limited income, I didn't take lessons for very long ..."

Chapter 46

It's noon, Wednesday, the day before Thanksgiving, when Michael, Carla and Johnny arrive at Bishop Philip Arlington's home in Lake Charles, New York. The Arlington house is a three-story Adirondack stone structure. It is built on a hill with fifty acres of wooded land around it. There are patches of snow in the more remote areas stretching beyond the carefully tended land adjacent to the imposing building. Lampposts topped with white globes surround a large parking area close to the house. A long driveway is lined with neatly trimmed evergreen trees. At the entrance to the long driveway is a white double-door iron gate mounted on two carved granite lamp posts again with more white glass globes.

Dressed formally in a suit and white collar, Bishop Arlington greets Carla, Michael and Johnny at the front door. "Welcome, my dear," he says, embracing Carla warmly.

"What a sublime setting," Carla says, as she returns the bishop's embrace. "Let's go in before you catch cold."

"I'm used to this cold weather," the bishop says as he turns to greet Michael. "It's wonderful to see you again, Michael. I'm glad you could all come."

"Hello, sir, hello," Michael says, greeting the bishop warmly.

"And of course this is my grandson and young friend Johnny," the bishop says, extending his hand, and then hugging him affectionately.

"Hello, sir," Johnny says.

Bishop Arlington guides the Hartleys into a vestibule leading to a high ceiling foyer where his wife waits. The ceiling and walls are decorated with large religious murals. On one wall is an image of Jesus and on the opposite wall an image of the Virgin Mary holding the Christ Child. Carpeted circular stairs lead from the foyer to the upper floors. There is an elevator door to the left of the stairs. To the right, just beyond the foyer, is a large office. To the left is the living room.

"This is my wife, Grace," the bishop says.

"Welcome to our home," Grace says as she kisses and embraces Carla.

Then she turns to Michael. "And this is Professor Hartley, Carla's husband."

"Yes," Carla says, "my husband, Michael, and our son, Johnny."

Grace Arlington is a tall, dignified and attractive woman. She has white hair and hazel eyes, but she appears more youthful than her age. She wears a simple crimson dress, with a light pink scarf at her neck. A gold leaf pin with a large pearl in its center is clasped to her dress. Despite her dignity, she seems a little tense. "Won't you please come in the living room," she says, leading them to the warm, cheerful room and inviting them to sit down.

"You have a beautiful home," Carla says.

"Thank you," Grace Arlington replies.

There are two heavy, elaborately carved oak doors on either side of the living room. One leads to a library that adjoins an auditorium, both of which can be seen from the living room. The auditorium can accommodate an audience of fifty or more people. The door on the opposite side opens onto a long hallway leading to several bedrooms.

"Did you have a pleasant flight?" the bishop asks.

"We did," Carla says, "except for a long wait at the Ashton airport for the car we rented so that we can drive to Byron later. I guess it's because we're from out of state."

"These delays can be annoying. Let me just give you an idea of our program. Mother lives with us. She has a suite upstairs and she's looking forward to meeting all of you."

"We would love to meet her," Carla says.

"Great," the bishop says. "Then our daughter Elizabeth will be coming with her family from Stratford very shortly. Christine and her family will arrive from Ashton later this evening. She'll bring her children with her. I'm told that Ron will drive another car and bring Alexia and her roommate, as well as Ron's roommate with him. We have a small chapel on the ground floor, and we like to celebrate Evening Prayer at 5:00 You're all invited to join us if you'd like, but please don't feel you have to come."

"We'd be glad to join you," Carla says.

"That's right," Michael says. "We'd like that."

"How about you, Johnny?" the bishop asks turning to Johnny with an affectionate smile.

"I'd like that too, sir."

"In the morning, at about 7:30," the bishop continues, "we have Morning Prayer on Thanksgiving. Again, you're all invited, but don't feel obliged to go. You may prefer to sleep late. It's traditional in our family that on Thanksgiving, and when everyone is here, we worship together. We do the same on Christmas Night. As I said, you're all invited and welcome to join us, but do whatever makes you all comfortable. I expect that Christine and her family will join the service tomorrow, and hopefully Alexia and her roommate will join, as well as Ron and his roommate. We'll see how the young people feel."

"I would love to come at 7:30 tomorrow," Carla says. "Michael?"

"Yes, that sounds good."

"And Johnny?" the bishop smiles.

"I'll be there, sir."

"Splendid. Would you like to read the Prayers, this evening, Carla?"

Carla appears surprised. "Yes, of course. Would you show me when and what to read?"

"The Bible will be on a podium, in the center of the Chapel, my dear. It isn't difficult. I'll give you the passage you'll be reading before we go down. I'll also give you a signal when it's time for you to read."

"Thank you," she says, appearing slightly uneasy.

"Christine, I am sure," the bishop says, "wouldn't mind reading the first lesson tomorrow. She's done that many times. And I'll ask Elizabeth to read the second lesson. She's also done that many times. I'll of course read the Holy Gospel. If you like, Carla, you can read the Prayers of the People on Thanksgiving tomorrow too."

Yes," she says, still somewhat uneasy, "I can do that."

"I think Elizabeth and her family have arrived, Philip," Grace says to her husband.

"Good. I thought they'd be here soon. You may remember that Elizabeth is the one with twins. They're fifteen. Young Bryan is a few minutes older than Jennifer. He was named for Elizabeth's husband, who's an industrial engineer and takes care of our family's business in Stratford."

Carla, Michael and Johnny listen politely.

Elizabeth Arlington Robinson and her husband Bryan Robinson, with their twin children then walk in. Carla and Elizabeth immediately walk toward each other and embrace warmly.

"It's so good to have you join the family," Elizabeth says. "It means so much to us."

"I'm happy to be here, very happy," Carla says.

"So are we all," Elizabeth says. "This is my husband Bryan, and these are our twins, Bryan and Jennifer. I understand that you also have twins."

"Yes, and we brought one of the twins with us, our son Johnny. Alexia is coming with Ron from Byron. She and Ron met at Ivy. And this is my husband, Michael."

Michael embraces Elizabeth, and her husband, Bryan, embraces Carla. Then Johnny shakes hands with both of them and their two children.

"Mother is waiting upstairs," the bishop says. "Christine and her crowd won't be here for a few hours. Why don't we all go upstairs to greet Mother. She's very eager to see Carla and her family."

"Philip," Elizabeth addresses her father.

"Yes, my dear."

"Why don't you and Grace go with Carla and her family upstairs in the elevator, we'll take the stairs and follow you."

"Yes, that's a good idea."

The elderly Mrs. Arlington is in a wheel chair when the bishop, Carla, Michael and Johnny enter her suite. Carla and the bishop go in first. "This is our newly found daughter, I can tell," the elderly woman says, then looks at Carla closely, "Oh, Philip, you're absolutely right, she is Christine's double," the elderly woman exclaims, extending her hand to Carla. "What a miraculous thing!"

Carla walks toward her and shakes her hand gently. She then bends over, to kiss her. "Hello, it's so nice to meet you," she says.

"I am so happy to meet you," the bishop's mother says to Carla. "You have no idea how happy I am to see you. God works in mysterious ways. Yes, it is wonderful. Is the gentleman behind you your husband?"

"Yes," Carla says, now feeling the emotion in the encounter, "this is my husband, Michael Hartley."

"And is the young man your son?"

"Yes, this is our son, Johnny."

"What a nice looking young man! And he looks like Ron, Christine's older boy. Come closer to me, my dear," she continues, extending her hand to Johnny, "I want to kiss you."

Johnny walks toward the elderly woman, shakes her fragile hand very gently, bends over her and hugs her as she embraces and kisses him.

"Do you have only one child?" the elderly woman asks.

"Johnny has a twin sister," Carla says nervously, "but she couldn't come with us, she's coming with Ron, whom she met at Ivy University. Ron and his roommate and Alexia and her roommate are all coming together in Ron's car."

"Like our younger granddaughter, Elizabeth. Maybe Philip told you that she too has twins."

"Yes, and we've already met them."

"I'm so glad I'll have a chance to see your other child. Only God knows how much I prayed for your mother. He was listening, I know that now. What a glorious thing! It's just marvelous."

"Would you like to join us for the Evening Prayer, Mother?" the bishop asks his mother, raising his voice.

"I wouldn't want to miss that. What do I call you, my dear?"

"'Carla,'" Carla says, now raising her voice. "My name is Carla."

"Yes, come to think of it, Philip told me your name is Carla. It's a very nice name. Your mother named you for her father. That was good. What a delightful evening! Come closer, Carla, and sit near me. This is a great occasion. I'm so happy it turned out this way. God is merciful."

Chapter 47

"My goodness, Mike," Carla whispers after their visit to the bishop's mother, on their way to the chapel on the ground floor, "did you hear Elizabeth call her father 'Philip,' and her mother 'Grace?'"

"That's why he wants you to call him 'Philip.' Michael whispers back.

A wide-open side entrance with a wooden arch of oak leads to a small chapel on the ground floor of the Arlington home. About fifty empty chairs are placed facing the altar. On the altar wall, between two similarly arched small stained glass windows, is a mural depicting Christ on the Cross. The sidewall opposite the entrance has another pair of arched, clear glass windows overlooking a garden. There are two rows of benches on either side of the chapel, between the first row of chairs and the altar. These benches are at right angles to the altar, two steps higher than the chapel floor. There are two arched side doors, with stained glass, one leading from the altar to the Sacristy, and, on the opposite side, the other leads to the garden. The floor of the chapel is of mosaic tile.

Elizabeth wheels her grandmother through the entrance and into the center of the chapel, placing her between the two sets of side benches so that she faces the altar. She then seats herself with her husband and two children on one of the benches to the right.

Carla, Michael, Johnny and Grace sit on the opposite side benches, facing the Robinsons.

All except the elderly woman kneel as they wait for the bishop to come in from the Sacristy.

At the stroke of five, the bishop, carrying a Bible and a Book of Common Prayer, enters.

They all stand up except the bishop's mother, who remains seated in her wheel chair.

"Brothers and sisters in Christ," the bishop begins: "One of the great joys of our being is to freely choose to share ourselves with our human family. We call this kind of generosity 'Love.' Now, all human free choices are derived from God, because only God is absolutely free. Only He can make absolutely unconstrained free choices. God chose to share Himself with humanity by creating us in His own image. This is because God's nature is Love. This is why Love is an essential joy of our being. And if the joy of Love is something we derive from God, then the authenticity of each one of us depends upon giving the Love we derive from God to our human family. Our human wholeness and happiness are absolutely contingent upon this. Amen."

"Amen," they all say.

"Page 115 of the Book of Common Prayer," the bishop then says, giving a sign to Carla.

Carla walks to the podium. She appears very nervous.

All eyes are trained on her.

She examines the pages of responsive reading before her, and begins to read in a low and uncertain voice:

The congregation, in unison say, Lord have mercy, after each of her paragraphs of the reading.

Let my prayer be set forth in your sight as incense, the lifting up of my hands as the evening sacrifice ...

Lord have mercy

Grace to you and peace from God our Father and from the Lord Jesus Christ ...

Lord have mercy

Worship the Lord in the beauty of holiness; let the whole earth tremble before him ...

Lord have mercy

Yours is the day, O God, yours also the night; you established the moon and the sun. You fixed all the boundaries of the earth; you made both summer and winter ...

Lord have mercy

I will bless the Lord who gives me counsel; my heart teaches me, night after night. I have set the Lord always before me; because he is at my right hand, I shall not fall

Lord have mercy

Seek him who made the Pleiades and Orion, and turns deep darkness into the morning, and darkness the day into night; who calls for waters of the sea and pours them out upon the surface of the earth: The Lord is his name ...

Lord have mercy

If I say, "Surly the darkness will cover me, and the light around me turn to night," darkness is not dark to you, O Lord; the night is as bright as the day; darkness and light to you are both alike …

Lord have mercy

Jesus said, "I am the light of the world; whoever follows me will not walk in darkness, but will have the light of life

Lord have mercy

Carla walks back to her seat.

The Bishop says: Let us confess our sins before God our Lord.

The Congregation:

Most merciful God,

We confess that we have sinned against you,

In thought, word and deed,

By what we have done,

And by what we have left undone,

We have not loved you with our whole heart;

We have not loved our neighbors as ourselves,

We are truly sorry and we humbly repent.

For the sake of your son Jesus Christ,

Have mercy on us and forgive us;

That we may delight in your will,

And walk in your ways,

To the glory of your name

Amen.

The Bishop:

Almighty God have mercy on you, forgive you all your sins through our Lord Jesus Christ, strengthen you in all goodness, and by the power of the Holy Spirit keep you in eternal life.

Amen

"It was a lovely service," Carla embraces the bishop after the service.

"You read very well. I am delighted that you could join your family in this service."

"Thank you very much. I'm glad you asked us to come, and asked me to read."

"All of us enjoyed the service," Michael comments.

"Thanks for joining the family in prayer. I hope the service wasn't too long for all of you."

"Not at all," Michael says.

They all return to the living room when the doorbell rings.

"That must be Christine and her family," the bishop says.

"Yes," Elizabeth replies. "I'll answer the door."

When Christine, her husband, Dean, and her younger son, Scott, enter the living room, Christine and Carla immediately walk toward each other and embrace warmly, forgetting formal introductions.

"Even I can see that we're sisters," Christine says.

"Yes, we must be," Carla says.

"When Philip described the resemblance we have to one another," Christine continues, "I wondered what to expect, but now I can see what he means. I feel like I'm looking at my double."

"I feel the same way," Carla smiles.

"That's phenomenal. Well, let me introduce my family. This is my husband, Dean, and this is our son, Scott. Ron and Alexia and their guests were behind us. They'll be here soon, I'm sure."

"And this is my husband Michael, and our son John, we all call him Johnny."

"I can even see resemblances between our children."

"Yes, I can too."

"Wait until you see Ron. He even looks like Johnny. I'm sorry we're a little late. We had to wait for Ron and Alexia and their friends to arrive. They arrived about one hour later than we expected."

Chapter 48

The doorbell rings again.

Elizabeth rushes to the door. "Hello, hello, come right in, hello, Ronny, bring your guests in and introduce them to everybody. I can tell, this is Carla's child, Alexia," Elizabeth says, embracing Alexia.

Fatigued, frightened and quivering, Alexia looks at Elizabeth Arlington Robinson, not knowing who she is, gently releases herself from the embrace and awkwardly extends her hand. "Hi, yes, I am Alexia," she says in a faint voice. Anna-Marie to her side, and following Ron and Brad, she looks toward the spacious living room, where she immediately spots Johnny, her dad and her mom standing with a small group of men, women and kids waiting, none of whom looks familiar to her. She relaxes a little and begins to feel safer. Her quivering subsides somewhat, but she is still nervous and frightened, not knowing what to expect when she meets the monster, Bishop Arlington. Then, out of the corner of her eye, she spots a tall, handsome elderly man with white curly hair and deep-set, serene blue eyes and a ruddy face. He is dressed as a cleric, and stands a step or two in front of everyone, as if waiting to receive her and her friends. This must be him, the bishop, the rapist and the philanthropist Anna-Marie admires, she tells herself. Observing the remarkable resemblance he bears to her mother, about which she heard so much, she is astounded by it. An elegantly dressed, attractive, elderly woman is at his side. As she and her friends inch closer, the clergyman begins to resemble Ron, the newly discovered cousin she is secretly smitten by. The clergyman makes a few steps to meet her and her companions. She looks at him intently, as if to verify that he is real. She is stupefied in her own reaction to him. He's human all right, she decides, agreeing with what her brother Johnny said about him earlier, and may even be nice. No, he isn't she rebukes herself, he isn't. He can't be. He's a rapist and a criminal. She takes another look toward her parents and Johnny, who exchange loving smiles with her. A feeling of comfort and confidence now begins to settle within her, but she is still unsure of herself, and doesn't know how she will react when the clergyman comes closer to her.

"Hello, my dear Ronny, hello, how good to see you," he finally says, in a familiar voice, embracing Ron, her favorite Ron, then quickly turning to Brad and shaking his hand. "I am Philip Arlington, Philip, just Philip, please. I am Ronny's grandpa, but Ron calls me Philip. All members of our family call me Philip. So please call me Philip."

"Thank you, sir," Brad says.

"Brad is my roommate at Ivy, Philip," Ron says.

"I'm delighted to meet Brad," the bishop says. Then turning to Alexia, the bishop's face lightens. A gentle, child-like smile forms on his countenance. "I know this must be Carla's child, Alexia, our beloved Alexia," he says softly. "Who is the lovely young woman with Alexia?"

"Yes, this is Alexia, Philip," Ron says. "We invited her roommate, Anna-Marie, to come with us."

Alexia is now intrigued. She begins feeling herself being absorbed into a fascinating movie. Yet she is still frightened.

"May I give you a hug, Alexia?" Bishop Arlington asks Alexia very gently as he comes closer to her.

The bishop's words shock her. She is instantly petrified. She is shaking involuntarily. She wants to say, keep your hands off me, but she is unable to speak. Yet as she looks at the smiling bishop, she continues to be intrigued. Even as she struggles, his child-like face and smile disarm her. Nodding her head approvingly, she finally mumbles, closing her eyes: "Yes, you may."

"Alexia is shivering, my dear," the bishop whispers to his daughter Elizabeth. "She must be feeling the cold. Can you get her a heavier sweater? Please turn up the heat a little in the house. Our family members from Virginia are not used to the cold of the Northeast."

Alexia, holding Anna-Marie's hand tightly, then rushes toward her brother Johnny, embraces and kisses him, then introduces him to Anna-Marie. Holding Johnny's hand tightly now, and motioning to Anna-Marie to follow her, Alexia runs toward her mother first, her eyes watering. She kisses and embraces her mother warmly. "I love you, Mom. I missed you so much."

Carla returns her embrace, holding Alexia close to her. She rubs her eyes, unable to speak.

Alexia then runs to her father with more kisses and an embrace, leaning her head on his shoulder momentarily.

"Alexia, my love," Michael says. "You've lost a lot of weight, Darling."

"This is my roommate, Anna-Marie, Mom." Alexia introduces her roommate without responding to her father's observation about her loss of weight. "You've already met Anna-Marie and you remember her, Dad."

"I do indeed," Michael turns to Anna-Marie and embraces her. "You are an angle. Thank you so much for looking out for Alexia, Anna-Marie."

Blushing, Anna-Marie remains quiet.

"Yes, we are so very grateful, Anna-Marie," Carla adds.

Anna-Marie blushes again. She continues to be quiet.

Ron then leads Alexia, Anna-Marie and Brad to the other members of his family, and introduces them, except for the bishop's mother, who has not yet joined her family. She is still in her own suite on the second floor of the mansion.

After the introductions, Alexia and Anna-Marie move to sit near Alexia's immediate family.

"Are you all right, my dear?" Michael whispers to Alexia. "You've lost weight, have you been eating well? Have you been sick, Sweetheart?"

"I'm alright, Dad," Alexia whispers back to her father. "It's just my worry about my courses and study, but I'm fine, Dad. Don't worry about me." She turns to her mother. "I missed you a lot, Mom. I've missed Dad and Johnny a lot too. And I miss Joan, do you ever see her, Johnny?"

"Yes, I've seen Joan on campus. She always asks me about you. Haven't you called her, or written her?"

"I should've written her more. I will again when I go back to Byron."

"How do you find college?" Alexia's father asks. "It's quite different from high school, isn't it?"

"Yes, it is," Alexia says, "but I was surprised how similar some of the courses I took in high school are to the college courses I am taking. There are differences, but some things about them are very similar."

The Hartley family then excuse themselves, after agreeing to join the entire Arlington family for supper at seven that evening. They go up to the third floor of the Arlington mansion, taking Anna-Marie with them. They have been given a spacious private suite there.

When they arrive at the suite, Carla takes Alexia and Anna-Marie to a pleasant room which they will share. It is next to a similar room for Johnny.

Carla and Michael's more spacious room is on the other side of the suite, next to a living room. "Let's sit in the living room for a little bit before we eat," Carla says to Alexia and Anna-Marie. "It's next to our bedroom on the other side of the suite. You can't miss it. Relax a little if you'd like to, then come back and join us. Take your time, and we'll wait for you."

In the living room of the suite, the Hartley family and Anna-Marie sit together, at first admiring and discussing the Arlington mansion and its beautiful setting. Then the conversation turns to casual questions about Alexia's experience at Ivy.

"What's your biggest surprise?" Alexia's father asks Alexia.

"My biggest surprise, honestly, Dad, was how much I missed my family and friends. I really didn't expect that." Alexia's eyes tear. "I think that I learned a lot from that. Feeling homesick forced me to think, to reflect on many things. I discovered that I was too confident, too sure of myself, almost arrogant. Being away from home has been a humbling experience for me."

"That's good, Sweetheart. I know going away from home for the first time is quite an experience. We missed you too, Alexia. We miss you a lot. Your mother and I think about you day and night, my dear."

"I know, Dad," she says, still tearing. "I know I'm being emotional, but seeing you, Mom, seeing you Dad, and seeing Johnny, all this reminds me how much I need my family, all my family. I didn't realize how much I love you guys, but I do know now."

"We all love you, Alexia," Alexia's mother Carla tries to reassure her daughter.

"I know that, Mom," Alexia chokes. "I'm sorry I have not been grateful."

"Of course you have been grateful, Alexia," Carla says. "All families have disagreements sometimes, dear, and that's part of life, part of growing up, of maturing and of living. That doesn't mean those who disagree with each other are ungrateful toward one another."

"I know, Mom," Alexia says, wanting to become close to her mother again, yet still in her heart wishing that she would pull away from the bishop, "but I caused you, all of you, a lot of grief. I know I did."

After Alexia calms down a little, Michael whispers to her: "Go wash your face, Sweetheart. We'll wait for you."

"OK," Alexia says, appreciating her father's suggestion. She goes back to her room, while her family and Anna-Marie wait for her.

"Alexia needs help, Mr. and Mrs. Hartley," Anna-Marie says in a low voice. "She's the sweetest, the kindest and one of the smartest people I know, but she needs to be helped, maybe because of the traumatic experience she had speaking with her grandmother about the rape incident. Alexia shared part of that conversation with me. She's very troubled, and she needs help."

"We know," Michael says. "We'll be going to Byron directly from here. We'll speak with her about seeing a counselor tonight or tomorrow. Thank you, Anna-Marie. This is on our minds day and night."

"It is," Carla says. "Maybe someone at Ivy can help us find someone she could be comfortable with."

"I'm sure that can be arranged, Mrs. Hartley," Anna-Marie says.

Johnny, not saying a word, just looks down, visibly concerned and shaken.

"Please give your parents our greetings and good wishes for Thanksgiving," Michael then says to Anna-Marie. "When will you see them next?"

"We'll stop at my home in Green Meadow for a few hours, before we continue to Byron."

"All of you, Ron and Brad are going with you also?" Carla asks.

"Yes, all of us, the four of us are going together."

"We'll follow you the very next day," Michael says, "the three of us will join you for a day or two. We would like to take all of you to dinner. Are you all taking the bus to Byron?"

"No," Anna-Marie says, "Ron is borrowing his Mom's car again, so Alexia and I will ride with Ron and Brad."

"The two young men, Ron and Brad, are going with you and Alexia to your home in Green Meadow then?" Carla asks.

"Yes, I invited all of them," Anna-Marie says. "Mom is preparing dessert for the four of us. I wish you all could join us."

"It's going to be difficult on this trip," Carla says, "but when we arrive in Byron, we'll take all of you out for dinner," she repeats.

"Thank you, Mrs. Hartley, but you needn't trouble yourselves."

"This is the least we can do," Michael says.

"You've been wonderful, Anna-Marie," Carla then says. "You have no idea how much we appreciate you, and your kindness and friendship with Alexia. I would love to meet your parents. Michael and I have talked about that. We hope to invite your family to visit us in Valley Town, not during the summer, when it is unbearably hot, but maybe during the winter. We'll be in touch with you."

"Thank you, Mrs. Hartley. My parents would love to meet you, I know, and I'm sure they would love to visit Valley Town."

"We'll expect you to come with them."

"I will, Mrs. Hartley."

Alexia comes back, looking refreshed, relaxed and comfortable. The conversation with her family resumes. "I'm sorry I was a little emotional," she continues, "please forgive me, but as I was trying to say earlier, I never realized how weak and vulnerable I am, and how much I need my family, all my family. Although this has been humbling, I found it very revealing. I discovered that I'm dependent on you guys, and on my friends in many ways. I guess we're all dependent on one another, and need each other. Anna-Marie has been a true friend, a strong and wonderful friend. I don't know what I would've done without her. I also decided that no matter how bad some people may be, there's always a good side to people, there can be goodness in everyone, even in the very worst of us. Anna-Marie and I have had many philosophical discussions about forgiveness. I wish I could have the strength, to be as forgiving as Anna-Marie, and I'm determined to work on it."

"That's wonderful, Alexia," Michael says to his daughter.

"I'm not there yet, though, Dad," she hastens to say. "And please don't hold your breath. I'm still struggling with my own feelings about all this." She pauses again. "Yet no matter how reflective I try to be," she continues, "and how hard I try to become a good, forgiving person, I find myself falling short. Whenever I convince myself that I should heed Anna-Marie's words about forgiveness, the voice of Grandma Rose-Anne begins to haunt me again and again. A horrible feeling of guilt then overwhelms me. I become depressed and weak. Horrible pain creeps through my whole body. Although it's I, myself, on my own, without pressure from anyone, who agreed to come to Lake Charles, the place I've dreaded, simply in response to Ron's irresistible, but casual invitation, and in order to be with my family, I find myself, even right now, with an unbearable feeling of guilt. I'm always, and constantly, plagued with anxiety and fear, all of which I can never understand or explain, and much worse, bear. Yet not wanting to be a selfish, or a self-absorbed person, or a burden on anyone, I go on with my life, as if nothing is wrong with me, but deep inside me I know better. I know there's something wrong going on inside me, but I don't know what. I also know that I'm weak, very weak, because I'm always depressed."

Her family and Anna-Marie listen, not commenting or saying a word.

"For example now," Alexia continues, "I know that I must join all of you and go back to be with Bishop Arlington, Philip, whose rape of Grandma Rose-Anne haunts me day and night. I know that I must show Bishop Arlington respect, as though nothing of what I mentioned exists, as though he never raped Grandma, whom I've loved, with all my heart. I know that I must be gracious to him and to his entire family. I know that I must work on my inner self, in order to love and forgive him. I know that I cannot and should not hate him. I know that I must not allow myself to even think about hating him. Yet a distant but powerful voice constantly nags and rebukes me. In the most heart-wrenching way you can imagine, that voice implores me not to love or ever forgive the man who raped and injured the person I was so close to, the person I loved and still love and will always love, Grandma Rose-Anne. That voice tells me and begs me even to hate the man who raped Grandma, and to despise him with all my mind, and with all my heart. Who should I listen to? Who should I listen to? I am torn. I don't know what to do. And what is worse is that I don't think that any doctor, or any therapist, or psychiatrist can resolve, or help me resolve this horrible conflict I find myself in. I like to think of myself as a reasonable and intelligent person, but no degree of reason or of intelligence has been able to, or perhaps can, bring comfort or harmony to me. Now, I know that we must go to join our host for supper. I know that we can't wait any longer." Standing up, Alexia looks pale. She is distraught and in pain. "Let's go," she says in a low and trembling voice.

"Before we go, Sweetheart, may I say a few words?"

Not expecting her father to speak, Alexia is bewildered. "Of course you may, Dad," she finally says softly.

"I just want to say, Sweetheart, how much I appreciate what you've just said. What you've said is so frank, so honest and revealing to me, that I now understand how you feel a lot better. There's nothing wrong, Sweetheart, with hating what the bishop did to Grandma Rose-Anne, and you shouldn't feel guilty about that at all, my darling. And I don't think that you have to feel rushed to forgive him. You don't have to feel that you need to forgive him instantly, or ever, my dear. You don't have to feel guilty if you cannot forgive him now, or ever, for that matter. These things take time, Sweetheart. You were very close to Grandma Rose-Anne, and even the bishop himself, I feel reasonably sure, does not expect all of us to forgive or to forget what was done to Grandma. This has been very hard on you in particular, Sweetheart, because you were the closest member of the family to Grandma. So don't feel badly about how you feel, Alexia."

"I agree with every word Dad said, Alexia," Carla says. "I couldn't have expressed it better. I just want to add that I too feel badly for my insensitive reaction to my discovery of what happened to Grandma. I didn't know that Grandma had shared, with some detail, what happened to her with you before her death. Had I known that, Alexia, I would've been more sensitive to your feelings. I just needed to say that. I agree with Dad that for you in particular it isn't easy to forget or forgive what was done to Grandma and to her family. I hope that you find what I'm saying helpful, Alexia."

"It's helpful, Mom," Alexia says, tears in her eyes again.

"And I'm sure that Anna-Marie would agree that it isn't easy for someone in your position to forgive," Michael says.

"No, it couldn't be easy," Anna-Marie says. "When we had our discussion about forgiveness, Alexia, maybe you remember that I said if it had been me who went through what you went through, I wouldn't be able to forget or to forgive. I never wanted our discussion to put an additional burden on you, Alexia. I was discussing the idea of forgiveness in general, like from the standpoint of society, not from our own individual point of view. I truly agree with what Mr. Hartley said."

"You're all very sweet," Alexia says. "Your comments Dad and Mom, and Anna-Marie, are very comforting. They're very reassuring, but I still need to work on my own feelings. I'm sure that I'd feel better, much better, if I could honestly say that I've forgiven Bishop Arlington. I hope that one day I'll be able to say that."

Alexia follows her family to the Arlington's dining room, Anna-Marie by her side.

Chapter 49

The bishop's mother is in a wheel chair in the dining room chatting with her two granddaughters.

When the Hartley family and Anna-Marie arrive, Ron immediately takes Alexia and Anna-Marie to meet the grandmother.

"I'm so happy to meet you, Alexia," the elderly woman greets Alexia. "I've heard so much about you. Ron really likes you, he admires you very much. You and your brother Johnny are twins. Did you hear that my daughter Elizabeth has twins too?"

"Yes, I did," Alexia says, "and I'm glad to meet you too." Suddenly, she begins to hear her beloved Grandma Rose-Anne again: *...The next day ... the rapist's mother returned to our apartment. Mother angrily told her about my condition. she snapped at Mother, ... stop screaming, and don't you dare scream at me again.' 'I'm sorry,' Mother said, 'but my daughter is - ah - to say the least, is very upset.... we all are upset and feel terrible,' the woman shouted at Mother again. 'My husband and I are sick over it. We want to pay for our son's horrible behavior.' 'My daughter is upstairs, and I'll certainly tell her what you've said, but she wants to miscarry.' Mother was intimidated... Would we go to jail for it? I just don't know... Mother said. 'What are we to do?!' Mother asked. ... 'I don't know what to do,' Mother cried, 'but my daughter is determined. She is adamant, Mrs. Arlington. She doesn't want the baby.... as long as it doesn't make things worse for everybody, we will pay any and all expenses for whatever your daughter decides to do.' 'Thank you,' Mother told the woman... that's why I want you to be careful. I want you to be careful always. Do you understand now? .... Yes, I do Grandma ...*

"Look at Alexia," Michael says to Carla from the other side of the room.

"She's daydreaming again," Carla says.

"Let's all get seated," Grace says. "Carla, you may sit next to Philip, there," pointing to the chair to the right of the bishop. "Michael, you can sit next to me here," pointing to the chair to her right. "Alexia, please come and sit right next to me here," pointing to a chair to her left. "And Johnny will sit next to Philip in the chair to Philip's left. Please wheel mother to her chair in the center. Anna-Marie and Brad will sit next to Mother, one to her right and one to her left. The rest of our family may sit in any of the chairs, as they wish."

Everybody is seated now. There is a moment of silence. "Philip will say grace," Grace says in a low voice.

"Our Lord God, Great Creator of the universe, architect of all things, bless this food we are about to eat, bless us to your service, strengthen all of us, your weak and humble family, in a bond of friendship and love, forgive us all our sins, and give us the strength to forgive and love those who have sinned against us. Amen."

"I have a question," Carla says, speaking to the bishop after supper, and before retiring to the suite. "I hope you can answer it for me."

"I'll try," the bishop says.

"I noticed that Christine and Elizabeth, as well as their husbands, and even their children call you by your first name, Philip. I know when you were at our home in Valley Town, you asked Mike and me to call you Philip. This is unusual, but I'm sure we'll learn to do it and get used to it. Is this a family tradition?"

"We want it to be a family tradition, my dear. If you don't mind, I'd like to address it during the service tomorrow. I'll say something about it in my sermon."

"Oh, good, we'll look forward to that."

Carla, Michael, Alexia and Johnny, as well as Anna-Marie, all retire to their suite on the third floor of the bishop's home. Alexia and Anna-Marie go to their room, and Johnny to his. Michael and Carla go to the living room.

"That young man Ron," Michael says to Carla, "has a strong resemblance to Johnny."

"He certainly does. Although Christine has been saying repeatedly how wonderful it is that Ron and Alexia go to Ivy, and have met there, I didn't dare comment on that, or say anything about it. I don't want to embarrass or upset Alexia. As I may have said before, I think that she likes Ron, and may have been smitten by him, the way she looks at him. I think it's platonic, though."

"It better be, they're cousins."

"Alexia said that Ron told her to consider him her brother."

"That's nice."

"But I think she has a crush on him, and that's why she came, Mike. She'd never have come otherwise."

"We don't know that, but what makes you think Alexia has a crush on him?"

"I know Alexia, and it kind of seemed like it, as I said, the way she acts around him and looks at him. Maybe now that she's found out that she has a cousin at Ivy, who's respectful of the bishop and who loves him dearly, that'll make her more amenable to forgiving the bishop, but her statement before supper tore my heart, Mike."

"It got to me too," he pauses. "It also scared me."

"The comment you made after that was very good though."

"I only hope that it helped. I could tell, Carla, that your support of what I said made Alexia feel good."

"I hope so."

Chapter 50

Shortly after Carla and Michael retire to their bedroom, they hear a tap at their door.

"Who is it?" Carla asks.

"It's me, Mom, can I come in?"

Carla opens the door for her son. "I'm glad you came, Johnny," Carla says. "Dad and I want to speak with you."

"Yes, come in, Johnny. Come in, I guessed that you might come." Michael is somber. "What's on your mind?"

"I'm restless, Dad," Johnny says, "and I'm worried, more than I can say."

"What's the matter?" Carla asks.

"I'm uncomfortable about the whole visit here, Mom, but I'm mostly worried about Alexia now, very worried about her."

"We all are, Johnny," Carla says.

"You're referring to what she told us before supper, aren't you?" Michael asks.

"That's right. I don't know. I just think she might be feeling more miserable and down than we all realize. That makes me feel awful. Alexia needs help, soon, very soon, Dad."

Michael flinches.

Carla stares, but says nothing.

"What are you too going to do?"

"I want to get her to a therapist, or doctor in Byron as soon as possible," Michael says, "but you heard what she said about that at the end of her conversation."

"I know, she doesn't think anyone can help her, but we need to do something very soon, without delay."

"We can't assume that she won't accept treatment, though," Carla says. "We must see to it that she's treated, even if we have to take her to a counseling center or to a hospital ourselves."

"We can't force her," Johnny says. "That won't work. It'll just make her resist all the more."

"That's right," Michael agrees, "we can't force her, and we don't want or need to admit her to a hospital. A counseling center at the University, or elsewhere, maybe."

"There must be a counseling center at the university, and that's what we should try to convince her to consider, Dad."

"Yes, but we have to do something fast," Carla says.

There is a moment of silence.

"That evening service, I really didn't like it," Johnny then says.

"Why didn't you like it?" Carla asks, seeming to be surprised.

"It was sort of creepy, and that seating arrangement at supper was weird," Johnny says.

"I think Grace wanted to seat us her own way, and more formally, which is all right. I don't see anything wrong with that," Michael says.

"But why didn't you like the Evening Prayer, Johnny?" Carla asks.

"It depressed me," Johnny says. "It made me uncomfortable and restless. It really annoyed me even."

"Why would it annoy you?"

"Maybe because I'm worried about Alexia, I'm sorry."

"We're all worried and concerned about Alexia," she says.

"Maybe because of a discussion I once had with Alexia about God and religion."

"Whatever, but we should be respectful."

"This is the way I feel, Mom."

"Forget it."

"I'm sorry, but I'm now remembering a heated discussion I once had with Alexia about God and about this whole sad thing, after we met the bishop the first time at our house, and I now know that Grandma Rose-Anne described to Alexia in painful detail how she was raped by the bishop. I really didn't want to make a big deal about it. I want to talk about having Alexia treated. Alexia needs professional help without delay, right away. Anna-Marie has told us emphatically that Alexia needs help. She also spoke to me privately about it. She asked me to tell you that it should be done really soon."

"I agree we should do it right away," Michael says, his face grim, "but how do we persuade Alexia? That's what's most important now."

"Speak with her about it before we leave here, Dad."

"I'll do that."

"Anna-Marie thinks that Alexia should be admitted to a hospital immediately. She's been living with Alexia, and she should know what she's talking about."

"Alexia will never agree to that," Carla says. "I now agree that we need to discuss it with her gently first."

"I can discuss it with her," Johnny says. "Do you want me to talk to her about it?"

"Dad's the one who should talk to her first," Carla says. "She's more comfortable with Dad. Let Dad speak with her first," Carla sighs. "I'm very scared, and I can't think clearly now. What do you think we should do, Mike?"

"Yes, I think I should be the one to speak with her, and I'll speak with her first, Johnny. I'll do that in the morning," Michael says. "I agree that it's better if I spoke with her first."

"About the Evening Prayer, Johnny," Carla resumes, "the bishop is an older man now. He's a devout and gentle soul. Religion and faith are part and parcel of his life, my dear. That shouldn't bother us. Can we look at it that way?"

"Yes, we can, but…"

"I can really understand how Johnny feels, Carla," Michael says. 'Let's leave it at that for the time being, we have other and more pressing things to worry about."

"What exactly disturbed you about the Evening Prayer though, Johnny?" Carla asks.

"I don't know, Mom, but I felt that the whole service was inappropriate."

"How?"

"Couldn't you see the pomposity of the bishop assembling his family, rising above them at the altar and preaching at them? Drawing on his superior knowledge, wisdom and holiness in this setting is inappropriate. It's kind of creepy to me. It makes me doubt God if the likes of Bishop Arlington are his servants. This is a common struggle with many young people, Mom. You should hear Alexia talk about all this."

Carla is speechless. She only stares at her young son.

"The whole service turned me off."

His head down, and his hands clasped, Michael looks at his silent wife and continues to listen to his son.

"I just feel that life is full of hypocrisy. I'm sorry, the whole thing felt wrong. Maybe he, the bishop, in this setting, out of respect to Grandma, and in deference to us, especially in deference to Alexia, who's haunted by Grandma's words day and night, and who's suffering more than all of us combined, should say: 'Our loving God, I've sinned against one helpless and innocent Rose-Anne Riley.' Not 'we have sinned against you.' He should say: 'I've been responsible for making her pregnant against her will, and bringing her daughter, Carla, to the world, and I've caused Carla and her family a great deal of suffering and pain. I'm donating ninety percent of all my fortune to the poor, and to the sick, and to the hungry, and to the victims of rape, as a token penance for my sin, and I'll continue to do more as long as I live. Take away my incredibly lavish home and give it to the homeless and to the deprived, to the victims of rape, and to the hungry in honor of Rose-Anne Riley.' We'll all say: 'The Lord be with you ... Let us pray.'"

"He's already done that, most of that. Let us be reasonable. I guess we're all tired and upset," Carla says.

"Didn't you like what I said?"

"I'm getting very tired and I need to go to bed now. Why don't you just sleep late tomorrow..?" Carla covers her face, puts her head down and sighs.

"Do you guys mind if I sleep on the couch in the living room? I don't feel comfortable in the bedroom."

"We don't mind," Carla says, "I'm sorry the Evening Prayer made you uncomfortable."

"I think I'm going to hit the sack," Johnny says.

"We should too," Mike agrees.

Carla and her husband wrap themselves in each other's arms as they stretch on the king size bed in their luxurious bedroom.

John stretches out on the couch in the living room, covering himself with his bathrobe.

"I too am very uncomfortable, Carla," Mike whispers. I agree with Johnny, a service for one's family shouldn't be too formal. I can see how the bishop would seem to young people as pompous and condescending. Close family members who haven't seen each other for some time are getting together, and they have us as new members to get acquainted with. To Johnny and to his generation, the bishop shouldn't behave in this way. To the younger generation this is crazy. As father and grandfather, the bishop in effect withdraws from his family to assume a priestly role, while the family in unison says Amen. Were it not for the sad tragedy that constantly looms in our minds, the whole service would have seemed comic."

"We don't know how priests and ministers conduct themselves at home. So, Ron and Alexia went out together. I'm frankly surprised that she'd even think of going out with a grandson of the bishop."

"I must say that I'm surprised too."

"Maybe it's because he looks like Johnny. I'm sure that she realizes that they are first cousins and that there'll always be a limitation to such a relationship."

"She must realize that."

"She won't date anyone seriously, I'm afraid. She never dated anyone seriously in high school, but if she were to get to know, and become close to a cousin, a grandson of the bishop, wouldn't that give her a different prospective, and maybe lessen her anger at the bishop? I guess I'm a wishful thinker, hoping for some miracle to come and make my Alexia whole again."

"Maybe through her cousin she'll begin seeing boys in college, like Brad, let's hope."

"And when she finds out that there are young men nice enough to date and become friends with, maybe that will soften her attitude toward the bishop. That would be better than any professional treatment, or any visit to any doctor, but I know Alexia."

Chapter 51

While Johnny is having a conversation with his parents in his parents' bedroom in the Arlington mansion, Alexia and Anna-Marie are having their own conversation in their bedroom.

"I have always heard that Mom resembles the bishop, but I didn't expect the resemblance to be so striking," Alexia tells Anna-Marie.

"It is striking." Anna-Marie pauses. "What did you think of him?"

"You mean the bishop? Philip?"

Anna-Marie giggles.

"I was so scared of him, that I didn't want to get anywhere near him, but he kept creeping toward me."

"I noticed that, and I was worried about you."

"I was out-of-control trembling, I was afraid I'd literary faint."

"You did very well."

"When I saw him smile, and heard him speak gently, I immediately recognized his voice, and I began to relax a little. I was relieved thinking maybe he won't bite me."

Anna-Marie giggles again.

"Thank God, I saw my brother Johnny with Mom and Dad, and I became a little stronger and more comfortable."

"It worked out."

"When he greeted me, and asked me if he could hug me, I began to shake again."

"But you said, yes, you may. I was very proud of you."

"What else could I say or do? And this is why I feel horrible about myself and about everything. What did you think of him?"

"Well, I don't have the disadvantages, or maybe the hang-ups that you have, and I found him to be a gentle and kindly soul, who's trying to be gracious to his guests."

Alexia scowls. She is irritated.

"I was touched to see him hug and kiss Ron the way he did. To me he's just any loving grandfather who's delighted to see his grandchildren and to be with his family."

Yes, Alexia says to herself, I saw him hug and kiss Ron too, and I saw Ron hug and kiss him the way he did. Oh, Ron, how could you do that?

"I was sure he really wanted to be kind to you, Alexia," Anna-Marie continues.

"He probably sensed my discomfort."

"He probably did."

"Poor man, but I couldn't help it," Alexia finally says. "I still don't want to be anywhere close to him. I'm still scared to be near him, afraid of his touching me or speaking to me again."

"I know, and it's sad, but I feel for you and for him."

"Why for him?"

"I have a feeling that he wants to be closer to you. And he wants you to forgive him, but he doesn't want to impose on you. As you say he probably senses your discomfort, and I think that if you give yourself a chance to know him better, you may find something interesting about him, and you may even like him. Not many people in the world are willing to give away so much of their fortune. It takes a special kind of person, who's noble and able to feel for the poor, the hungry and the destitute, to give up so much of their wealth for them. I can't help but admire that kind of nobility in any human being. Do you see my point?"

"Sure, I do, and I also realize that no one is perfect, or without certain flaws, and I also would like to admire that kind of human being, but as you say I have a hang-up that keeps me scared of him. I guess I'm in a rut."

"No, you're not in a rut. You're doing your best. I was so proud of you when you had the courage and the kindness to let him hug you, Alexia, especially knowing how hard it was for you to do that."

"Thank you, I think we should go to bed now, what do you think?"

"I think we better."

"And we need to get up early tomorrow to join everybody in the Thanksgiving service at 7:30 in the morning."

"I'm glad you're going. I'll come with you. That's good, very good, Alexia."

"I want to give myself every opportunity, Anna-Marie. I want, very badly, to be able to love and forgive him, if only I could."

"I'm sure you will one day. Good Night, Alexia."

"Good Night, Anna-Marie."

Chapter 52

Two floors below, on the other side of the Arlington mansion, Bishop Arlington and his wife Grace discuss the bishop's first encounter with Alexia.

"Did you see that poor child, Carla's daughter, Alexia, quiver when she entered our home?" the bishop asks.

"I didn't really notice that until you mentioned it. She appeared embarrassed when you asked for a warmer sweater for her. She declined the sweater we brought her."

"I realized when she declined the sweater, that she wasn't really cold, but that she was probably scared of me, that monster who attacked her beloved grandmother. When I visited the Hartley home last August, I met everyone, except her. Carla was apologetic and felt awkward that Alexia, the other twin, didn't come to meet me then. I found out that from her childhood the young woman was very close to her grandmother, and I suspect that she just didn't want to have anything to do with me, the monster in her mind who assaulted and abused her grandmother. How can I blame her? So when she entered our home, most likely after someone had twisted her arm hard to come, probably mercilessly hard, she was petrified at the very thought of being close to me."

"We don't know any of that, Philip. The poor girl is barely eighteen. She has been going out with Ron, she and her roommate have been going out on double dates with Ron and Ron's roommate. She likes our grandson."

"I'll bet you that she was scared of me, scared out of her wits, and when I asked her permission to hug her, she was speechless for a while, then she said, yes you may, with such a faint low voice that I could hardly hear her. She broke my heart, and when I got close to her to hug her, she closed her eyes, Grace, and couldn't wait to be freed from me. I'm sure she thinks I am horrible."

"I wouldn't worry about that, Philip. She'll get used to you, and to us. I'm sure she will, Philip."

"I hope so, and I would do anything to make that family whole again, Grace. I would give my eyeteeth to make that lovely, innocent and frightened young woman feel safe around me. I know it's difficult, if not impossible. I have so much hard work ahead of me, my dear, for if that young woman accepts and forgives me and becomes comfortable around me, then I feel sure that our Lord will accept, forgive and be comfortable with me."

"I'm sure He will. Good Night, Philip."

"Good Night, my dear."

Chapter 53

"Blessed be God, Father, Son, and Ho-ly Spi-rit," the bishop chants at 7:30 the next morning.

The four members of the Hartley family, as well as Anna-Marie, Brad, Christine and Elizabeth, with their children, and also the bishop's wife and the bishop's mother are all in attendance in the family chapel on the ground floor of the Arlington mansion. They all sit on chairs facing the Altar. The bishop's mother sits in her wheelchair facing the Altar.

"And blessed be His kingdom, now and for ev-er. A-men," they all respond, chanting in unison.

Quivering, feeling cold and frightened, Alexia stands, stares at the bishop, without being able to utter a word.

Standing, the bishop reads:

"Lord God Almighty, who hast made all peoples of the earth for His own glory, to serve Him in freedom and peace: Grant to the people of our country a zeal for justice and the strength of forbearance, that they may use their liberty in accordance with His gracious will ..."

"Amen," they all say.

Christine Arlington Barton, attired in a priestly garment, walks to the podium, ready to read the first lesson.

"A reading from the Book of Samuel:

And the Lord sent Nathan unto David. And he came unto him: There were two men in one city; the one rich, and the other poor. The rich man had exceeding many flocks and herds: But the poor man had nothing, save one little ewe lamb, which he had bought and nourished up: and it grew up together with him, and with his children: it did eat of his own meat, and drank of his own cup, and lay in his bosom, and was unto him as a daughter. And there came a traveler unto the rich man, and he spared to take of his own

269

flock and of his own herd, to dress for the wayfaring man that was come unto him; but took the poor man's lamb, and dressed it for the man that was come to him. And David's anger was greatly kindled against the man; and he said to Nathan, As the Lord liveth the man that hath done this thing shall surely die: And he shall restore the lamb fourfold, because he did this thing, and because he had no pity. And Nathan said to David, Thou art the man...

The Word of The Lord."

"Thanks be to God," they all say. Standing they all sing the Song of Praise:

Blessed art thou, O Lord God of our fathers;
Praised and exalted above all forever.
Blessed art thou for the Name of thy Majesty
Praised and exalted above all forever.
Blessed art thou in the temple of thy holiness
Praised and exalted above all forever.
Blessed art thou that beholdest the depths,
And dwellest between the Cherubim;
Praised and exalted above all forever.
Blessed art thou on the glorious throne of thy kingdom;
Praised and exalted above all forever.
Blessed art thou in the firmament of heaven;
Praised and exalted above all forever.
Blessed are thou, O Father, Son, and Holy Spirit;
Praised and exalted above all forever.

Then Elizabeth Arlington Robinson walks to the podium, ready to read the second lesson.

"A reading from The First Letter of Paul to The Corinthians:

Grace and Peace to you from God our Father and the Lord Jesus Christ. I am always thanking God for you. I thank him for his grace given to you in Christ Jesus. You possess full knowledge and you can give full expression to it, because in you the evidence for the truth of Christ has found confirmation. There is indeed no single gift you lack, while you wait expectantly for our Lord Jesus Christ to reveal himself. He will keep you firm to the end, without reproach on the Day of our Lord Jesus. It is God himself who called you to share in the life of his son Jesus Christ our Lord; and God keeps faith. I appeal to you, my brothers, in the name of our Lord Jesus Christ: Agree among yourselves, and avoid divisions; be firmly joined in unity of mind and thought.

The Word of the Lord."

The Congregation: Thanks be to God.

The Bishop proceeds to the podium.

They all stand and chant:

"Al-le-lu-ia, al-le-lu-ia, al-le-lu-ia.

Show us your mercy, O Lord, and grant us Your sal-va-tion."

Raising the Bible high, the bishop says: "The Holy Gospel of Our Lord Jesus Christ According to Matthew:"

"Glory to you, Lord Christ," they all say.

The bishop reads:

When He saw the crowds he went up the hill. There he took his seat, and when his disciples had gathered round him he began to address them. And this is the teaching he gave:

How blest are those who know that they are poor;

The kingdom of Heaven is theirs.

How blest are the sorrowful;

They shall find consolation.

How blest are those of a gentle spirit;

They shall have the earth for their possession.

How blest are those who hunger and thirst to see right prevail;

They shall be satisfied.

How blest are those who show mercy;

Mercy shall be shown to them.

How blest are those whose hearts are pure;

They shall see God.

How blest are the peacemakers;

God shall call them his sons.

How blest are those who have suffered persecution for the cause of right;

The Kingdom of Heaven is theirs.

The Gospel of the Lord.

Congregation: Praise to you Lord Christ.

The bishop delivers his sermon:

"I would like to address a question which Carla asked me last night. The question is: Why do I ask you, my children and grandchildren, to call me by my Christian name, 'Philip.'

You see, while it may be the custom for children to call their parents 'Dad' and 'Mom' or 'Father' and 'Mother,' I actually don't feel that I have a fatherly authority apart from Jesus. Our Lord Jesus has often spoken strongly, but graciously and mercifully, to remind all of us, especially the clergy in Christ's Church, of our place and our duty. We have no absolute authority as fathers and mothers, as sisters and brothers, or even as our own selves. Jesus is our father and mother and sister and brother. He is us. This is so that we can find our true selves in Him, so that the world can see each one of us and see Him in us, and so that we, seeing one another, can see Christ.

This is so that our lives can represent Jesus in everything we think and say and do.

Whoever wants to be a good father, or a good mother, or a good brother, or a good sister, or a good person, my dear Carla, my dear mother, my dear wife, my dear children, my dear grandchildren and my dear friends and guests, must be a servant of Jesus and must see Him day and night.

Whoever wants to have life must always remember Christ and be simple. He must be detached from the world, the flesh, and the devil. He must be focused upon Christ, and be poor, chaste and obedient.

Our Lord Jesus, Himself, has said that whoever will be humble in this way, will come to joy and peace, and will come to exaltation.

And so, I want to be humble, and I want to be poor. I do not want my children to think of me as anything but a meek and ordinary being, who is like them in every way and who is a servant of Christ.

And that is why, my beloved, I prefer that you and all my other children and grandchildren and all my friends and guests, call me by my Christian name, 'Philip.' Amen."

"Amen," they all respond.

The Bishop returns to the altar. He sits on his chair in silence for a long moment. Finally, he motions to Carla.

Carla proceeds to the podium. She reaches for her pocket and unfolds a paper on which the Bishop typed the Prayers of the People for her to read. The crackling of the crisp paper is the only sound heard in the quiet Chapel. All eyes are trained on her. Her voice very low and quivering, she reads:

"During this Thanksgiving Day, let us offer our prayers to God, saying: Lord, have mercy:

That our gracious Savior may rouse us from sleep and make us attentive to the nearness of His presence, let us pray to the Lord."

All: "Lord, have mercy."

"That we may discover God's word in every sound of this world, God's touch in every human embrace, and God's love in every gesture of self-sacrifice among us, let us pray to the Lord."

All: "Lord, have mercy."

"That divine energy and holy grace may bring our hearts to vigilance and make us see the Christ who suffers in his peoples' agonies, let us pray to the Lord."

All: "Lord, have mercy."

"That we may come to recognize on this Thanksgiving Day, that Jesus the Christ is with us, here, to make our songs of praise and pleading His own, let us pray to the Lord."

All: "Lord, have mercy."

"That God's coming into our lives may be always new, always brimming with light, let us pray to the Lord."

All: "Lord, have mercy."

Carla then prays muttering under her breath inaudibly:

Help, guide and protect Alexia and Johnny from all harm.

Help Alexia overcome her anger toward Bishop Arlington.

Let her love and forgive him for the horrible sin he committed many years ago against my mother, her beloved Grandmother and mentor, Rose-Anne.

The bishop then says:

"Prepare us for your coming, O Lord. Receive our prayers in the name of our gracious Savior, Jesus, the Christ. Have mercy, O Lord on those who preceded us to be in your company. Have mercy on your servant, Ronald Arlington, my father. Have mercy, O Lord on an innocent woman against whom I committed a great sin, Rose-Anne Riley Perry, and all victims of rape. Embrace Rose-Anne with your love, O Lord, for the love and care she gave to her daughter and mine, Carla, whom I fathered against Rose-Anne's will. Open the gates of heaven to Rose-Anne for her courage. Comfort her for the undeserved pain and suffering I caused her. Help Rose-Anne's innocent family, O Lord, defeat the pain which I have caused them, the pain which endures until this day. Give patience and solace to Rose-Anne's daughter and mine, Carla, and to Rose-Anne's grandchildren and mine, Alexia and John, and others I have not met. Give me the strength, the integrity and the wisdom to obey your command, O Lord, and sustain me as I do penance for my sin by helping the poor, the sick, the hungry, the homeless and those who are victims of rape, in Rose-Anne's memory, and in your service. Help me, O Lord to earn her and her family's forgiveness, in order to be worthy of your forgiveness. I make this earnest appeal to you, my Lord, in the name of your beloved son, Jesus Christ, Amen."

"Amen," they all say.

Turning to his family, the bishop says in a strong clear voice:

"The Peace of the Lord be with you."

"And also with you," they all respond strongly and in unison.

The bishop, having concluded the service, goes to his mother. He bends over her wheelchair to embraces her as she kisses him on both cheeks.

"What a beautiful service, Philip," she says to her son. "I'm very proud of you, Philip. You're a good man. God will forgive you, my dear. I have no doubt about it." She wipes away her tears.

The bishop then goes to Carla and Michael and embraces each of them. "I know that these are tears of relief, my dear," he says to Carla.

"Thank you, you are a good man," Carla says.

The bishop looks toward Alexia.

She is trembling, unable to move.

Johnny and Anna-Marie come to the bishop to embrace him.

"Thank you very much for this service and for your moving sermon," Anna-Marie says to Bishop Arlington. The tears in her eyes do not hide her admiration of his forthright presentation.

"Thank you, thank you so much," Johnny says to the bishop, hugging him warmly and shaking his hand.

"I am so glad to see you, Johnny," the bishop says, returning Johnny's warm embrace.

Finally, the bishop comes to Alexia. "Good morning, my dear. May I offer you the Peace of our Lord?" Bishop Arlington asks softly.

Panicked and unable to speak, she slowly turns to allow his embrace.

"May the Lord keep you and save you," the bishop prays, placing his palm on her head gently. "May He bless you, look after you and give you his Peace. Amen."

"Thank you," Alexia says, tears rolling down her cheeks. "Thank you very much."

His face reddening, and sweating profusely, the bishop moves on to his daughters and his other grandchildren.

Her face still pale and her knees weak, Alexia sits in her chair weeping.

Anna-Marie rushes to her and sits down right next to her, extending her hand to her friend. They watch the bishop's two daughters and their children gather around him and receiving his embraces and prayers.

Holding Anna-Marie's hand tightly, Alexia closes her eyes: "Thank you, Anna-Marie, thank you. I have forgiven him, I have forgiven him, I am sure I have. I will pay a heavy price for that. I know I will, I know I will, but I have no alternative now. I have no alternative," she continues crying quietly.

The bishop continues to greet and hug each member of his family, as they all turn to one another, exchanging hugs, kisses and embraces.

"Thank you for addressing my question," Carla says, "and for your thoughtful concluding prayers."

"Your question was a very good question. I hope I addressed it adequately."

"Yes, you did. In fact I was moved by your approach to that issue. Thank you ever so much."

"I'm glad Alexia and Johnny joined our family in this service." He then turns to Michael. "You have a lovely family, may the good Lord bless all of you."

"Thank you, Philip, it was a lovely service. You are a good man. It's an honor for us to be with you and your family in your home."

Chapter 54

"Did you notice Ron, Christine's older boy, the young man Alexia likes?" Carla asks her husband after the service, on their way to their suite.

"Yes I noticed him. He really was into the service, wasn't he, singing loud and chanting with all his heart. He was really moved by the service.

"He kept looking at Alexia throughout the service, and she kept looking at him. What do you make of that."

"Nothing, they just care for each other."

"And he has a good voice, which I am sure Alexia noticed, but I still wonder how Alexia will react to him now, after observing his obvious religious devotion."

"Yes, I noticed that she kept looking at him. She must've realized how devoted he is to his faith. I'm sure she'll sort all that out."

"Although she kept looking at him, and he at her, I'm afraid she was in another world."

"Maybe, but she was very attentive to what the bishop said about Grandma Rose-Anne. I'm sure she was."

"Yes, she was, and the bishop's concluding prayer brought tears to her eyes. That really caught her attention, and I also know that Ron's hearty response to the service got her attention too."

"The whole thing may be a good experience for her, but it's a lot to digest in, Carla."

"I'm willing to guess that it will soften her heart toward the bishop, but how much, and for how long?"

"I'm sure that the bishop's concluding prayers touched her, you're right about that, but after listening to Johnny's reaction to the Evening Service last night, I can't help fearing that a young and distraught person like Alexia might implode."

Carla winces.

"And I can't help wondering how she'll feel about Ron after this, now that she realizes how attached he is to the bishop, and how committed he is in his faith."

"I wouldn't know my dear."

"More importantly, Carla, how will Alexia react to the bishop's public acknowledgement of his offense against Grandma Rose-Anne? Will that and the moving prayers that followed, make her feel any differently? So that eventually she could accept the bishop's sincere remorse and forgive him?"

I know that Johnny has changed his mind about the Bishop. I saw him walk to him, thank and embrace him warmly."

"I saw that too, but we'll have to wait and see."

At the stroke of 1:00 on Thanksgiving Day, the Bishop, Grace, Christine and Elizabeth and their families, Carla and her family as well as Anna-Marie and Brad, all gather outside the dining room.

The turkey has been carved and placed at the center of the table. There are the traditional Thanksgiving foods. The cheerful spacious dining room is lit by large chandeliers. The table with sixteen antique Queen Anne Chairs around it, is set with bone china and sterling silver, befitting the occasion. Two servants are busy making sure that everything is ready to be served. They finally leave the room. Gradually, all take their seats and wait quietly.

"I have asked Christine to say grace," the bishop says in a subdued voice, breaking the silence.

"Our Lord God," Christine begins, "we thank you for this Thanksgiving day, and for every day. We thank you for this food, for the gathering of our family, for the presence of our friends and for all your blessings. Make us always aware of the needs of others, the poor, the hungry, the homeless and the elderly, who have no one to care for them. Amen."

"Amen," they all say.

"It's so good to have all of us, here," Grace says, "please everyone, we want you all to feel at home."

"It's not unusual to have snow in November in this part of New York State," the bishop says. "Let's hope that there won't be heavier snow tonight. I'm glad Ron and Alexia and their friends have decided to delay their travel until tomorrow. Tomorrow should be a nicer day. We're promised a little sunshine."

"Do you like the snow, Carla?" Christine asks.

"I love it, I think it's beautiful, and it doesn't seem to be too cold."

"I love your winter overcoat, Alexia," Grace says. "Did you bring that with you from Virginia, or did you buy it in Byron?"

Alexia is surprised that the question is addressed to her. She hesitates at first, wondering why Grace cares. She wants to hear my voice, she quickly decides. "I bought it from Byron, Mrs. Arlington," Alexia speaks in a soft but clear voice. "Anna-Marie helped me select it, so she deserves most of the credit, but I'm glad you like it."

"It's a lovely shade of blue," says Elizabeth.

"Alexia," says the bishop's mother, "what a beautiful name, my dear. I'm so glad that you and Ron have met. How did you meet? Did you meet in one of your classes?"

"No, Grandma," Ron says, "Mom gave me Alexia's name, told me that we're related and suggested that I go meet her, so I went and found her at her dorm."

"Isn't that nice?" the bishop's mother says. "And how did you hear about Ivy, Alexia? Are there other students from your high school class attending Ivy?"

She really wants to hear me speak, Alexia says to herself. "I don't think there are other students from my high school class attending Ivy, Mrs. Arlington," Alexia says in a low but distinct voice. "Grandma Rose-Anne was the first to suggest Ivy to me. When I asked my advisor and some of my high school teachers about it, they encouraged me to apply. Two of my teachers wrote very kind letters of recommendation for me, and my school was supportive."

"That's nice," the elderly woman says. "Your grandmother gave you good advice, I'm sure. She was a highly educated woman herself. I'm sure you'll do very well, my dear. Ivy's a great institution, one of the very best."

"Thank you, Mrs. Arlington."

"We're very happy that Ron and Alexia met," Carla says. "That was very nice of Ron to go and find Alexia. Now they both have family to rely on while they're away from home. Thank you Christine, we're very grateful, we appreciated that very much."

Alexia remains quiet, hoping that no more questions will be addressed to her.

After a few moments of silence, the bishop resumes: "So, Brad's Ron's roommate, and Anna-Marie's Alexia's roommate. That's very nice! You're also in the College of Engineering at Ivy, Brad?"

"Yes, sir, I'm in Chemical Engineering, with Ron."

"And Anna-Marie?" The Bishop turns to Anna-Marie.

"I'm in Human Ecology, Bishop Arlington."

"And Alexia's in Arts and Sciences," the bishop turns to Alexia.

Uneasy, her voice hardly audible, Alexia says softly: "That's right, sir, but I haven't yet selected a major."

Visibly uncomfortable and blushing, the bishop's voice suddenly becomes unsteady. "It takes time to decide on these difficult choices, my dear," he finally says. "Well, well, well," he then changes the subject, "the political season will soon be upon us. "I suppose our family in Virginia will soon be supporting the young George Bush to be our next president. I guess the country has had enough of Mr. Clinton. We need a change."

"Actually, we like President Clinton," Michael smiles, "and we don't like the younger Bush that much. We voted for his father, but we're afraid of the younger Bush."

"How's that, Michael?" Bishop Arlington asks.

"Carla and I have discussed it, and we both think that the younger Bush may make snap decisions, without much reflection, and we don't think he knows much about world affairs or the global political economy."

"We're Democrats, Philip," Carla jests.

"Oh, that's what it is," the bishop laughs. "Actually, Grace and I are Republicans."

"But we rarely vote along party lines," Grace hastens to say.

"That's right," the Bishop now concedes, "we both voted for Clinton the second time, not the first time though."

"You'll be proud to know, Philip," Ron says, "that Brad and I will be active in the Ivy Republican Club."

"How about Alexia and Anna-Marie?" the bishop's mother asks.

"My family and I are Democrats, Mrs. Arlington, but I don't know about Alexia," Anna-Marie says.

"Like Mom and Dad," Alexia says, "I'm a Democrat too."

"I bet Johnny is a Republican," Bishop Arlington jests again.

"The Virginia crowd are all Democrats," Johnny smiles, "and we're not Southern Democrats either, who have more in common with Republicans, we're real Democrats."

"Well," the bishop smiles broadly, "except for Christine, the rest of our family in the Northeast are all Republicans."

"It shouldn't really matter at all," Elizabeth says. "We're all Americans."

"That's right," the Bishop agrees.

Chapter 55

It is nearly 2:00 pm, Friday, the day after Thanksgiving. The four friends had lunch in Lake Charles before embarking on their trip.

After lunch, and before the drive to Green Meadow, Alexia and Johnny have a private, but short conversation. Alexia informs her brother that she is ready now to forgive the bishop and to put the whole tragedy behind her. She confides to her brother, however, that she will pay a hefty price.

Concerned, Johnny pleads with his sister, against his parents' earlier advice, to consider therapy and treatment.

Alexia is shocked that Johnny would take it upon himself to make such a bold suggestion to her, feeling that the difficult question of her treatment is strictly between her and her parents. She hoped that Johnny would be on her side on that issue. She tells Johnny that since she has been able to forgive the bishop, she does not need any such treatment anymore, that it is she who has to address her own problems and work on them herself.

Hoping to strengthen his position, Johnny makes the mistake of telling his sister that even her friend Anna-Marie thinks that Alexia needs treatment, and that Anna-Marie had spoken about it to their parents.

Alexia is jolted by her brother's revelation. She is visibly shaken by it. She tells her brother that Anna-Marie had no business telling their parents what medical treatment she, Alexia, may or may not need.

Johnny, now obviously realizing that he blundered, does not know how to retract or correct his blunder.

Alexia, however, noticing her brother's bewilderment, hugs him and gives him a kiss. "Don't worry about it, Johnny," she tries to reassure him. "It's okay."

In the meantime, Bill Falvo and his wife Maureen, with their two younger children, sit in their family room in Green Meadow waiting for Anna-Marie and her friends to arrive. The four young students arrive in Green Meadow shortly after 4:00 pm.

The contrast between the Arlington Mansion in Lake Charles and the modest Falve home in Green Meadow is striking. The Falvo home is a small white two-story colonial built on a half-acre lot in a suburban community of about fifteen thousand in upstate New York.

The Falvos have prepared tea, coffee and dessert for their guests, who will then continue back to Byron in the station wagon Ron has borrowed from his mother.

Anna-Marie's parents and younger siblings receive their daughter Anna-Marie warmly when she and her friends arrive. She hugs her younger brother and sister, then introduces her friends to her parents and siblings.

Although Anna-Marie's parents had already met Alexia on her first day at Ivy, and had continued to hear about her from Anna-Marie, Alexia is nevertheless politely reserved and says very little. Yet she is more relaxed at the Falvo home than she was at the Arlington mansion.

"We missed you yesterday," Maureen Falvo says to Anna-Marie. "We wished that you could've invited your friends to our home for Thanksgiving, but we realize that we couldn't compete with Bishop Arlington's gracious invitation."

Turning to Ron, Maureen resumes: "Thank you for inviting Anna-Marie. It was an honor for us and for her to be invited to the home of the bishop."

"You're welcome, Mrs. Falvo," Ron says. "We really appreciated your letting Anna-Marie join us."

"We're happy she could join you," Maureen continues, "so now, we hope you like the dessert we have for you. We know that you had lunch at Lake Charles before you left, and you need to get back, so we kept it simple."

The four are urged to help themselves to cakes, fruit and tea which they bring to the dining room. Maureen sits at one end of the table and waits for the others to be seated. "We didn't have Anna-Marie with us on Thanksgiving yesterday," she says, "so we're happy to have her with us today along with the three of you.

Mr. Falvo then offers a brief prayer. "Our Lord, God," he begins, as they all bow their heads, "we thank you for this Thanksgiving Season. Bless our food and bless our family, and bless Anna-Marie's guests, Alexia, Ron and Brad. May this time of year be a happy one, not only for those of us who are comfortable, but also for the very many of our countrymen, as well as others around the world who are hungry and homeless. Amen."

"Amen," they all say.

"Alexia," Bill Falvo says, "I hope you're enjoying your experience at Ivy. Anna-Marie writes us regularly. She's so happy to have you as her roommate and friend."

"I'm very happy to have Anna-Marie as my roommate and friend, Mr. and Mrs. Falvo. She's a true friend, very kind and very sweet. Thank you for having us at your home. I'm enjoying my experience at Ivy, very much Mr. Falvo. My parents are coming to Byron tomorrow. They'd love to see you, and my brother Johnny will be with them. He's my twin. He would love to meet all of you too, hopefully soon."

After dessert, the four students continue on to Byron. Alexia sits next to Anna-Marie in the back seat.

"When will your parents arrive?" Ann-Marie whispers to Alexia.

"They said they'll arrive tomorrow afternoon."

"That's good, and then you'll have a little more time to spend with them."

"I hope so," Alexia says.

"What's the matter, are you tired?"

"I'm exhausted."

"I am too, to tell you the truth. Well," Anna-Marie continues, "thank God it didn't snow last night. There aren't always flurries this early. How do you like the snow?"

"Well I like looking at it from inside! But I dread walking in the snow, especially when it's really cold. I'm sure I'll get used to it."

"Doesn't it snow a little in Valley Town?" Anna-Marie asks.

"The ice storms are the worst in Virginia," Alexia says. "So I actually should get used to the snow here."

"I'm sure you will."

"I hope so," Alexia repeats in a low voice.

"I'm hoping you liked Mom's dessert."

"I did, very much, your family is nice, but as much as I am happy to be with Mom and Dad and Johnny tomorrow, I'm worried a little."

"Why, Alexia? Your Mom and Dad are so nice, and so is Johnny."

"I know they are, but they're going to pressure me to get medical treatment, and I'm not up to that now. I want to be left alone for a little while. I want to think, you know. Now that I've mustered the courage to acknowledge that the bishop is sincere in his repentance, and deserves forgiveness, I don't feel like I need any therapy, or counseling. I need to concentrate on what I'm going to do with my life."

"Alexia, you should be happy now. Your grades are improving and you should be OK. I'm so happy for you, for being able to realize that the bishop deserves forgiveness, I'm very proud of you. I don't think that after these traumatic few weeks, a little therapy or counseling will hurt you, but it's your call, it's up to you what you want to do. This thing the bishop did so many years ago, for which he's clearly remorseful, and we agree on that now, I've thought about it, especially after his sermon yesterday, and I think, tragic as the whole story you told me about him may be, you shouldn't still be worrying about it. I mean you shouldn't even be thinking about it, or telling people about it, or letting it upset you anymore. This horrible thing happened so many, many years ago, when he was really young and didn't know what he was doing. Now he's an elderly, decent, kind and prominent man, a bishop, a father and a grandfather. As you know he's also a very generous man. He's a philanthropist. Of course God will forgive him, especially now that you can forgive him. And what he did should be forgotten and no longer be allowed to dominate your thoughts, when there's so much out there for you to do, like you said, and right here at Ivy. So may be a counselor could help you put the awful history in its place, where it won't any longer sort of hobble you. What do you think?"

Alexia is pained, but she tries to hide it. Her face betrays her, however. She stares out the car window.

"It isn't that I don't understand how painful this has been," Anna-Marie hastens then to say, appearing to notice her roommate's pain. "I do, Alexia. I feel very terrible for anyone who's a victim of rape, and for that person's family, but I just thought that perhaps, for your own sake, for your own peace of mind, Alexia, you can somehow with a little help maybe, put the whole thing in its place. You know, that tragedy doesn't deserve to be ruling you! You shouldn't be thinking about it, or even talking about it to anyone."

Alexia turns her face away from her roommate and looks at the distant hills passively.

"Have I said something wrong?" Anna-Marie asks. "Did I go too far? I'm sorry, Alexia," Anna-Marie says, her own eyes tearing. "I know I said something that upset you, but I'm worried about you. What's the matter, Alexia?"

Alexia does not answer.

"Did I upset you? If I said something wrong, I am sorry."

"Did you say anything to my parents about my needing help, or about my being admitted to a hospital for treatment?"

"Yes, Alexia, I mentioned that to them, what you and I talked about before."

"Don't worry about what I said to you about the bishop, I am sorry I upset you with it," Alexia says, fighting back the tears. "You're my best friend, and I trust you."

"I really want so much to help you," Anna-Marie says, now herself becoming more tearful. "You don't have to apologize to me. I just felt that the bishop's troubles of years past, now that you feel he deserves your forgiveness, are none of anyone's business anymore. You're a very good and very thoughtful person. I know you are. You're my friend, and I care and worry about you."

Alexia continues to stare out the window, wiping away the tears with her bare hands.

Anna-Marie reaches for her pocket, gets out two fresh tissues, hands one to her roommate, and tightly clutches the other. "You do understand, don't you, Alexia? You're my friend, and I care about you."

Alexia continues to look through the car window into the emptiness. As the car speeds along the highway toward Byron the familiar voice comes back: *"... Daddy's suicide marked the tragic beginning of my push into the cruel, but broader world beyond our farm ... Nor could I have believed that the world for this little farm girl, who was once raped by a horrible and murderous monster in Stratford, would so expand that she would become a professor at a large and respectable university ...* Alexia continues to stare into the emptiness. The music and lyrics of a song she had written and composed in the Music Room of her dorm begin to ring in her ears.

The ceaseless flow of water sings
As I glimpse the Angels wings
Bubbles float and music cheers
Life beyond human spheres

Then she remembers Anna-Marie's words in a previous discussion:

" ... What does a perpetrator of a horrible crime have to do to be forgiven by us for his crime, Alexia ... In my estimation, Bishop Arlington has done a lot, as a step toward giving him that forgiveness ..."

Alexia shakes her head in bewilderment.

Chapter 56

"Thank you, Philip," Carla embraces the bishop as she and Michael and their son Johnny say their goodbyes to Bishop Arlington and his family the next day. "This has been a memorable visit. We'll always remember it as long as we live."

"We're delighted you came. All of us are. We're especially happy that Alexia and Johnny came. I'm sure you can see how the whole family has reacted to your coming home, Carla, especially Mother. I'm so glad that Mother met you and Alexia and Johnny. You have no idea how much this means to me, to all of us. I hope and pray that this is the first of many visits, my dear. Now this is your home, and we are your family."

"I know that," she says, embracing the bishop warmly again, "I know I am, and I look forward to seeing everyone again."

"Good! And always give our love to the children, especially to Alexia. Tell her we all love her dearly and look forward to seeing her again soon."

"I will." Carla says. She, Michael, and Johnny get into their car and wave goodbye as they drive down the long driveway and set off for Byron.

"Now we can all relax," Johnny says to his parents.

"It wasn't really that tiring, was it?" Carla asks.

"No, it wasn't physically tiring, but emotionally it was exhausting, and the religious thing isn't for me, Mom, I'm sorry to say. I'm glad I attended the service yesterday though. That was very moving, not for the religious part, but for the bishop's own personal thoughts which he kind of put into the prayers. Those sincere honest words were really great. They touched me. That also touched Alexia, believe it or not. I almost fell off my chair when she admitted to me that she was touched by the bishop's remorse. She even said that she is ready to forgive him now."

"She told Dad and me that too."

"What do you make of it, Dad?"

"I agree, that was great," Michael says, "but we have to wait and see."

"I still worry about Alexia," Johnny tells his parents.

"How, was there anything else she said?" Carla asks.

"Not really, but just the day before, she was still saying that the bishop was a farce. I'm worried about her changing her mind so fast."

"After the service," Michael says, "I changed my mind a great deal about the bishop too. There isn't an iota of doubt in my mind now that his remorse is sincere. After that service, I would think that Grandma Rose-Anne herself would be willing to forgive him. I wouldn't worry about Alexia, give her more time. She's smart, and very fair in her judgments. She saw for herself and heard the man acknowledge what he did to Grandma Rose-Anne, she heard him express his painful remorse and pledge publicly to help the victims of rape, in honor of her beloved Grandmother. What else can any reasonable person ask for?"

"I agree, but I don't think that you, or Mom, have any idea of Alexia's weakness and true feelings about all this."

"We do, my dear," Carla says.

"Alexia is still very hurt, I'm telling you, she's still upset more than you can imagine."

"We know all that, and she was very close to Grandma Rose-Anne," Michael says, "but now I have a feeling that she recognizes that the bishop is truly remorseful, and is willing to do all he can to honor the memory of Grandma Rose-Anne."

"All this is true, but she's still in trouble, she isn't out of the woods. You're right, Dad, she was very close to Grandma Rose-Anne, closer than Mom even, and Alexia used to think that Mom was indifferent to Grandma's misery."

"That has changed, didn't you see how she hugged and kissed Mom? She needs Mom, and Alexia is very happy to be with Mom now."

"I know that she loves Mom and needs Mom, but Alexia is still hurting, Dad, trust me."

Carla and Michael remain silent for several minutes. Michael continues driving steadily through the cold white rolling hills, not looking right or left. Carla stares out the window.

"What's on your mind then, Johnny?" Michael asks his son.

"What's on my mind is that Alexia still needs treatment, Dad."

"We know that, Johnny, and we all agreed that I would speak to her about it. Why, son, did you mention it to her? Why did you have to tell Alexia that Anna-Marie spoke to us about her?"

"I did that because I am worried about her, Dad."

"I'm just afraid that what you did, Johnny, is bound to make Alexia think that Anna-Marie is betraying her. Can't you see that? Why did you do that, my boy? Didn't we all agree that I'll be the one to approach Alexia about it?"

John puts his head down, covers his face with his right arm and says. "Oh, my God, oh, my God, I blew it. I know I blew it, and that's why I'm more worried about her than ever, Dad."

"What's the matter, Michael?" Carla asks. "What is it that Johnny said?"

"Don't worry about it. He knows he made a mistake."

"A big mistake," Johnny covers his face with both hands.

Michael looks in the rear view mirror at his son. "Don't worry about it, Johnny, it'll be all right."

"If I were you," Johnny says, "I wouldn't mention treatment or going to the University Counseling Center, or admission to the hospital to Alexia now, Dad, not now, Dad, you need to wait."

"I agree," Carla says, "I think this would turn her against Anna-Marie, and it would make things worse, much worse."

"Oh, my God, what got into me? Why did I do that?" Johnny rebukes himself.

"It's done, my dear, let us not dwell on it," Michael says, "but I agree, let's not bring the issue of admitting Alexia to a hospital, or getting her treated now. Let's wait on that."

"It's horrible, Dad, but I dread that too, I dread waiting, Dad."

"How far are we from Byron?" Carla asks.

"I think we're about a hundred miles from Byron now," Michael says.

"Johnny is crying?" Carla whispers to her husband.

"He's upset with himself and worried about Alexia."

"She'll be all right, Johnny," Carla tries to comfort Johnny.

"I hope so."

When they arrive in Byron, they immediately go to Alexia's dorm and find Alexia and her roommate, Anna-Marie, waiting for them in the hall.

Having agreed with Alexia's parents beforehand not to join them for dinner with Alexia, Anna-Marie discretely begins to excuse herself in order to go up to her room.

Alexia tries to persuade her roommate to join them, but Anna-Marie declines firmly and politely, saying that she expects a phone call from her parents.

Alexia begins to worry about the conversation she and Anna-Marie had about the bishop on their way back from Lake Charles. She also worries about having put Anna-Marie on the spot for advising her parents that she, Alexia, should be treated medically. She broods a little, but quickly recovers.

Alexia then goes out for dinner with her family and has a good and pleasant time with them. She repeats to her parents how impressed she was with the bishop's concluding statement in the Thanksgiving Prayers. She expresses relief that she now believes that the bishop's remorse and sorrow are genuine. She reiterates her determination to forgive him and to go on with her life.

Her parents commend her, and assure her that she has taken a good step forward. Neither one makes any reference to medical treatment or hospital admission. They only praise Alexia, and again express delight at what she has told them.

Not participating in the discussion, Johnny remains quiet.

"I have thought about getting help for my occasional depression and distress, as you mentioned the other day, Dad," Alexia tells her father, "but I really believe that I'll be able to manage on my own now. I'm comfortable that I can do that now. If I should find that I can't cope, or that I need help, I'll go see the nurse at our dorm, or someone at the counseling center."

Her parents listen, saying nothing at first.

Then her father says, "Alexia, my dear, we have to rely on your judgment, sweetheart, and if you want to discuss this further with me or with Mom before we go home, we can still do that before we leave. We have plenty of time. I'd feel better about it if you and I or you and Mom, or you and Johnny could consult someone about your worries, my dear, but as I said, we'll leave that decision to you. We'll rely on you, Alexia."

"I am sure I'll be all right, Dad, but I'll think more about it."

"Yes, please think about it," Carla says. "We're hundreds of miles away, and we would like to do the right thing for you. We don't want to make you uncomfortable, and we'll do whatever you feel is right."

"I know, Mom, I know," Alexia says to her mother, affectionately placing her head on her mother's shoulder.

"And after we leave," her father says, "call us anytime you feel you need to speak to us about it, or about anything at all. We'll try to reach you more often ourselves. I still think that it won't hurt to get a little professional counseling before we leave, Alexia. What do you think?"

"That's not necessary, Dad. I'll call all of you more often, and I need to hear from all of you. You too, Johnny, why are you so quiet?"

"I'll call you, Alexia, you know I will," Johnny says.

"We're so glad that you have these wonderful friends, sweetheart," her father says.

"And it makes us comfortable to know that you and Anna-Marie are very close," her mother says. "And your newly found cousin, Ron, he seems like a good person, and he cares about you, dear. It's good that you met him."

"We can take you back to your dorm now, and we'll come and pick you and Anna-Marie up tomorrow for breakfast. Is there a place to have breakfast on Sunday that's near the University?"

"I'm sure we'll find one, Dad," she says. "I just hope that Anna-Marie isn't mad at me."

"Why should she be?" Michael asks.

"Well, she didn't want to come to dinner. She and I had a little discussion, not really an argument, and I hope she doesn't also opt out of breakfast."

"I'm sure she won't, sweetheart. Do you mind if I ask what your discussion was about?"

"You know, we spoke about the bishop, and about my getting medical treatment, but she's a good person. I'm sure she wouldn't be mad at me for too long."

Her parents listen.

"All right, Dad, I'm ready to go back to my dorm, and I'm sure you're all tired and need to rest. You have a long day ahead of you tomorrow."

"We do, sweetheart."

Michael, Carla and Johnny then drive her back to her dorm.

Chapter 57

"How was your dinner, where did you go?" Anna-Marie greets Alexia when she returns to her dorm. Anna-Marie is downstairs waiting for Alexia.

"It was great. My family loves me, Anna-Marie, and I'm so glad that I've become close to my mom again. I need my mom and I love her. The falling out I had with her over the bishop was mainly my fault. I was being unreasonable, but I do understand now better why Mom needed to see and know her natural father. It was natural for her to want to meet him. And my dad is a sweet man. I guess everyone thinks his or her own dad is wonderful, but Dad is really super, and I've always been very close to him. Johnny was quiet tonight, and that worries me a little. I hope he didn't have any disagreement with Mom over anything."

"You really do have a very nice family. I love your family."

"I love yours too. I guess you must know that. I hope you're not mad at me, Anna-Marie, over our discussion in the car on our way back."

"Don't be silly, of course I'm not mad at you."

"Thank you. Even though I've reconciled myself to the fact that the bishop is going to be part of my life, and I believe now that his remorse is sincere, and that he merits forgiveness, I still have to work hard on myself. It's no longer the bishop's problem, as far as I am concerned, that I need to address, it's my own problem. I can't blame my anxiety and my distress on the bishop or on anyone else anymore, I have to face my own situation myself, don't you think?"

"Of course you have to address your own concerns. You're right about that."

"And I don't want to isolate myself anymore. I want to go out with you and with Ron and Brad, and date other guys, and get myself out of my rut. I want to go out with Doug again, for example, what do you think?"

"That's exciting. We can do all that, especially with Ron and Brad. I like them a lot."

"I like Ron and Brad too," Alexia says. Then she begins to think about Ron and the Thanksgiving religious service. She remembers Ron's face reddening with joy as he sang and chanted during the service. She remembers his looking at the bishop with unquestioning devotion. She remembers his going to the bishop after the service and embracing him strongly. She remembers how the bishop opened his arms as Ron was approaching him saying, Ron, my dearest Ron, may the blessings of our Lord be with you always, my dear Ron. So, Ron, Alexia sighs, is not what I thought. He's not for me, and I'm not for him. Ron belongs to the bishop in a way that I can't.

"Don't you agree that we can go out with Ron and Brad, and have fun with them?" Anna-Marie asks Alexia.

"Yes, we can go out with them, and I want to continue doing that as Ron suggested and we agreed, but I think that Ron's too religious, Anna-Marie, and I'm not like that. That doesn't mean that I don't like him, or don't want to go out with him again, but I think that religion is a big part of his upbringing, which I don't fault him for, but I'm not wrapped in religion the way he is. That's why it would be good for us to date others as well, as we continue to date Ron and Brad. What do you think?"

Anna-Marie listens to her roommate. "I think it's a good idea."

"It doesn't mean that religion shouldn't play a role in people's lives, I'm not saying that. And don't misunderstand me. I'm not against people who are religious and devout."

"I'm not either. I grew up in the Catholic faith, and I went to church with my parents every Sunday as a child, and that's why I didn't feel uncomfortable with the service the bishop gave on Thanksgiving Day. I was familiar with that kind of service, and I found it uplifting. Did you go to church as a young girl?

"Not regularly; my family took us to church only on holidays, like Easter and Christmas. My parents aren't very religious. I think that my mom is a little more so than Dad. Dad grew up in the Episcopal Faith, like the bishop, and so did my mom, but Dad's more secular. My parents took Johnny and me to Sunday school occasionally, more as a cultural experience than a religious one, more or less, but I found that boring as a young girl. Neither one of us received serious religious upbringing. My dad's a very enlightened and tolerant person though. He's respectful of all religions. He taught Johnny and me, from the time we were very young, that all religions are good. He always said that religions were designed to make people better human beings, and that we should be respectful of all religions. He also mentioned to Johnny and me one time that we shouldn't argue with other people about their religion, or their religious beliefs, and that we should never tell anyone that his faith or his religion is not good. I've often discussed with my brother Johnny the role that God plays, or does not play in human life, in a general sort of way, and philosophically, but I never discuss that with other people."

"Sometime I'd love to hear your views on the role God plays in our lives."

"You may not like my views," she smiles.

"Why not? Maybe I can learn something new."

"Maybe some other time."

"Maybe we can discuss that with Ron and Brad sometime."

"Not with Ron, Anna-Marie, if I were you, I wouldn't discuss religion with Ron."

"Why wouldn't you? Ron seems very tolerant and very smart."

"I'm sure he's smart and tolerant, and I'm still very attracted to him, but didn't you watch him during the service? Didn't you notice how he was waving his arms, singing with emotion, very loudly, God's blessings and what have you, and getting emotional about the whole thing? I have a feeling that if he knew where I stood on that sort of thing, he wouldn't be too happy with me." She suddenly feels heat going through her body, as she remembers her first sweet encounter with Ron, when he came to her dorm to meet her. She is sad.

"I'm not sure he'll not be happy with you, if you weren't comfortable with that type of church service, but what's wrong with his liking it, or singing very loud?"

"I'm not saying something is wrong with it or with him, not at all. There's nothing wrong with him, or with anyone liking it, but that's not how I feel about religious services and about religion. I think that a discussion about it with Ron wouldn't be smart, but you may find it interesting. Who am I to say?"

"Maybe you're right."

"So let's have breakfast with my family tomorrow, all right?"

"Yes, of course, that'll be fun."

"Would you like to go to the music room, for a little while now, and before we go to bed? They play good '80s music now."

"Yeah, sure."

While Alexia and Anna-Marie have their discussion in their dorm at Ivy, Michael, Carla and Johnny continue their discussion at the Byron hotel about Alexia and her problems.

"I'm still very concerned about Alexia," Johnny tells his parents. "I think that Alexia's calmness and seeming relaxed mood is deceptive."

"Why do you say that?" Carla asks. "She seemed completely poised and in complete control of herself. What do you think, Mike?"

"I agree with you, she was very much in control of herself at dinner. She even seemed relieved that she has reconciled herself to the bishop, and to his being part of her life and family. I think, like all of us, she was moved by the bishop's admissions, and prayers for Grandma Rose-Anne, but I'm also always respectful of Johnny's sixth sense, especially when it comes to Alexia."

"Mom, Alexia is a depressed young woman. She's depressed, Mom. She may even be suicidal."

"What do you say, Johnny?" Carla is visibly shaken. "Please don't use that horrible word, Johnny. Please don't say that. Let's be thoughtful and reasonable. Let's not exaggerate the situation."

Michael remains quiet. His face grim, he only stares at his son in bewilderment.

"Before we go anyplace, Dad and Mom, we should get Alexia admitted to a health center."

"She'll never agree to that, and we'll only make things worse," Carla says. "Remember, you even thought so, so we've got to be careful."

"I know it isn't easy, but I changed my mind, it has to be done. One of us should stay behind. We can't leave Alexia here by herself. Alexia is very depressed, believe me, I know what I'm talking about."

"Who should stay behind, and what excuse would we have to give for staying behind?"

"I don't know, Mom, but either you or Dad, in my opinion, should stay behind. One of the two of you, not me, should stay behind with Alexia. That's what I think."

"Why do you think it should be one of us, and not you, Johnny?" Michael asks.

"Because I'm her equal, and I don't have the moral authority of a parent, that's how she feels, Dad."

"Let's think about it then. I need to get some sleep, but let's talk about it in the morning, son."

"That's fine," Johnny agrees.

In their bedroom at the hotel, Carla and Michael continue to talk about their concern for Alexia.

"I believe that Johnny, being her twin, Carla, may have a more accurate read of his sister than you or me, and we should take that into consideration in what we decide to do."

"I can't agree more, but he really shook me up."

"He shook me up too."

"What are we going to do?"

"Maybe you have to stay behind with Alexia yourself. Now that her affection and love for you are rekindled, I think that it would make more sense for you to stay with her for a week or two, or as long as it takes until we feel that she's really safe. You'd have the time to persuade her to get help, if you felt she needed it."

"I'll do whatever I have to do, but we need to find a way to let her know why I'm staying behind, a convincing way."

"We have to be honest with her, she'll respect that. We have to tell her we're concerned. I think that it should be you who tells her, that you're concerned, that you did not have the heart to leave her behind by herself. I think she'll be touched by that. And we can hope that she'll take it to heart."

Carla reflects a little. "I agree. I'll stay with her as long as it takes."

"I know you will."

Chapter 58

The next morning, after having breakfast with Alexia and Anna-Marie, Michael and Johnny go up to their rooms at the Byron Hotel to prepare for their trip back to Valley Town. Carla stays downstairs in the Hotel restaurant with Alexia and Anna-Marie.

"I think I'm going to stay in Byron for a few more days, Alexia," Carla says.

"That's great, Mom. Where will you stay?"

"I'll stay here, at the same hotel, dear."

"You could move in with us for a few days, Mom. I could sleep on a mattress on the floor, and you could sleep in my bed."

"We can make it work, Mrs. Hartley," Anna-Marie says, happy with that prospect.

"Yes! Move in with us for a few days."

"I think I may," Carla says, "Let me think about it."

"Did you tell Dad you're going to stay behind, Mom?"

"I did, and he approves, dear."

"Does Johnny know?"

"Yes, he does."

"This is exciting. I'm so happy you can stay for a few more days. You can come and sit in on some of my classes."

"I'd love to do that."

"And we can do a lot of things together. It'll be a nice change for you too, Mom."

"I'm sure it will be, dear."

Michael and Johnny, returning to the restaurant with their suitcases, re-join Carla and the girls.

"Dad," Alexia exclaims, "thank you for letting Mom stay with me for a few more days. I'm so excited. I wish you could stay with me too, and Johnny, but I know you guys have to go back."

"I'm glad Mom could stay with you, sweetheart. I'm sure you'll enjoy each other."

"Alexia and Anna-Marie have invited me to stay in their room while I'm here. What do you think, Mike?"

"It's up to the three of you, but that sounds good. Would there be room?"

"Plenty of room, Dad, Anna-Marie and I will manage. I'll sleep on the floor, and Mom will sleep in my bed."

"How long will you stay, Carla?" Mike asks his wife.

"I'll stay a few days, or until Alexia and Anna-Marie are fed up with me."

"You can stay as long as you want, Mom. We'll never be fed up with you."

"Yes, Mrs. Hartley, you're most welcome to stay as long as you want, we have plenty of room."

"I'll leave the rental car for you, Carla," Michael says, "it's all gassed up, and you can turn it in when you're ready to come home. Johnny and I will take a cab to the airport."

"I can drive you to the airport, to drop you off," Carla suggests.

"No, you don't need to do that. We'll manage, my dear."

"Will there be a place for me to park the rental car near the dorm?" Carla then asks.

"We'll take care of that, Mrs. Hartley. Don't worry about it," Anna-Marie says.

Michael and Johnny embrace Carla and say good-bye.

Tears in her eyes, Alexia says good-bye to her father first. "I wish you could stay with me too, Dad," she says, "but we'll be in touch. I'll write you soon. She then turns to her twin brother, puts her head on his shoulder. "I love you, Johnny. We'll be in touch. I'll write you too, soon. Take care."

Mike and Johnny then turn to Anna-Marie.

"Thank you, Anna-Marie, and thank you especially for letting Carla cramp your style, sweetheart," Michael jokes.

"I'm glad she could stay, and she won't cramp our style a bit. It's going to be fun having her with us."

Carla stays for a week at her daughter's dorm, during which they grow even closer. Carla pampers Alexia, loves her, comforts her, and counsels her. Carla refrains, however, from intruding on her daughter's privacy. She allows her and Anna-Marie all the freedom they need, to study, to listen to music in the dorm's music room and of course to go to classes. Carla goes with Alexia to two or three classes and encourages her to keep up with her studies. Carla does not bring up the matter of Alexia's health, nor does she suggest that she seek medical treatment. She speaks with her husband daily, and reports on Alexia's condition. She advises her husband that, as far as she can tell, Alexia is leading a normal and healthy life, eating well, going to classes regularly, enjoying social activities and in short appears to be content and happy. She tells her husband that suggesting to Alexia that she visit a doctor, or seek a counseling center, or consider admission to a hospital would be, in Carla's opinion, very unsettling to Alexia and do more harm than good. On the basis of these observations, Michael agrees with his wife that no mention should be made of either seeing a doctor or being admitted to a hospital.

A few days later, having considered her discussions with her husband, Carla tells Alexia and Anna-Marie that she plans to go back to Valley Town in two days.

Alexia accepts her mother's plan gracefully. While helping her mother pack and get ready to leave, she begins to compose six letters, one to her parents, one to her brother Johnny, one to her best friend in high school, Joan, one to her English Literature high school teacher, Margaret Bates, one to Bishop Arlington, and finally one to Anna-Marie.

To her parents, Alexia wrote:

"Dear Mom and Dad:
    I know that the news of my suicide will be an unbearable shock to you, but I couldn't go on living with all of the distress, anxiety, grief, fear and depression that has been haunting me for several months. The death of Grandma Rose-Anne, after she revealed to me the details of a gruesome rape she suffered shook me to the core. I cannot cope with life anymore, despite the loving support you have given me during these intolerable months. I know you will grieve for me, but feel happy that all the pain I have been enduring will no longer plague me.
    Thank you, Mom and Dad, for your love and support. Thank you, Mom, for a most precious few days of your love and company. Thank you, Dad, for letting Mom stay with me during the last few days of my life. Thank you both for your unconditional love.
    Love,
    Alexia"

To her brother Johnny, she wrote:

"Dearest Johnny,
    The only reason I waited this long to end the pain of the past several months, and to end my life, was the constantly nagging knowledge of how devastating it would be for you. Yet finally I could not endure any more, Johnny. I wanted to rest in peace and be with Grandma Rose-Anne. I know

that you will grieve for me, but be happy that the pain and suffering that have been destroying me will be no more.

Please ask Mom and Dad to bury my remains next to Grandma's.

I hope you will forgive me, Johnny, but I could not go on any longer. I also hope that you will have a full life, with a good family and loving children.

You deserve the very best.

I love you.

Alexia"

To her high school friend, Joan, Alexia wrote:

"Dear Joan,

I know that the news of my suicide will shock you, but I have been in constant pain which has become unbearable. I had to end that. Your friendship and love will always be a part of me. Thank you for that. I know that you will grieve for me, Joan. Be happy for me and know that the miserable pain and suffering I have been living with for months will now be gone forever.

Love,

Alexia"

To her high school teacher, Ms. Bates, Alexia wrote:

"Dear Ms. Bates,

The news of my suicide will no doubt surprise and shock you, and shock my other wonderful teachers from high school, but I have been living with constant pain and unbearable suffering, Ms. Bates, all of which resulted from learning that my Grandma Rose-Anne, who died during my last year in high school, was raped when she was my age, and that my mom was a product of that horrible crime.

Please convey to all my very kind teachers my deep respect and affection.

Your literature courses, Ms. Bates, were among the very best courses I had in high school and in college. Jane Austin's "Pride and Prejudice," and "Sense and Sensibility," were among the very best I read in high school. I hope that one day, someone will write a novel about the consequences of rape, and about the pain and suffering it brings to its victims, and to their families, generation after generation.

I want you to know that you are the very best teacher I ever had.

Love,

Alexia"

To Bishop Arlington, Alexia wrote:

"Dear Bishop Arlington,

You will, I am sure, hear about my suicide. I don't know how you will react to it, but I wanted to let you know, that your very kind and remorseful words about Grandma Rose-Anne, and your genuine sorrow and grief for her family, have meant a lot to me and to my family. I am now convinced that you are a gentle and kindly person, caught in the contradictions of life.

I want you to know that I have forgiven you, and I wish you success in your efforts to heal all victims of rape.

Sincerely,

Alexia Hartley

Finally, to her roommate Anna-Marie, Alexia wrote:

"Dear Anna-Marie,

I write to apologize to you, my dearest Anna-Marie, for shocking you with my suicide. It was inevitable. I am confident that if you knew the extent of the suffering, the severity of the constant pain and the intolerable agony I have been enduring, you would understand my action, if not forgive me for it.

Your kindness and your love for your friend I would not have found in anyone else.

Thank you for the care and sympathy you gave me, for the counseling and refinements I received from you. You are an angel, as my Dad believes.

I hope that you will have a long and full life, with a good family and loving children of your own. You deserve the very best, my dear Anna-Marie.

Love,

Alexia"

The day before Carla's scheduled departure to Valley Town, at about 4:00 pm, Alexia tells her mother and Anna-Marie that she is going down to mail a few letters to some of her friends.

With the six letters she composed the night before in her hand, and wearing her light blue overcoat Anna-Marie helped her select, Alexia takes the elevator to the first floor of her dorm. It is a cold, wet and rainy day. She goes to the Music Room and sits for a few minutes by herself reading the verses she had written a few days before. Then she begins to quietly sing them. She decides to change the second line of the lyrics. Instead of : "And heal my soul again," she decides it should be, "And will heal my soul with rain." She continues to sing softly:

Death will free me from my pain
And will heal my soul with rain

When I lie beneath the bridge
To Love and Peace I will pledge

The ceaseless flow of water sings
As I glimpse the angels' wings
Bubbles float and music cheers
Life beyond human spheres

Let me die and live again
Let me end my spirit's drain
Let me die in dignity
In peace and anonymity

Let me end my spirit's drain
Let me heal my soul with rain
Then with love and humility
I will pray for humanity

When I see the angels peering
I will know Grandma's nearing
And when the angels rise and sing
To grandma's arms I will cling

No one is there to see the tears rolling down Alexia's cheeks. She looks around briefly then leaves for the post office.

On her way out of the dorm, she walks up to the desk where she first met her cousin Ron. She stops for a moment, smiles at the young student sitting there, and walks out.

After a few steps in the rain, she looks back at her dorm for the last time then continues to the Post Office.

And when I hear the angels sing
To Grandma's arms I will cling

She drops her letters into the post office box.

Let me die and live again
And end the pain, my spirit's drain

Alexia walks toward the Van Cliff Bridge, the highest bridge on campus. As she approaches it, she stops, struck by its magnificence and the perfection of its design. She goes on, her heart pounding.

The ceaseless flow of water sings
As I glimpse angels' wings
Bubbles float and music cheers
Life beyond human spheres

She notices a fence constructed around the platform of the bridge and examines it. She then looks down at the turbulent water in the three hundred-foot-deep ravine and begins to shiver.

The ceaseless flow of water sings
As I glimpse the angels' wings
Bubbles float and music cheers
Life beyond human spheres

She stares at the bridge, momentarily stunned by its grandeur. Then she begins to examine the fence around the wet platform again.

She knows that the fence is designed to discourage intruders like her.

Yet she convinces herself that she is making a farewell pilgrimage to this sublime edifice for a worthy purpose: To eradicate forever the pain and suffering which have eroded her spirit, and to allow the restoration of her soul.

She examines the fence more closely and detects a hole in it. The maintenance people must have neglected to repair the fence, she muses.

Now she is more nervous, shivering as she did when she faced Bishop Arlington for the first time at his home in Lake Charles. In spite of her anxiety, she begins to feel relief and a strange sense of strength. She walks toward the hole in the fence slowly, squeezes her trembling body through it gradually. Then she climbs up to the platform with dignity and confidence. She sits on its flat surface for a moment to calm her nerves and quell her fears. At last she turns to lie serenely on her back and the familiar soothing strains come again:

Death will free me from my pain
And will heal my soul with rain
And when I lie beneath the bridge
To Love and Peace I will pledge

The ceaseless flow of water sings
As I glimpse the angels' wings
Bubbles float and music cheers
Life beyond human spheres

Let me die and live again

Let me end my spirit's drain
Let me die in dignity
In peace and anonymity

Let me end my spirit's drain
Let me die and live again
Then with love and humility
I will pray for humanity

When I see the angels peering
I will know Grandma is nearing
And when the angels rise and sing
To Grandma's arms I will cling

Suddenly, Alexia hears the voice of a woman whose words have been blurred by distance: "Look at that beautiful young girl lying flat on her back on the wet platform of the bridge. She's about to roll herself into the ravine!"

Alexia Hartley does indeed peacefully and unhesitatingly roll her shivering body from the platform of the Van Cliff Bridge at Ivy University into the deep ravine below, to her death.

Chapter 59

Two hours go by. Carla and Anna-Marie wait restlessly in the dormitory for Alexia's return.

Anna-Marie decides to go down to the entrance hall. She steps into the Music Room, where Alexia frequently stops to listen to music. When she does not find her roommate, her heart begins to beat faster. She asks the girl behind the desk if she has seen Alexia. The girl tells Anna-Marie that the last time she saw her was about two hours before, when Alexia was holding letters in her hand, and that she would assume now that Alexia was going to the post office to mail them.

Another hour goes by, and there is no sign of Alexia.

Anna-Marie goes back to her room and finds Carla choking back tears. "I'm sorry, Mrs. Hartley," Anna Marie says, "I have no idea where Alexia is."

"Do you think we should call the police?" Carla asks in a trembling voice, indeed her entire body shaking.

Anna-Marie herself begins to cry. "I don't know what we should do, Mrs. Hartley. It's getting dark, and we must do something."

"Please call the police," Carla says. "I'm too upset to do anything. I think I'd better call my husband."

Several days after Alexia's death, a memorial service is held in her honor at the Auditorium of the Valley Town High School. Several hundred students, teachers, friends and relatives attend the service. They come from Virginia, California and New York. An atmosphere of sadness prevails. Several people speak, including Ms. Bates, Bishop Arlington and Anna-Marie.

"The most brilliant student I ever had," says Ms. Bates.

"She is now in heaven, surrounded by the angels, who will deliver her to the loving arms of her beloved grandmother," says Bishop Arlington.

"She is the sweetest, the kindest and the most beautiful human being I ever met," says Anna-Marie.

A few days after the Memorial Service in Valley Town, the Ivy Daily on the college campus writes an article about Alexia's suicide with the following lead:

"ARTS FRESHMAN ROLLS FROM BRIDGE'S PLATFORM TO HER DEATH."

The article continues:

"Grieving for a recently revealed rape committed against her deceased grandmother decades ago, Alexia Hartley of Valley Town, Virginia, rolled to her death from the platform of the Van Cliff Bridge. Alexia's mother was on campus when the suicide took place. Her father as well as her twin brother had left Byron only a few days before. The young deceased's roommate, Anna-Marie Falvo, was admitted to the University infirmary in shock. Several suicide notes had been mailed to relatives and friends.

Chapter 60

"Why do you suppose Johnny won't let us see or touch the note Alexia wrote him?" Carla asks her husband after the Memorial Service.

"He's distraught, my dear."

"And maybe blames me for Alexia's pain and suffering. What else could I have done?" Carla weeps quietly.

"We did all we could." Michael Hartley stares into the emptiness outside the window of their home. "Alexia is gone," he chokes. "She's gone! She's gone! And Johnny must feel that we don't deserve the honor of seeing or touching his own note, maybe we don't. He must feel that we're responsible for Alexia's death. Are we?"

"He must feel that I'm the one responsible," Carla says. "I'm sure he feels that I saw the Bishop as an opportunity for monetary gain, regardless of the feelings of anyone else. He feels that Alexia paid the price of my greed. He must hate me," she begins to weep again.

"He doesn't hate you," he continues to weep. "He's just distraught."

Epilogue

Three years pass after Alexia's suicide, during which Alexia's twin, Johnny, drops out of college and moves to Ohio.

Carla's husband Michael continues to grieve for his daughter. He often weeps privately. He takes a leave of absence to look for Johnny and travels to Ohio looking for him. When he finally finds him working at a garage of a gas station, he desperately tries to convince his son to return to Valley Town to complete his studies, to no avail. He finally accepts early retirement from the University and stays home most of the time.

Carla has remained stoic. She resumes her social and business activities, and continues her contacts with Bishop Arlington and his family. At the same time she forms a charitable organization for the prevention of suicide among young teen agers.

Then, Bishop Arlington dies suddenly of a massive heart attack. Carla is immediately notified of the death of the bishop by the bishop's older daughter, Christine.

"Hi, Carla," Christine's voice is somber, "I hope all is well there."

"Hi, Christine," Carla says, "as well as could be expected under our circumstances. How're you all? How's Philip?"

"I have very sad news, Carla. Philip had a severe heart attack a few hours ago. We rushed him to the hospital, but he didn't make it. He was pronounced dead upon his arrival at the hospital."

"Oh, my God," Carla cries. "I never expected that. Did he have heart problems before?"

"No one thought he had any." Christine is crying.

"I'll fly to Ashton first thing tomorrow morning," Carla struggles to maintain her composure, "and if I can get a flight tonight I'll leave tonight."

"Thank you, Carla, please let me know your plans. I'll meet you at the airport in Ashton. I'm so sorry to give you this sad news."

"I'm very sorry too," Carla is in tears, "I'll see you soon."

"Thank you, Carla."

While trying to make reservations for a flight to Ashton that evening, and before informing her husband Michael of the Bishop's death, Carla's uncle Clifford calls and tells her of the Bishop's death.

"Thank you, Uncle Cliff, Christine called me a few hours ago. I'm trying to make reservations for a flight to Ashton, but I couldn't find a flight for tonight. The earliest flight I could get is tomorrow morning at 11:30."

"That'll get you in Ashton close to five in the evening, if you don't have to wait too long at JFK."

"I think they said I could arrive in Ashton at 4:45, Uncle Cliff."

"That wouldn't be too bad. Do you want me or Don to pick you up at the Ashton Airport, my dear?"

"No, you don't have to. Christine said she would pick me up."

"That's good. Do you want Don and me, and possibly Anita and Norma, to come to the funeral home during calling hours?"

"Yes, of course, Uncle Cliff, I think that would be very nice."

"I know there'll be a lot of people, and I don't know how Don feels about it, and we don't yet know anything about calling hours and funeral arrangements. All that'll be in the paper tomorrow, I'm sure."

"That's right. Could you call me early tomorrow to give me all that information, Uncle Cliff, before I leave?"

"Yes, I will, my dear."

"I could've asked Christine about that, but I didn't have the heart to ask her, she was so broken up over this."

"I'm sure she was. It was a big shock, especially only a few months after his mother's death."

"Yes, I know, so let's speak again tomorrow."

"We will. Good Night, my dear, I'll call you tomorrow, and as soon as the paper arrives."

"Thank you, Uncle Cliff. Good Night."

Carla is shocked and saddened by the unexpected death of the Bishop, to whom she has become very close. She speaks of her shock and sadness to Michael, who expresses sorrow about the news. But for the most part he remains quiet.

The next morning, Carla herself calls her uncle Clifford. She is uneasy and cannot wait for his call. "Uncle Cliff," she says, "I hope it's not too early for you."

"No, it isn't, my dear."

"Were you able to see the obituary in the local paper about Phil's death?"

"Yes, sweetheart, I was. Do you want me to clip it and mail it to you?"

"Yes, could you?"

"There's also a long article about him in the local section of The Stratford News."

"Does the obituary mention his survivors?"

"It does."

"Is my name mentioned?"

"It isn't."

"Just Christine's and Elizabeth's?"

"And their spouses and children. Of course his wife Grace is mentioned."

"Thank you, Uncle Cliff." She begins to tear.

"I'm sorry, Carla," her uncle tells her.

"I know you are."

"The Bishop's family's probably afraid to mention you in the obituary lest they draw attention to what happened to Rosy. But you're mentioned in his will as a daughter, according to the article in the paper, my dear," her uncle tells Carla.

"I don't care about that," she mutters.

"I'm sorry," her uncle repeats.

"Thank you, I know you are. I don't think I should come to Ashton, Uncle Cliff, I don't think I could."

"You can come and stay with us. Maybe Christine would come to see you at our home."

"I don't think I could do that, Uncle Cliff."

"I understand, my dear."

Carla puts the phone down. She walks slowly toward her husband. "I'm not going to accept their money, I don't want it."

Michael Hartley remains quiet. He only muses, Alexia's gone. She is gone.